Laura Kay is a wi~~~~~~~~~~~~~~~~~~~~~~~~~~~~~~nerican History from the University of Sheffield, and now lives in East London with her wife and cats. In 2018 Laura was selected as one of the ten PRH WriteNow mentees. *The Split* is her first novel.

Praise for *The Split*

'Full of humour, kindness, cake and a cat, this is the novel
to turn to in difficult times'
Katie Fforde

'*The Split* has everything I love in a novel. It's hilariously funny,
it's so uplifting, and its characters are irresistibly loveable'
Beth O'Leary

'A warm, funny, comforting read with such loveable
acters – and it actually made me want to start running again!'
Ruth Jones

'A hilarious tale of friendship and community'
The Sun

'More than just a standard romcom but with gay characters,
this nicely written, engaging debut squeezes in ambition,
anxiety and cake galore'
Daily Mail

'Perfectly capturing the agony of a break-up, you'll want to
wrap them up in a hug, while eating a freshly baked cake'
Heat

'This ferociously funny book about family, friendship and finding
yourself will give you a warm glow'
Red

'Guaranteed to have you chuckling, this is a book with heart'
Prima

'A feel-good depiction of love, friendship and family, which is very
funny, but with moments of true poignancy too'
Holly Miller

the split

LAURA KAY

QUERCUS

First published in Great Britain in 2021
The paperback edition published in 2022 by

QUERCUS

Quercus Editions Ltd
Carmelite House
50 Victoria Embankment
London EC4Y 0DZ

An Hachette UK company

A CIP catalogue record for this book is available
from the British Library

PB ISBN 978 1 52940 982 6

10 9 8 7 6 5 4 3 2 1

Typeset by Jouve (UK), Milton Keynes

Printed and bound in Great Britain by Clays Ltd, Elcograf S.p.A.

Papers used by Quercus are from well-managed forests
and other responsible sources.

For the Kays.
And for Arthur, who I love madly and
who tolerates me in return.

1

Overboard

The kitchen was smaller and darker than it had felt before, even with the orange sun setting on the windows. The crisp winter air cut through the heat of the boat's tiny wood burner and I shivered. The cupboards seemed too close together, every door crashing into another. Not enough surfaces, not enough space.

I was more animated than usual, clattering about, talking loudly, laughing obnoxiously. I was trying to catch Emily's eye to somehow bring her into the room, which she'd walked into minutes before but still failed to completely occupy. I wished I'd cleaned up a bit, noticing my laptop and several dirty mugs on the table. I adjusted my hair into a neater ponytail. I was suddenly and ridiculously self-conscious of being in my Kermit the Frog pyjama bottoms, as if Emily had never seen me in them before, as if she hadn't worn hers the night before. I found myself talking non-stop about my mundane day, about Malcolm, who sat on the bookshelf looking bored by the whole sorry scene, about what I was cooking, about strange Mr Jeffrey's noisy building project next door which now seemed to be taking the shape of a kennel and should we be worried that he was getting a dog?

Emily sat at the kitchen table and looked out of the tiny round window on the side of the boat, through which you could just about make out the shapes of trees and the deep green of the murky river. Every time something I said elicited a response greater than a nod or a murmur I felt triumphant, clinging to those 'yes', 'no' and 'maybes' like the sweetest and most tender declarations of love. Emily alternated between fiddling with a loose button on her shirt and running her fingers through her long dark hair, pushing it roughly away from her face as if it stung every time it touched her. I thought the more I talked, the more likely she was to come around. I couldn't stop looking at her. I wanted to see her relax. But Emily's eyes wandered, filled with that strange kind of sadness that you impose on yourself a few times in your life when it's for the best, in the long run.

When I finally paused to put the dinner plates on the table, I immediately knew I should never have stopped, but by then it was already too late. That was my fatal mistake. I wished I could have stood in the kitchen for ever, making pasta and small talk until I finally said the thing that convinced Emily she was about to make a terrible mistake. I should have filibustered her into staying. There must have been a magic combination of words that would have worked. Instead I allowed that dreadful silence to envelop us, thick and heavy, as the first tears fell from Emily's eyes.

'I'm so sorry, Ally.'

Don't be, I said in my head. Just don't be and we'll forget this moment ever happened and we'll just eat our tea and sit on the sofa with Malcolm between us and carry on for ever.

'I can't do this anymore.'

I put my head in my hands, unable to watch.

'We both know that things haven't been right for a long time, don't we? Please look at me, Al. Don't make me be the one who has to do this when we both know.'

I didn't look up. I didn't know.

'We're just not right together anymore, are we? I think we've both grown up so much and we've both changed. Well, I know that I've changed.'

I told her that I hadn't noticed any change, which made her incredibly angry very quickly and after that there were fewer tears on her part. In fact it seemed I had unwittingly given her a renewed conviction. She sat up straighter and banged her hand on the table in frustration, which made Malcolm shoot out of the cat flap at lightning speed.

'Of course you haven't noticed a change! Of course you haven't.'

She shouted this, a kind of high-pitched, wobbly shouting that I had never heard from her before. If the moment hadn't been so completely horrible I might have laughed. It might have been something that I could have done an impression of in a few days' time with my arms wrapped around her waist and she would have slapped me on the arm and protested, but she would have laughed too.

'You never notice anything, Ally! It's like you've stopped bothering to engage at all. Do you know how hard it is to be the energy for two people? To have to coax you into coming out with me? To have to coax you into doing literally anything? It's exhausting.'

I told her that I didn't understand how she could be exhausted by me doing nothing, but I knew what she meant. I'm not stupid, but how do you respond to that? Maybe I could have apologised and tried to explain or reason with her, but I could see that she'd already made up her mind. In her head she had already stepped outside. I looked down and saw that she hadn't even taken her shoes off.

Emily said some things then that made me squeeze my eyes shut and grit my teeth until the ringing in my ears drowned out the sound. It was an attempt to block the memories ever being made. I knew it all anyway; tired, bored, done.

'I'm going to stay at Sarah's tonight,' Emily eventually said, breaking through the self-imposed sound barrier. She pushed her chair back and made a move towards the door.

Instinctively I got up too and stood behind my chair, gripping the top until my knuckles went white, prepared to shield myself from what I knew was coming.

'Sarah from work?'

I said this as incredulously as possible. As if it was the most ludicrous thing I had ever heard in my life. As if Emily had said she was going to stay at Father Christmas's house. But as I said it, watching her really squirm for the first time that evening, months of memories started flooding my mind. Tiny snapshots of late nights and distracted conversations and working on weekends. These memories that I had locked away in a tiny inaccessible part of my brain. I hated her then for thinking that I didn't notice, even though I hadn't realised that I had.

I shook my head and started to laugh – an absurd reaction to feeling that you've just taken the worst beating of your life and then been run over by a lorry.

Emily started to speak to me like you might speak to someone standing on the windowsill of a tall building or too close to the edge of a tube platform.

'Listen.' She put her hands up to indicate she meant no harm, that she wasn't going to make any sudden movements to make me jump. She didn't move any closer, but she did take her hand off the door handle.

'I never meant for any of this to happen, OK? I honestly never intended for any of this to happen, but seriously Ally, I feel like you checked out such a long time ago and so I just kind of felt like I could check out too. I meant to tell you sooner, but I just . . . it's been really hard. I really loved you, you know that don't you?'

She loved me. Past tense.

Emily carried on. She didn't see the word hanging in the air in front of us.

'And this thing with Sarah hasn't been going on for very long, a couple of months, three months I suppose. But she's not the reason for us breaking up, you understand that? We're not right and I should have done this sooner and I'm sorry for that.'

It was too much to process all at once. I slumped back down on my chair and nodded not so much in acceptance of her apology as in admission of defeat. I wouldn't keep her there that night.

'I'm going to go now,' Emily said very gently like a mother putting her child to bed without the light on for the first time.

'I'm going to come back tomorrow so we can talk about this all properly, OK? When things aren't so fresh.'

I nodded again, sick at the prospect of being alone to face the staggering realness of it all.

Emily looked irritatingly satisfied, as if we'd made some progress. She grabbed her bag. It was already packed, next to the door. How had I not noticed that? She stepped outside. She closed the door and took the breeze with her.

The kitchen got even smaller. The ceiling lower, the light dimmer. Time moved torturously slowly in the few hours after she left. I sat at the table in the deafening silence and cried, great wracking, gut-wrenching sobs, the kind that make your head feel like it might explode, that make your throat feel like sandpaper. I cried until I was exhausted, got up, turned on the tap in the kitchen sink, stuck my head under it and drank and drank like Malcolm does when someone tries to do the washing up. I picked up my plate of cold pasta studded with soggy bits of courgette and sad blobs of cold tomato sauce and ate the whole thing. Then I took Emily's and ate all of that too, this time covered with a pile of grated cheddar. I felt briefly comforted.

There was no way I'd be able to sleep that night, so I found myself lingering over ordinary bedtime things. I brushed my teeth for a full twenty minutes, until my gums bled and the brush tasted only of my own metallic saliva. I actually completed the lengthy cleansing routine I always vowed to do, which involved all sorts of rigorous wiping and steaming and several layers of moisturising. I put on fresh pyjamas, and finally, when there was absolutely nothing else to do, I stood in the doorway of our tiny bedroom, stared at the unmade bed which that morning had contained both of us, grabbed the duvet, shut the door behind me and made my way to the sofa.

My plan had been to watch TV all night, but the moment I lay down, I fell into a deep, dreamless sleep. I forgot to check if the door was locked or set a 'burglar trap' (a clothes horse in front of the door with lots of coat hangers on it for maximum noise). I didn't run through every single scenario in my head of the boat catching fire or Malcolm drowning or a serial killer prowling around the riverbank. I simply closed my eyes and slept and slept.

The next morning my mouth was dry and my eyes were puffy. I had been crying in my sleep, which was just about the most pathetic thing I could imagine. It was still dark outside, 6 a.m.

Basically the middle of the night. I switched my phone off airplane mode expecting to see at least one message from Emily checking I hadn't chucked myself overboard in the night, but there was nothing. Anger pulsed through me. There was no way I was going to wait around all day for her to come and speak to me. I couldn't bear the thought of her sitting in front of me telling me her plans for how I could move out and when. She would probably be planning to move Sarah in. I vaguely recalled meeting her at some Christmas drinks, but she was just a shape with a blank face. Not important enough to remember, I'd thought.

I grabbed my suitcase and started to pack as many clothes as I could. I'd be coming back soon, I thought. Yes, when everything had calmed down. It would blow over. Nothing we couldn't sort out. My thoughts were racing. I felt feverish, almost. The only place I could think of going was to Sheffield, home to my dad's. All my friends in London were Emily's friends too. I shuddered, wondering if they had known what was going on. Had they all discussed it? Had they offered her advice on how to break up with me? Whose idea had it been to have a bag packed? No one had reached out to me yet, to ask if I was OK.

I picked up my phone to text my dad.

Dad. This is an SOS. I need to come home for a while. Emily broke up with me. Is that OK? I'm sorry. I know it's early.

He replied almost immediately. I imagined him lying in bed scrolling through his phone, probably playing Scrabble.

You don't have to ask. I'll pick you up if you let me know what train you're on. Bring your big coat. It's cold.

Just as I was on my way out, Malcolm emerged from his spot in front of the wood burner. He stretched lazily before flopping back down again, exhausted by the effort. He looked up at me. I looked deep into his eyes for some sign of sympathy or understanding, but all I could see was *Breakfast?* Before I had the chance to make a conscious decision, I walked over to the bed and pulled Malcolm's carrier out from underneath. Somehow, perhaps because it all happened so quickly, he let me pick him up and wrestle him into it with relatively little fuss. A bit of bleeding was to be expected. My heart thumped as I paused in the doorway, a performance of thinking things through as if I hadn't already made up my mind. Malcolm yowled as we stepped off the boat.

The train was late. And it cost me more than £100. There ought to be some kind of discount for those travelling at the last minute with broken hearts. I thought about billing Emily and the look on her face when she saw the request pop up on her phone. Tempting.

The swell of anxious people rolling suitcases and the babble of screaming children on the platform was giving me a stomach ache. Every rogue shriek from a baby set a fresh burst of adrenaline pumping through my chest. I tried to block them all out. Crouching down, I poked a tentative finger through the slats of the carrier resting on top of my suitcase. Malcolm hissed.

When the train finally arrived, I heaved myself, my giant suitcase and giant cat onto the train, nearly bursting into tears at the sight of a luggage rack with space. This little accomplishment, getting onto the train and securing an unreserved seat, felt like a triumph.

I was suddenly ravenous. As other passengers organised themselves around me, and the train slowly rolled out of St Pancras station and into the grey January day, I got my Marks and Spencer ploughman's and packet of cheese puffs out of my bag and thought of nothing else for a few blissful, cheese-filled minutes.

I have never experienced a loss of appetite except when severely poorly and even then I stare longingly at the food other people eat, miserable at the wasted opportunity.

The romance of train journeys used to appeal to me. Once, even this East Midlands train that smelt like toilets and cheese and onion crisps would have relaxed me. But today I felt no joy or peace. The journey felt slower than usual and was punctuated only by Malcolm's occasional yowl, a guttural reminder that he was there against his will, and I realised, with a pang of guilt, that I hadn't given him breakfast before we left. I pushed a crisp through the bars of his carrier, but he just looked at it in disgust, insulted by the bleakness of the offering. I pressed my forehead against the window and as the next heart-wrenching lift of St. Vincent's guitar from my 'feelings' playlist burst through my headphones, I felt a cinematic rush of sadness and a fresh wave of tears flowed down my cheeks, turning the green hills and the winter sun into one big, beautiful green and orange smudge. I had been vaguely aware of people giving me a wide berth on account of the cat and the weeping, but in that moment it was just me, the train, and my pounding, anxious, broken heart hurtling from one home and into another.

When the train pulled into Sheffield, I hobbled onto the platform along with hundreds of students lugging their nice clean laundry. I realised, having had my phone safely back on airplane mode all morning, that I was going to have to switch it on now in order to find out where my dad was. He'd probably left at least two concerned voicemails. I took a deep breath before taking the plunge and swiping. My phone instantly lit up with messages coming through too fast to read, although I had my suspicions. Stopping at a pillar near a piano where someone was attempting to play 'Für Elise', I stabbed at my phone, squinting my eyes in an effort to see as little as possible. I lifted it to my ear to listen to a voicemail, expecting to hear Dad's voice telling me which car park many, many minutes from the station he was in.

'You've taken the fucking cat, I can't believe it.'

A surge of adrenaline flooded through my body. Emily.

'I knew you were going to be upset, Ally, but I didn't know you'd be so insane that you'd steal my cat.'

He's not *your* cat, I replied in my head. He is *our* cat.

'You need to bring him back immediately. Don't you dare ignore this, I will ring your dad and tell him.'

This didn't concern me. It was an empty threat, as Emily had never once bothered to come to Sheffield in the seven years we'd been together. I was also not sure what Emily thought my dad would do about it. He is not a cat bounty hunter.

I hung up, satisfied that she was experiencing at least some level of the turmoil I felt. As I put my phone away, I looked up and was surprised to find Dad hanging about in the entrance of the station craning his neck, looking around for me instead of doing snail's pace laps of the car park so he didn't have to pay. Seeing him search for me in the mass of people made the tears swell all over again and my heart lurch into my throat. I might have been five again and lost at the supermarket, or alone at a party desperate to go home. He was the physical embodiment of a lifeboat. I rushed towards him as fast as I could (given my furious, furry luggage) and threw myself at him, thrusting Malcolm's carrier into his spare hand and burying my face into his neck. I noticed that he felt shorter than I remembered, or slighter. He smelt like the shower gel I'd bought him for Christmas.

'All right, love?' he said, giving my head a little pat and pretending not to notice that I was crying, which I was very grateful for.

'Let's get these bits in the car, shall we?'

I nodded and together we moved slowly towards the car, which was parked down a side road, not saying anything. Just before he opened the boot Dad seemed to notice for the first time that the holdall in his hand contained a cat, but his only reaction was to raise his eyebrows and pop him in with a 'Here we go then.'

'Good journey?' he asked, adjusting his mirrors.

'Yeah,' I said, 'I had a ploughman's.'

'Lovely.'

There was something inherently comforting about sitting in the passenger seat of Dad's Peugeot. It smelt faintly of the ancient pine air freshener hanging limply from the rear-view mirror and far more strongly of a forgotten orange peel curled up in the compartment of the passenger's side door. I closed my eyes and in the comfortable silence of the journey felt my shoulders loosen a little bit as we rode through the city and out into the hills. Even with my eyes closed I knew exactly where we were going, each twist and turn and strain on the car's engine. I opened my eyes as he began his parallel parking ritual, which mainly consisted of turning a bit red and calling Brian next door's very reasonably sized people carrier a 'fucking monstrosity'. Once we'd finally managed it, I went to the boot to grab my bags, and followed Dad, who was carrying Malcolm, inside. I could hear our dog, Pat, barking excitedly on the other side of the door. I felt another pang of guilt for subjecting Malcolm first to this journey and then to an elderly but enthusiastic Jack Russell.

My dad put Malcolm's carrier at the bottom of the stairs before ushering Pat out of the back door to let off steam in the garden. I dumped my bags and fumbled about in the dark for the hallway lamp, but when I finally located the switch, the bulb had gone. I shivered as I took my coat off and hung it on the end of the bannister. I wondered when Dad had last had the heating on.

'Let's get you a cup of tea.' Dad's head popped around the kitchen door.

I nodded and slipped my shoes off, kicking them in the general direction of the shoe rack, something I could only get away with when there were actual tears on my face.

'Now then, what will um . . . what will Malcolm have?' He gestured at the carrier, acknowledging for the first time since he'd picked me up that I had brought the giant cat with me. Malcolm was staring out at us, quietly seething. Pat, who we'd always thought might chill out with age, could still be heard barking her special 'reserved for cats' bark through the back door.

'Could he have some water, and,' I paused, knowing I was pushing my luck, 'do you have any cheese? It's just that he loves cheese, and it might calm him down to have a treat.'

I knew full well that the nonsense of asking for cheese for the cat would only be tolerated for a short amount of time, possibly for today only, so I had to really take advantage while I could.

Dad raised his eyebrows but didn't protest. 'Cheese it is.'

I opened Malcolm's basket, very happy to turn my attention to him. He let out a low moan and crawled out, showing off his enormous tail so that everyone in the room would be rightly intimidated and frankly embarrassed about the size of their own tails.

He sniffed his way over to Dad, who was grating cheese onto a saucer, and after an intense inspection begrudgingly started to nibble on it.

We left him to his snack and took our mugs of tea into the living room. Dad settled on the big green armchair which was an old relic from Grandpa Arthur's time, and I sat down opposite him. The room hadn't changed since I'd moved out eleven years ago, with its bumpy painted walls and sausage dog doorstop. I didn't have to worry about the unknown in this room, it was like a time warp. A picture of Mum and Dad on their wedding day sat in a silver frame on the side table next to me. I wiped my finger over the front of their smiling faces to remove a layer of dust. Since Mum died, Dad and I hadn't put up any new photos in the house. Time stopped circa 2004.

'So how long do you think you'll be home?'

I took a sip of scorching hot, very strong tea. I hadn't had tea with anything but plant milk in it for over a year. Emily had become a vegan and insisted I at least give up milk if I could not commit as fully as she had. It tasted ridiculously, wonderfully good.

'Not that it matters,' he said quickly.

'Thanks, Dad. I don't really know. I kind of don't really have any plans yet, everything's a bit . . .' Despite myself I heard my voice waver and felt my bottom lip tremble again.

'A bit up in the air,' he said, nodding. 'It's all just a bit up in the air at the moment.'

I nodded because I couldn't speak, and reached forward to grab a chocolate Hobnob from the coffee table. My favourite. It was an unopened packet so I knew he had bought them especially for me.

'It will get better. And that . . . that awful girl will realise what she's missing soon enough and I tell you what.' He paused, looking as though he couldn't quite decide how to actually tell me what. 'She'll never find anyone as good as you.'

We were quiet for a minute. It was very much not like Dad to be so forthcoming, so he'd said it all very quickly, looking down into his cup of tea. I resisted the urge to slide over to him and plant a kiss on his cheek, getting my snotty, teary face all over his.

'Thanks, Dad,' I said through a mouthful of Hobnob, and he nodded at me, pleased he'd said his piece and that I wasn't going to make a song and dance about it. We fell into companionable silence as we drank our tea.

In the kitchen I found Malcolm lying on his tummy at the back door staring curiously at Pat, whose face was pressed up against the glass, tail wagging furiously. After making her promise through the window that she wouldn't chase Malcolm, I let Pat scamper in and give him an excitable sniff. Malcolm immediately swiped Pat across the face with an open paw, which was met with utter glee. She loved a game. I wondered if they might get along fine after all. I dragged my suitcase up the stairs, letting the wheels bump on every step, and then went back downstairs to fetch Malcolm from under the kitchen table. He went entirely stiff in my arms but didn't bite me or try to escape, which I chalked up as a success.

When I walked into my bedroom I was freshly overwhelmed with love for my dad. The room was spotless, with lovely green and blue floral bedsheets I'd never seen before on the single bed. He had laid me out a towel and lined up all my old teddies on the desk. I wondered if he kept this room ready for me to come home, or if this was this morning's labour of love. I quietly closed the door and plonked Malcolm on the bed, then had to immediately reopen the door for him as he started scrabbling at it ferociously. He was not interested in an afternoon nap and certainly not with me, his captor. I lay down on the bed and looked up. The ceiling was covered in glow-in-the-dark stars.

I had never been in my single bed with Emily. Her soft skin had never touched these sheets. I had never felt her hot breath on the back of my neck in the middle of the night within these four walls. I was transported to a land before Emily, to a place where she had never existed, where we had never existed. I didn't feel hopeful or happy, but for the first time in twenty-four hours, I didn't feel completely crushed. Just exhausted. I reached into my bag and pulled out my phone to find a white noise playlist (intended for babies but downloaded exclusively by anxious adults) and played it as loudly as I could get away with. I put a pair of squishy earplugs in my ears, stuffing them in until they started to hurt. Satisfied that I couldn't be disturbed, I drifted off to sleep.

*

17

I woke a few hours later to Dad gently prodding my shoulder. It was getting dark outside and there was a little puddle of drool on my pillow. My playlist had long finished.

'Just checking on you.'

I yanked the earplugs out of my ears and nodded as he asked me if I'd like fish and chips for tea and whether I might want to pop down and watch *Pointless*.

He turned to head back downstairs but stopped at the door.

'I forgot to mention, you know Karen's boy, Jeremy? You know, big Jeremy? Brown hair, he's you know,' he tipped his head towards me.

This meant gay. He was gay.

'Anyway, he's back home too. Has been for a while. Maybe you two could meet, try and cheer each other up.'

I nodded absent-mindedly, thinking only about the fish and chips, the fact that I had barely eaten anything but plants for tea in a year and how thrilling it was to do something that Emily would hate so much.

From: Alexandra Waters   12 January 2019 at 23:05
To: Emily Anderson

Subject: Important information regarding your recent break-up

Hi Em,

Remember we used to write emails like this all the time when we first met? Everyone emailed instead of using WhatsApp. I wish people would email more now. Sometimes it would be nice to receive a thousand words instead of ten. I'd write you a letter if I knew where to send it, but I guess you're staying at Sarah's now.

I can so clearly remember the first time I emailed you. I bet I could even recite that email word for word. I agonised over it for so long. I pretended I wanted to ask you something about an essay we had to write but it was really a love letter. It feels weird to say that to you. I always tried to act cooler than I was around you, but it's silly to pretend now. Silly and far too late.

I think you know this already but the moment we met I fell hopelessly in love. I was sitting in the back of that mouldy old lecture theatre doodling on my notepad while that lecturer (I don't remember his name, do you?) the new one who looked like he'd just done his GCSEs was reading off the first slide of his PowerPoint presentation. I'd just settled in for an hour of sleeping with my eyes open when you dashed in at the back, a mass of untameable, windswept hair and an enormous backpack. You threw yourself down next to me, flustered. While you struggled to take your coat off, I couldn't help but stare. You looked so pretty even with bright red cheeks and your fringe sticking to your forehead. You were wearing that thick, woolly jumper which you've brought out every winter for the past seven years and complained about how itchy it is. Maybe time to throw it away, eh, Em?

I'd hoped to catch your eye so we could bond over how bored we were but I realised you were going to actually listen to the lecture. You were so wide-eyed and transfixed at this really, truly terrible presentation. It was very endearing. Squished into those tiny seats it felt like the top of your arm and your leg were burning into mine through several layers of jumper and jeans. I did my best not to move at all for the rest of that hour. I kept expecting you to turn and look at me. I was literally vibrating next to you. I swear I haven't felt the same way about knitwear since.

I stayed madly in love with you even when I found out you had a girlfriend. You always claimed not to have noticed my obvious disappointment when I found out about her and although you've joked that I was 'waiting in the wings' and 'ready to pounce', I truly wasn't. At the time, being your friend didn't feel like a con-solation prize, Em. Sitting with you in a big group of people and catching your eye and knowing exactly what you were thinking, strolling home on late summer nights, laughing uncontrollably and not being able to explain the joke to anyone else. These were the things I loved. It was impossible to not want to be your friend. I have fond memories of how it felt to love you then, even on the days where my heart ached and my stomach hurt with wanting you, it was uncomplicated and perfect. I didn't have to worry about how you felt about me because it didn't matter. My feelings for you existed in their own bubble outside of our friendship and our real lives.

You were the Daphne to my Niles.

I know you think I'm daft and nostalgic for bringing this stuff up but if I can get you to remember how things were all those years ago then maybe there's something we can do to fix this? It's not too late.

I'm sorry I took Malcolm without telling you. Maybe you could come and get him and we can talk?

He's OK here though, Pat loves him. Dad even gave him cheese (I know, I know, it was just a bit.)

Love,

Ally xxx

From: Emily Anderson   12 January 2019 at 23:45

To: Alexandra Waters

Subject: re: Important information regarding your recent break-up

Ally,

It's not OK that you took Malcolm, I honestly didn't know you were capable of this. I know you're hurt and I completely understand why that is but you just don't steal someone's cat and then refuse to answer your phone and then send a gushing email (?!) about it. You don't.

You know I'm not going to be able to make it up to Sheffield anytime soon, NOR SHOULD I HAVE TO. You can't steal something from someone and then ask them to make a five-hour round trip to get it back, that's not how it works. Please bring him back ASAP. I don't believe he's getting on with Pat, don't say things like that to try and make this seem OK. It's absolutely not OK.

I don't think you're daft or nostalgic – I think you're a thief.
Let me know what the plan is re: returning Malcolm ASAP please.
Em

P.S. I don't need to remember those things because I haven't
forgotten. That's not the problem.

P.P.S. The jumper is really warm. I like it. I'm keeping it.

2

My First Beard

My misery does not love company. I needed time to wallow alone. I quickly settled into a routine at my dad's. Waking up just as he left for work when he popped his head into my bedroom to say goodbye. I then lay in bed and scrolled through Instagram until I was satisfied I'd seen every fostered kitten and every brunch and confirmed that Emily had still not posted anything. I also looked at Sarah's page, scrolling back to her first post and handling my phone as carefully as if I were working for a bomb disposal unit. She was a Sara with no H, it turned out. Of course she was. She always seemed to be posing next to trees and had the physique of someone who exercises for fun and swims naked in ponds. All muscle and no bits sticking out. There was no question who would win in a fight. She had tall person energy even though it was impossible to actually determine her height from the tiny square photos.

Every now and then Emily and I had gone on 'off grid'

weekend camping trips, which I desperately wanted to enjoy but never really did. Emily has one of those families that go camping in the south of France every summer and she just knows how to do these things. She doesn't get bitten by insects, she tans easily. I had a vivid memory of sitting next to Emily in a cafe while she spoke fluent French and looked like Audrey Hepburn while I picked ice out of her Diet Coke to hold against my mosquito bites.

I found one picture of Sara and Emily. It wasn't on her grid, but they had both been tagged in it. It was from several months ago at a work event. A whole line of women who'd clearly had several glasses of champagne smiled blearily at the camera. Emily and Sara were on the end of the row squeezing together to get in the photo, their arms around each other. I stared at that for a long time trying to bring it to life, to somehow see the minutes before or after. Did they keep their arms around each other after the photo was taken? Was something already happening between them then?

Once I'd exhausted the morning Instagram stalk, I'd shuffle downstairs in my old slippers, make a cup of tea, and put *Frasier* on the TV while reading the news on my laptop. I tried to make Malcolm sit with me, but he was still grumpy and preferred to glare at Pat from the comfort of Pat's own bed. At about 10 I would change into my baggiest T-shirt and joggers. I could not stand to put on proper clothes in those first few days – my skin felt too delicate, everything scratched and stung. I would then take Pat for her walk. Pat was in her twilight years and not accustomed to too much walking, but once we'd been out a few minutes she'd get into it. The walk was an hour-long loop through the woods, and the cold air and the other humans going about their daily life made me feel normal. I wondered how many of them were trying to feel normal too.

After lunch, when Pat and Malcolm were fast asleep, I'd tentatively start looking for a job. Looking for a job had been my full-time occupation for about a month since I'd quit working as an English teacher. Teaching was something I'd fallen into mainly because my parents were both teachers and it sounded impressive and useful and I was keen to be both of those things. I cared about my students. Well, some of them anyway. The ones who weren't audibly discussing my outfit or openly doing each other's (banned) make-up during my lessons. And my teaching job had subsidised taking classes at the weekend and evenings. I learned how to bake and sold a few elaborately iced cakes to friends and family, fantasising about my alternate reality in a little French boulangerie filled with delicately iced confectionery and pastel macaroons. Every time I brought cinnamon buns out of the oven or placed a perfectly executed tart on the table, Emily would gasp gratifyingly and gush about how delicious everything was. Or she used to. Then she became a vegan and cut down on eating 'refined sugar' and me and my baking both seemed to lose our appeal.

She had remained supportive though. She had, hadn't she? *You need to leave this job*, Emily had said when I had come home in floods of tears after yet another nightmare day at work where

I hadn't managed to drink any water or take one bite of the sandwich I'd bought, and one of the students had stolen another one's shoes and thrown one out of the window and one at my head. Again. *Start doing what you actually want to do, this is killing you, why can't you see it?*

Emily had offered to pay the bills for a while until I was back on my feet and this had been such a generous offer that it hadn't really occurred to me that, although I was unhappy at work, I had no idea what it actually was I wanted to be doing. Full-time birthday cake maker? Pastry chef? I was underfunded and underqualified for everything apart from being a (terrible) English teacher.

So now: no job, no home, no girlfriend. Each day, as these facts settled like a heavy weight in the base of my stomach, I would allow my feet to lead me into the kitchen and I'd start to bake. The first day it was squidgy and soft salted chocolate chip cookies, which I ate dipped in tea. The second day was a Victoria sponge filled with thick buttercream and lots of strawberry jam, which we had for pudding and then my dad took to school for the staffroom (it went down a treat, I was told). These were the things that made me feel warm and comforted and like myself.

One day, a week into my new routine, I was just finishing eating raw carrot cake mixture out of the bowl, chasing the last orange strings around with my fingers, when the phone rang. Assuming it was Dad ringing to check up on me, I wiped my sticky hands down the front of my jumper and snatched up the phone.

'Hello Father!' I exclaimed, elongating my vowels in the silly posh voice we sometimes do for each other. There was a confused silence on the other end of the line and then a small voice,

'Oh . . . is Ally there please?'

I only just managed to resist the urge to hang up the phone. I cleared my throat.

'Yes, this is Ally – sorry, I thought you were my dad.'

'Oh right, sorry, no it's not,' the voice said, 'it's actually Jeremy, my mum said to call you? I'm home as well . . .' he trailed off.

'Yes, I heard.'

I couldn't believe he was actually calling. I don't think we'd ever spoken on the phone before. All previous meetings had been arranged by our parents. My heart sank. I had nothing against Jeremy in particular; it was more that I currently had an issue with all human beings. I couldn't successfully hibernate if there were going to be people calling me – and on the landline too. Unacceptable.

There was silence on the end of the phone. I didn't know whether I was meant to be elaborating. I went with, 'It's weird isn't it?'

'Yeah,' he said quickly, 'really weird. So do you maybe want to meet up or something?'

My instinct to say no was so strong that my mouth opened to form the shape. I couldn't bear the thought of someone coming in and bursting my little bubble of quiet and Dad and Pat and Malcolm.

But he was quiet, waiting for me, and I knew that he was sad too.

'Yeah OK, are you free tomorrow? We could always go for a dog walk.' I reasoned with myself that I would have been doing that anyway. He could tag along.

'Yes!' said Jeremy, more excitedly than I'd expected. 'I'll come by tomorrow after lunch.'

'Great, see you then.' I hung up, hoping I had successfully concealed how put out I was.

Dropping the phone back onto the sideboard I darted over to the kitchen timer, catching it thirty seconds before it was meant to go off and cancelling it. I hate the sound of the buzzer. I took the cake out of the oven and sat heavily on a kitchen stool, picking at the charred sultanas poking out of the top.

I'd known Jeremy since I was six years old. From the day he'd joined my primary school in year one I had insisted that I was going to marry him. He was my first beard. We had drifted apart when we went to secondary school, but were brought together every so often when our mums were having cups of tea at each other's houses and at Easter and on Christmas Eve.

Once, when we were twelve, Jeremy and his mum had come to our house after school. Hearing Jeremy thumping up the stairs to my room I'd opened my door and peered over the bannister to see our mums having a hushed conversation.

I'd glanced at Jeremy and saw that he had red eyes and his face was blotchy. What with being twelve I felt so wildly uncomfortable about his visible distress that after letting him into my bedroom, and perching on the end of my bed while he sat on my swivelling desk chair, I didn't say anything for a torturous few minutes before finally managing: 'What's that about then?'

Jeremy had shrugged and stayed quiet a few moments longer, kicking off his shoes and gently swivelling side to side on the chair, his knees pulled up to his chest. I assumed it was to do with Jeremy's dad. He'd left Jeremy's mum for the first time a few years earlier. He'd been back and forth since then – long enough to create Molly, Jeremy's little sister – but had recently moved out of Sheffield altogether and in with his new girlfriend 'down south'. He never came back after that. There had been a lot of quiet conversations between my parents about it over the years when they thought I'd been out of earshot. 'Just up and left apparently. No concern for the kids. Graham, I swear to God if you ever even think about it I'll . . .'

Jeremy had picked up Tim, my scraggly teddy bear, from the bedside table and was fiddling with his loose eye, plucking it away from his head until the thread was just threatening to snap and then letting it ping back again.

'Came out,' he mumbled.

'What?' I genuinely hadn't heard him, distracted as I was by Tim being tortured in front of me.

'Came. Out,' he repeated very slowly and deliberately, as though he was talking to someone who didn't understand English. He looked up at me, obviously hoping to gauge a reaction where there wasn't yet one available – I was still processing, and it sometimes takes a while for my brain to get going. He took my silence for still not understanding, and rolled his eyes.

'AS GAY,' he explained, exasperated.

'Yeah OK, I know!' I'd always known. That was probably why I had been so keen to marry him. 'What did your mum say?'

He shrugged again and opened his mouth to say something before reconsidering. We fell back into silence until eventually he glanced up, and I noticed his hands were shaking.

'She cried. I've never made her cry before.'

And then tears started to roll down his face, thick and fast, which made me so uncomfortable that I started to cry too. After a few minutes I passed Jeremy my box of tissues left over from Christmas covered in pictures of mistletoe and he took one, and I took one and said, 'Are you hungry?' and he said, 'Yeah,' so we went downstairs. We walked past the closed living-room door where the hushed voices remained hushed, and into the kitchen where we found an unopened box of Chocolate Fingers. We sat at the kitchen table with the radio on and methodically ate every single finger.

Another year passed before I managed to say to Jeremy, 'I am too.' And by that time my mum was already ill so no one had the time or energy to cry over my deviant sexuality.

When Mum died, Jeremy's mum would breeze into our house twice a day. She'd let herself in. Quiet as a mouse. Lamps would switch on in dark rooms, mugs would disappear from tables.

Plates of food would be placed gently in front of us, and pints of milk would appear in the fridge. Sometimes she'd bring Jeremy and Molly who was just a baby, and we'd all sit in silence watching TV. *Pet Rescue* was on a lot. We'd sometimes not say a word to each other and then when *Pet Rescue* was finished they'd get up and go home. I don't remember them hugging me or crying or saying sorry, but I remember the feeling of two warm bodies squashed in on either side of me on the couch, sticky fingers around a carton of Ribena, and emotionally investing in the health of a swan for half an hour. Jeremy's mum magically knew when I was ready to go back to school because one day my uniform, washed and ironed, was hanging on the back of my bedroom door. Dad and I went back in on the same day and for one time only I let Mr Waters, Head of Maths, walk me from the car and into the building.

That evening I sat down with Dad eating carrot cake and watching *Masterchef*. We talked for the thousandth time about how we wished we could taste the food through the TV and cursed science for not having made that breakthrough. Malcolm sat pointedly on Dad's lap and, although Dad rolled his eyes and dusted imaginary stray fluff off his trousers, I noticed that he slipped him a bit of icing when he thought I wasn't looking. As we cleared up our plates and took them through to the kitchen, I told him that Jeremy was going to pop around tomorrow.

'Oh really? That'll be nice,' he said. It was an unconvincing display of surprise. He had obviously already spoken to Jeremy's mum about this development. 'It will be nice for you two to see each other. You did have fun. I seem to remember attending a wedding at some point.'

'Yes, my first husband. It will be good to see what became of him.'

I made my way up to my room and inspected myself in the mirror as I carefully changed out of my jogging bottoms and jumper, my skin still somehow bearing the brunt of my heart-ache, tingling with hurt. My full tummy, round and soft, poked out more than ever, and I gave it a little pat. I had never minded my tummy and it seemed to be growing here. I was paler than ever and I peered at the mirror, screwing up my face at the dark circles under my eyes and my limp, greasy hair tied back in a ponytail. Not great, but the best that I could manage at the moment. I couldn't remember the last time I'd washed my hair and vowed to at least do that before seeing Jeremy. I lay in bed clutching my phone and thought about Emily.

From: Alexandra Waters   19 January 2019 at 22:41
To: Emily Anderson

Subject: re: re: Important information regarding your recent break-up

Emily,

Do you remember how we finally got together? Recently I've been playing it out in my head like a film. Although in my version

I'm two inches taller and I've not spilled the dregs of a lime Calippo down my front.

It was the last night of our final year just before we all went home for the summer. We were sitting in the park drinking cans of gin and all the vodka from various bottles we'd accumulated over the year and attempting to cook things on that disposable BBQ. I remember being thrilled that your girlfriend had gone home for the summer already. I'd even heard rumours that you'd argued, whispers that it might not last. We sat around on a couple of blankets taken from our actual beds, chain-smoking badly rolled menthol cigarettes as if it was our last night on earth. God I miss smoking, do you? I know you say you think it's gross now but do you really? I don't think I do. The sun on my back, a glass of wine in my hand and the first drag on a cigarette is one of my favourite feelings in the world.

As the evening went on and we all got drunker and either silly or serious depending on what we were drinking, we split into groups of shriekers and whisperers. I became very aware (from the shrieking camp) of you and that boy James (whatever happened to James?) having what looked like a very serious, very slurred conversation. You looked shocked and a bit teary (gin?) and kept glancing over at me and then putting your head down for a new flurry of intense whispering. My heart was pounding and not just from the Red Bull we'd been mixing with the vodka.

Eventually, emboldened by a swig of warm white wine sophisticatedly poured from a box, with a newly lit cigarette in my hand, I wobbled over to sit on the blanket next to you and James and asked what you were talking about.

It was only when you looked at me that I realised I was significantly drunker than you.

'Nothing,' you said.

I'll honestly never forget that moment, Em. Never in my life has a nothing hurt so much as that nothing. If at five years old I had asked my parents what I was getting for Christmas and they had replied 'nothing' it would not have punched me as hard in the guts as that 'nothing' from you. I would probably not have been so drunk in that first scenario, but still.

I couldn't say I was in good spirits on the way home because inside I was almost certainly dying, but I remember being obnoxiously loud. We had a group hug with the people going the opposite way and all shouted about how much we loved each other and would desperately miss each other (we don't even speak to any of them now!). Eventually everyone peeled off and just you and me were left.

I only had a dress on and your T-shirt and jeans weren't much warmer. The cold came on all at once and deflated me. It was one of those times where in a heartbeat you go from totally drunk to as sober as a person could be, in every sense of the word.

Do you remember how we walked those last few minutes in silence and at the end of my road where we'd usually say goodbye we stopped and looked at our feet and then at each other? You know that I'm not normally one to allow any kind of sincere

34

moment to pass uncommented on. But before I could say anything you stepped forward and kissed me. It was gentle at first, just our lips brushing together, but before you could get away, before the moment could be anything but real and happening to me, I put my hand up to the back of your head and pulled you right against me and kissed you hard. Two years' worth of wanting, gone in one moment. I couldn't believe I could be so lucky, to feel this way about the best person on the planet and have her feel it too.

I really have been happy ever since. I was so excited to move to London with you, but Em. It hit home this week that in the seven (seven!) years since then you have never visited my family in Sheffield. You've never seen my bedroom, or cooked dinner in the kitchen or walked Pat with Dad. You've never seen my primary school, or the tree I got stuck in or the bench I had my first kiss on. Do you even care that you've missed those things? Did you ever?

That's why I took Malcolm. I thought that even if you didn't care enough about me to get on a train for two hours, you might care enough about him. Also, he is half mine. I know he was technically a present from your parents, but let's be honest Emily, he doesn't like you very much. He knows you're responsible for the diet he's on and you're always trying to brush him. He likes to be at home with me watching TV and sharing a sandwich. He knows you would never share a sandwich with him. Would Sarah even like Malcolm? Did she even know that's what she was signing up for?

I am not going to bring him back, Emily. If you want to come and get him, fine. If you don't, then he's mine.

Love, Ally xxx

From: Emily Anderson   20 January 2019 at 08:17
To: Alexandra Waters

Subject: re: re: re: Important information regarding your recent break-up

Ally,

Obviously I remember that stuff, I was there too. Maybe I don't remember it in technicolour like you do but that doesn't make me insensitive or uncaring like you're insinuating. It was a little different for me. I don't regret it for a second but I'm not proud of it either. I was with someone at the time wasn't I? So not one of my finest moments.

It's a shame we never got around to visiting your dad together. I know it means a lot to you. I've always been so busy, it was just never the right time. That does not justify holding my cat hostage. And yes, he is my cat. Mum and Dad bought him for me for my birthday. He was my birthday surprise. He can't be half yours if he was MY birthday surprise. And he does love me just as much as he loves you. What a horrible thing to say. Love isn't just letting him eat sandwiches and disregarding his health, love is thinking about his future, wanting him to be the healthiest he can be. Love is paying his vet bills, Ally. Love is making sure he doesn't get hairballs and changing his litter tray and brushing his teeth with that fucking disgusting cat toothpaste even though he hates it.

You know full well it is Sara, no H. Don't ask about her, Al. This isn't about her. She hasn't signed up for anything but for the record she loves cats and she'd love Malcolm. Not that it matters.

I will pay for your train back down to London – let me know when you would like to come and I will book it.

Em

P.S. I wasn't crying because of the gin. You were wearing a skirt and a top, not a dress. I don't miss smoking but I miss that feeling you describe, you describe it very well. Bring back the cat.

3

Cakes and Cigarettes

I spent the morning before Jeremy arrived consumed with petty resentment at having my routine interrupted. I added his profile to my morning Instagram stalk. I knew that he'd gone to university in Manchester but other than that I had no idea what he'd been up to. He'd posted a couple of heavily filtered pictures of the riverside path near his house recently, but to get any real insight I had to scroll way back. There were plenty of photos of breakfasts dappled in sunlight and cocktails held up against impressive city views. And lots of photos of a good-looking boy sitting at restaurant tables posing with glasses of wine. There were several of a holiday in Spain. There were hardly any photos of Jeremy, but there was one of him laughing. His eyes were squeezed shut and his head thrown back, his hands clapped together in glee. It was from nearly two years ago. I pressed Follow.

Since I couldn't go on my dog walk yet I went to the kitchen to bake – making chocolate brownies studded with thick blobs of peanut butter was top priority, visitor or no visitor. I began the process of beating eggs, sifting flour, and melting chocolate (and nibbling chocolate) and the rhythm of the day seemed to fall into place a little more easily.

I looked at the clock and wondered, peanut butter spoon dangling from my mouth, what time 'lunchtime' was and then what time 'after lunch' might be. It was midday, which to me, seemed like a very reasonable lunchtime, so might he arrive at 1 p.m.? I reached for my phone to text and ask when I realised that he'd rung Dad's home phone and so I had no idea what his number was.

As predicted, at 1 p.m. I heard a gentle knock at the door. So gentle in fact that I wouldn't have noticed it had Pat and Malcolm not whipped their heads around, furious at the intrusion to their all-day naps. I ran to the door, peering through the peephole. Jeremy.

He'd always been tall but he was much broader than I had remembered, much bigger. His hair, dark and curly, looked as untamed and unbothered with as ever, and I noticed as he smiled at me shyly that his eyes looked just like mine, very tired and lined with big purple bags. I tried to remember when I'd last seen him and couldn't.

'Jeremy!'

I wasn't sure whether we were doing hugs or not so I went with a little wave as I ushered him in.

'Hey!' he said, lifting his hand slightly in return.

We hovered awkwardly in the hall for a moment before I switched into 'mother' mode, insisting he take off his shoes and come through for a cup of tea. He did as he was told and followed me down the hall and into the kitchen.

'Oh wow, those look amazing,' he said, talking to the brownies instead of me, leaning in for a closer inspection before suddenly snapping back as though he'd realised it wasn't good manners to plant his nose in the baked goods. The presence of our parents was strong; we weren't used to seeing each other without them.

'Thanks,' I said, also addressing the brownies, suddenly unexpectedly embarrassed at having gone to the trouble of baking even though I would have done it anyway. 'Do you want some?'

He said that he did and of course I did, so I cut two huge pieces and put the two mugs of tea down on the kitchen table.

There was a brief silence as we each took a sip of tea and a first bite of cake.

'I'm really sorry if it's weird that I came over, I just felt like my mum would never shut up about it if I didn't.' Jeremy said this quickly, shovelling brownie into his mouth as if to put a stopper on the words.

I laughed, relieved that we were going to be honest with each other.

'If you hadn't have come here I'm sure that my dad would have frogmarched me around to yours soon enough. He's probably getting sick of me hanging around the house moping, which,' I took another bite, 'is fair enough.'

Jeremy nodded.

'Have we . . . ever hung out without them? Just the two of us?'

I thought for a moment, then shook my head.

'Not since school. We were left to our own devices surprisingly often, weren't we?'

'Yeah, why did they let us walk to the park by ourselves? It's miles away!'

'Terrible parenting.'

We were quiet for a moment. Chewing. I thought of my mum waving us down the hill towards the park shouting instructions about when to be back and who not to talk to.

'They probably thought they'd have got rid of us for good by now,' he said.

'Do you mind if I . . . why are you back?' I asked.

'Well, I lost my job.'

I nodded sagely.

'And my boyfriend broke up with me.'

He paused before the word boyfriend like he wasn't quite used to saying it.

I continued to nod, feeling horribly, selfishly satisfied that I wasn't the only person in the world going through this waking nightmare. Perhaps my misery did love company after all.

'So that happened about eighteen months ago and I kind of had a bit of a—' He stopped, searching for the right word. 'A bit of an episode.' He shook his head immediately, realising he had not chosen the right one, that 'episode' was someone else's word. His mum's, probably. 'A breakdown, I had a breakdown.

And I, you know.' He sighed heavily. 'I ended up taking a lot of stuff to try and make me feel better. Too many drugs. Way too many.' He shook his head. 'Messed me up a bit.' He smiled grimly, like he was trying to downplay what he was saying, to make it somehow more palatable for me. It didn't quite reach his eyes.

I opened my mouth to say something but no words came.

'So I'm back here,' he popped a piece of brownie into his mouth with one hand and gestured around his head with the other, then continued to talk with his mouth full, 'because I lost my job so I lost my flat, and I moved so I lost my friends. It's been a bit shit actually.'

He stopped abruptly, dropping his fork with a clatter onto his plate, and I felt my heart start racing. I lifted my hand to my chest as if to calm it. He looked up at me, waiting for some kind of response.

'Jeremy. I don't know what to say,' I whispered, feeling like I might cry and telling myself not to bloody dare cry.

'I'm so sorry that happened to you. Is happening to you. Do you feel any . . . better now?' I silently cursed the inadequacy of my question.

Jeremy nodded. 'Most days I feel better. It feels like such a long time ago now. Another world.'

We sat in silence for a bit, sipping tea and taking in everything Jeremy had said. My heartbeat returned to somewhere near normal pace. I got the sense that he hadn't heard those things spoken out loud in a long time.

'You know,' he said, after a couple of minutes, 'these brownies are fucking delicious.' He picked a bit straight out of the pan with his fork, all of his initial reserve gone. As if being so honest had broken a spell.

'Thanks, they're super easy to make. The trick is less flour, more chocolate, always. And salt. I love to do it actually. I sort of want to do it properly.'

'You mean like professionally?'

'Yeah I suppose so. Why, do you not think they're professional-grade brownies?'

'They definitely are! But you're a teacher aren't you?'

'Well, not anymore. Since I packed it in.'

'But I mean you don't want to go back to teaching?'

I shook my head.

'No, I don't think so. I want to do something that makes me happy. Or at least something that doesn't make me sit in the toilets and silent scream into a rolled-up jumper.'

'Dare to dream!'

I grinned. 'Are you working at the moment?' I asked tentatively.

'Yeah, I've got some shifts at a call centre in town. I do not recommend. It is not for the faint-hearted.'

'Lots of rude people?'

'Oh yes.'

'What were you doing before?'

'It wasn't much better, to be honest. I was at a start-up doing customer service for an app that tells you smart ways to invest your money.'

'But does that at least mean you have loads of money invested in clever places?'

He smiled. 'Absolutely loads. That's why I'm living with my mum.'

'Oh shit, yeah.'

'Al, do you mind if I smoke?'

Jeremy was already out of his seat and halfway to his coat out in the hall before I could answer.

'No, of course not,' I called after him, 'best do it out the back door though, Dad will go mad if he smells smoke in here.'

I grabbed my coat too, along with the brownie pan and our forks, and followed him out to sit on the back step. Malcolm trotted out after us and settled in a patch in the middle of the lawn in order to judge us from a distance. It was freezing cold and the grass was wet so he sat hunched like a loaf of bread, looking utterly miserable.

Jeremy nodded towards him as we sat down.

'That one's new.'

'Yeah. A long story.'

'He's very fluffy.' He patted the step next to him as if to beckon Malcolm over.

'I wouldn't waste your time with that, he won't come if you want him to.'

'Treat them mean, eh?'

45

'Exactly. And it works.'

He nodded and took a cigarette out of the packet and popped it in his mouth before offering them to me. I started to say no and then changed my mind and took one.

'Cheers,' I said, tapping my cigarette to his as he handed me the lighter, 'I haven't smoked in years.'

'What? Oh my God, why?' He sounded genuinely shocked, as if I'd said I no longer drank water or breathed air.

'Well, I heard it isn't good for you . . .' I smiled and nudged him. 'And Emily hated me smoking so I stopped when we got together.'

He stared at me. 'Even when you're out?'

I laughed properly for the first time in days. His expression was one of pure horror.

'Even when I'm out, even when I'm a bottle of wine down.'

He shook his head. 'Well, I'm sorry I've brought you back over to the dark side.'

I took a drag of my cigarette and smiled, enjoying the giddy, heady sensation you only get after a long time without nicotine.

'I don't mind.'

We sat for a long time on the back step chain-smoking and picking at chocolate brownies from the pan. I got up at one point to put the kettle back on but instead of suggesting we go inside to the warm, it made sense that afternoon to bring our fresh mugs of tea outside where it was chilly and not very comfortable. We both seemed much happier there. We made each other laugh talking about when we were teenagers and trying to remember the last time we'd seen each other. I thought it had been at a family BBQ for my dad's birthday when we were just about to leave for university. I insisted I was right because I distinctly remembered having to take turns to help Dad out while he stood swearing under a big umbrella, refusing everyone's suggestions that we just do it on the grill inside. Jeremy thought there had been a Christmas Eve in the pub with our extended families since then, after we'd spent our first term at university and I'd come back with a tattoo on my forearm that was the talk of the table.

'I just don't understand why it had to be a *mermaid*!' Jeremy hissed, his eyebrows raised as high as they could go, eyes wide with horror in such a perfect impersonation of his mum that I couldn't stop cackling.

I pulled up my coat sleeve and inspected the offending article. 'I mean she's right, it's not great, is it?'

I offered my arm to Jeremy and he had a good look up close. She was a little mermaid, no bigger than three inches, halfway up my forearm. Her green tail was faded now and her long blonde hair a very sad shade of yellow. The lines on her arched chest looked as though they could use a touch-up.

'I like her,' Jeremy said, gently giving her tail a little prod. 'She's very you.'

'What, a bit of a mess?'

He smiled and put down his cigarette to rest on the saucer

which was our makeshift ashtray. He pulled up the bottom of his jeans and rolled down his sock to reveal the name Ben in an elaborate font scrawled on his bony ankle.

'Oh no,' I whispered, half horrified, half thrilled, 'you didn't!'

Jeremy nodded grimly. 'We both did. I know I should get it removed, but I just can't seem to bring myself to. Plus it's so expensive.' He took a final drag of his cigarette before stubbing it out. 'So I'm stuck with him for now.'

'And he's stuck with you.'

Jeremy barked with laughter. 'I doubt it.'

'Why did you . . . how did things end? If you don't mind me asking?'

He shook his head.

'We were together for two years and it was one week before my birthday.' He took another cigarette out of the packet but didn't light it. Just rolled it around in his fingers.

'He was very stressed but I thought it was just work. He woke up one morning, a Saturday morning. Turned around to me in bed and told me he didn't love me anymore. He just . . . didn't. There was no one else. And he didn't want to meet anyone else. Said he wanted to be single for a while. Have some space to think.'

'How can you just fall out of love overnight?'

'I think about that a lot.'

'It seems so unfair. That you can fall in together, but you have to fall out one by one.'

Jeremy sighed and nodded, then looked at his watch. 'I'd better go, I didn't realise what the time is.'

We'd been sitting there for three hours.

I faffed about in the kitchen while Jeremy fetched his shoes. We stood in the hallway as he put them on and looked up when the buses were.

He looked around before he left, peering behind me and up the stairs as if he were trying to take it all in.

'I feel like I've stepped back in time, Al.'

I nodded, knowing the feeling well.

'It was good to see you, I actually feel a bit normal this afternoon.'

'Good! Me too.' He stepped outside the front door and hovered on the porch, jiggling about on the spot to keep warm.

'Do you want to come again?' I asked.

'Yeah, when?'

'Tomorrow?'

'OK, see you tomorrow. After lunch.'

From: Alexandra Waters   20 January 2019 at 23:14
To: Emily Anderson

Subject: From Sheffield, with love

Dear Emily,

I miss London. I miss you. I even miss the boat. I miss feeling seasick in bed. I never thought I'd say that. I feel like it's odd not to be texting you all day. Isn't that ridiculous, that the thing that feels like the biggest loss at the moment is asking what you want for tea and sending you pictures of Malcolm?

It's not that I don't love my dad, but this is not real life. Well, it is, but it feels like my real life fifteen years ago. I couldn't have ever imagined that I would end up back here. It's like a dream where I'm myself but I'm not and this is my house but it's not quite, and I'm trying to move but my legs are stuck in mud and I can't quite gather the strength to push forward. We don't talk about you here, it's like you never existed.

I think I should be angry. I have read that I should be feeling anger, but I haven't felt it yet. I know it's something that always bothered you. So here goes, here is something I don't understand, perhaps even something I'm angry about: how could you have let me quit my job without finding anything else when you knew you were going to leave? I am mad about that! I am mad about the fact that you let me give it all up thinking that I could rely on you when you knew you were about to pull the rug out from under my feet (a rug that we bought together, Emily!).

Anyway, let me know when you'll be coming up and we can talk about all this properly, maybe we can even go back home together? We can work it all out I think.

Love, Ally xxx

P.S. I saw Jeremy today. Did I ever tell you about Jeremy? We were best friends in primary school and then our families became friends because we got married. We've never really hung out just the two of us – not since we were kids anyway but it was actually really nice to see him. I made your favourite brownies, he loved them too. He's having such a terrible time. I'll tell you all about it when I see you.

From: Emily Anderson   21 January 2019 at 14:11
To: Alexandra Waters

Subject: re: From Sheffield, with love

Dear Ally,

It's not that I don't want to see photos of Malcolm, it's just that I don't think it's a good idea for us to text all day. I don't want you to get the wrong idea, or to continue to have the idea you've already got. These emails will have to stop too at some point. I'm not coming up to see you, Al, and we're not going to go home together. I have packed all the rest of your things. I know you don't want to hear that but I have. I think I'm being very reasonable giving you lots of time and letting you get away with stealing my cat for the moment. You will have to bring him back soon though.

You can come back to London and find another job. This is an example of what I'm talking about – it is not my responsibility to come and get you and decide to bring you home. You are not passive, Ally! You can make a choice! I always had your best interests at heart. You're remembering things differently to how they actually happened. I didn't force you to give up work. I offered to help out for a bit until you decided what you wanted to do and you accepted. What you actually did, was nothing. I am sorry it left you in such a tricky spot, I really am. I didn't think I'd end up leaving when I did and I feel bad about it but you are not my responsibility, Ally. I couldn't keep on taking care of you.

Em x

P.S. I think you told me about Jeremy. Gay kid you married? It's nice that you have someone to keep you company there. Of course he loved your brownies, they're the best.

4

Game Plan

Jeremy did visit the next day, and the day after that. He started coming as soon as he'd finished work and it became our new routine to take Pat for her walk, sometimes the long route and sometimes just a couple of laps around the block depending on the weather and on Pat's mood. We'd always come back past the shop and buy flour and sugar and whatever else that day's concoction required. Jeremy was not a naturally gifted cook but he improved under my watchful eye. He was set to work measuring and stirring and greasing tins for our increasingly elaborate creations. We talked a lot about school and the people we used to know. We talked a lot about Emily and Ben. We didn't know how to lift each other out of our perpetual wallowing and sadness so instead we plotted and planned ways to win them back. We laughed about it, the schemes getting more and more ridiculous, but each one sustaining a glimmer of hope. I tried to inject my schemes with enough reality that they seemed possible. Unlikely, but possible.

A couple of weeks into our new joint routine, hovering over my shoulder as I piped roses onto the side of a giant pink and white sponge, the sweet rose scent filling the kitchen, Jeremy said to me, 'Al, can I tell you something?'

'Yeah of course.' I wasn't properly listening, concentrating on trying to wipe away a phantom hair that I could feel tickling my face with the side of my wrist as I bent over the cake in the hot kitchen.

Jeremy was silent for a second, watching me.

'Ben is here.'

I frowned, the icing wasn't coming out how I had hoped it would. 'What do you mean?'

'He's here. In Sheffield. Well, he was. Visiting someone I think, or maybe he's moved here finally. We did sometimes talk about it before.'

I spun around, still clutching the heavy icing bag,

'You're joking.'

I scrutinised Jeremy's face, trying to see if he was just playing one of our games. Ben is here and we're going to find him. Ben is here and I'm going to win the lottery and woo him back. I realised that Jeremy wasn't playing. Ben was just here and there was no plan.

'How do you know? I thought you'd had a Ben cleanse.'

'I saw him, when I was at the shops with Mum. He was

54

running past. Not running away from me,' he clarified quickly, 'I mean, he was on a run.'

'Did he see you?'

'No, definitely not, he had his head down.'

'If he had his head down . . . I just mean are you absolutely definitely sure that it was . . .'

I stopped, meeting his steely eyes.

'I know what Ben looks like,' he said flatly. 'Do you not think you'd know if you saw Emily jogging past you?'

I thought about all the times in the past couple of weeks when I'd been sure I'd caught a flash of Emily. At night I willed Emily here with such intensity that I felt sure that when I looked out of the window the next person around the corner would have to be her. Or the next. Or the next.

I shook my head. Jeremy's eyes were lit up and he was animated in a way that I hadn't seen him since we'd reunited.

'So, what's the plan?'

He grinned.

'Well, I happen to know that he's running the half marathon.'

I was about to ask how he knew, but Jeremy was scrolling through his phone and shoved a screenshotted photo in my face before I had the chance. The photo was of someone's race entry confirmation posted with the caption saying 'no going back now' and the 'scream face' emoji. One person called Ben86 had commented – it simply said '*eek*'. The emoji was the monkey with his head in his hands. This didn't scream solid evidence to me but I didn't feel I could say so to Jeremy when he seemed so happy and full of purpose.

'I still don't understand the plan. What are we going to do?' I frowned. 'Cheer him on?' I had a mental image of Jeremy, alert and anxious, clutching a home-made banner while a horrified Ben ran past him.

'No, Al,' he looked at me wide-eyed as if I was missing the most obvious thing in the world, 'we're going to run it!' He smacked his hand on the table, which wobbled precariously and we both made a grab to steady the cake.

I burst out laughing. I couldn't imagine running a lap around the block let alone a half marathon.

'Jeremy. I'm not running anything with you.'

'Of course you are!' Jeremy was unperturbed, prepared for the possibility of resistance. 'You need something to focus on as much as I do. It will show your dad you're doing something. He's not going to let you slob about here for ever.'

'I'm actually job hunting,' I said indignantly, but even as the words came out of my mouth I was aware that I hadn't actually applied for any jobs, the ten minutes or so browsing on LinkedIn proving almost too much most days. I couldn't bear the idea of getting a job here. Or in London. Or anywhere at all that didn't involve Emily. I preferred the limbo of the perpetual Groundhog Day I'd created for myself.

'I think you can cope with a second thing on your agenda,' Jeremy said. 'We could run with Pat instead of walking her.'

We both looked at Pat who was lying on her back in bed fast

asleep, one grey foot twitching every now and again as she chased the rabbits in her dreams.

'Or maybe,' he said, 'we could go back out for a run after we've walked Pat and then come home and bake.'

'I can't run!'

I felt a familiar swell of nausea. In the past I'd had a complicated relationship with running, with exercise in general, in fact. PE at school was never a problem because I was really good at just not doing it – standing last in line for gymnastics and continually swapping with the keen kids until the hour was up, volunteering to play 'deep fielder' in rounders so I could chat to my mates, occasionally raise an arm to wave in the ball's general direction and then make a disappointed face when I missed it.

'Of course you can run, don't be daft!'

'I can't. Don't you remember PE?'

'Al, that was more than a decade ago, there's a chance you've evolved since then.'

'No, I haven't! Cross-country running scarred me for life. A whole mile first thing? It was horrible. I was always last, and Miss Miller was so bloody patronising.'

I screwed up my face into a condescending smile. 'Come on Alexandra, it's not far is it?' I mimicked her voice, clipped and haughty. She had probably never broken a sweat in her life.

'Oh yeah, she was a right cow, wasn't she?' Jeremy sat back in his chair to reminisce. 'Do we think she was a community member?'

I looked at him, trying to figure out if he was serious.

'Obviously, Jeremy! I have never met a more lesbian lesbian in my life! God she was so annoying, I hated her.'

'You loved her.'

'No, I hated her, she ruined my life with those runs.'

'You loved her and you hated her because you couldn't believe you fancied someone who wore a stopwatch around their neck all the time even when she was being a substitute teacher in maths.'

I thought back to all the times I'd dragged myself to PE just so I could see Miss Miller. Her blonde hair pulled back into that severe, vein popping ponytail, her arms not soft and weak like my own, but strong and toned, gripping her clipboard as she stared us down for the register. I had known in a roundabout way that I didn't want to address the fact that when she bellowed 'Alexandra Waters' the flip of my stomach was more than nerves about the weekly mile of torture.

'Perhaps,' I conceded.

'So you're basing this decision on some teenage angst. We were all shit at PE, Al. It doesn't mean you can't do it now. It's a run, it's not a hockey match, you don't have to have any skills. Plus,' he continued just as I opened my mouth to protest, 'this is exactly the kind of thing Emily would be surprised to see you do, right? Committing to something outside of your comfort zone? Seeing it through? Looking all sexy in your Lycra?'

I couldn't deny that he had a point. Emily was always doing this kind of thing. A jog around the park for breast cancer here, a 10k for refugees there. I turned down her invitations to join in so many times that eventually she stopped asking. I looked at Jeremy and couldn't help but smile as he gave me his best puppy dog eyes. He took that for a definite yes.

'Yes, Al!' he cheered and grabbed my arms, making me do a little floppy victory dance. 'You will not regret this, we're going to have so much fun!'

'I'm still not saying I can do it,' I said, untwisting from him and turning back towards the unfinished cake. 'I can try, I suppose,' I spun around pointing the icing nozzle at him, 'but if I don't like it after one go I can give up, OK?'

Jeremy nodded at me, still grinning from ear to ear. 'Loud and clear,' he said. 'I'm going to make it fun though, I promise, I'll plan a beginners' route. I'm a beginner too.'

I stuck a finger in the icing bowl and brought it to my lips. Jeremy was now scrolling furiously through his phone, presumably trying to find the perfect run to convince me to actually do it.

I thought back to a day last summer trying to catch up with Emily as she stormed along a busy street in Hackney. She was expertly dodging day-trippers and kids on scooters and sausage dogs in a way that is magically possible when you're absolutely furious. I'd not only turned down the opportunity to save the children by running around Victoria Park with her, but I'd also been extremely late. So late in fact that I'd missed her running altogether. I thought about Sara with no H. She probably runs all the time. I knew for a fact she was always doing those terrible assault courses where you pay to drown in mud and scale walls. She was probably doing one right now. I allowed myself to imagine what it would be like to cross the finish line of a half marathon. I would be glowing, my hair magnificent. I would be only slightly out of breath and sweaty in a sexy way. For some reason Sara with no H would be standing on the sidelines cast in shadow, grey and tired and desperately jealous of my phenomenal achievement – and of my legs. Emily would be there too, weeping gently with pride and regret.

I finished icing the cake and admired my handiwork for just a moment before taking the big knife from the sideboard and slicing it right down the middle. Jeremy winced.

'I didn't even get a chance to take a photo!'

'It's not for looking at, it's for eating.' I set about transferring half the cake into the biggest Tupperware box I could find and sealing it with foil for Jeremy to take home.

'Al, if you're going to be a professional cake artiste then you need evidence of your masterpieces! Next time take a photo. If it's visually pleasing, people will want to eat it. People eat with their eyes first, remember.'

'OK, thank you, Mary Berry.'

As he left, Jeremy turned back to me. 'I've got a really good feeling about this, Al, I'll bring my running shoes tomorrow.'

I rolled my eyes and shooed him away. 'God, what have I got myself into.'

*

That night, long after Jeremy had gone home, by the blue light of my laptop glowing in the dark of the kitchen, I felt the gears in my brain grinding into something that felt vaguely like focus. I recognised the thrill of possibility mixed with the anxious knots writhing in my stomach. As I scrolled through page after page of on-sale trainers, high-vis tops and sweatbands (which I had previously only ever worn decoratively circa 2002) I felt as though I might be about to turn a corner. Perhaps I could run to fill the time until Emily changed her mind. Perhaps the act of running itself would change Emily's mind. I clicked on a website called Women's Running and devoured every article, from the best posture to how to fuel your body in order to reach your maximum potential. I was disappointed to see that cake was not recommended as a high-performance breakfast option. That night I skipped the sneaky cigarette I'd taken to having before bed. I had two chocolate Hobnobs dipped into a cup of tea instead, for the oats (slow burning energy), and the starchy carbohydrates (not sure to be honest), and felt on the path to something, at least.

5

Our Everest

Growing up, I had a lot of stomach aches. Most days I could handle the dull pain, ignore it, forget about it even. On good days it never appeared at all. But on bad days it became me. On those days Mum would sit on the edge of my bed, shake her head and stroke my hair. She'd tell me I could stay at home and the relief washed through me like a tide. The prospect of not having to speak to anyone for the rest of the day was always guaranteed to untwist the knot in my stomach. I could eat as many bowls of Coco Pops as I liked for breakfast, and recline on the sofa in my dressing gown. If I could have spent every day by myself instead of going to school, I would have.

Since Emily and I broke up the stomach ache was a daily occurrence. Every morning I lay in bed listening to Dad getting ready to leave for work. The sound of the fridge opening and closing, footsteps up and down the hall, the clatter of keys being snatched from the kitchen table. I closed my eyes and I could have been fourteen again, taking a day off school because I'd said I had a tummy ache, which was both true and not true. I didn't have a bug I could pass on, I had the same tummy ache that would flare up at four, and fourteen and probably at forty. I pictured the seed of worry swelling and mutating and multiplying like cells swarming through my veins and eventually settling painfully, uncomfortably in the pit of my stomach.

I heard the door open and then some shuffling about, I could just picture Dad patting himself down for his wallet and keys before grabbing his backpack and sandwich from the bottom of the stairs. I felt a swell of love and nostalgia so strong, tears pricked at my eyes. He did this every day. Soon after there was a slam, which was my cue to shuffle my feet into my slippers and head downstairs. Malcolm was having a very relaxed wash in the middle of the kitchen floor, meaning my dad must have fed him. I had left my phone downstairs overnight to stop myself compulsively checking for messages from Emily. I did a pretend routine where I pottered about the kitchen nonchalantly putting the kettle on and rooting about in the cupboard for my favourite mug before wandering through to the living room where I just happened upon my phone. My heart pounded as I switched off airplane mode and waited for messages to pop up. There were some junk emails, and a text from Dad.

Have a good day, Al. Thanks for the cake, I'm sure it will go down a storm apart from with Mrs Jones who has gone gluten free. I'll give her a bit that's all icing.

I simply couldn't believe that Emily had given up on getting

Malcolm back so quickly. Perhaps she'd email when she got to work, I thought, trying to buoy myself for the morning and not just crawl back into bed and a pit of despair. I was strangely grateful for the grim distraction of the upcoming run with Jeremy.

I hesitantly opened WhatsApp to look at the chats I had been ignoring. There was a group of all the women teachers from my last school that I had muted – The Coven: witch emoji, cauldron emoji, laughing face emoji – a reference to a text from a student teacher that had accidentally been sent to one of the faculty describing the female staff. I realised they didn't know what had happened. It felt oddly soothing to think that in the minds of my former colleagues Emily and I were still together. There was another message from my favourite Coven member Fran saying, 'School is shit without you! I am going to murder a child!! No joke?!!! Wine soon please?'

There were also a couple of messages from Beth of Tom-and-Beth, a couple we knew from uni. They had been Emily's friends from her course and both were now high-flying lawyers and owned their one bedroom flat in Stoke Newington that they shared with a sausage dog named Stephen. The first message she'd sent had been the day I left London and the latest was from two days ago saying simply, 'Let us know if you need anything x'. I wanted to reply. There was so much I needed but nothing that Beth or Tom could do for me. I thought about all the lovely evenings I'd spent sitting on their expensive sofa, drinking posh wine and stroking Stephen's tiny little head. It was so cosy and the light was just right and they always had some cool music playing that I'd never heard of but still enjoyed. We'd have proper conversations too. Not just bitching about people from work or slagging off our other friends. I wondered if Emily would take Sara with no H there now. Whether they'd ask her about the things she cared about. Plastic probably. Sustainable coffee cups and responsibly farmed courgettes. Stephen will have forgotten all about me. I closed WhatsApp and threw myself down on the sofa on the opposite side of the room, away from my phone and all the people inside it.

The time that Jeremy usually came over crept up on me and I ended up madly dashing between mine and Dad's room desperately looking for something that looked vaguely like sportswear. I settled on a pair of leggings that I would usually pair with a big jumper for lounging about the house in, and a vest top I hadn't worn since I was about sixteen. I would have to wear a normal bra, the only one I'd brought with me in fact, as I had never had the need to invest in a sports bra. I inspected my body in the mirror at the bottom of the stairs, a mirror Mum had once described as 'not very flattering'. I grimaced at my grey skin with the spatter of spots across my right cheek, and the deep circles under my eyes which I just couldn't seem to shift despite the tragically early nights of the past couple of weeks. The circles cut into the shape of my face as though the fresh healthy skin had been gouged out and I was left with these sunken, hollow bags to carry around. The vest top clung to places I was certain it hadn't all those years ago and the shape of my rounded tummy felt unnecessarily highlighted. I didn't mind the way I looked when I was in my usual clothes, but I did mind that I didn't look like someone you might expect to see going on a run. The clothes made me feel like an imposter. I could already picture people staring at me, how my arms would mottle pink and white as I got hotter and where the sweat patches would appear. I grabbed a hoodie from a coat hook, feeling instantly less conspicuous. I paced around the kitchen in some old, worn-out trainers, sipping water and trying to keep calm. I thought about Emily. I desperately wanted her to know what I was doing. I desperately wanted to tell her that I was trying. I picked up my phone with the blank screen and wanted to scream.

By the time Jeremy knocked on the door, I'd managed to get so worked up that I'd all but decided to tell him I couldn't do it at all. But seeing him grinning in his slightly too tight T-shirt and what looked like some old swimming trunks, his very pale legs poking out of his old gym trainers, made me realise that was not an option.

'Ready?' he said as I opened the door. 'Had some breakfast to keep you going?' He didn't come inside, choosing to hover about on the doorstep instead, as if stepping over the threshold might somehow burst his energy bubble.

'Obviously I've had breakfast,' I said indignantly, having never knowingly skipped a meal in my life. I paused. 'Jeremy, I'm really nervous.'

'No need to be, we're just going to see how far we can get

today in half an hour and we even get to walk some of it.' He waved his phone at me. 'I've got a training plan.'

Half an hour seemed like a horribly long time to me, that was more than an entire episode of *Frasier*, that was a full *EastEnders*.

'Where are we going to run?'

'Well, I thought we'd start here and head up towards my nan's and then back again.'

I looked at the hill that we'd have to run down and then back up again and looked back at Jeremy.

'It's fine!' he said. 'You'll probably get a burst of adrenaline at the end anyway, I read about that somewhere.'

I took a deep breath. 'Right, shall we get this over with?'

We took off together and awkwardly tried to keep in rhythm side by side. I felt as though I was trotting along taking three steps for his every one, my five foot three no match for his six foot. We took off down the hill at what felt like a pretty decent speed and it didn't seem so bad – it was actually quite fun. I'd forgotten the feeling of running like you might not be able to stop. We reached the bottom of the hill looking a bit pink but otherwise great and headed off on the long, flat road at the bottom. That is where things started to fall apart. Every step along the flat road was harder and I became very aware of the sound of my own breathing becoming more laboured by the second, interspersed with little involuntary grunts. I glanced over to Jeremy and he seemed to be doing fine. Purple, but fine. I dropped my pace a little from slow shuffle to brisk walk and waved at him to carry on ahead. I felt a thick pain at the back of my throat that spread to my jaw and tongue. I briefly wondered if this was what drowning felt like. The breakfast I'd eaten earlier sat solidly in my stomach, in fact it seemed as though every meal I'd ever eaten was piled up inside me, weighing me down, making me feel extremely sick.

I glanced up. Jeremy was gesturing at me with a grin on his face, which looked a little more strained than before. He was holding his open hand up and exaggeratedly mouthing at me, 'FIVE.' The first thought that flashed briefly through my mind was 'miles' and then it was replaced with the horrible realisation that he meant minutes. I had been running for five minutes and my whole body was on fire.

'When are we stopping?' I yelled with a surprising amount of power given I felt that every breath was possibly my last.

'At the end of this road,' he gestured vaguely at the endless flat path in front of us, 'we can walk for two minutes.'

The end of the road seemed impossibly far away. I was surprised to feel tears pricking my eyes and I rubbed them away quickly, feeling my cheeks sticky with sweat. Fixing my eyes on Jeremy's lolloping body ahead, I carried on. As we finally approached the end of the road, Jeremy began to spin around to give me a thumbs-up every few seconds, doing a sort of backwards jog. I don't know why, but it was the most intensely irritating thing that had ever happened to me. I looked everywhere but at him, refusing to acknowledge the thumbs-up until finally he slowed to a stop and I lurched up next to him a full minute later. As soon as I stopped, all the irritation melted away and I'd never felt such relief and joy at standing still before. Never again would I take standing for granted.

'You're doing great, mate,' Jeremy said, slapping me on the shoulder and steering me back along the pavement into a fairly pacey walk, 'we can't stop though, just walking for two minutes.'

Up close Jeremy looked as absolutely awful as I felt, which made me feel miles better. Perhaps he wasn't finding it so easy after all. Perhaps I would soon be the one giving the world's most patronising encouragement.

The next twenty minutes were some of the slowest of my life. I hated both the stretches of running – pure, unadulterated pain – and the gentle walks during which my legs wobbled, and I could barely enjoy the relief of being able to breathe before taking off again. I couldn't think of a time that I'd felt quite so conscious of every single part of my body, apart from maybe during sex, but this was obviously distinctly less exciting. I was intensely aware of my stomach and hips shifting from side to side seemingly of their own accord, and the waistband of my leggings folding down so I had to yank it up every thirty seconds. At first I'd been self-conscious every time we ran past anyone, adjusting my posture and trying to make my struggling less obvious, but by the second half of the run I'd completely given up trying to look casual, instead opting for elaborate hobbling and loud groaning. It was oddly freeing. The approach to the hill at the bottom of my road was part of a well-timed walking stint, but we walked in silence, aside from the thick panting breaths and, I'm ashamed to say, spitting. We spluttered our way to the bottom of the hill and looked up. Our Everest.

'OK,' said Jeremy, even his bright and shiny attitude dulled somewhat by the prospect of a vertical finish. 'One last stretch, this is going to take us thirty seconds max if we try and go as fast as we can.'

The idea of trying to run 'as fast as we can' up a hill so ridiculously steep the council had put in a handrail would have seemed preposterous to me only thirty minutes earlier, but now I just wanted to get home as quickly as possible. I thought about a cup of tea and a biscuit with the longing of someone who'd been trekking without sustenance for days. I nodded.

'Three, two . . .' said Jeremy, and I steeled myself, eyes fixed firmly ahead on the lamp post at the top of the hill. Just got to get to the lamp post, I told myself, and we're home.

'One, go!'

I took a few quick steps forward, bounding up the first few metres and felt surprisingly OK. *Perhaps this is going to be fine after all*, I thought, *perhaps I am an athlete now*. But then, too soon, my body caught up, as if the sudden burst of speed had taken a few seconds to register. My legs seemed to drag behind the rest of me, full of lead and shooting pains. Catching my breath was now out of the question; no matter how many breaths I took my lungs remained empty, hot and burning.

Every single inch of my body compelled me to stop; it would

have been so easy to stop. But something inside kept my legs moving. I could barely even hear Jeremy at the top bent over by the self-imposed finish line, cheering me on while trying not to be sick. I just kept staring at the lamp post. One step closer to the lamp post, two steps closer, until I slapped my hand against it as if I'd finally made it home after the world's shittest game of It. I stopped, crouched down, and bent my head over my knees, dizzy with breathlessness and utterly elated that I'd reached the top. The tears that had been threatening to spill the whole time we'd been out finally did and Jeremy and I walked wordlessly to the front door, his arm resting gently and awkwardly over my shoulders.

We went inside, kicked off our shoes and noisily drank water out of pint glasses until our breathing returned to normal.

I sat at the kitchen table, wiped my sweaty forehead with the back of my hand and said to Jeremy, 'So how far was that? How many of those would we have to do?'

Jeremy fiddled about on his phone. 'Erm,' he said squinting at it and grimacing slightly, 'that was nearly 4 km.'

'What's that in miles? I only know miles.' I got up to refill my pint glass, feeling as though I might never fully rehydrate.

'That's two and a half miles.'

I nodded, impressed. 'Well, that's not too bad! How long is the race?'

'Just over thirteen.'

Even Jeremy, who had been channelling Mr Motivator all morning, seemed horrified at the prospect of running more than five times that distance. The contrast between the man bursting with energy and enthusiasm on the doorstep that morning and the crumpled, dejected one sitting at the table was too much to bear. The idea that he might give up seemed too terrible to contemplate and, unbelievably, I found myself talking him back into running thirteen miles together.

We sat in front of my laptop unshowered and eating second breakfasts of peanut butter on toast while reading training plans and other unfit people's accounts of running races. Pat and Malcolm sat in the middle of the floor staring at us, both confused by the switch-up in routine and extremely interested in the peanut butter. Smiling faces beamed out of the screen at us, looking positively radiant having just run a marathon, and I wondered whether that could really ever be us. Some of the people looked like professional athletes, all white teeth and flat tummies and toned calves under colourful Lycra, but others looked closer to actual human beings just giving it a go. We had another brief browse for proper running gear but balked at the prices before deciding we'd be best off going into town to see what we could find. Then we each signed up for the race, solemnly passing the laptop between us in silence.

'Eight weeks,' I said, looking up at Jeremy. Eight weeks ago I had been living with Emily. A lot could change in eight weeks.

'We can definitely do it,' he said earnestly, his vigour restored by toast and sugar. He shook his head as though stunned by his own brilliance. 'Ben is not going to believe this. I just feel like I want him to see *this* me, you know? I don't want the last thing in his memory of me to be, well . . .' He trailed off.

'I know,' I said, dunking a digestive into my now cold tea, still ravenous. I still wasn't entirely convinced that running this race was the way to win Ben back, or that Ben was even definitely running the race, but I understood why Jeremy needed to do it. Plus there was a part of me that felt that it was so thoroughly impressive and out of character, such a bold move, that I didn't know how Ben could fail to take notice. I made a note to let Emily know later. I hoped that she would tell Sara with no H and that she would rightly be threatened by my burgeoning athletic prowess.

Jeremy eventually sloped home for a shower and a recovery nap. In the fresh silence of the house, I could finally take in what we'd done. My legs, which were still nippy from the wind, wobbly in their rubbish leggings, were beginning to form a dull but not completely unpleasant ache. It was impossible not to feel pleased with myself, and I found it inconceivable that Emily not only didn't know about this, but that I had done it without her altogether. I decided that it was all too confusing and sad to process so I stuck the kettle on again, grabbed Malcolm, and went through to the living room to switch on the TV and get lost in the screen until lunchtime. Malcolm walked out of the room the moment I put him down and sat down on the other side of the doorway to wash absolutely every bit of fluff I'd had the gall to touch with my disgusting human hands.

I sat there until I was freezing cold, my still clammy T-shirt

sticking to my lower back, and I realised with some disgruntle-
ment that I would have to shower. I had been avoiding showers,
especially showers that involved proper hair washing and body
shaving, because the quiet was too much to stand. There was
nothing to drown out the incessant internal monologue or the
constant humming sadness, and I would be forced to confront
some of the feelings I tried most days to drown out. Every
shower I'd had since coming back to Sheffield had resulted in
dramatic underwater sobbing.

I trudged upstairs, grabbed the pink fluffy towel hanging in
the airing cupboard and pressed it to my face, breathing in that
homely, soapy smell. I thought about how nice it was to have an
airing cupboard and how these are things you only get in
houses not bloody boats, where towels always seemed to be
ever so slightly damp because there's nowhere to hang them
up. This was the first time that thinking of the boat didn't trigger a wave of nausea but instead a wave of indignation. I didn't
like living on that boat, and I didn't like always having a damp
towel. I wondered if I might be making progress. Then I stepped
into the shower, switched on the scalding hot water, and howled
for a full twenty minutes.

Getting dressed, I inspected my lobster pink legs in the mirror for any signs of muscle growth. Even though rationally I
knew that one hellish plod in the cold couldn't possibly create
beautifully sculpted and inexplicably tanned legs, I still felt a
little bit disappointed. It seemed like in return for all that effort
there should be some physical reward other than aching feet

and a massive blister. I picked up my phone and stared at the home screen – a photo of Malcolm wearing a Santa hat. Well, of Malcolm having a Santa hat held every so slightly above his head by Emily while she said to me, 'Take the picture, quick, quick before he gets me!' I pressed my finger onto the screen against the hand in the picture. We'd been happy then, hadn't we? Do unhappy people take photos of their pets in fancy dress?

I might have cried had I not just used up all my tears in the shower. Instead I put my phone down, hobbled over to my bedside table, and rummaged inside the drawer of miscellaneous 'bits' until I found what I was looking for. I sat back down on the edge of the bed and gently eased the safety pin into the blister on the side of my big toe. Water ran down my foot and the blister sank in on itself like a punctured bicycle tyre.

6

Run Direction

I normally walk everywhere with headphones in, but I was all the way down the hill and about to cross the road before I realised I'd forgotten them. I gazed helplessly back up towards the house but knew there was no chance I could be bothered to head back up. The throbbing in my legs from earlier had barely died down yet, so for the first time in a long time I set off on a walk by myself without anything to distract me.

This walk was one I'd done hundreds, possibly even thousands of times as it took me past the turning for my old secondary school. I'd trudged along these streets rain or shine for five years. The quiet of the roads was eerie but familiar. There were ghosts everywhere. There was me nipping across the road in front of honking cars because I was late for school. Laughing so hard outside the gates I thought I'd be sick. Walking home arm in arm or sometimes even hand in hand with a girl I was madly but silently in love with, and the ghost of me dreaming of her for the rest of the evening long after we'd said goodbye. Teenage Ally would never believe it, but now I longed for that feeling. I hadn't appreciated the excitement and sweetness of pining for someone like that then. I'd give anything to swap out my hollow gut and constant sickness for that dizzy daydream.

As I approached the row of shops, I walked past the news-agent and the Tesco Express, and tied Pat up outside the new bakery, Bread and Butter (anything that had cropped up since I left for university was 'new' in my book). Pat's eyes were darting about, her tiny mouth wide open in anticipation, recognising all signs pointing towards treats. I stepped inside and smiled nervously at the staff, who looked young and cool and not at all the older ladies I'd expected them to be. Another customer came in and began chatting away, which was a huge relief as I could browse the counter properly instead of rushing to make a deci-sion in order to get out of there as quickly as possible. I chose a loaf of bread studded with green olives, a giant cheese scone, and, just as I was paying, decided on a doughnut, sprinkled gen-erously with sugar, oozing with chocolate custard. I stuffed the lot in my backpack and headed out to retrieve Pat, already excited to head home and eat.

I could have turned around and quite happily walked home then and there. All the resolve I'd felt that morning to go and get the kit that would turn me into an athlete had completely faded and I was convinced I'd fallen prey to one of those 'run-ner's highs' I'd read about, where exercise tricks you into feeling happy and calm for a period of time afterwards because of 'endorphins'. Those endorphins were well and truly gone. However, I'd already talked myself into this excursion and knew it would be exhausting to have to go through this whole rigmarole again tomorrow. Pat and I strolled to the end of the row and stopped outside a shop called Run Direction. Pat had little to no interest in running but was keen on following my backpack with her nose and so dutifully scampered through the door as the sound of the little bell announced our presence to the empty shop. I hovered in the doorway, already hating the experience with every fibre of my being. After a few moments it became clear that nobody was rushing out to greet us and that we were very much on our own. Pushing aside the creeping paranoia that I'd unintentionally broken into a closed shop or someone's house with a very unusual name and design aesthetic, I started to inch forward towards a rack of T-shirts that were all brightly coloured and absolutely tiny. I was halfway through systematically touching every single pair of tiny leggings on the rack when finally there was a sign of life behind the counter. A woman backed her way out of the staff door carrying an enormous cardboard box with a mug balanced precariously on top. In her mouth was a stack of letters, gripped tightly between her teeth. Such was her concentration on not spilling the drink or dropping any of the letters in it that she didn't acknowledge my presence aside from a quick eyebrow raise as she caught my eye.

'Do you want a . . .' I offered, half-heartedly gesturing towards the mug.

The girl shook her head slightly as she lowered herself into a tentative squat trying to keep the box completely upright. We both watched as the mug threatened to slide down, but she managed to drop the box to the floor and grab the mug all at once. She pulled the letters from her mouth, bounced back up quickly, and dropped them on the counter, looking up at me, triumphant.

'Hi!' she exclaimed, laughing at her dramatic entrance. 'What can I do for you?' She had a Yorkshire accent. Stronger than mine. Not softened at the edges by years of living with someone who had '*barths*' and '*darnced*'. She reached up over her head and ran her hand through her hair. It was kind of floppy in the front and kept flicking in her eyes. For some reason I felt even more self-conscious than usual. I suddenly felt embarrassed at the prospect of explaining to this girl with her skinny jeans, her toned arms and zero body fat, that I thought none of the clothes in here would fit me, that some of them were Pat sized. I tugged at my jumper underneath my unzipped coat, somehow trying to make it cover up more of me. I was acutely aware that I was wearing old, shapeless jeans and hadn't bothered to put any make-up on.

'Well,' I spoke carefully, feeling like such an imposter that I needed to check I was using the correct words, 'I've started running. Today, actually.'

The girl raised her eyebrows. 'Oh wow, did you run . . . here?'

'Er, no,' I said glancing at Pat slumped at my feet who, lovely as she was, was not in any kind of shape to be going running, and then down at myself – also deeply unlikely.

I looked up and realised the girl was teasing me.

'So, you've started running and you need some proper gear?' the girl suggested to me, picking up her mug of tea and taking a sip. She wrapped her hands around it as if to warm them through. Her nails had chipped blue nail polish on them.

'Yes!' I said. 'Yes, exactly. I only have old leggings.'

'Old leggings won't do,' the girl said. 'So how much running do you think you'll be doing? A couple a week? A 5k?'

'I'm doing the half marathon,' I announced confidently.

'The half marathon here?' The girl pointed down at the floor as if the marathon might be taking place in this very shop and involve thousands of tiny laps. 'The one in a couple of months?'

'Er, yeah? I know, it's probably impossible.'

'No, no, no,' said the girl, putting her drink down and lifting a hand up to stop me. 'It's not impossible. It's a challenge, but it's certainly not impossible.'

'Do you think?' I said earnestly, immediately placing deep value on this stranger's opinion. I mean, she looked like a runner and worked in a running shop, so surely if she thought it possible then maybe it really was.

'Absolutely,' she said firmly. 'We'll get you kitted out in all the proper gear and I'm sure that you can smash it.' She stepped out from behind the counter and gestured for me to follow her over to the back of the shop, about three strides away.

'OK, yes, thank you!' I was thrilled to have someone not scoff in my face and to be taken seriously in my new identity as A Runner. She didn't laugh me out of the shop. It was a fantastic start. She inspected the clothes on the rack as if she'd never seen them before, or had to look at them in a whole new light to work out how best to serve this unusual customer. Pat had lost interest in the whole thing and was staring longingly at my backpack, willing the zips to spring apart and the doughnut to fall out. As the girl started pulling clothes off racks and plonking them on the counter, I watched her closely. Her hair was dark blonde and looked as though it had once had highlights that were now just at the ends, ready to be snipped out. She furrowed her brow and screwed up her face as she clumsily tried to detangle hangers from each other and eventually gave up on one particular top, choosing instead to rip it off the hanger and fling it down on the counter. She was tall, and her long limbs knocked into everything. It was a bit like watching Bambi go shopping.

'Right!' she announced, snapping me out of my trance. 'Why don't you see what you think of some of these?'

We waded through tops, deciding on one with longer sleeves because the weather was, as Dad would say, 'perishing', and one with short sleeves in case of unseasonably warm weather on the day. I voiced quiet concerns that nothing would fit me and was assured that they absolutely would and that tight running clothes are essential so that there's nothing flapping about. 'Streamlined' was the word she used. I nodded, making a vow to remember this later when I squeezed them on at home. We decided on some knee-length running leggings because I was a 'naturally warm' person and because they were marginally cheaper than full-length ones. They looked vaguely reminiscent of the kind of pedal pushers I'd worn to school discos circa 1999, which made me like them more. The girl tried to get me to consider buying some new trainers, but having looked at the prices (eye watering) I decided that they would have to wait until another day. I did give in and buy a single pair of socks, though, which cost £7, and which the girl assured me would 'cushion my feet' and 'give a bit of bounce'. It seemed like a lot to ask of a bit of towelling for your feet, but there you go.

As I stood at the counter to pay, my eyes landed on a flier which looked like it had been photocopied on a machine running out of ink. It read:

Come run with us!

Have you always wondered if running is for you? Then try it out! We don't discriminate, we don't check times, we don't talk about nutrition. The aim of the game is to simply get around the route – no person left behind!

If you fancy giving it a go then we meet every Thursday at 7 p.m. outside Endcliffe Park gates.

Email: Jo.runs@gmail.com for more info.

The girl caught me reading the flier. 'That's my group,' she said.

She continued to fold away my new clothes into a bag before stopping and looking up at me, so obviously thrilled at her own epiphany a lightbulb practically glowed above her head.

'*You* should come!'

I started protesting, but she was already thrusting a flier into my hand.

'Yes! I can't believe I didn't think of this straight away, we're always looking for new recruits. It's perfect for you.'

I opened my mouth again, but she ploughed on.

'We can't promise to get you half marathon ready but we can promise it'll be fun!"

She sounded like a children's TV presenter. I enjoyed her unabashed cheesiness. She seemed unaware of it. The girl handed over the bag and took the credit card from my hand without even pausing to tell me how much it was before shoving it in the machine.

'I don't know,' I said, taking the card machine off her and wincing at the amount on the screen, which I wasn't certain was even available on this card. 'I'm very new and very slow—' I hadn't finished speaking but the girl jabbed her finger at the piece of paper in my hands.

'No person left behind!' she read out loud very slowly as if maybe I had not been able to read the flier and that was where my reluctance was coming from.

She handed me back my card and grinned triumphantly.

'So, see you on Thursday at 7 p.m. then.'

It wasn't a question. Usually I would have said something non-committal, but there was something about this girl, her certainty that I could do it. And her enthusiasm was so genuine and contagious that I found myself quite helplessly smiling back.

'Well, yes, OK. OK, I'll see what I can do.'

I turned around to leave, scooping up a now virtually comatose Pat, and then turned back.

'I'm Ally by the way.'

'Hi Ally, I'm Jo.'

On my way home I sent a picture of the flier to Jeremy with the caption: *Get in bitches we're going running.*

He replied almost immediately, *Yes, Al! That's the spirit – I knew you'd get into it. Count me in.*

From: Alexandra Waters   3 February 2019 at 17:25
To: Emily Anderson

Subject: Anybody out there?

Hi Em,

I haven't heard from you in a couple of days. I really thought you'd be wanting to come and collect Malcolm but I guess you're too busy at the moment what with everything that's going on. Have you moved everything of mine out of the boat now? I left some stuff there and I can't stop thinking about you sitting there with all my things around you. I don't mind if you've got rid of it all but I'd like to know. I've got everything I need up here so don't worry about that. I completely understand.

So you won't believe this but I'm going to run a half marathon in April with Jeremy – you know my old friend who I told you about? I've got eight weeks to train which seems a bit mad I know, but it might really be doable. I didn't really think I'd be here that long but in a way it feels nice to have a marker you know? I felt like I was sinking a bit and now I have something to swim towards (well, run towards). It also means that you have eight weeks to come up and visit?

Eight weeks. It sounds like a lifetime but eight weeks ago we were living a different life. I lived in my home with you and I thought our future was all mapped out. So how could we possibly say where we'll be in another eight weeks?

Anyway, I will be very busy training for the run now but I will always have time to see you.

Al x

P.S. Are you still with Sarah? I don't want to ask. I hate it that I'm writing this question but I just have to. The image of you two together is burned into my brain. It feels so real, like I've seen it a million times. Have you liked her since you met her? I keep trying to remember when she started working with you but I can't. Has it been two years? More? Did you know then that this is what you were going to do? Have I been so blind for such a long time? I can't even begin to tell you what it feels like. You have no idea because no one would ever do this to you.

From: Emily Anderson   4 February 2019 at 11:06
To: Alexandra Waters

Subject: re: Is there anybody out there?

Ally,

I don't even know where to begin. Sorry I haven't been in touch but I did say that I'm busy at work at the moment and that I think we ought not to speak every day for both of our sakes.

You know that I do want Malcolm but it seems like you're not planning on bringing him back and I have no intention OR TIME to come up and get him. I can't even think about it at the moment and I trust you're looking after him so for now let's leave things as they are. The thing is Al, if you'd just asked me to come and see you I might have done it but something really sticks in my throat about being forced to come up because you stole my cat. Did you really think that was a good way to get what you want? I guess you just weren't really thinking at all.

Obviously I haven't got rid of all your stuff! How on earth can you think I'd do that? That's such a weird thing to say, Al. I haven't thrown away your things. I haven't thrown you away. I'm not trying to cut you off or cut you out. Please stop thinking like that.

As for the run, wow. That's unexpected! But good for you. It'll be nice for you to have something to focus on. Eight weeks though, that isn't very long!

Is your dad fine with you staying? Do you not have plans to move back down to London? It's just people miss you here and you haven't been answering anyone's messages. Beth told me she's sent you three and you haven't even read them? It seems a little like you've upped sticks and just switched off this part of your life. This wasn't just my life. This was your life too. You belong here too, even without me.

Maybe I've got that all wrong. But regardless, Ally, I think you should speak to people that love you and are worried about you. You don't have to cut them out. They're your friends too.

Good luck with all the training.

Em x

P.S. Yes. I think you know that I am still with Sara. Not to hurt you, Ally, but it is just the truth.

7

Organised Torture

I discovered a new photo on Sara with no H's Instagram page. It had been uploaded the evening before and I recognised it instantly because I had taken that same photo hundreds of times. It was the view of the sun setting from our boat. From Emily's boat. If you sit on the roof at the right time you can catch the sun in the trees and the shadows on the river. It was a picture I never got tired of taking. It was oddly satisfying to see it there on her page. Like picking a scab and making it bleed.

Emily had still not updated hers. She had not uploaded any stories. I wondered if she had approved this photo or if she would scold Sara with no H for it when she saw it. Perhaps they had been sitting next to each other when it was taken. I screen-shotted the photo before putting my phone back onto airplane mode and getting out of bed.

It was our first running club that evening, so Jeremy and I

had agreed to forgo our lunchtime meeting and see each other at the park instead. I was just settling in for a day of TV and existential dread when I heard the key in the lock. I looked at the clock. It was midday.

'Hello?' I called out into the hall.

My dad walked into the living room followed closely by Malcolm, who was hoping he might get double lunch.

'All right, Al?' he said, leaning against the door frame of the living room.

'Yeah,' I replied into my mug, leaving it slightly too long before saying, 'you?' I was annoyed with him for being home and for catching me still unshowered and in my pyjamas at lunchtime.

He ignored me.

'I had a free period before lunch so I thought we could go for a walk.' It was clearly not so much a suggestion as an instruction, but I attempted to protest anyway.

'Dad! No, I'm too tired. I'm not even dressed. And it's freezing anyway.' I stared at the TV, knowing already that my resistance was futile.

'I'll just get my walking shoes on and then I'll be ready to go,' he said breezily, 'get Pat's lead and the bags will you?'

He disappeared into the hall.

I sat still for a few more moments, gearing myself up to go outside. I didn't like the sound of this walk. This was not my dad's style. Still, I dutifully pulled on some jeans and put my wellies on. I coaxed Pat away from eating Malcolm's food.

Malcolm was lying flat out in the hall like he'd been shot so that on our way out we had to step over him.

'You need to not be so fussy,' I told him. 'You snooze you lose.' Then, to Dad, 'I hope he's OK.'

'He's fine,' he said. 'Look at him.' Malcolm rolled over, his eyes closed.

We chatted a bit about the horrible weather as we set off, as if this was a perfectly normal, not at all coerced family walk.

It was muddy in the woods and as we adjusted to the quiet and the squelching, we fell into silence. We walked like that for a few minutes. We passed a couple of dog walkers to nod at, and one man running speedily in a luminous backpack, but it felt very much like we had the place to ourselves.

'How are you doing then?' my dad finally said. He sounded strained, as if he was the one there against his will.

'Yeah, I'm all right.'

'No.'

I didn't look at him but could tell he was shaking his head.

'You're not all right, tell me how you're doing.'

He didn't sound cross exactly, but definitely impatient. It was so unlike my dad to ask a question like this. To ask a question at all, in fact. I found that I was compelled to answer him.

'OK then. I'm really sad, Dad.' I thought perhaps he'd say something, but he just carried on walking silently next to me.

'I feel like I'm seventeen again, except I'm twenty-nine and I've got nothing to show for the past twelve years. I'm back at square one. And I miss Emily. And I'm so furious with her. And feel so sorry for myself. And I'm so cross with myself for being so pathetic. And I just have no idea what I'm doing.' I laughed a bit, to ease the pain of hearing some of those words spoken out loud.

Out of the corner of my eye I could see my dad nodding as if he were agreeing with me. Quite rude.

'You've every right to be cross with Emily and you've every right to be sad, but you've got to stop this, Al.'

'Stop what?'

'Stop moping about. Stop feeling sorry for yourself! Do you think sleeping in and sitting around the house is going to change things?'

I didn't say anything. My bottom lip wobbled.

'I'm not just moping around the house – I went for a run with Jeremy.'

'Right, and did he pay you for that then? Is that your new job?'

I glanced at him, but he was staring resolutely ahead. We squelched along past a family with an enormous, extremely muddy golden retriever. We both offered embarrassed apologies for Pat's growls at its friendly advances.

'No,' I said eventually. 'I know I've been a bit . . . it's just that I really thought I'd have my shit together a bit more by now.' I'd never got into the habit of swearing in front of my dad and involuntarily bit my cheek.

'You're twenty-nine!' Dad exclaimed, breezing right past the errant 'shit'. 'Why would you have it together?'

'It's just, well . . . you and Mum had me by the time you were twenty-nine. When you were my age I was six years old!'

My dad honked with laughter, or something like it.

'I wouldn't use having a kid as a measure of doing all right. Do you think me and your mum were sorted just because we had a kid? Let me tell you, those were the hardest years of my life. Jesus Christ.' He shuddered, the memory of my early years haunting him.

'Cheers.'

He softened. 'Good years, obviously. But bloody hard work. I didn't feel like I had everything together when I was twenty-nine. Thank God I had your mum, but it wasn't all hunky-dory and it wasn't what I thought it would be like, either. You can't expect everything to go to plan. And you can't just fall apart when it doesn't. That's not an option.'

We were both quiet for a minute. Thinking of Mum.

'She was the best, wasn't she?'

My dad rubbed his hands together to warm them up.

'Yes. And you know what she'd be saying to you, Al?'

I thought for a moment but I couldn't conjure her. 'I actually don't, Dad.'

He paused. Perhaps the words he imagined her saying didn't come as easily as he'd hoped to him either.

'Maybe "pull yourself together"?' I offered eventually. 'Maybe "there's plenty more fish in the sea"?'

'Perhaps,' Dad nodded. 'I think she'd say, "you've always got us".'

The 'us' was like a knife to my heart, slicing it softly like butter even after all these years.

'Look, I know I can't just keep on living with you. I'm sorry, Dad. I've come crashing back in uninvited like an overgrown teenager.'

'You're not uninvited at my house. It's *your* house too.'

Just as I began to protest, he carried on, 'Although obviously I know what you mean. What if you start paying rent? Will that help you stop feeling like a teenager?'

'Of course I'll pay rent! I don't actually *want* to be a freeloader.'

'All right, suits me fine. We'll work something out. Happy to help. But you know, Al, in order to pay rent you'll have to get a–'

'Yes, a job. Thanks, Dad, I know.'

'Doesn't have to be a teaching job if you don't want that. Although I do think it's a waste of all that training.'

I started to tune him out.

'Maybe you just haven't found the right school. You know I could see if there's anything coming up at–'

'No thanks, I'll sort it.'

I started sweating at the mere thought of working in the same school as my dad, the same school that I went to and dreamed of escaping.

'Right, well. As long as you're not just sitting about the house all day anymore. I can't stand it, Al. It makes me depressed just looking at you. You're better than that.'

'Got it.'

I decided that today I could gloss over the fact that my dad had quite heavily implied that I was an unplanned arrival that ruined his twenties, and focus on the part where he'd opened up to me a bit.

'It's nice to talk to you properly. Even if it is to get told I'm a layabout,' I said, as we both naturally turned around at the tree that we'd decided years ago marks the halfway point of this particular walk.

'Well, who else is going to tell you? I want you to be happy. I wish you'd talk to me more, to be honest. I know you think I won't understand like your mum would have, but you don't give me a chance.'

We walked mostly in silence on our way back, commenting only on the muddiness of our boots and the changing colours of the sky as the clouds shifted. As we got closer to home we talked about how hungry we suddenly were and of all the things we could eat for lunch since Dad would be home from school for once. We tried to decide what we might have. Absolutely no green vegetables was a given. I floated the idea of another round of fish and chips before spontaneously adding, 'And it's on me!' What was one more thing on the credit card? Running clothes and chips surely cancel each other out in some way?

In a classic annoying Dad way, he immediately threw his hand up to his chest as if the very idea of such generosity from his daughter had given him a heart attack. I ignored him as we approached the edge of the woods and emerged back onto the street.

'It's a one-time offer! It will expire.'

'I'll have one of everything then please.'

I bumped my head into the side of his arm and he reached around with his other hand to give my head a little pat. We were friends again.

'You can do me a favour actually. In lieu of financial reimbursement.'

I looked at him but he was staring resolutely ahead. He'd obviously been planning on saying whatever was coming up for ages, I could tell. I wondered if that's what this whole 'walk and talk' had really been leading up to.

'What's that then?'

'It's a fun job, I think.' He was still staring straight ahead, squinting slightly into the middle distance. 'We need someone to hand out pop on Friday evening at the lower school disco.'

'Oh, no thanks.' By which I meant to say – absolutely not.

'Ally,' he turned to me, 'we need someone to do it. It's just standing behind a table and handing out pop.'

'Stop saying pop. What do you mean, the lower school disco? I thought they didn't do discos anymore.'

He looked flustered.

'It's for the year 7s – they're throwing a disco for Syria.'

'Bloody hell. I'm sure Syria is thrilled about that. Just what they need.'

'I'm sure they are, they've raised £100, Ally.'

'Right. I'm not sure that it's a school disco though, is it, Dad? It's not 1995 . . .'

'A school *dance* then. That's right. It's a dance.' He clicked his fingers as if it was all coming back to him. 'There's a theme . . . yes, it's seaside themed.'

'The seaside?'

'Yes, yes.'

'Which seaside?'

'You know. *The* seaside. Seasides, Al. You've been to Clee-thorpes. Sea, sand, buckets and spades!'

It was no accident he did not mention 'sun'.

'Cleethorpes themed?'

'I suppose so.' He nodded. 'We gave them a choice, it was the seaside, winter wonderland, or outer space.'

'How did you land on those?'

'Well those are the decorations we already have.'

'Right. OK. None of this makes any sense. It's February.'

'They voted, Al! It was all done fair and square.'

Good grief.

'I'm not sure why you need my help anyway, surely there are enough teachers to do it.'

'We've not had enough volunteers! It's a Friday night, *most* people have been working all week.' He looked at me pointedly. Can't argue with that.

'You can bring Jeremy if you want. As I say, it's just standing behind a table and handing out—'

'Yes, I get it! Handing out pop. Bloody hell. How long is it?'

'Just a couple of hours.'

'Fine. That's not too bad.'

'We need you an hour before that obviously to set up, and an hour afterwards as well to put it all away.'

'Right.'

'It'll all be over by 10 p.m., Al. Latest. Come on.' He reached over and squeezed my shoulder. If we'd have been different people he would have reached over and got me into a headlock kind of hug where I had to squeal to be let go and agree to do it. This was Dad's version. 'I'll buy you a drink after.'

'All right, done.'

Listen Jeremy, Dad's roped us into this thing on Friday night. It's a dance at the school to raise money for charity – he keeps calling it a disco for Syria. Anyway we just have to help set up and hand out drinks, and clear away. Dad says he'll buy us a drink after and I think there might be a fair amount of free snacks in it for us. Sorry. This is one of the most tragic messages I've ever sent. Truly, one for the ages.

I can't deal with Disco for Syria. What do we wear? Leg warmers? Will there be a glitter ball? I will be there, obviously.

The bag of running clothes was still sitting in the corner of my bedroom where I'd dumped it a few days before. Malcolm had taken to alternately sitting in it and ripping it apart so it was looking a bit worse for wear. I put a pair of knickers on, the elastic gone, grey from the washing machine, ten years old at least. The age and familiarity of the terrible knickers somewhat softened the aggressive newness of the running clothes which I had already decided to hate. I took my time pulling the tags off the trousers, chewing through the bit of plastic with my teeth exactly as I had been taught not to. They were covered in cat hair. Eventually I sat on the bed and pulled them on, not really believing that I'd even be able to get them over my knees. I had to stand up and wiggle about a bit, thrusting backwards and forwards. They pulled up high over the top of my belly button, which I liked and, although they clung uncomfortably to my knees, overall they didn't feel too bad. They were tight but not in the way jeans felt tight in a changing room, they felt like they were meant to be tight, as if to hold all of each leg in one place.

Putting the sports bra on turned out to be a feat so complicated and strenuous it took my mind off everything for a very confusing few minutes. Jo had assured me that it was the right size and yet it seemed so small and inflexible that I found it very hard to believe I was ever going to be able to fit it around my body. I stretched, lifting my arms up and down until it shifted into place. When I exhaled I was surprised to find it didn't feel as though I was being cut in two. I pulled on a short-sleeved grey top that clung to all the areas that were spilling out of the sports bra, but I had to concede the overall effect was not as horrible as I'd imagined.

My dad waved me off as I left to meet Jeremy. I could tell he was pleased to see me get out of the house, even if it was to my unpaid running gig. And he was clearly amused by my running gear.

'Good luck, Mo! Go for gold!'

'Ugh. Bye Dad.'

*

'We must be the first ones here!' Jeremy said as we approached the gate of the park, but as we got closer I spotted a gangly girl with a long ponytail bobbing about in a green luminous jacket surrounded by a few other dark shapes, and immediately recognised her. Something fizzed in my stomach.

'That's them,' I said, nudging Jeremy and pointing towards the small group. There were four of them including Jo, which was much less nerve-wracking than the huge group of Lycra clad running machines I'd been expecting.

As we approached, I lifted my hand into a half wave and Jo squinted for a second, trying to work out who it was from a distance and then, to my delight, her face lit up and she waved back enthusiastically and gestured for us to come forward and join them.

'You came!' she exclaimed once we were within hearing distance. 'I'm so pleased you came, that's great!' and to my surprise she stepped forward and gave me a little hug. She smelt like freshly washed hair and I cursed myself for wallowing in my own filth all day, knowing full well that my hair smelt like the cheese toasties I'd made at lunchtime and liberal amounts of dry shampoo.

'And you brought someone,' said Jo, turning to Jeremy. I did introductions and Jo gave Jeremy a hug too before turning to the group. 'Everyone, this is Ally and Jeremy who are going to be running with us today – they're running the half marathon in April so they're trying to step up their training.'

I thought that was an extremely kind way to put it. Stepping up my training by adding not one, but two runs to my repertoire.

'Ally, Jeremy, this is Jane, Jim and Jas.' She waved her arm around introducing the entire group as one person.

'Ooh, all Js,' I said.

'Pardon dear?' said Jane.

'Um, it's just you're all . . . Js.'

Jo smiled. 'Yeah, so we are,' she said, like you might to a child who had correctly identified a colour.

She turned to the group and began explaining the route as I continued to die inside and Jeremy stifled giggles next to me. He jabbed me in the side as we started shuffling back towards the gates of the park.

'Come along, Jalexandra.'

We were all encouraged to run at a pace at which we found it 'comfortable to talk', which didn't really exist for me, so I just tried to run at a pace which kept up with everyone else. I settled at the back just trailing behind Jane who was running with her head down staring at her feet. Ahead of me I could hear Jeremy alternately chatting and panting to Jo. I focused on observing everyone in front of me, trying to assess how hard they were finding it. I kept my eyes glued to Jane's feet and noticed that her trainers were bright white with pink stripes – quite obviously, I thought, brand spanking new. They looked absolutely huge, like someone had strapped pillows to her feet.

I felt compelled to keep up with her and tried to fall into pace alongside her. Jo made it all look completely effortless. She was looking up at Jeremy and nodding encouragingly as he tried to answer her questions and breathe at the same time, which looked increasingly difficult. His easy smile had been replaced with a grimace. I was aware that while I didn't mind if Jane or the others could hear my ragged, uneven breaths, I really didn't want Jo to. I didn't want her to know that I struggled or sweated or that my hair was stuck to the middle of my forehead.

As we approached some traffic lights Jo reminded us all that we had run 'nearly a mile!' and we all made noises varying from 'wow' to 'bloody hell' and then it started to rain. Not just a light drizzle but a heavens-opening, end of days, full-on downpour as if someone was holding an infinite bucket of water above our heads. The rest of the run was a blur of fat raindrops and sweat pooling at the tip of my nose and dripping into my mouth. Despite the discomfort of soggy feet squelching in my trainers and of my hoodie getting progressively heavier, the run somehow became easier. Everyone slowed down to avoid slipping, the noise drowned out the sound of our gasps for air, the streets cleared, and the smell of wet leaves filled the air. We finally rounded the bottom of the hill that would lead us back to the park entrance. Despite the muscles in my calves and the rasp of my breath begging me to stop, something inside screamed at me to keep going. I decided I'd keep plodding on until I fell, which was unnecessarily dramatic – there were metres to go before the finish line. As we slowed and finally stopped at the foot of a large tree, Jo turned to face the group and wiped water from her face.

'Well done everybody,' she bellowed against the sound of the rain. 'Thanks so much for coming, I'm so sorry about the weather.' She said this completely sincerely as if she really had summoned the clouds herself. 'I really hope to see you all again next week, hopefully we'll all be slightly less soggy,' she added as I lifted the bottom of my hoodie and wrung it out. As everyone said their goodbyes, Jo sidled up to us. Jeremy and I were discussing whether or not to shell out for an Uber to drive us back instead of waiting for the bus.

'So what did you think?' She grimaced at our unimpressed faces and chattering teeth.

'Honestly I didn't mind the rain!' I was keen to reassure her. 'I am really glad that I came in the end,' I said, and to my horror I reached out and patted the top of her arm. Jeremy grinned irritatingly next to me.

'You wouldn't believe how close we were to bailing,' he said to Jo.

'Well,' she said, 'I'm really glad you came. See you next week?'

'Yes, we'll be here,' said Jeremy, answering for us both.

'Great. See you then. Why don't you give me your number in case you're running late so I know that you're not just bailing on me.' She winked at me and my heart leapt.

I didn't dare look at Jeremy, but I could feel him effervescent with excitement, emitting a tiny noise on a frequency only audible to the hysterical.

'OK sure, yes, that makes sense.' I reached out and entered what I hoped was my number into Jo's phone. 'Should I . . . get yours?'

'You've got mine, silly! It's on the flier.'

Of course, this was a formality. She probably took everyone's number down, it just made sense. Although I couldn't help but notice she did not take Jeremy's.

'OK guys, get home safe.' Jo grinned and, to my utter disbelief, jogged away in the other direction. More jogging!

'I should probably get your number,' Jeremy was saying in a high-pitched voice as we shuffled off, united by an unspoken agreement that we had too much to discuss now to simply have a five-minute Uber ride together. We needed to walk. I allowed myself to imagine that maybe Jo wanted my number for non-organisational reasons.

As we turned out of the park we spotted a pub on the corner. It still had lights in the window from Christmas; a snowman blinked at us. It looked like the most inviting place in the world.

'We could just quickly . . .' I gestured in the direction of the pub.

'Let's do it.' Jeremy linked arms with me and we power-walked pubwards.

We were unlikely to bump into anyone from school at this pub. It was at the top of a hill so steep that you really had to commit to going, and was generally full of older gentlemen and the strong smell of a carpet saturated with the dregs of beers past. We were more likely to bump into someone's grandad having his Thursday evening pint, or teenagers trying it on, than anyone our own age. Confident that we could relax, we slung ourselves into two armchairs next to a not-quite roaring fire and took turns to buy packets of crisps and pints of the cheapest lager. We reminisced about the many evenings we'd spent here in what seemed like another lifetime. Sixteen-year-old me desperately hoping not to be ID-ed, eighteen-year-old me sitting at the top corner of a table on a stool that was too high for it, feeling horribly in the way but unable to go home just in case the girl I was madly in love with paid me even the smallest bit of attention. I thought about what it would have been like to bring Emily there as a teenager and knew that she wouldn't really get it. I couldn't imagine Emily ever drinking sickly, sticky pints of cheap cider or diligently persevering with smoking Silk Cuts stolen from her nan until the choking subsided and the sweet headrush kicked in.

By the end of the second pint, when we had properly dried out and warmed up, we had a merry debrief of the evening. We were both incredibly smug, like athletes who'd just nailed a PB.

'Mate, I think actually I was born to run and now I've found my sport there'll be no stopping me.'

'No definitely, definitely, I know what you mean. I wasn't even that out of breath, was I? I don't think I was. It was more the rain.'

'Yes! It was the rain. Honestly, we were both great. This is going to be fine.'

'It's going to be a breeze and . . .'

He looked at me cheekily over the top of his pint.

I glowered at him, daring him to say what he was about to say, knowing exactly what it was.

'And,' he popped a crisp in his mouth, crunching loudly for dramatic effect, 'you're going to bang Jo.'

'JEREMY!' I shrieked, giving his shin a little kick under the table. 'I am not going to bang,' I paused slightly, recoiling at the word, 'Jo. I haven't even thought about it.'

I picked up my pint to finish off the dregs.

'You're a liar, but OK.'

'I haven't!'

'Ally, you literally have. You basically didn't stop staring at her, it was borderline creepy.'

'No it wasn't! I wasn't!'

I knew he was winding me up, but the part of me that constantly feared finally being exposed as a massive creepy lunatic was starting to wonder if there was some truth to it.

'I'm teasing, Al – well, not about wanting to bang Jo.'

I rolled my eyes. We were quiet for a minute.

'Do you know who would hate Jo?'

Jeremy shook his head.

'Emily would *hate* her.'

Jeremy looked scandalised. And thrilled.

'Why?' He patted his shorts pocket, a reflex, looking for a packet of cigarettes to accompany his gossip. He stopped, disappointed, as he realised he had not brought them to running club.

'She's just so,' I waved my hand about looking for the word, 'nice. She'd think that she was putting it on or that she was bland. She hates niceness, she thinks it's boring.'

'She sounds like a treat.'

I shrugged. I couldn't really defend her nor lay into her. I'd deferred to her opinions on people for a long time.

'So, do you think she's bland? Or fake?'

'No! Well, I don't know. I don't know her well enough to judge.'

'Just well enough to know you want to bang her.'

I nodded, giving up trying to change his mind.

'You know what Emily would hate even more than Jo? *You* and Jo.'

I looked at him blankly.

'Together. As in she would hate it if you and Jo got together.' He rolled his eyes at me for being too slow.

'I don't know. She and Sara with no H are shacked up together having a great time no doubt. She probably wouldn't even notice.'

'Of course she would! She'd hate it. That would one hundred per cent get her attention, Al. Running this half marathon with your hot, young personal trainer and *lover*.'

I burst out laughing.

'OK, first of all, please never say *lover* again.'

I considered what he'd said properly.

'It's just that the idea of being with anyone apart from Emily makes me feel a bit sick.'

'I know. But that's only temporary. And if she can crack on with some other girl then you can too. It doesn't have to be a big thing, just a bit of fun. Try and think of it as a way to get her attention.'

'I don't know. I mean, would Jo even be interested in me? I'm not exactly at my best at the moment.' I dusted crisp crumbs from the front of my hoodie. 'Plus we don't know that she's even into women, do we?'

'Of course she is! No one is straight anymore. She got your number, she invited you running, didn't she? Have a bit more confidence in yourself. Just think about it, open your mind up to the possibility of a *fling*, Al. You don't have to fall in love with her. You don't have to marry her.'

'I just have to get with her and then tell Emily about it.'

'Basically, yeah.' He glanced around to look at the bar to see if it was busy. 'Another one?'

Without proper food (there are not enough crisps in the world to constitute a meal in my opinion) another pint might tip me over the edge from fun drunk to complete mess. I hesitated. I also desperately did not want to go home by myself.

'Do you want to get some food and then see after that?'

'Yes, yes, a thousand times yes.' Jeremy clattered up from the table. We were both well on our way.

'Hey,' he said quietly, grabbing my hand on our way out and giving it a little squeeze, 'thanks for this.'

We went to an Indian takeaway a few minutes' walk up the road, halfway between the pub and my house and, once we'd collected our food – in a crate, which I think indicated that we may have over-ordered, along with the chuckle from the man who handed it over – trudged the final few minutes back to mine in the quiet, dark streets. The rain had almost completely stopped, but people had yet to venture back out.

We stood by the door to my house while I fished around in the zip-up pocket of my tiny Lycra trousers for my house keys. I was reminded of being sixteen and preparing to 'act sober' for my dad after a night on the Bacardi Breezers. We finally clambered inside and shouted through to see if Dad was in. He was already on his way towards us, lured by the smell of tikka masala.

'All right, Al?' he said walking up the hallway. 'All right, Jeremy?' He extended his hand. 'Long time no see,' he said, matter-of-factly.

'Hello Graham,' Jeremy said seriously, shaking my dad's hand, doing his absolute best impression of a sober person.

'What have we got here then?' Dad said, eyeing up our crate of food, ignoring our dishevelled appearances and the fact we'd been due home at least two hours ago.

'We were starving after our run,' I said pointedly, but his eyes didn't stray from the plastic containers.

'Yeah, do you want some, Graham?' Jeremy offered. 'We got loads.'

'I reckon I could take some off your hands, yeah.'

And so, Jeremy, Dad and I sat in the dim light of the kitchen, plates piled high with brightly coloured curry and poppadoms the size of our heads, and ate in amiable silence – only breaking it to pass each other different containers, complain about the music on the radio (which none of us bothered to change), and at one point grab three beers from the fridge (curry doesn't taste right without it according to Dad). With the terrible music on, the plentiful carbohydrates, a cat and a dog sitting companionably under the table waiting for us to drop our food, I felt content for the first time in a long time. That evening, things were as they were supposed to be. I enjoyed the warmth of the kitchen, my fuzzy head, and pleasantly aching body.

'So you'll be helping out at school next week will you, Jeremy?'

'I will, Graham! I hear we're throwing a disco for Syria.'

I kicked him under the table.

'Hmm?' my dad said, squinting at his beer bottle, holding it as far away from his face as possible, trying to read the label.

'I'll be there.'

'Grand.'

Jeremy left to walk home and finally have a shower. Once the front door slammed, the house felt incredibly empty.

'So, how was running?' Dad said after a lengthy silence. He sat back in his chair, swigging on the last of his beer.

I began stacking plates in the dishwasher, my back turned to him.

'Good, thanks.'

I realised he was waiting for more and when I turned around, he was looking expectantly at me. He looked suddenly much older. Tired from his long hours at work and from his miserable daughter. I could see how desperately he wanted for things to be getting better.

'Well. I managed it.' I smiled and raised my eyebrows.

'And how was it?' He ignored my raised eyebrows completely and began nibbling on some leftover poppadom from the bag on the table.

'It was OK actually, apart from getting totally drenched.'

'Great!' he said and smiled broadly. 'So you've had a fun evening.' He said this as more of a question than a statement, keen for me to confirm that I'd had a good time, that I'd been OK for a few hours.

'I have, Dad.'

He beamed and announced he was making a cup of tea and heading upstairs to bed. As he stood waiting for the kettle to boil I stood behind him and wrapped my arms around his waist, resting my head on his shoulder. My dad is not a cuddly dad, so it was very rare that we had any physical contact when we weren't greeting or leaving each other, but after a couple of moments he tilted his head to rest on mine. I felt him exhale.

We stood like that for a few moments more before I gave him a big squeeze and he made a noise as if he was winded to really ensure the sincerity of the moment was well and truly over. I told him I was going to have a shower, and went upstairs.

It was only when I was back in my bedroom, naked and blow-drying my entire body to get warmed up, that I realised the shower hadn't made me cry.

*

From: Alexandra Waters   6 February 2019 at 23:47
To: Emily Anderson

Subject: Update – I'm an athlete now

Emily,

It's OK I knew you were with her but I just had to check. Sometimes things get worse in my head than they are in reality so I just need to know the situation. Thanks for not throwing my stuff away. I can't even think what's in those boxes, is it just clothes and stuff? I feel like all the proper stuff is probably yours. I guess if you think it's worth keeping you can just bring it up with you when you come to get Malcolm.

I don't know if I'll be back in London. I know I need to get back to everybody but to be honest Em, they don't really care about me, do they? They were always your friends really. Maybe I'll meet them for coffee one time and they'll tell me how sorry they are and how absolutely nothing will change and how they aren't taking sides but that isn't the truth. They're yours. And I was part of your package. And now I'm not.

It isn't your fault. It's my fault for allowing myself to just become an extension of you for the past few years. You're really great and when I was with you I thought I was really great too but I think, actually, it was all just you and I forgot about my bit. Maybe that's why you don't want me anymore. It's easy to discard someone who isn't really there. I hope you know what I mean. It doesn't feel as though I'm explaining myself properly.

That's why I feel like I might stay here for a bit. Certainly for the next couple of months, especially with the run coming up. You can come any time.

I went running today with a club. I thought it would be horrifying but it wasn't. The girl who organises it is really nice.

I paused after typing *nice*. She *was* nice, but was that really the right word to use to make Emily care? What could I say that would drive her mad?

She was really hot.

Ugh, no. I sounded like a teenage boy.

She was really mysterious.

I have never described anyone as mysterious in my life. I am not Peter André.

She was really interesting.

Interesting! Bingo. She'll hate that I didn't elaborate.

She makes me feel like I might really be able to do it. She even took my number!

Or should I say she even asked for my number? Which was true. But did it sound like too much of an obvious brag? Although I was trying to obviously brag, so perhaps that was what I should go for.

She makes me feel like I might really be able to do it. She even asked for my number!!

That's the one.

I also ate a chicken curry with Dad and Jeremy. That's right. I eat chickens now.

Anyway, I hope you're OK. Maybe you won't even reply to this. I haven't heard from you in a couple of days.

Love, Ally xxx

From: Emily Anderson   8 February 2019 at 08:30
To: Alexandra Waters

Subject: re: Update – I'm an athlete now

Hi Al,

I know it's been a couple of days. That is not an unreasonable amount of time to leave before replying to an email – I think most people would even consider that prompt.

I don't even know what to say to you, your email upset me. I don't want it to be true but if I'm honest with myself I know that it is, at least in part. I didn't fall in love with an extension of me though Ally, I fell in love with you. A whole you. You are a complete person. I don't know what happened to make you feel otherwise. I hope it wasn't my fault.

For what it's worth, it's not nice to be put on a pedestal like that.

Remember that promotion I was up for? It must have been two years ago now. I worked so hard and the whole time you'd just been utterly convinced I would get it. No doubt in your mind. And then I didn't, and I took it really badly and I went out and got pissed with people from work and I came home and I think I must have looked awful. Red wine lips and my make-up everywhere and I'd failed. And you looked at me in this way like you'd pulled back the curtain and seen that it wasn't magic after all. I know you swept into action and took off my make-up and made me a sandwich and told me it would all be OK, but I saw that look you gave me when I got home. You were unsettled when I wasn't 100%, disappointed even, and that's a lot of pressure for one person.

Of course your things are worth keeping. They are not all mine. I think this is something you've made up. This was your home. Your things are not worthless.

I am not that surprised that you eat chickens now. Believe it or not I knew about your penchant for drunken late-night chicken nuggets. Do whatever you want! I am not in charge of your diet, but I'd like you to remember – I never have been. I feel as though I have morphed in your mind into some kind of omnipresent, authoritative monster. I think I am sometimes guilty of being a bit overbearing, but I'm not a tyrant and it's unfair to paint me as one.

Running club sounds like a great idea, it's nice that you've found somewhere so encouraging and with such a friendly instructor (who has taken a shine to you?!). I really hope your training goes well.

How is Malcolm? I can't even bring myself to type the words asking you to bring him back again, but you know what to do!

Em x

8

Scouts

Over the next week, two things happened that upgraded my life in Sheffield from that of a sad overgrown teenager to somewhat functioning human adult. The first was that I got a job. The second was that I socialised with someone other than my dad and Jeremy.

The job came first. On the Saturday after running club I took Pat for an early-morning stroll, having woken up at 6 a.m. with no chance of going back to sleep. Pat was experiencing no such problems and was furious with me for dragging her out of bed at such an ungodly hour, but once we were out in the winter sun she perked up. We took a familiar route past the shop where I had bought my running clothes and I peered through the window as casually as possible just in case Jo was there. It was empty. The bakery where I'd bought the custard doughnut, however, was already a hive of activity despite the closed sign on the door. I stopped at a small notice in their window.

Staff wanted – enquire within.

I was surprised to find that my heart leapt upon seeing it. I hadn't realised how much I wanted to work, how much I'd missed having a purpose – for myself as well as to keep my dad happy. And more specifically, how much I wanted to work in such close proximity to those doughnuts. I rapped on the window, catching the attention of a woman with a clipboard who was standing at the counter. She frowned as she came over to take the latch off the door and I realised I probably could have waited until the shop was open.

'Hi!' I was suddenly nervous, thrown by my own rash behaviour. 'I saw your sign in the window and I wanted to . . . enquire?'

'Oh!' Her face softened. 'Amazing! I literally put that up about ten minutes ago, what an early bird!'

I smiled and sort of gestured at Pat as if to say, 'You know what it's like'. Pat looked at me with disgust at the suggestion that this was her idea.

'So basically we just need your CV.' She hesitated, leaning on the door frame and realising I probably did not happen to have my CV with me at 6 a.m. She pushed her round tortoiseshell glasses on top of her head. 'Do you know what, since you're here, can you just give me a quick rundown?'

Initially I was horrified by the impromptu interview, but soon realised I had plenty to say. I relayed my several years of waitressing experience as a student and then told her about my cakes and the courses I'd taken, which, when described out loud, actually sounded pretty impressive. I could see in the woman's face that she was pleased with what she was hearing.

'That all sounds great. Listen, why don't you come back in some time next weekend – Saturday maybe? We'll have a proper chat and you can do a few hours behind the counter. Treat it as a trial shift? It'll be very early, mind you, so maybe not if you have big plans on Friday night . . .'

I shook my head. Perhaps a bit too quickly. I mean, is Disco for Syria a big plan?

'Yes! I mean yes, I can do Saturday. That's great for me. No big Friday night plans.'

I walked away from the shop buoyed by a rare feeling of pure luck and a sense of lightness that lasted all morning. I decided to text my dad who was teaching an extra Saturday morning class for gifted and talented students – something I'd fortunately never had to endure.

Guess who's got a job? Not me! But nearly! I have a trial shift next weekend at Bread and Butter – that bakery. The lady was really nice and she seemed pleased with all my experience so fingers crossed. Soon I can pay you all the rent in the world . . . within reason. Anyway, see you later.

He replied almost instantly. Definitely had his phone under the desk. *Glad to hear it.*

And then before I had a chance to put my phone away another message flashed up. *Good luck . . . not that you knead it.*

I groaned.

DAD. Get back to work.

*

·I was still so upbeat that at lunchtime when I received a message from Jo asking if I was free, I didn't panic and immediately say no. I read it, reread it, and calmly ate a few handfuls of salt and vinegar crisps from an open bag on the counter before washing my hands, picking up my phone and responding, 'Sure, why?'

That afternoon I rode the wave of spontaneity. I didn't question why Jo would want to see me, or whether she had had her phone stolen and I was being catfished. I had a brief panic when she didn't respond for several minutes, but then my screen flashed.

Do you fancy going for an extra training run? Thinking of trying a new route in the Peaks. Would be good to have a go at some hills . . .

Now, I obviously did not fancy an extra run. I did not want to 'have a go at some hills', but I definitely did fancy hanging out with Jo, just the two of us. I considered how I would tell Emily. *Jo and I have been doing some extra sessions. One on one.*

OK yeah where shall I meet you? Promise to be gentle with me. I can't handle hills!

Haha I'll be gentle, I swear. I'll pick you up, where do you live?

I ran upstairs to put on my one and only running outfit, which had been in the wash several times and finally stretched out enough to feel genuinely comfortable. I paused at the mirror wondering what to do about the whole hair and make-up situation. Ordinarily for running club I'd never consider putting anything on my face or running a brush through my hair, but today was no ordinary running club. I tried not to think too hard about why I found myself unscrewing the lid on my ancient mascara and quickly running it through my eyelashes until they were appropriately battable, or smearing concealer under my eyes in a bid to make myself look somewhat 'well'. I brushed my hair, glossier than usual from the infrequent washing, and pulled it back into a half ponytail. Halfway down the stairs I turned back to add some lip balm to the equation. Tinted. I didn't look in the mirror in case I changed my mind.

As I was tying my shoelaces I heard the deafening honk of a car horn outside. Hastily grabbing my phone and keys before heading out the door, I immediately wished I'd brought a waterproof as I slammed it behind me and noticed the darkening sky. There was an ancient dark red Fiat a few metres down the road, the engine grumbling about the hill. I waved and let myself in the passenger side. The second I shut the door I was struck by the intimacy of being in such a confined space with someone I didn't know very well. It was a small car and my hand brushed hers as I clumsily buckled my seat belt. She didn't appear to notice or care as she was far too busy admonishing me for the hill my dad's house was on.

'It's like a mountain, Ally!' The car stuttered and stalled suddenly as we lurched forward, and I saw her cheeks redden, the first time I'd seen her remotely flustered.

'So how was your day?' she asked when we finally got going.

'It was good,' I said to the dashboard. 'I'm going to start a new job – at Bread and Butter. Opposite the running shop actually.'

'Amazing! Congrats! Where are you working at the moment then?'

'Erm, nowhere presently.'

'Oh right, OK. Wow, well, that's great!'

I dug my fingernails into the palms of my hands.

'So how was your day?'

'Good, good. Fine. Quiet day at the shop.' She was distracted, concentrating on the roundabout.

The radio was on and our conversation lapsed into silence. I was very aware of my body in this tiny space. I looked out of the window, occasionally stealing glances at her face as she concentrated on the road. There is something about a woman driving me about that I find uniquely attractive. I'm not sure if it's because I can't drive and consider it a miracle that anyone can successfully manoeuvre a vehicle, or because it's something about relinquishing control to someone else. I have tried not to analyse it too much lest I ruin my harmless driver fetish for myself.

When we arrived at the designated spot we clocked the dark clouds, which looked even more menacing from up high in the Peaks. Jo did some sort of stretching up against the car so I lamely copied her, knowing full well there was very little I could do for my poor under-used muscles now. I had walked the route she was planning before and found that hard enough. Still, she was an expert and thought I could hack it – plus I still couldn't shake off the memory of our first exultant run together. I wasn't going to give up this time with her, even if it was going to be painfully spent.

'So the new plan is to beat the rain,' Jo said. 'I think we can do this route in forty-five minutes if we really try.'

I really appreciated her use of 'we' to mean 'you'.

'We can try,' I smiled.

We set out at a pace that was comfortable for approximately forty seconds before I was out of breath. Jo did the kind thing after a few minutes and took off ahead instead of waiting around and listening to my ragged breaths. Running on the grass instead of roads felt like what I assume running through sand is like. Or wading through concrete. Hill followed hill before the ground briefly levelled out again, meaning I could never quite get into a rhythm. I felt like the clumsiest mountain goat in the herd, hobbling about at the back. I'd been tricked into climbing a hill instead of doing a run. By the time I was anywhere close to making it back to the car, Jo had long ceased to be a dot in the distance. For all I knew she had driven off and was halfway home while I was left out here to fend for myself. As I approached, I saw her leaning on the fence at the edge of the field directly facing me. She had her arms crossed and I just knew she was smiling. She didn't do anything as annoying as try to high-five me or, God forbid, hug me as I reached her, she just said 'good job' and handed me a bottle of water. The very moment she did, the clouds parted and rain came hammering down. It was the kind of rain where you are immediately thoroughly drenched. I had emerged from hour-long baths drier than I was when I wrenched open the door of Jo's car and threw myself in. We laughed as the windows steamed up and we tried to wipe our dripping faces on our dripping hoodies.

'I'm sorry! I don't have a towel,' Jo said, looking around desperately as if one might suddenly appear, horrified at the social faux pas of inviting someone into her car and not being able to adequately provide for them.

'It's fine. I wouldn't expect you to keep a towel in your car.'

'Well,' she said, wiping away a fresh avalanche of water pouring down her face since she'd tipped herself upside down to look fruitlessly under the seat, 'maybe I should be more prepared.'

'You were obviously never a Brownie.'

'Well, no, I insisted on being a Scout.'

She took her hoodie off and sat back in her seat.

I stared at her. I have always had terrible gaydar and, like a lot of lesbians I knew, a propensity to make judgements based on outdated and frankly offensive stereotypes. I hadn't clocked Jo when we first met, but all the gay cogs I had in my arsenal began whirring at the mention of Scouts. Shorts? Building fires? I pictured a tiny Jo collecting her DIY activity badge and even though I knew it was ridiculous (I'd been to Brownies, after all) it was like puzzle pieces falling into place. The relentless interest in sports! The severe PE teacher ponytail! Scouts for God's sake, Scouts!

'Oh?' I said, casual as anything.

'Yeah,' she tapped on the steering wheel but made no actual moves to get the car started to take us home, 'I just wanted to do what my older brother did. Plus,' she continued, this time with much more conviction, 'I didn't want to wear those bloody culottes.'

I laughed, 'Hey, I wore those culottes!'

'And I'm sure they looked great on *you*.'

I smiled at her compliment to nine-year-old me. I was starting to relax.

'So,' I said after a pause, 'you were a Scout and then . . . you worked in a running shop?'

'Oh no, I'm still working through Scouts, just getting my running badge.'

'Ah, good luck!'

'Thanks.'

She smiled at the windscreen, her fingers still tapping the wheel, before leaning back in her seat.

'I'm just finishing my MA. I've been doing it the past two years. I'm working in the shop to pay for it actually. Took a gap year to save up too, but man, those things are expensive.'

'Oh my God.' I looked at her aghast, the phrase 'gap year' filling me with dread. 'How old are you?'

'Twenty-four.'

She began to laugh at my gobsmacked face.

'I don't know why,' I began, shaking my head, 'I assumed we were around the same age.'

'Why? How old are you?' Concern crept in to her voice. What if I was secretly forty?

'I'm twenty-nine.'

'Oh!' she said, relieved. 'Not that old!'

'Not *that* old?'

'Not old at all! Just the way you were freaking out! It's not a big age difference at all!'

She grinned.

'No, it's fine, it's just that I didn't know you were still in uni, you seem very . . .' I reached around for the word, 'very together.'

She snorted. 'OK.'

'What's your MA in?'

She pushed her seat backwards and gestured for me to do the same. It seemed as though we were going to be staying in the steamed-up car for a while, at least until the torrential rain stopped, but I found that I didn't mind at all sitting in this damp car in my damp clothes with this damp person. I didn't mind if we didn't move all day.

'It's in History.' Her inflection made it sound more like a question than a statement. She didn't even look at me before starting to apologise for it.

'I know, I know, it won't take me anywhere. I know I should have done law or chemistry or like . . .' she was gesticulating in the air above her, staring up at the car ceiling, 'dentistry or something. But I just don't care about any of those things.'

She finally looked at me, searching for signs of judgement.

'Why would you do dentistry?' was all I managed. 'I would never have done dentistry even if they let me, which they wouldn't have – I'd have been a danger to people's teeth. And lives.'

'I know, it's just people keep asking me what I'm going to do and I keep telling them that I'll probably get into teaching or something, but I just . . . don't mean it? Like maybe I'll just work in the running shop for ever and that would be OK.'

She looked at me for confirmation and I suddenly felt a thousand years older than her. And not one bit wiser.

'It would be OK,' I confirmed. I decided not to reveal that I was a failed teacher.

Jo shook her head. 'Anyway,' she said emphatically as if we'd been talking about her for hours, 'tell me about—' She stopped abruptly, clearly realising she didn't even know where to begin.

I decided to save her.

'Well, I've only been back for about a month, but I grew up here,' I said, mentally counting the days since I hauled my sad suitcase and furious cat here.

'Oh yeah, what brought you back?'

'Just missed the sunshine, you know?'

'Oh yeah, it's almost too much vitamin D here.'

We were both quiet for a minute.

'I left my job. And then my girlfriend broke up with me.'

'Oh wow. Shit, I'm sorry, Ally.'

'Yeah thanks, it's OK,' I said, which was a ridiculous thing to say. 'It will be OK anyway,' I corrected myself.

'Were you together long?'

'Yeah. Seven years.'

'Shit,' she said again. 'So did you meet at uni?'

I nodded. It suddenly felt too hot and sticky in the car. I'd been enjoying the intimacy of the steamed-up windows and the moody, dark peaks as our backdrop. It felt reminiscent of Kate and Leo on the *Titanic*. Except with more Lycra. But the more I thought about Emily, about missing her, it was increasingly claustrophobic. What did I think was going to happen in this banged-up old car with basically a teenager? I wanted to open a window, but the rain was still lashing down. I wondered when we'd be heading off.

'My parents met at uni – I always thought I'd meet my person there too,' she said. Despite my discomfort I couldn't help but feel a slight thrill at 'person' instead of 'boyfriend'.

'But you haven't?'

'No. There's been a few relationships.' She put air quotes around the word 'relationships' as if she was questioning the very concept. 'I've just never really liked anyone enough, I guess.'

'I literally cannot understand what that must be like.'

'What do you mean? You always like people . . .'

'Too much,' I finished for her. 'I think,' I said, forming some on-the-spot self-analysis, 'I put people on pedestals and then they don't really know how to live up to it.'

She nodded. 'I think that it's a good thing overall though. To love so much.'

I began to protest, but she interrupted. 'But your girlfriend was more like me?'

'Didn't love me enough, you mean?'

She nodded again, grimacing slightly at the bleakness of the question.

'I think she loved me. I don't think she could have loved me like I had loved her. Maybe that was always going to be the end of us. I think perhaps by the end, I'd become quite difficult to love.'

Jo didn't try to tell me that she was sure that that wasn't true, which I both appreciated and was quite offended by.

'Do you think there's any chance you'll get back together?'

'I hope so,' I said quite hopelessly. 'I know I'll have to see her again at some point because she needs to come and collect our cat.'

Jo nodded at this but didn't ask any further questions, confirming to me that she was already familiar with lesbian relationship politics.

'It sounds stupid but, I felt like maybe if I could do this bloody run and prove that I could really commit to something outside of our relationship then maybe I could just show her . . .' I realised I didn't really know what I meant. I couldn't tell Jo that I wanted Emily to see me with her. That I wished that I could send out some sort of transmission signal to inform her where I was and who I was with.

'I understand,' Jo said. I'm not sure she did, but it was a nice thing to say and I chose to believe her.

'And you're going to smash it.' She said this with a lack of conviction but with such kindness that I burst out laughing and she did too. And with that, our sad, weird, sticky bubble was burst and we moved our seats forward so we were sitting upright again and Jo finally put the keys in the ignition. She pulled out of the parking space and onto the empty road, the rain still lashing down onto the windscreen, but not before she turned to me and smiled.

'Thanks for running with me this afternoon.'

'Oh, you're welcome,' I said, 'you're really improving, more and more every time I see you.'

She slapped me playfully on the knee and I grinned the whole way home.

That evening, after a very long, very hot shower, I sat with Dad and watched rubbish Saturday night TV with our tea in our laps. Malcolm sat in between us, his eyes fixed on my plate. Dad hadn't known what to make of it when I'd returned home after my afternoon with Jo, soaked from head to toe, shivering and grinning from ear to ear, but he basically threw me into the bathroom and insisted on getting me some proper food. Sitting with Dad on the sofa, eating a battered sausage off a fork bite by bite, laughing out loud at an inane game show, I felt peaceful in a way that I hadn't for a long time. I wasn't worried about what I was going to do with myself the next day, or distracted by the ball of sadness in my tummy. I sat in the moment with Malcolm, my chips and my dad, and relaxed.

As I got into bed, I took my phone off airplane mode and held my breath waiting to see what came through. There was

a message from Jeremy confirming our Sunday Runday Funday
the following day (running on a Sunday followed by a pint and
a roast dinner), and a couple of junk emails. Nothing from
Emily. And nothing from Jo. The familiar disappointment
washed over me, but it wasn't overwhelming. It felt habitual,
routine.

Once I had composed the email to Emily that I'd been planning in my head all day, the lines practically writing themselves,
I put my phone down on my bedside table, safely back in airplane mode. When I closed my eyes, instead of the same
slideshow of old, fraught memories, all I could think about was
sitting with Jo in the hot, damp car and a hand sliding down
the steamed-up window.

From: Alexandra Waters   15 February 2019 at 22:34
To: Emily Anderson

Subject: re: re: re: Update – I'm an athlete now

Emily,

Yes thank you. Malcolm and I are both well.

Training is good, I went out for an extra run with Jo today,
just the two of us. There were lots of steep hills and she took
off super fast but I kept up with her the whole way! I think I'm
really getting somewhere. It started to rain just towards the
end, we got DRENCHED, it was so funny. We just had to sit in
the car until it eased off. It was good to chat actually. She
thought I was twenty-four. Can you believe it? I guess that's

because she's twenty-four and also people do say I look very youthful.

She's a very interesting person. She asked about you. I think one-on-one training is going to prove very useful.

Anyway, hopefully see you soon.

Love, Ally xxx

9

Disco for Syria

'Oh God, that smell,' Jeremy said as we walked into school at 6 p.m. on Friday night.

There is no smell quite like that of your old high school. It is very specific. Sour. It's lunch and sweat and hormones. Feet and Lynx Africa and hairspray.

'I know. It's making me feel a bit ill.'

'I feel like that smell is about to call me a poof.'

'Right. It's really pushing me into the lockers. Christ. Sorry about this, Jeremy.'

'It's fine. We get free crisps, don't we?'

I was nodding in reply as my dad approached looking extremely stressed.

'Thank God you're both here. There's so much to do. Ah, glad to see you've got coffee, very sensible,' he nodded at the Keep-Cups full of white wine that Jeremy and I were clutching. 'You'll need the energy.'

'Oh, you know us, Graham. Very prepared.'

'Indeed. Right, come along, I'll show you where we need you.'

It turned out Jeremy and I actually had very little to do, but as long as we did it very slowly then we could get away with not helping the rest of the teachers, ties undone, shoes kicked off, with putting up streamers and carrying seemingly thousands of chairs out of the hall. We set up two tables just outside the doors leading into the hall and very carefully started lining up pre-poured fizzy drink in compostable cups (how times have changed) as if we were to be handing them out at a cocktail party. We were thrilled to discover the school had ordered quite literally hundreds of bags of crisps.

'Crisps for Syria,' Jeremy said wryly, popping another prawn cocktail in his mouth as he poured lemonade into the final cup on the table.

We admired our handiwork as we sipped our wine and every time someone stressed rushed past we simply ripped open cardboard boxes or inexplicably picked up an armful of 2-litre bottles of Coke and gave them a sympathetic look. We had both spent enough years working in jobs we hated to perfect the art of looking busy.

My dad came by to inspect our work at ten minutes to seven, or what he described as 'ten minutes 'til kick-off'.

'Great work, guys. So I just need you to stay behind this table all night. Someone must be manning the table all night, you understand? The kids will go wild if someone isn't supervising the pop.'

'Understood. Man the pop.' I gave him a little salute which he ignored.

'Right,' he looked at his watch, 'just enough time to get into my costume.'

'Dad! No! You are joking. This is a joke?'

'I'm certainly not joking.' He looked at me, concerned. Perhaps I had misunderstood the concept of a theme.

'What are you going as, Graham?' Jeremy was thrilled.

'A lifeguard.'

He looked very pleased with himself.

'Oh my God, Dad. Please keep your shirt on. I beg you.'

'Anyway, I'll see you in a bit,' he said, ignoring me. 'Remember, one pop per person. Two pops if they look very thirsty.'

'You don't know what these kids are taking, do you? That's the thing,' Jeremy said, straight-faced.

My dad didn't hear him, thankfully.

'See you later, Graham!' Jeremy waved my dad off as he jogged towards the boys' toilets.

The problem with a seaside theme for eleven- and twelve-year-olds in February at a school is that the kids are very much not allowed to wear seaside themed clothes even if they voted for it 'fair and square'. Or they are, but extremely modified versions. Swimming trunks but with a T-shirt. Swimming costume with a skirt on over the top and a cardigan for good measure. Absolutely zero tolerance policy on bikinis. Everyone was wearing flip-flops, which quickly got discarded after they all immediately got blisters. One girl showed up in what looked to be her big sister's heels and fell off them before she even got in the hall. There was quite a lot of excitement then because she needed a plaster. The thing about year 7s is that they are actual babies, which, when you're at high school, you really don't realise. Jeremy and I spent most of the first half hour when they were all arriving on the verge of tears, chanting a chorus of 'oh bless them, oh BLESS them', on a loop. We'd had a lot of wine.

'God, Al,' Jeremy was sitting on a plastic chair, reclined as far as he could go, with one leg rested up on the table, 'it's all giving me a stomach ache.'

'Yeah, well I'm not surprised, I think you've had about 150 bags of crisps.'

'No. Being back here. Do you remember we had one of these in year 7?'

I nodded, trying to think back to those dark days. I'm sure I'd tried to wipe a lot of those memories out.

'Yeah, but there wasn't a theme though?'

'No. We just paid a pound and then we could run around hyped up on sugar for two hours in the dark.'

'Honestly would pay a pound for that now, as an adult.'

'Ugh, I think back to that little me and I just wish I could tell him . . .'

He paused, not really knowing how to finish the sentence. He shook his cup – empty. I passed him a lemonade and we sat in silence for a bit.

'I wish I could tell him he was fine, you know? I always felt on the verge of being found out. It made me second guess everything I did. I literally remember being here looking at all the other boys wondering if my hair looked like theirs, if my trainers were the same. I was so anxious that nothing looked out of place in case it gave me away. I was so sad, Al. I sometimes think, even after all the shit I've been through since, I've never been as sad as I was then.'

I looked at him. Huge now. A giant in his plastic chair, gripping his tiny cup of lemonade. His eyes all shiny.

'I'm really sorry, Jeremy.'

'Why are you sorry? You were going through it too.'

'No, not like that. I wasn't sad, I was clueless. I had no idea what I was, I thought everyone felt the same way as me. And I knew you were sad. And I just couldn't deal with it. I couldn't understand what had happened. I knew your dad had left but I didn't know what to do about it, so I just . . .'

'Al, you were eleven. You don't have to apologise for eleven-year-old you.'

'I do. Well, I want to. I'm really sorry. I wish I'd done more. I wish there was another version of me and you at that dance. If I could go back in time, I'd come and find you and dance with you all night.'

'Dance it all off.' He smiled.

'Exactly. Just dance it all off. I was too busy racing around after that horrible group of girls who I thought were *so* cool. Every time a song came on that I liked, we had to go back to the toilets to put more lip gloss on or go out in the corridor to talk about a boy.'

'See, that's the experience I was actually looking for.'

We were quiet for a minute as a group of boys came running past, slick with sweat, chasing each other with a can of deodorant. I briefly wondered if I should do something to stop it, but they were so fast. It's character building, I thought to myself.

'You know, I was so sad my mum took me to the doctors once,' Jeremy said.

'What? I didn't know that.'

'She thought I had some kind of virus. Something making me tired all the time. She'd be all like "he's not running around with the other boys, doctor! He just sits and stares out of the window."'

'In your silk dressing gown? Holding a martini?'

Jeremy laughed.

'Yes. Sunglasses on. Cigarette in one of those long holders.' He patted his pocket instinctively. They were there.

'So the doctor said I needed to run around more. It would be good for me, make me happier. He said maybe I should play football. Exercise. Make some friends.'

'Christ. When has football ever made anyone happier?'

'I know. It was literally years later before anyone suggested I get some therapy and then years after that before I got any medication.'

'Did it help?'

'What?'

'Either?'

He shrugged, peeling the compostable cup into strips like a banana.

'Things help sometimes and then they don't. And then something else does. And then nothing. Sometimes I'll have a run of bad days even if things have been good for months and then I worry that it's all going downhill again, but then I start to feel better. Sometimes I don't. Sometimes I have something to actually feel shit and anxious and depressed about and then I worry that it's not real. Takes a while to figure out whether I can trust a feeling or not.'

He looked at me, chewing the inside of my mouth next to him.

'I'm pretty good at the moment though, Al.'

'Do you think it's all the running around though? Was that first doctor right?'

Jeremy poked my leg with his foot.

'Oh yeah, maybe I'll take up football next! I don't know – no. Yes? A bit? On some days? I like the routine. I like the fresh air. I like *you*. All those things help. But they help you too, right? That's just a human thing, I think. For me, anyway. It's not a cure.'

I nodded.

'So it's like . . . just maintenance then? The exercise helps keep you ticking along when you're in good shape, but like if you're broken down it's not going to help to just . . . top up the oil every day? You need a mechanic to look at the engine.'

'Why are you using a car analogy? You know I can't drive.'

'I can't drive! It just came to me. Quite good though?'

'Yeah, pretty good.'

He passed me his peeled cup, all splayed out with the bottom of the cup in the centre.

'A flower for the lady.'

I accepted it and tried to tuck it into my top pocket like a buttonhole.

'Do you think it's easier for them now?' I asked him.

'The gay kids?'

I nodded.

'I hope so.'

The kids cottoned on pretty quickly to the fact that Jeremy and I didn't care if they took one or two or forty drinks.

'Miss, do you work here?'

'Nope!'

'Miss, are you even a teacher?'

'Nope, I'm not even a teacher.'

'So can I have another bag of crisps?'

'Yep.'

'I've had five bags, miss!'

'Cool!'

Just before 9 p.m. my dad came out of the hall, alarmingly sweaty. I hoped to God he had not been dancing. He was wearing a bright red T-shirt with 'lifeguard' emblazoned on the back, tucked into a pair of jogging bottoms which looked enormous on him. He had a pair of sunglasses perched on his head and a whistle around his neck.

'Ally, Jeremy! They're about to play the last song of the night if you wanted to come in?'

'Is it going to be "Flying without Wings"?'

'What?'

'Don't worry.'

I was about to tell him that we really didn't want to go just as Jeremy said, 'Oh cheers, Graham. Come on, Al,' and grabbed my hand to pull me up from my chair.

The hall was dark apart from some sad lights emanating from the mobile DJ booth. The smell was out of this world. The floor was sticky somehow, as if we were in a club. The teachers were all leaning wearily against the walls, on their phones. I got the sense that the kids could have been doing tequila shots and lines off the windowsills and no one would have noticed, apart from my dad of course – him and his whistle.

Ariana Grande, 'One Last Time', came blasting out of the speakers and the kids all started screaming and running around and hugging each other, like it was the end of the world.

'Dance with me?'

'Jeremy . . .' I whined.

'Ally, come on, you can't abandon me at another disco. Not at Disco for Syria!'

'You said I didn't need to apologise!'

'Not if you dance with me now.'

So we slow-danced, my hands on his shoulders, his hands

on my waist. We stepped side to side, keeping as much space between us as possible to respect the tradition of the slow dance. Somehow surrounded by pre-teens and teachers, in a school hall that smelt like sweat and sickly sweet body spray, I found myself laughing my head off.

'Another wild Friday night for us.'

'Can't stop us! When will we calm down?'

Jeremy spun me around and I caught my dad's eye. He was watching us, a little smile on his face. He waved and then looked at the clock. The song just about finished before the clock struck nine and my dad blew his whistle. It was deafening. The fluorescent lights immediately went on. Incredibly jarring.

'That's it folks!'

My dad was herding children like sheep out of the hall, his arms out in front of him, whistle in his mouth.

'Do not forget your flip-flops,' he was yelling. 'Any unclaimed flip-flops will be BINNED. Do not waste these flip-flops folks, think of the environment. Think of Syria!'

Once we'd cleared away and my dad had changed out of his costume and back into appropriate attire, we all met out the front of the school. It was freezing cold.

'Right, I did promise you a drink, didn't I?' My dad zipped up his coat and looked at us both. 'Will you be joining us, Jeremy?'

'Yes please, Graham. Never knowingly turned down a drink.'

We trudged off to the pub around the corner and my dad

bought us all a pint. Most of his was gone moments after he sat down. I realised we had not served him at the pop station.

'Those things are exhausting.'

'Yeah, that's a lot of tween energy to keep under control.' I took a sip of my drink, peering around to see if there was anyone in the pub I recognised, but it was mostly just men my dad's age.

'Any gossip from tonight, Graham?' Jeremy asked.

'Ah, no. One twisted ankle. An argument about being left out of a dance routine.'

I smiled.

'You know how they say school days are the best of your life? They're definitely lying, aren't they?'

'I don't know about that. You liked school, Al.'

'Did I?'

'When you were little you did.'

'Well, it's nice when it's all just arts and crafts and playing the recorder, isn't it?'

'Mmm. Before you actually have to do any work.'

'All right, Dad.'

We were quiet for a moment. Dad started building a tower out of coasters.

'This is a nice pub,' Jeremy said, looking around. 'It's cosy.'

'Yeah I like it. Although they've changed it now. Got all this trendy stuff going on.' My dad pointed vaguely around him – a comfortable-looking chair, a nice lamp on a table.

'We used to come here with Mum, remember, Ally? It wasn't

all la-di-da. But they had board games, we used to sit around and play Scrabble for hours.'

'I remember.'

'You always used to lose, didn't you? Always came last.'

'Yeah, I was a child, Dad! Playing against two adults!'

'Mmm yes, I seem to remember that excuse then as well.'

Jeremy asked my dad a question about the beer we were drinking and I drifted out of the conversation. I looked around, trying to remember where we'd sit back then, but Dad was right. It was all different now. None of the same tables and chairs. A different layout. Mood lighting. I tried to imagine Mum sitting around the table with us, but I couldn't quite conjure her. It didn't make sense. She was too young. Frozen in time. She looked all wrong. My dad's coaster tower collapsed and I was briefly overwhelmed with a flood of sadness for him.

'Did you want another one, folks?'

I interrupted Jeremy on the verge of saying yes.

'I'd better not, I've got work first thing. I don't want to be hungover on my first day.'

'Very sensible, Al.'

We said our goodnights and Jeremy headed off to get a bus. Dad and I were walking the fifteen minutes home.

We spent most of it in companionable silence aside from the odd involuntary shiver and the chatter of teeth.

'Thanks again for tonight.'

'It's honestly fine, Dad.'

'It was nice to have you there.'

When we got home the house was freezing as usual. I threw my keys down on the table in the hall and went to switch on the lamp. The bulb had been replaced. The glow illuminated the faces of two hungry creatures staring at us out of the darkness.

'Yes, yes, we're home,' my dad said, reaching down absent-mindedly to stroke Malcolm on the head. 'We're home.'

10

Bread and Butter

I love the peace of a house filled with sleeping people and creatures. Creeping down the stairs in the dark hours of Saturday
morning I felt like the only person in the world who was up
and about. I pushed open the kitchen door where Pat was fast
asleep in her basket and where the only sound was the ticking
of the clock on the wall. As I shuffled about, Pat's head lifted
wearily and she stared at me through squinting, sleepy eyes,
wondering if it could possibly be breakfast time. Quickly deciding that it was just a dream, she buried her head into her wispy
tummy again with a little sigh.

I wondered vaguely about what Emily was doing and whether
she was lying in our old bed with Sara with no H. Were they
wrapped around each other or sleeping with their backs
turned? Maybe they'd woken early too and were having lazy,
sleepy, just-woken-up sex. The kind we used to have when
hungover and only half awake, all closed eyes and smells and

prickling skin. The wandering thought was as curious as it was painful. It felt like prodding a bruise rather than sticking my fingers into a fresh wound. Progress, I thought, as I walked over to the sink and rinsed my empty mug under the hot tap until my hand burned.

In the end, as is always the way for me when I get up early and feel as though I have all the time in the world, I found myself suddenly late and running out of the door with only fifteen minutes to do the twenty-five-minute walk to the bakery. By the time I arrived I was certain that when I pulled my beanie off to arrange my hat hair there would be actual steam rising off me. I tapped on the door gently so as not to make the person behind the counter jump, but she whipped around anyway. She smiled when she saw me. It was a different woman to the one who I'd spoken to before – she was shorter and had cropped blonde hair. She wore huge round glasses that took up at least half of her small face, but which somehow looked very cool. I wondered when giant round glasses had gone from deeply unfashionable (circa 1998 when I had been wearing them to school) to cutting edge style. Maybe I had always just been twenty years ahead of the curve.

'Good morning!' The woman smiled at me. She didn't have a Sheffield accent but a Scottish one. 'Charlie said to expect you today and it still gave me a shock! I'm in my own little world. I'm Sophie.'

She stepped aside so I could come in. The interior looked so different when it was empty, with just one of the very cool low-hanging lights switched on giving it a gentle glow. I breathed in and let out a little involuntary sigh of pleasure. 'Oh my God, it smells amazing in here!'

She laughed. 'Yes, I've just got the first batch of croissants in.'

'You make them here?'

She nodded. 'We'll see how you go and maybe get you on pastry by the end of the week.'

I nodded enthusiastically, thrilled that before my trial was even started we were discussing the end of the week. I went to hang up my coat and grab an apron as instructed and, as I was doing so, Sophie kept up a steady stream of chatter from the other room where she was jabbing at the till, somewhat fruitlessly it seemed judging by the amount of random swearwords punctuating our conversation.

'So Charlie won't actually be in today because . . .' she trailed off and was silent for a moment before exclaiming, 'fuck!' And then, 'Sorry. Charlie won't be in because she's not feeling well, so it's just you and me this morning, I'm afraid.'

'Oh, OK!' I called from the tiny room where the aprons hung. I tried to get my hair into a ponytail that felt neat despite the lack of a mirror.

'In fact,' she continued, 'it's an absolute godsend you're here because I don't know what I'd have done on my own, no one else is coming in until later and obviously no one is checking their phones this early in the morning.'

I detected a note of irritation in her voice. It seemed to me when I met her that Charlie was the owner of the shop, but per-haps I'd been wrong.

I appeared from the back, aproned, sweaty, and ready to go.

'Put me to work!'

Barely looking up from the logbook she sighed and said, 'Well, first things first, shall we have a cup of tea? The kettle's on downstairs.'

I nodded and headed down. Tea first. I'll like it here, I thought.

We spent the next couple of hours before opening time hur-riedly kneading and mixing and baking. Sophie was pleased that although I needed filling in on specific recipes, as soon as she'd explained things once she could leave me to it. Soon trays and trays of delicious things filled the counter. Sophie made beautiful loaves of sourdough bread in enormous batches (nor-mally we'd have more variety, she told me apologetically, but no time today!) and filled huge baskets with them. We worked quickly and in amiable silence for the most part. There was simply no time to waste chatting. When it came to opening time she dramatically wiped her brow and patted me on the shoulder.

'Brilliant.' I loved the way she said it and resisted the urge to parrot her.

I had a few minutes to sit down with an almond croissant and a coffee before we flipped the 'open' sign on the door and the day flew by. I didn't have time to think about anything other than mastering the basics of the till, putting cakes and bread into paper bags as delicately as I could, and running downstairs to stick trays into the giant oven. We raced through lunchtime, when a boy who looked about eighteen came in and started his shift. By the time there was a lull long enough to look at the clock it was 2 p.m. and I had been there for seven hours.

'Ally!' Sophie exclaimed. 'You saved the day!'

The boy smiled and rolled his eyes and Sophie jabbed him in the side with her finger. It turned out his name was Nick and he was Charlie's nephew who was at university in Sheffield.

'Seriously, we couldn't have done it without you.'

'I'm so happy it went well,' I found myself gushing, 'I've really enjoyed myself!'

I cringed at how earnest I sounded, but it was true, I'd never had a day at work like this in my life.

'You should head off now,' she said, looking at the clock again, 'since you've barely had a break. But when can you start properly? We really need someone in to do the shift you've just done a few days a week.' She saw my face and mistook my expression for worry about the workload.

'It won't always be as manic as this, I promise! Normally it will be me, you and Charlie first thing – it makes it so much more manageable.'

'No, it's fine, I just–' I paused, resisting the familiar urge to say I wasn't sure, or maybe, or I needed time to think about it. 'Yes, that sounds really great!'

It felt good to just say yes to something and, as Sophie wrapped an arm briskly around my shoulders and told me she was thrilled, I knew I'd made the right decision, but there was a lump in my throat. I was now connected and committed to something in Sheffield, to something independent of Emily. I didn't realise how much I had been clinging on to the idea of me and Emily miraculously reuniting and walking off into the sunset together. Or at least back home. This felt somehow like a full stop that I wasn't quite ready for. But it was the right thing, I told myself. It didn't have to be a full stop, I was just mid-sentence. It was a comma at most.

I left in a daze, having turned down Sophie's offer to sit down and eat something before I went. I desperately wanted to be alone with my thoughts. Instead I took the fattest Nutella doughnut left and stuffed it in my backpack, wondering whether I'd be able to wait until I got home before ripping into the bag. I walked in the direction of home, but noticed in an abstract sort of way that I was darting across the road so I could pass the running shop.

I peered through the window. Inside, a man leant on the counter chatting animatedly. I couldn't see who he was talking to. He looked towards the window but didn't seem to notice me standing there. All of a sudden he was upright and marching towards me, then wrenching open the door. My first thought was that he was going to tell me off for looking in, but he stalked past without even appearing to see me. There was still no sign of Jo. I was just turning to leave when suddenly there she was, appearing from below a shelf full of brightly coloured energy gels. I leapt away from the window. I hadn't had any real plans of popping in, I just wanted to see if she was there. But it was too late. She'd spotted me and was beckoning me into the shop.

'Hello! What a nice surprise!' She looked happy to see me, but she seemed agitated.

'Hello!' I stood awkwardly in the doorway of the shop. 'Yeah, I just, I work over there so . . .'

'Oh of course, of course. Good day?'

'Yeah, sold a lot of cake.'

'Great.' We were quiet for a moment and she looked at me expectantly. She wasn't irritated exactly, but she was definitely on edge. Verging on twitchy.

'I erm . . . are you busy?' I gestured at the fully stocked shelves inside the empty shop. 'I'm sorry, I didn't mean to interrupt.'

'You've not interrupted. I just didn't expect to see you.' She was standing still, clutching a cardboard box in front of her like a shield.

Just as I was about to make my excuses and leave she sighed heavily and dropped the box to the ground. She peered behind me trying to discern if any customers were imminently coming in, and then she flopped down onto the floor, leaning against the shelves behind her. She gestured for me to do the same. I gingerly crouched down and sat opposite her. My legs crossed, my backpack in my lap.

'That boy. He used to be my boyfriend, and normally it's fine with us but . . . I wasn't expecting him to come in here today and it's thrown me a bit.'

'Oh.' I didn't really know what to say. It was hard to read how she felt.

'Yeah, we split up a few months ago, but it was a bit of a messy break-up, I've still sort of seen him a few times.' She went a bit pink when she said this. 'But a few nights ago when I saw him, I found out he had been seeing someone new and he *still* invited me over, so I left in a bit of a huff. I've not been answering my phone, hence why he's come to see me somewhere he knows I can't leave.'

'Had you just had a row when I got here?' I fiddled with my backpack cords feeling hugely uncomfortable and deeply concerned that this boyfriend might mean an end to my grand plans.

'Not a row exactly. More like . . . reaffirming what I'd already told him. He doesn't like things to not be on his terms, I don't think. He was embarrassed that I'd walked out.'

'But . . . he has a new girlfriend?'

She nodded and shrugged. 'Men,' she said in that conspiratorial way that people sometimes do. It didn't seem like a natural thing for her to say, like she'd heard other people say it and was trying it on.

'Ah well, I wouldn't know.'

'Lucky you. So . . . you've never had a boyfriend?'

It was strangely intimate to be sitting on the floor together.

I instinctively shook my head, but quickly corrected myself.

'Once. Well, not quite a boyfriend. When I was in high school there was a boy I'd sometimes snog at the back of the playing fields.' I grimaced at the memory. 'And then in uni there was one drunken night after a girlfriend broke up with me where . . . I experimented with my housemate.'

Jo laughed. 'That's what uni is for, isn't it?'

'Finding yourself, trying everything out.'

'Yeah, exactly.'

We were quiet for a moment. I was desperate to find out more about this boyfriend and whether there had been any girl-friends, but just as I was working up the courage to ask, the little bell above the door rang and we both scrambled to our feet. I spun around to see if it was Jo's ex-boyfriend again, want-ing to get a closer look now I knew who he was, but it was a middle-aged man in some expensive-looking and very reveal-ing cycling gear. One of those all-in-ones that looks like a Victorian swimming costume.

Jo greeted him and went back behind the counter. I picked up my backpack to leave and paused in front of her.

'Another ex?' I whispered.

She smiled broadly at me.

'Yes, how did you know?'

'The sexual tension.'

The man coughed, clearly trying to get Jo's attention.

'I'd better go, see you soon.'

'Hey, thanks for coming in. You've turned my day around.'

I didn't know what to say to that so I just waved and found myself grinning all the way home.

I was relieved to see that my dad's car wasn't in the driveway. I kicked off my shoes in the middle of the hallway to release my aching feet and drank an entire pint of water over the sink while listening to a voice note from Jeremy that he'd sent me on his lunch break. It was over five minutes long and although it was supposedly sent to wish me luck for my first day, it consisted almost entirely of him trying to figure out which colleague was stealing his milk.

It's got to be Nathaniel. He's always looking at me very intensely. Like he's daring me to confront him about it. Like he's been drinking it right under my nose and he's been getting a kick out of it . . . I'll keep you updated.

I grabbed my backpack from the hall and tore into the doughnut bag, taking an enormous bite out of one end, Nutella oozing onto my hand. I took my laptop, headed upstairs, and got into bed still fully clothed. Between my clean sheets I could smell butter and sugar either clinging to my skin or oozing out of my pores. I didn't mind it. I lay on my back, propping my head up on the pillows, and logged onto my emails, already steeling myself for disappointment. I inhaled sharply. There was one from Emily. I opened it, squinting at the screen to protect my eyes in case it was very short or somehow contained even worse news than her dumping me and shacking up with someone else.

From: Emily Anderson   22 February 2019 at 13:40

To: Alexandra Waters

Subject: re: re: re: re: Update – I'm an athlete now

Hey Al,

Good news that training is going so well. Are you still doing the training with Jeremy or is it just with Jo now? It sounds like you're spending a lot of time with her. That's nice. Does she have a boyfriend or anyone you've met? It's good that you're making new friends.

I have to say it feels very strange here without you. I mean in London. Everyone wants to know how you are. You haven't been banished Al. They really do care about you no matter what you think. This self-imposed exile made some sense at the beginning, but it's been weeks. Are you going to stay exiled for ever? Really never see any of us ever again? I just can't believe that that would make you truly happy. Even if by the sounds of it at the moment you're quite enamoured with your new friends.

Anyway, let me know that you're OK.

Em x

I stared at the screen. I read it a couple more times just to check that my initial reaction was accurate. I found myself grinning broadly, triumphant. *Does she have a boyfriend* indeed! It would have been reaching I think to say that Emily was jealous, but she was definitely rattled. Her interest was piqued by my nubile young running coach. I screenshotted the email to send to Jeremy and closed the laptop, deciding not to reply yet but instead to let her stew. I got up. I needed to wash the layer of butter from my skin. I was not in exile, Emily. I was free.

11

Personal Day

Reading Emily's email I had felt powerful and galvanised. But every moment after that brought me back slowly into myself, questioning whether my plan was working and whether, beyond mild curiosity, Emily thought about me in any meaningful way at all. Still, I persisted and focused on creating a semblance of a life for myself that didn't involve Emily for the purposes of flaunting it in front of her. She said our mutual friends were desperate to get in touch with me, yet I'd scarcely heard from anyone since the first few days after I'd left. Beth of Tom and Beth had long given up. Most of the other people I'd endlessly warmed houses with or spent afternoons stomping across the Heath alongside had never messaged in the first place. Partly I felt annoyed with Emily for taking them from me, but more than that I felt cross with myself that I'd allowed myself to live so long surrounded by people who didn't particularly care about me.

An important step I knew I had to take was leaving my house for something other than work and running club. This was easier said than done. Standing up for eight hours in a row punctuated with dashing up and down the stairs carrying heavy trays was leaving me so exhausted I'd found myself asleep by 8 p.m. on more than one occasion. On the plus side I felt certain that my job was contributing towards my race training. The big day was creeping up on us frighteningly quickly. Jeremy and I had been very keen to focus simply on the time we were running rather than the distance, and made a commitment to run twice a week outside of running club. As soon as Jeremy finished work on Mondays he'd come by my house to get changed and we'd head out. Headphones in – we'd soon stopped attempting to talk. It had never occurred to us that we might go running separately. We had even tried to add some 'fitness sessions' to our routine after our Sunday run, which involved holding each other's feet while we did sit-ups in my front garden. More often than not these sessions ended with us lying on our backs and sharing a cigarette while we watched YouTube tutorials on our phones of confident, tanned people doing squats and shouting.

Jeremy would gesture at the screen. 'I feel like, as good as he looks, he'd be the last person on the planet I'd want to go for a drink with. Do you know what I mean?'

'Yeah. Imagine,' I'd say, taking a drag on our cigarette, 'sitting there while he puts his gin and slim into his calories app. Depressing.'

But as much effort as we put in, it was impossible not to

notice that the distances we were covering were quite different to the distance we were expected to cover on the day – 'not even close!' my dad had exclaimed over dinner one night after Jeremy and I had been on a particularly horrible seven-mile run.

When we'd first signed up we'd shared the attitude that our future selves would be vastly different, enlightened beings and somehow able to pull running thirteen miles out of the bag like magic. As we approached the big day it became increasingly obvious that we were still the same sweaty lumps dragging ourselves around the streets every few days.

On the plus side I had taken to popping across the road after work to meet Jo on a pretty regular basis, by which I mean every day. Sometimes I'd just stop in to say hello and give her a piece of cake (I'd learned that banana was her favourite), and she'd eat it in about three gleeful bites while she spoke to me. The first time she did it I worried she'd choke, but it became apparent she'd developed some kind of evolved breathing method, the sort you'd use to play the didgeridoo. I never commented on it in case she stopped. It was mesmerising.

On other days, quiet afternoons in the shop, I'd spend longer with her. Once I spent a few hours doing inventory with her, which should have been the most boring job in the world, but the time flew by.

'Ally, I can't let you stay here and do this when you've been at work all day,' she'd said as she handed me a clipboard with an itemised list on it.

'It's fine – what am I going to do at home anyway?' Frankly I was thrilled at the excuse to spend the afternoon sitting in close proximity to her, even if it meant I had to count shorts.

'It's going to be so boring.'

She walked away from me and into the back room looking to retrieve a stepladder.

'Spending time with you could never be boring.'

This had been easy to say when she wasn't in the room, but was infinitely embarrassing once she'd re-entered it. We both pretended it hadn't happened.

'So,' she said, once she'd set me to work, 'is it very weird living at home again?'

'Yeah, it was quite weird at first but I'm getting used to it.'

'But, being back in Sheffield in general . . . I mean, do you keep bumping into people?'

'Like who?'

'Like old school friends? I don't know! Like . . . ex-girlfriends maybe?'

'Are you trying to ask me about my ex-girlfriends?'

'No! Maybe . . . I'm curious!'

I smiled. It was nice to have someone feel curious about me.

'I haven't bumped into anyone actually. None of my old friends live here anymore apart from Jeremy, they all stayed away after university. And in terms of exes – there is hardly a *crowd* of women I'm trying to avoid bumping into.'

'Really?'

'I haven't lived here since I was eighteen, Jo. I mean there were a couple of girls at school who kept me top secret, so I'm not sure they were my *girlfriends*.'

I recalled a night in sixth form where a group of us had managed to get ourselves served undetected at a very rough pub until one very small, nervous boy had blown our cover and we'd all been chucked out. Giggling and tipsy from downing our drinks before we left, we'd relocated to the local park and waited for someone's older sister to bring us alcopops and Lambrini from the off-licence, which she put a huge premium on: the delivery rate. In the thrill of the darkness, grabbing onto each other on the uneven grass, giddy and shrieking, my then best friend Clare and I had fallen in the grass. She went down first, slipping in her ridiculously wobbly and unsuitable shoes, and pulled me down with her, and I had landed with a thump half on top of her. We'd screamed and giggled, but as I pushed myself up on my arm which had landed on Clare's right side, our faces millimetres apart, the shrieking stopped and I felt her sweet, cider breath on my lips. Those few breaths felt like a lifetime before Clare's mouth formed a grin and she shoved my arm to move me off.

'Up you get, you big lezza,' she'd said affectionately, quietly so that only I could hear. We'd linked arms again and carried on with our night, swigging on nasty vodka and knock-off Smirnoff Ices until Clare was horribly, violently sick and I had to wobble home with her, attempting to silently push her up the stairs so that her parents didn't wake up. I managed to haul her out of her coat and into bed. I crept about trying to locate pyjamas for myself and got into her single bed with her like we'd done a hundred times before. Clare, hot and wriggly and immediately asleep, reached around and pulled my arm around her. I fell asleep that night with the ceiling spinning, a dead arm, and my head buried in the back of Clare's neck.

'Ally! That's really sad.'

'Oh no. It suited me fine.'

I thought about it for a bit. My early love life had for the most part consisted of drunken one-night stands and unrequited pining.

'I'm quite boring I'm afraid. Before Emily there was no one very significant.'

Jo nodded.

'When I go home, I literally always bump into my high school boyfriend.'

'Oh yeah? Where is home?'

'York.'

'Oh! I thought you sounded quite posh. Explains it.'

She ignored me.

'Chris Miller. We went out for six months and then he dumped me for Jessica Robertson. She got a car for her seventeenth birthday. I'm not saying those two things are related but . . .'

I smiled. 'And you never got over him?'

'I pine for him.'

When we'd finished for the day and locked up we hovered on the doorstep of the shop. Jo's house was in the opposite direction to mine.

'Are you really not going to let me pay you? You're owed half my money for this afternoon.'

'Absolutely not.'

'Will you let me buy you a drink then?' She peered up the street towards the pub at the top of the road.

The air tautened slightly between us and the yes was just on the tip of my tongue when suddenly she slapped her hand to the side of her face.

'Oh shit, shit, shit. Sorry. I've just remembered I've got to go out for dinner for my housemate's birthday. Oh God, I don't want to go, I think that's why I've banished it from my mind.'

'No worries at all. Honestly, I didn't mind helping out this afternoon. You don't owe me anything.'

'No, but I mind! I mind. And I want to buy you a drink and not go out for dinner. It's going to be rubbish, I know she's going to get so drunk she won't be able to eat anyway.' She looked at her phone and then back up at me, I think figuring out if she could feasibly bail on her housemate.

'Look, you go. It's honestly fine.'

She nodded, looking genuinely disappointed, which was gratifying.

'Another time?'

'Sure.'

We went our separate ways with a little wave and by the time I reached the end of the road I already had a message from her.

Will I see you tomorrow?

Don't worry you'll get your cake fix.

No, I want to see you! I don't know how I'm ever going to thank you for all the freebies.

A thousand responses rushed through my head that I would never send. As I typed and re-typed something appropriately flirty-but-not-too-much, she saved me.

Oh God. That sounded really bad. I mean. One day I will do something for YOU and not the other way around.

And then: *Is that even worse?*

I grinned.

Maybe stop now? Let me know when you're ready to pay me for my labour and cake. I accept wine.

Deal.

Charlie and Sophie invited me around for tea at theirs that Friday night after work. I hadn't realised at first because of my broken gaydar, but Sophie and Charlie are a married couple. They had bought Bread and Butter a few years ago when it was crumbling, and slowly built it back up again from scratch. Sophie told me all about it one morning as I was washing up enormous bowls and a seemingly never-ending pile of spoons. How they'd met at university and decided to stay in Sheffield, and how they'd made their own wedding cake in this very shop. They'd done all the parts together. A Sophie layer (chocolate and peanut butter), a Charlie layer (lemon) and a raspberry and rose layer that they chose together. They'd even made tiny brides to sit on the top, which had made everyone laugh because they were both terrible at fondant icing and the brides looked like little aliens. I'd done my best to keep it together while she told me this story, trying my hardest to convey my delight while also staring down at the suds in the sink, scrubbing furiously. I knew if I looked at her for a second I would burst into tears. I couldn't believe my luck, and I wasn't used to feeling lucky lately. In all my wildest dreams growing up in the house just a couple of miles up the road, a tiny gay cake enthusiast, I could never have imagined that I might find other people like me on this street. And the idea that I would know them and work for them, well, it would have been utterly unimaginable.

I was exhausted, but the prospect of doing something other than sitting around with my dad was very appealing.

Dad I've been invited for tea at the bosses' house so must be doing something right! See you later – don't wait up.

Finally some time at home for the lads . . . and Pat. Have fun. Don't do anything I wouldn't do.

Charlie and Sophie lived on the opposite side of town in an area I'd previously only associated with students and takeaways. I used to go there to eat occasionally, but as we passed what used to be cheap Vietnamese restaurants and Turkish supermarkets there were quirky-looking cafes with baby blue shop fronts, and craft beer shops. I pressed my nose against the bus window. Everything had changed. I put my headphones in to listen to a voice note from Jeremy.

Hiya babes. Work was so bleak today. Even more bleak than usual. I don't know why these people think I'm personally responsible for their shit broadband. I'm also pretty sure someone was wanking on the phone to me, which you know . . . in the right time and place . . . but not while I'm reading a script about troubleshooting, you know? I had a peruse on LinkedIn but I don't know. Do I want to stay in customer service for ever when I hate customers? No, probably not. Like I keep thinking, do I want to be a teacher? You were a teacher though and you hated it. Why was that? Maybe you just weren't good at it? No offence. Or like at least something where I'm helping people. But not with their broadband. ANYWAY. What are you up to? Off to the lesbians for tea, are you? Do you think they're going to ask you for a threesome? Fingers crossed, eh? Anyway call me later.

I rolled my eyes and started typing a reply as I listened.

Ew. People are disgusting. Imagine getting off on broadband.

No, don't stay in customer service. You hate it.

No offence taken. I'm sure you'd be a great teacher. What would you teach? Primary school? Seems on your level, hun.

Yes of course there'll be a threesome. That seems very likely. You're ridiculous. They're so wholesome. I think their house is going to be all quinoa and pictures by local artists. I bet they wear rainbow cardigans at home.

Their house was at the end of the row of terraces and had a bright coral-coloured front door. The window frames were all painted a dark grey and they had a little window box filled with pansies.

I knocked gently and Sophie immediately opened the door as if she had been standing behind it waiting for me.

'Ally! Come in, come in.' She ushered me inside and gave me a big hug. She took the very average supermarket flowers that I'd brought with me and rushed off to get a vase, shouting, 'Charlie, Charlie, will you *look* at these.' She was wearing a black T-shirt and jeans and, as soon as my coat was off, I noticed that their house was absolutely boiling hot. Like grandparents' houses levels of heat. I made a note to tell my dad. To guilt trip him into maybe having the heating on a bit more.

Charlie appeared at the door of the kitchen wearing an apron that said 'masterbaker' on it. She had a wooden spoon in one hand and a glass of red wine in the other. She looked uncharacteristically flustered.

'Ally! I'll be out in a sec. What will you have? Red? White? Beer?'

'Red is perfect, thanks.'

'I'll bring it through.'

Sophie led me through to the living room. Their house reminded me of Beth and Tom's lovely flat in Stoke Newington. All wooden floors and colourful accents and cosy rugs. The wall in the living room behind the sofa had an incredible dark, tropical wallpaper on it and a big gold-framed mirror. I paused at a black and white photo on the wall of them on their wedding day. They were sitting at a table screeching with laughter. Charlie was reaching over to cover Sophie's ears.

'All right?'

I was surprised to see Nick sitting in a grey armchair, feet up on a footstool, an iPad in his hand.

'Yeah, you?' I said, silently nodding my thanks to Charlie who passed me a large glass of wine and disappeared back into the kitchen. Sophie padded in carrying her own glass and sat down next to me on the sofa.

'Yeah.' He barely looked up from his iPad. He had a beer next to him on a coaster.

I wondered if they'd invited him for dinner too, although he seemed very comfortable. I noticed he was wearing slippers. I didn't know that he lived here. I'd assumed he lived in halls.

I turned to Sophie.

'Your house is lovely.'

'Oh thank you.' She beamed. 'We're very lucky. We bought it in 2010. It cost next to nothing then.' She sounded almost apologetic.

'Back in the good old days.' I took a sip of wine. It was delicious. 'I'll probably never own a house.' I didn't mean to sound self-pitying, it was just a fact.

'Where did you live in London?'

'On a boat. It wasn't mine though. My girlfriend . . . my ex-girlfriend . . . Emily bought it.'

'A boat! What was that like?'

'Um . . . not for me, to be honest. It was very claustrophobic, in the end.' Boat life had never really been for me. A montage of me walking into things began to play in my head.

We chatted more about the house. About decorating. About how Charlie loves to start DIY projects and never finishes them. She showed me their half tiled bathroom and a project in the spare room that Charlie was describing as 'upholstering and repurposing vintage chairs' despite never having upholstered or repurposed anything in her life.

'She's learning off YouTube,' Sophie whispered.

We sat down for dinner all squeezed in next to each other at a too-small table in their kitchen. There were so many candles and bottles of wine and glasses of water on the table I wasn't sure how we'd fit any plates in, but somehow we managed it.

'I can't believe you *made* ravioli,' I exclaimed, putting a whole piece in my mouth at once and immediately regretting it as lava hot ricotta spilled over my tongue.

'Oh, it's easy really.' Charlie waved off the considerable effort that the mess on the kitchen counters indicated and started dishing out salad to everyone. Salad which, upon closer inspection, had even more cheese in it than the pasta. No wonder Nick wanted to live here.

I took a sip of a different, equally delicious wine.

'This wine is amazing too. Are you fancy wine people? Do you know about the notes and the body and all that stuff?'

Sophie immediately burst out laughing.

'Excuse me!' Charlie tried to look outraged, but also succumbed to laughing.

'Sorry darling, but no. You are not a fancy wine person.' Sophie looked at me. 'She's going to claim to know a lot about wine, but she doesn't. She chooses by whether she likes the label.'

'I do not! I know loads about wine. I could be a posh wine

person if I wanted to be. I'd just need to put the effort in, and I don't have time.'

I thought about Frankenstein's chair upstairs.

'I don't know anything about wine. I just know what tastes delicious,' I pointed at my glass, 'and what tastes like it was made in someone's bath.'

Nick was silently shovelling ravioli into his mouth and staring straight ahead looking like he was willing the dinner to be over.

'You know my mum used to know loads about wine,' I said.

'Did she?' Sophie asked.

'Yeah, or I mean, she definitely *liked* wine a lot. No, I'm sure she used to know a lot about it. She lived in Spain once. Or Italy.'

Shit. How could I not remember that? I'd have to ask Dad.

'I remember going to the wine shop with her and my dad on a weekend and she'd choose a bottle for them. Huh. You know, I've only just remembered that. I'm sure it was my mum who chose and not my dad, he's not very discerning.'

'Is it just your dad now, Ally?' Charlie asked. Sophie glared at her.

'Yeah, yeah. Just my dad. Mum died a long time ago.'

'I'm sorry. I didn't know that,' Charlie said.

'Mine died last year,' Nick piped up, his mouth full.

Sophie looked absolutely horrified. 'Dead mums' was not on her list of suitable dinner party conversations. Nick didn't seem to notice.

'Oh shit. I'm sorry, Nick.'

'What did your mum die of?' he said.

Sophie put her fork down and very quickly picked up her wine.

'Oh, it was cancer. The usual story. You?'

'Heart attack. People don't think women die of heart attacks, but,' he paused to pop a bite of salad in his mouth, 'they do.' I wondered if he was going to elaborate, but he just shrugged as if to say 'what can you do?'

'Fuck. Nick. I'm sorry. It's just shit isn't it?'

'Yeah.'

'Right, well yes, good.' Sophie started loading up her plate with more pasta. 'What about holidays, Ally? Are you off on any holidays this year?'

After dinner Charlie insisted she'd wash up later, regardless of how many times I offered, so instead I persuaded her to at least let me clear the table with her. Sophie and Nick went and sat in the living room before pudding. I'd heard whispers about tiramisu.

'I didn't know about Nick's mum,' I said, lifting things randomly from one place on the sideboard and putting them down on another as I realised I had no idea where anything went.

'Oh God yeah, bless him. He's had an awful time.'

'Was she your . . .'

'She was my sister-in-law. My brother's a mess. Him and Nick never really got on, so it just makes sense that he's here for now.'

'Totally.' I dropped the fork I was holding. I'd had a lot of wine. 'He's really lucky to have you.'

Charlie smiled.

'He's so close to Sophie. You know he just adores her. She's so . . . I don't want to say sweet because that doesn't sound like enough, it sounds insipid, but you know what I mean? She has this side to her that I don't have, this gentleness. She's very maternal. I don't have that. I'm very practical, logical, you know. But sometimes you don't want logic. You want someone like her. Just listening.'

'You guys, ugh.' I put my hand to my heart. 'You give me hope.'

'Ally. You are twelve years old. Your life is just beginning. You're fine. You should be filled with hope. All the time.'

My lip wobbled when she brought the tiramisu out of the fridge.

The rest of the evening is a bit hazy if I'm being honest, but I know that we sat around talking for hours. Nick grew chattier as the night went on and I really felt as though we bonded with some deep conversations over tiramisu. Deep for Nick.

'You love cake, don't you?' he'd said, watching me sink another mouthful of tiramisu.

'Um, yes. I do. Don't you love cake?'

'Nah.'

'Oh right, do you not like working at the bakery then?'

'Nah it's fine. I like bread.'

'Oh well, that's something.'

'And I like working with you guys.' He said this matter-of-factly. Without a hint of sentimentality.

'Nick!'

'What?'

'That's so nice. I feel like I might cry.'

'OK.'

At around midnight, after another bottle of wine and at least forty-five helpings of pudding, they put me in an Uber which they insisted on ordering for me. They all waved me off at the door, including Nick, who, excruciatingly, I pulled into a massive hug on the way out.

'You're the best bosses ever. What boss makes ravioli for their employees? No boss! BYE NICK.' I was suddenly aware that I might have been shouting. On the way home, grinning in the back seat, my face entirely numb from alcohol, I knew it was a good time to voice note Jeremy.

Jeremy! Oh my God. They are so nice. Just angels. ANGELS. I've had so much wine. They just gave me so much wine, how nice is that? How nice! True love exists, Jeremy. It EXISTS. I've seen it with my own eyes. They love each other so much. They love each other and Nick and his mum is DEAD. SO SAD. IT'S SO SAD, JEREMY. But you know what, we're going to have that again, Jeremy. LOVE not DEATH. We are! OK I LOVE YOU. I'm shouting, am I? OK I'm going to go and have some water. OK love you. BYE!

He messaged me back immediately.

You are shouting. No threesome then? Rubbish. Love you, Al. Get home safe. Text me please. And yes we will have it again – love and death.

I sent my dad a text, jabbing at the screen.

URGENT!! Where did Mum live???? Spain? OR ITaly? WAs she a WINe genius? Xxzzz

When I woke up the next morning, bleary-eyed, I turned my phone over and saw the reply my dad had sent at 7 a.m. I could hear him pottering about downstairs chatting to the animals.

It was Spain. She lived in Barcelona for 6 months when she was 19 before she met me. She was very adventurous. Not many people did that kind of thing back then. I don't know what a wine genius is but she knew her way around a wine list. And she was good at drinking it. Like mother like daughter by the looks of it.

How rude.

By the Thursday two weeks before the half marathon I was seriously flagging. Jeremy had cancelled on our after-work runs two days in a row. On the first day I didn't mind. I was happy about it even – any excuse for a much-needed break. I believed him when he told me he had a headache. On the second day he didn't cancel on me. He simply didn't turn up at my house or reply to any of my messages although I could see that he'd read them. I decided to go to his house (assuming he was sacking off work as well as me) if I still hadn't heard anything and physically drag him to running club with me.

The walk to work felt even more brutally cold than usual, a sharp wind and the occasional burst of hailstones. I felt deeply sorry for myself and when I finally arrived at the steamed-up bakery door, my face chapped and my nose running from the wind, I didn't know how I would make it through the day. There was nobody upstairs, but I could hear the tinkle of the radio and I knew that either Charlie or Sophie would be downstairs already hard at work. I found Charlie pouring out three mugs of tea. I could have kissed her. The morning sped by as usual, with all three of us working for the most part in amiable silence. By the time Nick came in to start his shift, I was, despite being exhausted, feeling at least fifty per cent more human and able to face the day. I took the opportunity to have a sit-down for five minutes and eat a cookie, sticky with tahini and white chocolate. I scrolled through Instagram, absent-mindedly liking pictures of dogs I didn't know and elaborate cakes I fleetingly wondered if I could make. I opened Sara with no H's page to check for any new content (none) and while I did my habitual scroll to see if I'd missed anything, a message popped up on my screen from Jo. My tummy flipped.

Hey! Are you coming running tonight? A couple of people have dropped out but I am up for it if you and Jeremy are? What are you doing after?

I had been considering bailing on running club that evening, if I couldn't persuade Jeremy. But I couldn't seem to find the right words to say no to Jo. And I couldn't resist the thrill I still felt at seeing her in person, so I texted back.

Oh no! Don't worry J and I still in. No plans for after other than collapsing in a heap, why?

'What are you grinning at over there?' Charlie was leaning against the counter stirring sugar into a cup of tea.

My face was suddenly very hot. 'Nothing!'

'Rubbish! Who are you texting?'

'What's this?' Sophie's head appeared at the top of the stairs. 'Ally's got a girlfriend.'

'I have not! Oh my God!' I exclaimed, my inner teenager rising up to meet their best annoying parent impression. I turned back around to face the window and shoved another piece of cookie in my mouth.

'Then who are you texting?' Charlie continued as she picked up her tea and came and sat on the stool next to me, thrilled to have elicited such a strong response.

'No one,' I said with my mouth full, and grabbed my phone before she could, catching her eye as I did and starting to laugh.

'Fine! I'm texting the person who organises my running club if you must know.'

'The person?'

'The girl.'

'The girl!' They both squealed. I looked at Nick for some kind of support but he just smiled at me and shrugged. I suspected he had endured this same line of questioning many times himself.

'YES! She is a girl; her name is Jo. But she is not my GIRL-FRIEND.' I said *girlfriend* like I was an eight-year-old boy in the playground, absolutely disgusted by the very notion. 'She is only twenty-four, she's literally a baby, no offence Nick.' He nodded, barely listening.

'So this Jo,' Charlie said ignoring all my protestations, 'she single?'

'Yes, but I'm not—'

'She's . . .' she interrupted, gesturing at me with a head tilt and a hand gesture to mean gay, in an astonishing approximation of my dad's classic move.

'No! Yes. Maybe. I don't know.'

This thrilled them even more and so in the manner of people in long-term relationships who have not been on a date themselves in a very long time, they set about initiating a takeover of my love life, asking endless questions about Jo, about our previous interactions, about who'd been texting who.

When I told them that she'd asked me what I was doing after running club Charlie practically exploded, dictating texts that I would never send and coming up with scenarios I knew would never happen.

'Technically she asked what both Jeremy and I were doing . . .' I protested uselessly against the cacophony of instructions.

'Look,' Charlie said, looking at Sophie for support, who nodded sagely, instinctively knowing the unsolicited advice her wife was about to give. 'I know it's hard to consider putting yourself back out there after such a hard time with . . .' she reached about for the name, really underlining the depth of her knowledge of my situation.

'Emily,' I filled in for her. I pressed my fingers into the soft crumbs on my plate and started licking them off my fingers, trying to remember exactly how much about my current circumstances I'd actually told them.

'Yes,' she said, snapping her fingers like it was on the tip of her tongue. 'You have to try and get over Emily, and sometimes the best way to do that is to throw yourself into something else.'

'Is that not what I'm doing with running?' I asked petulantly, knowing exactly what she meant.

'Well yes, but I mean throwing yourself into some*one* else.' She widened her eyes, wondering if my mood was light enough to laugh at her innuendo. It was not. 'Even if it's just a bit of fun.'

Sophie was now back behind the counter and nodding. They both looked at me eagerly. Married people were always desperate for everyone to be having *a bit of fun*.

'OK fine!' I said, relenting, not even really knowing what I was agreeing to. 'I will see her after running club ... *with* Jeremy!'

They both seemed happy enough with that. Customers were still trickling in by the time my shift ended, which allowed me to sneak out with minimal intervention. I just heard the echoes of 'let us know how it goes!' as the door closed behind me. I smiled to myself as I stepped outside, the cold wind refreshing against my still warm skin. It felt unexpectedly nice, however irritating it was, to have people wanting to live vicariously through me. As I walked home, I wondered about what I'd write to Emily. I felt a thrill at the prospect of typing out the words 'I went out with Jo tonight'.

I got the bus to Jeremy's house. I didn't have the correct change and the driver tutted at me. I really hammed up my Sheffield accent as I apologised, not wanting him to think I was a student who didn't know what I was doing. I wanted him to think I was a local. I was, wasn't I? He gave me a funny look. The bus was much more expensive in Sheffield than in London. I looked at my Oyster card sitting in my purse and it made me suddenly homesick. I loved riding the bus in London. I'd get the bus even if it was going to take me hours to get somewhere that should take minutes. Looking down on the streets made them feel familiar, gave me a more intimate understanding of the city, which could feel so overwhelming. By the time I'd lived there a few years I understood the layout better than people who'd been there for their entire lives. Looking out of the window as we moved slowly through the streets towards Jeremy's house, I felt lost.

I knocked on Jeremy's front door, assuming I'd be there for a while. I knew that his mum would be at work and that I'd have to wait for him to wake up and get so irritated with the noise that he was forced to come down to shut me up. So I was surprised when the door opened almost immediately. It was Jeremy's little sister Molly, who was dressed in her school uniform, or a version of it anyway. She probably was not meant to be wearing a skirt that looked like it was from the Christina Aguilera 'Dirrty' video with knee-high black socks, but maybe things had changed since the days of white polo shirts and grey nan trousers. Molly was, and had always been, terrifying.

'Ally, Jesus Christ!' She rolled her eyes and walked away from the door leaving it swinging open behind her. I took this as an invitation to follow her inside.

'Thank fuck you're here, he's doing my head in,' she was

saying as I walked into the living room. She flopped onto the sofa and picked up the TV remote.

Bearing in mind I hadn't seen her since she was a child, I thought perhaps there might have been a bit more small talk.

'Is he OK?' I asked tentatively, as she turned up the volume on the TV and picked up her phone.

'Hmm?'

'Jeremy, is he OK?'

She looked at me properly for the first time since I'd arrived and I felt the ice-cold chill of a sixteen-year-old girl taking in my Lycra-clad body.

'He's just being a dickhead,' she said eventually. She was clearly irritated by the question and by my continued presence. I was meant to be taking Jeremy off her hands, not bothering her while she was so busy.

'Is he upstairs?'

She didn't reply, just opened her eyes extra wide at her phone as if the screen could sympathise with her about how annoying I was being.

Jeremy's bedroom door was closed. I knocked gently and then pushed it open. It was dark and smelt like boy. Like socks and unwashed hair and bad aftershave. Jeremy's bedroom hadn't changed since he was ten by the looks of it. There was a border running around the middle of the wall with pictures of trains on. In fact, I remember picking at it several times as a kid and drawing a face on one of the trains with permanent marker. As

I tried to locate my handiwork I thought back to the last time I'd sat in that room. I couldn't remember the exact occasion, but it must have been when we were sixteen or seventeen, and we'd not seen each other in a long time. We'd sneaked up here away from a gathering downstairs that was too boring for very cool teenagers. One of Molly's birthdays perhaps. We'd stuck our heads out of the window and shared a cigarette. It had felt like the height of sophistication. We were too old to be there. On the cusp of breaking free.

'Jeremy?' I whispered.

He grunted something unintelligible.

'What?'

'How did you get in?' he croaked. It sounded as though he might not have spoken out loud in a couple of days.

'Molly let me in.'

'Molly's meant to be at FUCKING SCHOOL,' he shouted towards his door at a surprisingly alarming volume.

'Fuck OFF Jeremy you actual WANKER,' rang through the house clear as a bell. I was amazed that she could hear over the volume of the TV. It was one of her frightening, magical powers.

'Al, look, I'm sorry I've been ignoring you, but I don't feel like talking, all right?'

He rolled over to face the wall and pulled the duvet all the way up over his head.

I went and sat on the edge of his bed.

'I've come all the way over here on the bus. It cost me £2.75

and the bus driver had a paddy at me, so I'm actually going to stay for a bit.'

He was silent for a while and then turned over onto his back, the duvet still pulled up over his face.

'Bus drivers are pricks,' he said in a muffled voice.

'Yeah or I'm a prick for trying to pay with a tenner.'

'Oh yeah. You're the prick then.'

I waited for a while until he eventually pulled the covers down so I could see his face. He was all creased, as though he'd been sleeping with his face pressed into his pillows.

'Jeremy, what's going on?'

He shrugged and then his face crumpled.

'Ugh.' He rubbed his eyes furiously.

I looked away, trying to give him as much privacy as possible while basically sitting on his leg.

'I don't know,' he said eventually.

I nodded.

'I was doing all right and then I just thought what the fuck am I doing?' He wiped his nose with the sleeve of his jumper. He said this almost as if he wanted an answer.

'Like am I really going to do a run to impress Ben. Am I that stupid?'

'Yes! Well no, not stupid. And I don't know about impressing Ben, but you're going to do the run.'

'Did I even see him, Al? Is he even running the race?'

'I don't know. Maybe?'

'Maybe.'

'But *we're* running the race.'

He was silent.

'He wouldn't even want to see me. That's the thing.'

'I'm sure he . . .'

'He's got a new boyfriend.'

'What? Since when? How do you know?'

'Instagram, obviously.'

'Oh, you can't tell anything from Instagram, what's the picture?'

Jeremy shoved his phone into my hand. The image on the screen was of a boy who I recognised as Ben. He was looking just beyond the camera to the person behind it and smiling broadly. The caption was simply a heart emoji. Very basic.

'Who posted this?'

'Someone from uni. Daniel, he played rugby. I knew they always secretly liked each other.'

'It doesn't mean anything. It's just a nice picture . . .'

I looked again. It was pretty damning.

'Look Jeremy, I'm sorry you've had to put up with all my shit when you're going through—'

He didn't let me finish. 'Oh, stop, it's not a competition, is it?'

'Well,' I said, 'you would win.'

'I'm fine, Al. I'm not . . . I'm just taking a bit of time to wallow and obsess over my shit life. You'd know all about that.'

He smiled weakly and jabbed me in the side.

'I do love a wallow.' I grabbed his hand, which was still poking my ribs, and held it for a moment. 'I was worried. You can't just stop speaking to me you know. We wallow together.'

He pulled my hand up and kissed it.

'I know. I'm sorry.'

He stared at me as if he was taking me in properly for the first time since I'd arrived.

'You look nice,' he said. 'Very . . . stretchy.'

'Thank you. Yes, I'm going to running club tonight. With you.'

'I don't think so, Al.'

'Well, why don't you just get into your running stuff and see how you feel? We can hang out here and then if you still don't want to go this evening then don't come. I'll go by myself.'

He thought about it a moment.

'Can I put it on and then get back in bed?'

'Sure.'

He nodded.

'Let me think about it.'

'Oh and then . . . out for a little drink?'

'A drink?'

'Jo has asked us out on a date.'

He sat bolt upright.

'Describe please.'

I pulled out my phone and showed him all the messages between us.

'Ally, you've not replied! You can't leave her hanging!'

'I needed your input.'

186

He took my phone off me and typed: *Cool! Well we could meet at 9ish? Pop home first?*

Perfect! Black Lion? she replied almost immediately.

Great. See you later!

'Right, OK fine, I'll come, but only because I have to witness this. And to a lesser extent because I've already told work I'm going to be off the whole week with conjunctivitis, so it'd be a shame to waste a Thursday night.'

'Yes! Let's get ready at mine together afterwards.'

'All right.' He was visibly perking up. 'Ooh, that means I can use that running backpack I bought. I knew it would come in handy!'

'And it looks so good.'

He smiled at me sarcastically.

'I'm not taking fashion comments or suggestions at this time, thank you very much. But if I was, let me tell you I would not be taking them from someone wearing pedal pushers.'

'Noted.'

Jeremy pulled back the duvet, removed his phone from the spot next to him, and patted the space where it had been. I climbed in.

'Do you want to watch videos of people crossing the finish line at the end of marathons? It literally always makes me cry.'

I nodded.

'Yeah, I feel like that's a good visualisation technique.'

I watched as Jeremy typed in 'hot man marathon' to Google, and looked away from the screen, afraid of the results.

After about twenty minutes of watching beautiful men sprinting effortlessly, Jeremy turned to me.

'That could be us, couldn't it?'

I looked at him, thinking he was joking, but he was completely sincere.

'Yes. Definitely.'

He smiled and turned back to the hot man marathon on the screen – a glimpse into our future.

12

Sheffield's Premier Gay Establishment

Running club really was just the three of us, and Jo took us on a ridiculous route incorporating as many hills as she possibly could. Enough hills that I honestly thought at one point my lunch was going to make a reappearance. Jo chose to keep pace with us instead of powering on ahead and annoyingly never looked particularly out of breath, but mercifully did not try and chat to us. By the time we finally stopped back at the park gates, I was questioning whether I'd even be able to make it back out for drinks at all. How could I even be thinking about what I was going to wear when at least one of my lungs was collapsing? Jeremy threw himself and his backpack dramatically onto the grass and lay out flat on his back, arms above his head, surrendering to the earth. He refused to get up for a full five minutes despite Jo's protestations that his muscles would seize up.

'I don't have any,' he moaned, 'I'll be fine.'

Once we were both upright and definitely not throwing up, Jo looked at us encouragingly.

'Guys, you're really getting there! If you can run for an hour and a half, you can definitely run a half marathon.'

'What,' said Jeremy, pausing to spit on the ground, 'what if in an hour and a half you've only just managed half of a half marathon. A quarter marathon?'

If she was at all worried Jo's face didn't give it away.

'You'll be fine. It's different on the day anyway, you'll be swept up with the crowds and you'll have all the extra adrenaline.'

We looked at each other communicating a silent 'true'. We'd not considered all that adrenaline; we'd practically been running on empty.

Once we were back at mine and showered, we had a tiny window of time to wolf down some food (spaghetti bolognese, very kindly brought up on trays by my dad so we had the luxury of having a fork of pasta in one hand and a hairdryer in the other) and get ready before meeting Jo again. We also had a couple of glasses of sauvignon blanc on the go, courtesy of Jeremy's mum (we'd popped it in his backpack on our way out). Dad's generosity was somewhat backhanded, given that it suited him to keep us upstairs away from his teacher pals who were having a board game night downstairs. I wasn't sure how many board games they were playing but, judging by the amount of shrieking and giggling going on, I was confident that many bottles of wine were being drunk.

It was thrilling not only to have an evening plan but to have an evening plan with two whole people and on a school night. After going for a run! I didn't recognise myself.

I cracked open a bag of fizzy jelly snakes for pudding.

'It's weird I haven't lost any weight doing this training,' Jeremy said, stroking his tummy, a bit of snake hanging out of his mouth as he chewed.

'You don't want to lose any weight,' I said, and I meant it. 'You are the perfect Jeremy.'

He looked up at me, surprised.

'Thanks babe,' he said, looking a bit embarrassed.

We chewed in silence for a while.

'Do you feel better for being out of bed and going outside?'

'I'd been out of bed, Al!'

'Oh. I'd just decided you'd been in bed for forty-eight hours straight, too sad to move.'

'I'd actually been as far as the bathroom, and the sofa once to watch *Border Force* with Molly. The kitchen to eat my dinner. The shop to get cigarettes.'

'Quite the adventurer! Sorry. I was worried you'd—'

'Just taking a few "personal days", Al. That's what my mum calls them.'

'But not . . . I mean . . . I want you to be able to tell me if . . .' I didn't know quite how to put it.

'I would tell you if I wasn't well, Al.' He paused. 'Or I wouldn't. I don't know. But Mum would. Molly would. You'd be kept in the loop. I'm good for now though.'

'Right. Good. Fine. Does Molly ever go to school then, or is it all personal days?'

'Yeah, to see her friends and sell Mum's fags.'

'For all the important bits then.'

'Anyway,' he said emphatically, slapping his hands on his knees. 'What are you going to wear to impress our Joanne?' Jeremy reclined onto my pillows, grabbing an old teddy bear of mine and placing it carefully beside him like a second member of the judging panel.

'Joanne? How do you know she's a Joanne? She could be a Josephine or a Joan or a . . .' I floundered.

'A Joward, a Jostepher?' Jeremy offered.

I threw a snake at him.

'I simply asked her,' he waved his hand in a flourish, 'and all was revealed.'

'Well whatever, I'm not trying to impress her,' I said weakly, knowing there was no point even bothering to protest.

'OK, well if you were trying to impress her then what would you wear?'

I actually had no idea. I was still living out of the one suitcase I'd brought with me from the boat. I had virtually nothing with me. A pang of sadness hit as I thought about getting ready to go out with Emily, inevitably borrowing a top from her. I used to watch her get dressed and marvel at how beautiful she was and how effortless it all seemed. She would sometimes do my make-up for me and we'd end up laughing, and I'd always end up looking like I was in drag but keeping the make-up on so as not to hurt her feelings. I could hardly remember feeling more loved than when she was finishing dabbing things on my eyelids, standing back to admire her handiwork and brushing a piece of hair from my face.

'I really don't know, Jeremy.' I felt suddenly snappy and despondent, like the fun had been sucked out of the evening already.

Jeremy sat up and fixed me with a look, the kind you might give a toddler who is just on the verge of a tantrum. Very kind but stern. A sort of visual, 'Now do you really want to ruin this lovely day we've been having?'

'Al, it doesn't matter what you wear! I was just wondering. Jeans and a top? That's what I'm wearing.' He pulled his outfit out of his backpack as if I needed evidence and laid out a white T-shirt and some black jeans. 'And then just my coat and trainers – not my running ones, obviously. I don't want to look like an *actual* dad.'

We looked through the clothes I'd brought with me. All neatly folded in one drawer. We decided on my black jeans, still nice even though they were slightly floury (we figured we'd give them a good shake in the garden) and a denim shirt that I'd pinched off Emily, oversized on her and a perfect fit for me. I wondered if she'd even noticed that it was gone. What if she saw a picture of me in it with Jo? She'd be annoyed *and* jealous. A perfect sartorial choice.

'Talking of stolen things . . .' Jeremy said as we relaxed back into our seats, the clothing dilemma officially resolved. He pointed at Malcolm, who was stretched out in the middle of my bedroom floor, a live animal skin rug. Malcolm's fang, permanently snagged on his lip, glistened.

'Yeah . . . he's not technically stolen though . . .' I said, failing to summon the enthusiasm to do the full spiel.

'OK, kidnapped,' Jeremy said without missing a beat. 'Is Emily coming to get him?'

'No, well, I don't know.' I sighed. 'I thought she'd come and get him straight away, like maybe there would be some dramatic reunion the night I left where she raced up here and we got to talk away from London and she'd realise she wouldn't be able to go home without us both. But actually, I think she's so wrapped up in her new life without me that after she got over being pissed off with me for taking him she's just . . . not bothered. About either of us.'

I realised it had been a little while since I'd spoken properly about Emily, it being a subject I avoided both at work and with my dad. I hadn't yet vocalised what I'd slowly come to realise, that perhaps my plan to get her back really wasn't going to work.

'Oh Al, I'm sure she does care,' Jeremy tried in his best pep talk voice, but even that didn't sound very convincing. 'She's just maybe . . . not that good at showing it?'

I laughed.

'I think she's not good at showing it because she's got me in the same category as Malcolm now. Sure she'll miss me, but now that I'm not there she'll just have lots more time on her hands, less mess to clear up.'

'Al! I am certain she's not thinking like that. She wasn't a monster, was she?'

I paused before conceding, 'No, she wasn't a monster.'

'And she's asking loads of questions about Jo? I thought you said you'd got her rattled.'

'I did say that. She is rattled. She's very interested for some-one who's in another relationship.'

'Well there you go then. It sounds like you've made a lot of stuff up in your head. Don't wind yourself up with it.'

I knew he was right, but it was easier said than done, and pretty irritating advice coming from someone who had signed up for a thirteen-mile run on the off chance we might spot his ex-boyfriend.

'So . . . how are you feeling about potentially seeing Ben, given recent events?' I wiped my sticky, jelly snake fingers on my trousers, right at the tipping point between the sweets giv-ing me energy and making me fall asleep.

'When?' Jeremy looked completely horrified.

'At the race! The whole reason we're doing this thing?'

'Well,' he waved his hand in the air, 'who knows if he'll even be there. He might be too busy with his new boyfriend.'

We sat in silence for a bit scrolling on our phones, Jeremy still going strong on the jelly snakes. I glanced at his face in profile, illuminated by the screen light, and wondered whether he ever really did believe Ben was here in Sheffield, but I didn't want to push it any further. I let him chomp away in peace.

'Am I going to be a third wheel?' Jeremy asked me for the thousandth time, swirling his drink around in his glass as if he was going to sniff it and tell me all about the bouquet.

'No! It's not a date! You can't be a third wheel when we're all just going for a drink!'

'OK,' he said, looking thoughtfully at me as I applied one final coat of eyeliner. 'And you're sure she doesn't think that me and her are going on a date and that actually you're going to be a third wheel?'

I smiled. 'I'm actually not certain about that. Love works in mysterious ways.' I put my eyeliner back down on the desk and looked up at him. 'Shall we go and find out?'

We both picked up our wines and necked the dregs, still desperately thirsty after our epic run and needing all the liquid we could get in order to replenish our stores.

The Black Lion at 9.30 p.m. on a Thursday night was packed with students. The intensity of the noise and heat from a throng of inebriated humans was almost enough to make me turn right around and go home. But the courage from the glass of wine and the physical pull of Jeremy's hand yanking me around the crowded rooms looking for Jo meant I had no choice. We found her waving madly at us from a tiny table that she had managed to nab and was obviously stressed about trying to keep from the groups of people circling her like sharks. We pulled her coat off one stool and her scarf off another and plonked ourselves down, grateful to have found a place within the chaos.

'I don't know why I chose here!' Jo launched into an exhaustive list of all the reasons why she was a complete piece of shit for suggesting this place and the many ways in which The Black Lion was hell on earth.

Jeremy immediately told her not to be silly and I was grateful to him for launching into his favourite 'The Black Lion' story: the night that he drank two bottles of rosé, lost his wallet, accused absolutely everyone inside of stealing it, was sick in the smoking area, found his wallet in his pocket, had no memory of getting home, and woke up surrounded by seven umbrellas, all of which he can only assume he stole in retribution for his 'lost' wallet. While he told this familiar tale (I remember my dad being horrified but also quite keen to get his hands on one of those umbrellas) I watched Jo listening to him, politely enthralled by his disgusting, deeply unimpressive tale. She was dressed in high-waisted blue jeans, Vans, and a plain white T-shirt which hung off her in all the right places. A hint of a black bra underneath. I'd never been the kind of person who could just make jeans and a white T-shirt look cool and felt wildly envious of anybody who could. I realised I had never seen her with make-up on before. She didn't bother with it for work or running club. She looked so different – quite beautiful, really – and now I felt even more awkward than usual around her. The feeling was not dissimilar to bumping into your maths teacher in Sainsbury's. Outside of the prescriptive familiarity of the classroom, you had to take on new roles. Were you equals in Sainsbury's? Were you just two ordinary people trying to buy some yoghurt? It took some re-negotiating in my brain.

I volunteered to brave the bar and offered to buy us all drinks; we decided on a bottle of house white between us, but when I got to the bar it was buy one get one half price and, never one to turn down a bargain or indeed an extra bottle of wine, I staggered back to the table with a bottle under each arm, three glasses wedged between my fingers, and a sheepish look on my face.

'Ally's getting on it!' Jeremy screeched as he wiggled a bottle free from between my arm and my stomach.

'Look guys, I had no choice, it would have been financially irresponsible not to.'

'I understand,' said Jo solemnly, reaching for a glass with a grin. As our running and fitness guru I was pleased to note she didn't seem at all disappointed in me.

Jeremy poured three enormous glasses and we all lifted them up for a toast. Jeremy and I looked at each other, suddenly stumped for something to celebrate.

'Guys!' Jo looked between us like we were completely daft. 'To running the half marathon!'

'Oh yeah!' We clinked half-heartedly. The prospect felt absurd, but her unfaltering belief in us felt good.

As the night progressed and two bottles of financially sensible wine turned into four, which meant – Jeremy passionately opined with the conviction and verbosity of a barrister – that we got a whole bottle free, the 'Cheers'-ing became increasingly confident.

'To being runners!'

'To finishing the half marathon!'

'To WINNING the half marathon!'

'To being the best friends and athletes in the world!'

It was nearly midnight by the time we decided to leave, the conversation having touched on every subject imaginable apart from relationships, which I was somehow both grateful for and disappointed about. We had considered two more bottles, but weren't able to justify drinking two bottles each over the course of the evening or simply buying one bottle (a disgusting waste of money), so it made sense to call it a night. But once we hit the cold night air I decided that I had never felt more awake in my life and the idea of going home was unbearable. All my senses felt extra acute, which can't have been true given the seven hundred units of alcohol I'd consumed. I just needed the night to keep going. When I looked at the other two they had the same bright eyes, looking at me expectantly. I realised I was meant to be ordering an Uber for us all.

'I don't know if I really want to . . . like, do you guys maybe want to . . .' I trailed off, realising there was really only one thing I could be suggesting at this time of night.

'Al. No.' Jeremy looked at me mock sternly, and then, 'Or . . . yes?' A tiny flicker of possibility crossed his face.

'I know, should we not?' I said, pretending it wasn't already a done deal.

'Guys, what?' Jo asked plaintively.

We burst out laughing and she hit me on the arm, her hand lingering there for a second. 'What?' she whined. 'Tell me!'

'Jo, have you ever been . . . to a little place called Tom's?' Jeremy asked her, with all the mysticism you might expect when asking someone if they'd ever been to the Emerald City.

'Oh my God, no,' she said, her eyes suddenly lighting up, 'but I've heard of it.'

'OK, it's decided, we're one hundred per cent going.' Jeremy grabbed my arm and linked his through it. 'Honestly, we're probably best off just walking.'

'I'm so excited!' Jo squealed and linked arms with me too so I had one of them on either side.

The three of us weaved our way off down the road towards the only place reliably open until the sun came up.

Tom's, for those not in the know, is Sheffield's premier gay establishment. A club open until the early hours of the morning. A club in which you can have fourteen bottles of Lambrini, a hotdog, a full English breakfast and a Sunday roast all within the same twenty-four-hour period. A club in which you can play pool and a One Direction megamix within fifteen feet of each other. It was a place Jeremy and I had frequented regularly as sixth formers, it being both the only gay club in Sheffield and the only place you could buy cherry Lambrini by the bottle. I hadn't ever thought I'd have the opportunity or misfortune to return, but there we were, staggering down the road towards it past shops long closed and groups of students desperately hunting for taxis and cashpoints. I resisted the urge to point out how cold they must all be in their tiny outfits and no coats. I was one of them tonight! Albeit a sensibly dressed one.

Stepping inside the club, the stark contrast between the crisp, cold breeze on the street outside and the thick, hot air and pulsating dark purple walls was an assault on the senses. The noise and the smells were overwhelming and I felt a rush of nostalgia as we made our way up the stairs and towards the bar. When we reached the top we swerved the cloakroom queue and chucked our coats onto a crushed velvet banquette next to a couple of guys who were kissing very enthusiastically.

'What do you want to drink?' Jeremy shouted at us before immediately answering on our behalf, yelling, 'Lambrini!' and gesturing at the man behind the bar.

'No, no, no!' Jo intervened, pulling at Jeremy's arm as he mimed 'three bottles' over the bar. 'I will die if I drink a bottle of Lambrini, all my teeth will fall out. I'll just have a beer.'

'Oh, me too!' I said quickly to the barman. It hadn't occurred to me before that there was the option of not drinking a litre of sugar with a straw here.

'Suit yourselves.' Jeremy grabbed his Lambrini and made his way towards the dance floor.

Jo and I stood awkwardly at the side. I kept glancing at her trying to gauge her reaction. I felt responsible for everything going on around us since I'd suggested Tom's. As if I had chosen the decor and the music, and if they weren't to her taste I would take it as a personal slight.

'I can't believe I've never been here,' she leant in to yell in my ear over the music, smiling widely, 'I love it.' It was the closest we'd ever been to each other and my stomach was doing somersaults.

'I'm so glad!' I yelled back. 'It's very much a love it or hate it kind of place.' We watched as a girl in front of us attempted to unstick her shoe from the floor. 'It's very down to earth.'

Jo nodded and took a huge gulp of her beer. I wondered if she was nervous.

'You know the first time I came here,' I bellowed in her ear as Little Mix faded and Britney began to play, 'I was eighteen. A huge group of us came because it was someone's eighteenth birthday and it was the only place that was open really late. I was out, but like, not out out, you know?'

I broke away from her ear to allow Jo a chance to nod.

'So we came here and we were all dancing and drinking so much. I mean,' I grimaced, 'so much. We'd been drinking before we came out and then I had my first ever tequila shots.' I paused to take a sip of beer and to make sure I was going to tell this story right. Jo was all ears.

'It was probably about 3 a.m. and I'd never been out so late and I was feeling like I was flagging a bit but obviously didn't want to be the first person to go home, so I was sort of dancing half-heartedly and this girl came up to me and started sort of dancing half-heartedly with me. At first I was embarrassed, like I thought she was taking the piss, and I started to go back to my group of friends, but she grabbed my arm and said in my ear,' I softened my voice from a bellow to really act out the story for her. 'She said, "Have I seen you here before?" and I shook my head at her and she really looked at me and said, "You seem so familiar to me", and I don't know what happened but she went from inspecting me to kissing me in the space of about three seconds.' I shook my head smiling a little at the memory of eighteen-year-old me being swept off my feet by an older woman, who looking back now was probably about twenty. 'After that night, we came back here all the time, but,' I surveyed the dance floor, 'I never saw her again.'

'Wow!' Jo looked at me seriously and was quiet for a moment. 'So are you saying that you . . . kissed a ghost?'

I nodded at her gravely. 'Quite possibly.'

She raised her eyebrows and then grinned at me. 'You're an idiot,' she said affectionately, 'come on, let's dance.'

We found Jeremy dancing with a gorgeous boy and his big group of friends. He waved us in to join them, but we hung around on the periphery, preferring to watch everyone, have easy access to the bar and, although it was unspoken, maintain our own little world. At some point Jeremy bought us each a shot of sambuca ('they were on offer!') after which the night became increasingly hazy. I had no idea how long we'd been there or what drink we were on, but at some point Jo and I had been dancing for a while without talking. Jeremy and his new friends had wandered off, and we were surrounded by strangers. My head was saturated by the beat of whatever club remix was on and it all felt so easy, I was at that stage of drunkenness where everything was fluid. I was liquid. I was the beat in the walls. I was all the hot and sweaty people pressing up against us. At some point Jo leant forward to me so close that I could feel her breath on my lips and then she shifted up to my ear.

'Have I seen you here before?' she said softly in my ear. I laughed and reached out to playfully hit her on the arm.

'Does that not work every time?' She was looking at me intently, a half smile on her lips. Before I had the chance to think, we were kissing. My hand was on the small of her back, touching the skin where her T-shirt ended and waistband began. We kissed for eternity. Or at least until the end of the song, where we broke apart and Jo burst out laughing because they started playing Celine Dion.

Not long after, we found Jeremy again, and decided to call it a night. There was a brief discussion about cabs outside without any of us really committing to anything. Suddenly, with an unnecessarily loud shriek Jo realised she'd left her coat in the club and dashed back inside.

'Oh my God,' I said quietly. I felt suddenly very sober.

'I knew it! Didn't I tell you that you'd get with her!' Jeremy was both thrilled and furiously texting (I assumed someone he'd just met inside) so wasn't quite able to give the situation the attention I felt it needed.

'Jeremy!' I demanded.

'Ally!' he said, in the same bratty voice I had used, but softened when he saw how much I was freaking out. 'What are you worried about? It's just fun! You're both single, aren't you?'

'Yes, I suppose.'

'Well then! Tell you what, you need to get in a cab with her instead of coming home with me. This is what we said, Al. You want to get back at Emily? You want to feel better and make her take notice?'

'No, Jeremy, I'm not going to go back to some student house and . . .'

'Yes?'

'Just no!'

'OK, OK, fine. I'm just saying don't turn this into a massive thing.' He said this just as my brain was busy forming the most enormous thing it was capable of. A monstrous mountain of a thing. I had genuinely not considered that anything like this might happen. I desperately wanted my own bed, but somehow the idea of being in the back of a cab with Jo driving to wherever she lived seemed thrillingly inevitable.

'Jeremy, she probably doesn't even want to go home with me,' I hissed, peering back towards the club where Jo was trotting down the stairs, one arm in her coat.

'Well, let's see, shall we?' He grabbed my shoulders and gave me a big kiss on each cheek. Before I could protest he'd given Jo a little wave and hopped into one of the cabs queued up on the pavement outside.

'Got it!' Jo exclaimed as she triumphantly shoved her other arm into her coat.

'Great!'

'Hey, where did Jeremy go?' She looked all around, as if he might be hiding from her.

'He really needed to get home. He said to say goodbye.'

'Oh, well tell him I say goodbye too.'

She was possibly even more drunk than I was.

We stood in silence for a couple of moments.

'Your house is quite a long way away, isn't it?' she asked innocently, knowing perfectly well that it was a fifteen-minute drive away.

'Yeah, I . . . it is I suppose,' I replied, acting as if I too had no idea where my house was.

'I was going to walk back to mine, there's lots of room if you want to stay?'

'You can't walk on your own! It's . . .' I scrambled around for my phone, 'it's 4 a.m.! Shit, when did it get to 4 a.m.?'

'I won't be walking on my own.' She smiled at me and then we were walking away from Tom's and on our way to Jo's house. I had a rare 11 a.m. start, having mercifully swapped with Nick the day before. As we walked we discussed how much we hated sambuca and consequently, how much we hated Jeremy. We talked about how close the half marathon was and how far I'd come. We kept a safe distance, our arms folded across our chests to preserve heat. The tone of the conversation was so light, so jovial, that I genuinely wasn't sure what was going to happen when we arrived. Perhaps I'd be put on the sofa with a sleeping bag.

At Jo's she tripped over a pair of shoes in the middle of the hallway and tutted about the mess her housemates had left. She washed up two mugs for us to drink water from. My mug had '18' printed on the side of it alongside lots of pictures of a teenage boy holding beers and grinning. It smelt like a student house, that combination of sweat and bins and old carpet, and I briefly had an out-of-body experience watching myself sip water out of someone else's mug in this strange environment. It felt impossible that I could be there, that I was not at home in my single bed, fast asleep.

'Ugh, it's disgusting in here,' Jo whispered, snapping me back into my body. 'Let's go upstairs.'

I followed her up the stairs and into her bedroom, a big room at the front of the house. It had two huge, single paned windows and a fireplace that looked like it had never worked. Her bedroom wasn't untidy, but nothing really looked as though it had a place. Piles of books were neatly stacked in random spots on the floor. She had no bedside table, so a lamp was just placed in the middle of the floor next to her bed, the wire trailing across the floor. Her bed hadn't been made, and there were piles of clothes on it. It looked like she might have had as much trouble figuring out what to wear as I'd had.

'God, it's bloody massive in here. Why are rooms in student houses so huge? No actual homes have bedrooms this big in them.' I was babbling and I stopped myself, embarrassed, as if I wasn't sure if it was OK to mention that I was in her bedroom.

'I know, it's massive and it's always cold.' She reached out to touch the radiator, which was, helpfully, located directly below the huge, draughty windows. She gave an involuntary shiver.

'Hey, you're freezing, you need to put some warmer clothes on.' My instinct was to move towards her, to pull her to me and stop her shivering, but I stayed rooted to the spot near her bedroom door.

'Yes, let's . . .' She trailed off and started rummaging. She handed me a pair of flannel pyjama bottoms and a grey T-shirt, reassuring me that they were clean even though she pulled them from a pile in the corner of her room. She said she'd left her pyjamas in the bathroom and dashed out of the room leaving me to get changed in peace. I paused before I got into bed and then once I was in it, between unfamiliar sheets that smelt of Jo's perfume, sort of floral and sweet, I wondered if I should text Jeremy. For some reason I felt out of my depth. I needed a pep talk. Before I could reach my phone, Jo came back into the room, accidentally slamming the door behind her.

'Oops,' she giggled. She was wearing the smallest pyjamas I'd ever seen.

'How . . . are they warmer?' I smiled, the mood was lifted somehow by the door slam, the tension broken.

'They're just what I had!' Emboldened by the alcohol and by being in her own space, she stood in front of the mirror to peer at herself in her tiny pyjamas. I watched her too. She smoothed down the front of her strappy top. Her long legs made the shorts seem even shorter than they were. She had a horrible purple bruise on the back of her thigh like the one I'd got last year after I misjudged where the armrest on the tube was. I wanted to ask her where she got it, but resisted. It felt too personal to talk about her thighs. When she finally got into bed, she switched off the lamp next to her, plunging the room into almost total darkness. Her curtains were thin and flimsy and the glow of the street lamp outside gave the room an orange tinge. She lay flat on her back.

'Ugh, the room is spinning, Al, we're going to feel like shit tomorrow.' She'd never called me Al before.

'We're going to feel like shit *today* you mean.'

'No! Oh God, you're right.'

We were quiet for a minute and I wondered if she'd fallen asleep. I felt neither relieved nor disappointed – only a pang of worry about what I was going to tell Jeremy. I could picture his face as I described our chaste sleepover. 'Lesbians,' he'd say, shaking his head sadly.

'What are you thinking about?' she whispered.

I smiled.

'What am I *thinking about*?'

'What?' she said, half laughing, half affronted. 'I genuinely want to know, I think you're hard to read.'

I paused. I was trying to think of something to say that wasn't 'Jeremy', but she mistook my silence.

'Are you thinking about her?'

'Who?' I obviously knew who she meant.

'Emily.'

'I actually wasn't. But that's usually a pretty good guess.'

'You think about her all the time?'

'All the time.'

She sighed.

'Why, what are you thinking about?' I turned onto my side to face her, my eyes adjusted to the not-quite dark. She was still on her back staring up at the ceiling.

'I'm thinking about how I'm lying in bed next to someone in, let's be honest, basically my underwear, who is thinking about someone else.'

I pulled myself up so I could see her better. She still refused to face me.

'I never said I was thinking about her! I literally just said I wasn't.'

'You said you think about her all the time!'

I smiled. There was something I liked about the fact that she was sulking next to me.

'Why are you smiling?' she demanded, finally turning to look at me properly.

'You're jealous. I haven't seen this side of you. I never really knew you thought about me like that.'

'Well, now you know.' She was still petulant. It only made me smile more, which wound her up.

'OK. So now I know.'

The words didn't sound like they were coming out of my mouth. Partly because I was drunk, but also because it was so surreal after seven years of sleeping with one person to be suddenly so intimate with someone new. And for it all to be so easy.

I watched my hand as I traced a line from the top of her hip down her thigh. I touched the bruise gently. She shivered again and then we were kissing and I finally stopped thinking about Jeremy.

We were drunk and clumsy and for the second time that night I experienced the feeling of having left my own body. I tried to make myself concentrate, but couldn't quite convince myself that I was really there. That it was me kicking off those horrible grey flannel pyjamas, that it was my arms lifting Jo's top above her head. She kissed me urgently, kept pulling my face down towards hers, her hand on the back of my neck. I wondered if she could tell that my mind was wandering. Every time I closed my eyes the bed spun. I felt like I already knew the smell of her, the taste of her skin. All those times we'd hugged goodbye or our hands had brushed or I'd watched her wipe her forehead slicked with sweat mid-run. At one point she pushed me onto my back and kissed me all the way down my body. Had I been sober, I might have cringed. Emily and I had got to the point in our relationship where sex could be funny, and we laughed, a lot. I remembered straddling her, pinning her to the bed and insisting on kissing every inch of skin before I would go down on her. She'd squealed beneath me, uncharacteristically silly.

'We'll be here for hours!' she'd wailed as I slowly made my way to the tips of her earlobes.

'*Sshh*, it'll take as long as it takes. Anything for you, *mi amor*,' I'd whispered huskily in my 'seductive' voice.

When Jo did it though, it didn't feel embarrassing. Nothing she did was ironic or self-conscious. I closed my eyes and let myself enjoy the sweetness of the feeling of someone gently kissing my ribs, my stomach, the tops of my thighs. I didn't look to see if she was watching me.

Jo fell asleep quickly afterwards. Disconcertingly quickly – I was slightly offended. My brain was going full throttle trying to process everything that had just happened. Shamefully, a message was forming in my head for Emily. I stared at Jo asleep next to me and wished Emily could see what I was seeing, could know what had just happened. I needed her to know.

I knew there was no way I'd be able to sleep in this strange bed or deal with the morning after. The thought of it filled me with a sudden, bone-deep horror. I looked at my phone; it was 6.45 a.m. I had four hours until work. As quietly as I could, I got dressed, ordered an Uber, and crept down the stairs and out of the house. Before I left, I stood over Jo for a moment watching her sleep, like a creep. She had one arm flung above her head. I gently brushed the soft skin of her inner arm with my finger and she didn't flinch. I bent down and kissed it.

In the back of the Uber I composed a text to Jo, not wanting her to think I was freaking out. My hands shook.

Hey, sorry I took off. Couldn't sleep and work at 11 (help!) speak tomorrow. X

The taxi dropped me off on my silent street. I let myself in to the house and tried to shut the door behind me as quietly as possible before dropping my keys on the table, which made an unimaginably loud clatter. Creeping into the kitchen, I saw that Dad had left the little lamp on the side switched on for me. The house was boiling hot. He had really taken my notes about sometimes switching the heating on seriously. Malcolm, who was half asleep on one of the kitchen chairs, looked up at me with bleary eyes and, I couldn't help but feel, a little bit of judgement.

'What?' I whispered to him. 'Don't give me that look.'

I was definitely still a bit drunk.

He fixed me with a glare before stretching and flopping back down to face the other way. He couldn't even stand to look at me.

I got a glass of water and drank, wondering if there was anything I could consume that would somehow give me the energy I needed to get through the day without collapsing and/or throwing up. I switched off the lamp in the kitchen and let the cat go back to sleep before heading upstairs and throwing myself face down on my bed. I picked up my phone, hoping Jeremy might still be awake.

What do you think of this? Is it too subtle? I really want her to know that I spent the night at Jo's but it feels too creepy. Is it too creepy? I obviously will wait until tomorrow night to send so it makes sense. Oh god. This is tragic. Message me as soon as you get this.

He messaged back immediately.

AL, spell it out! Isn't this what you wanted? To make Emily jealous? Make her really jealous!

*

213

From: Alexandra Waters   13 March 2019 at 07:24

To: Emily Anderson

Subject: re: re: re: re: re: Update – I'm an athlete now

Hey Em,

How's it going? How is Sarah? I take it you're still together.

I'm enjoying work still. You know it is my dream to be in the company of cake all day every day. I've become quite the expert at making croissants now. And eating them.

I've been running a lot. I have to, with the race creeping up. And I've been spending a lot of time with Jo. I didn't expect to meet someone who I clicked with so easily. She's really fun. She and Jeremy and I went out for some drinks last night and ended up at Tom's. I'm sure I told you about Tom's? The sticky walls? The dancing cage? It was great – she'd never been before. We were out so late. Until 4 a.m., can you believe it? Me! It was so late actually that I ended up staying at hers. It was weird to be with someone who isn't you. But in a good way I think. I thought that I'd think about you. And I did, a bit. But actually, it's quite easy to forget when you're with someone else. I guess that's what happened with you and Sarah.

I wanted to tell you for some reason.

I know that's weird. I'm sorry.

Al x

13

Date Night

Getting through the following day at work was nothing short of heroic. Every single smell hit me at the back of my throat. Simple tasks like kneading or stirring or opening the oven door were insurmountable. Every sip of tea felt less and less likely to stay down. I did some fuzzy calculations about how many units of alcohol I'd had, but gave up around the twenty mark, my brain unable to cope with those kinds of numbers. I hadn't been so hungover in years. Not since I was in university and had the luxury of dedicating entire, sprawling days to hang-overs. I longed for a day in bed where I could gossip and eat crisp sandwiches. I fantasised about being stretched out on the sofa, drinking a litre of Lucozade and watching music videos with nothing to do and nowhere to be.

Sophie and Charlie were gentle with me, which was only fair given that they basically insisted I went out. But by the time it reached my break time and I'd sat down with a pint of water and a banana (when my body is rejecting pastry I know it's a bad one) they'd obviously silently decided that I'd recovered enough and it was time to interrogate me. I could see them out of the corner of my eye before they even started, assembling, making eye contact, and nodding at each other, the universal sign of 'no, you say it'.

'All right?' I said, looking up from scrolling through Instagram on my phone, which was giving me an intense feeling of motion sickness.

'Are *you* all right?' Charlie grinned back at me, folding her arms and leaning back against the counter. I hated her for being so chirpy when I felt so close to death.

'I'm fine, thank you,' I said defiantly, taking a tentative bite of my banana and then quickly putting it down again. Too soon.

'Good night, was it?' She didn't budge from her spot at the counter. Sophie was fiddling about doing, I suspected, absolutely nothing at the till apart from listening.

'Yes, thank you,' I replied. I hadn't actually had time yet to decide for myself whether I'd had a good night or not. I felt like there had been fun, despite the weight of hangover shame and dread that sat solidly in the pit of my stomach.

They both stood there looking at me then, desperate for details. I took pity on them.

'We just went to the pub, OK? With Jeremy as well!'

Charlie's brow furrowed.

'To the pub?'

'Yes.'

'Just the pub?'

'Yes, well no, not *just* the pub . . .' I sighed, knowing resistance was futile when I couldn't even follow my own train of thought. 'We stayed at the pub really late and then we just didn't really fancy going straight home, so we went to Tom's. Just for a bit!'

Their eyes lit up, triumphant in their sleuthing, like gay Sherlocks.

'I knew it!' Charlie exclaimed. 'You've got night at Tom's written all over you. I can practically smell the Lambrini on you.'

'I actually didn't drink any Lambrini, so—'

'Well? What happened?' she interrupted me, not remotely interested in what I had or hadn't been drinking. 'You go to Tom's, you have a few Lambrinis, and then what?'

'And then I went home.' Technically not untrue. I had eventually gone home.

Charlie couldn't hide her disappointment that she had failed to uncover deeper and more exciting gossip.

'Wait a minute,' Sophie butted in, having given up all pretence of doing anything with the till. 'You didn't just go there, have a drink and come home. You didn't go to Tom's just for the atmosphere. What happened while you were there? Did you have a dance? Did you . . .' She trailed off, raising her eyebrows at me.

'We had a dance, Jeremy got some guy's number I think, and er . . .' I paused, groping for a reason why I ought to bite my tongue but not sure why. 'And I kissed Jo, all right, or she kissed me! I don't know, ugh.' I put my head in my hands. Saying the words out loud brought the whole moment back in screaming technicolour. I realised the song that had been playing at the time was a club remix of 'C'est la Vie' by B*Witched. The romance.

'Oh my God!' they both said in unison, not even noticing when I looked up to judge them for it. They flapped about a bit, not really sure how to continue their line of questioning now they had actual information. I decided not to tell them I'd gone home with her. They might pass out with excitement.

'So what? Do you really like her?' Charlie had come to sit next to me now on the other little stool by the window. I couldn't tell if it was so we could have a more intimate conversation or whether it was because she wanted to see if I was getting any texts. I picked my phone up and put it on the other side of my abandoned banana just in case.

'I honestly don't know. I mean yes, of course. Of course I *like* her, she's great. She's so sweet and fun, but . . .'

'But Emily?' Charlie asked gently.

I nodded and we were both quiet for a minute.

'It's hard . . .' I started, and realised I couldn't even begin to list all the ways in which it was hard.

Charlie frowned.

'It won't be when you meet the right person. You'll know.' She looked over at Sophie and smiled. The bite of banana threatened to make a reappearance. I used to say that to people all the time.

'But what do you do when the right person for you decides you're not the right person for them?'

Charlie was momentarily stumped.

'I guess you go out and snog your running coach,' she concluded and slapped me affectionately on the forearm. 'Right, up you get, no more moping.'

I rested my head briefly on the cool counter.

'I feel like shit, Charlie. And no one says "snog" anymore.'

'It's your own fault. Now come on, we want those trays bringing up from downstairs.'

I groaned, wrapping up my banana in a napkin for later. A sorry sight.

From: Emily Anderson   14 March 2019 at 14:05
To: Alexandra Waters

Subject: re: re: re: re: re: re: Update – I'm an athlete now

Hi Al,

I didn't realise things were like that with Jo.

I don't know if I'm glad that you told me or not. I want to know but I don't think that's a very healthy thing to want.

Are you happy?

Em

P.S. It is Sara with no H. You know that.

From: Alexandra Waters   14 March 2019 at 14:25
To: Emily Anderson

Subject: re: re: re: re: re: re: re: Update – I'm an athlete now

Yes, it surprised me too. I stayed around the next day and we had breakfast together and talked and watched films. I think I might see her again tonight. I just wanted you to know. I don't want to keep anything from you.

Let me know if you want to come up anytime soon for the cat.

Al xx

I felt a perverse thrill when I sent that one. And a sadness. And a bit of shame. Some part of me wished it was true. I stared at the screen waiting for a reply that didn't come.

I got several messages from Jo in the next few days. She had been extremely gracious about me disappearing while she was asleep. Some messages were casual, simply enquiring about my day. Mostly they were sweet and funny, she sent me an article about a dog that ran a marathon. She said she hoped I wasn't too overwhelmed with work and training. I replied to all of them but in a way that was entirely non-committal, and then felt dreadful about it. I knew what it was like to receive a *haha* or a *cool* in place of a proper response, but I just couldn't quite bring myself to fully engage. I still couldn't quite decide how I felt about what had happened. Mostly I tried not to think about it and then at night I'd let the memory of it creep into my head. Mortifying and thrilling. Me and not me. The hazy idea of Jo, entwined with the visceral experience of her. It wasn't that I didn't want to speak to her, it was that I didn't have the words to express what I wanted to say. It had meant something to me. I just didn't yet know what.

Jeremy despaired of me. One afternoon in a coffee shop after work he shook his head at me as if I was simply incomprehensible to him.

'I don't understand what your problem is, Al. She's a *nice girl*, you had a *nice time*, why are you making it all so difficult?'

He was smug because he'd been texting a guy he'd met at Tom's and felt suddenly superior to me in his handling of his love life.

'I don't know! I don't know. I just, originally the goal of all this was to . . .' I trailed off. It was pathetic to say out loud.

'Right, but it doesn't look like Emily is coming back, does it?'

'All right! Jesus Christ. It was your idea. Why are you being so mean about it?'

He sighed.

'I'm not being mean. I'm being realistic. Ultimately this was all meant to be a bit of fun. I don't get why you can't just treat it like that.'

'I can treat it like that, I can. I can be cool.'

'Yes. Try and be cool. And normal. Show me your phone.'

I chucked it at him half hoping it would hit him, but he

caught it one handed and began to read out loud. His Jo voice was weirdly spot on.

Hey, how's it going? Do you fancy getting a coffee or something?

Hey, I was going to go for a run this evening, do you want to join me?

Hey, just wondering if you're free sometime this week?

'Oh my God, Al. She is *into* you. Why are all your replies so shit? How are you claiming to be busy all the time? Obviously lies. Can you not just go for a drink with her?'

'Yeah I can. I will. I was going to ask if she wants to come around when Dad's at parents' evening.'

'Hot.'

I ignored him. 'Do you think that's a good idea?'

'Yes. Do it. Then if you don't want to see her again after that you can let her down gently.'

I read out loud as I typed a message to Jo.

Hey, sorry I've been so rubbish. Everything's been really hectic.

Jeremy snorted.

Do you fancy coming to mine tomorrow? We could make dinner together or something?

I was jittery before she arrived. Humming with energy and not sure what to do with it. My dad had been teasing me before he went out but stopped when he realised I was too wound up to find him funny.

'Have fun, Al,' he said to me as he was on his way out. 'This kind of stuff, it's meant to be fun.'

'I know. I'm sorry I'm such a grump.' I looked up at him while he was getting his coat on. He was wearing a blue tie covered in equations that I'd chosen for him with Mum one year for his birthday.

'Try and be less of a grump when she gets here, eh? And calm down a bit. You'll stress the poor girl out.'

'I will! I'm fine, it's all fine.'

The doorbell went a few minutes after Dad had left and Pat merrily launched into riotous overdrive, which sent Malcolm flying up the stairs. Once I'd dragged the tiny guard dog away, I opened the door and ushered Jo in, barely looking at her, too busy concentrating on apologising for Pat and deciding where to banish her to.

'I don't mind,' Jo said. 'She's very cute.'

'She's a wolf in sheep's clothing so watch out.' When I'd shooed the dog away I finally looked at Jo properly and she was smiling, the picture of calm.

'Noted.' She took off her coat and hung it on the end of the bannister. I realised I should have offered to take it for her. She was wearing black skinny jeans and she'd rolled up the sleeves of her soft grey jumper.

'Come through, come through.' I beckoned for her to follow me.

'Wine?' I asked, a little more manically than intended.

'Sure, yes please, that would be lovely.' She shook a bag at me.

'I've brought snacks. I know we're going to make dinner, but I'm starving.'

I tipped the bags of crisps she'd bought into bowls and set them on the kitchen table and then went about pouring wine into enormous glasses. I wondered if I could get away with taking a swig from the bottle without her noticing.

When I turned around she was feeding a sweet chilli crisp to Malcolm, who had crept back downstairs in order to inspect the stranger.

'Sorry!' she said, catching me looking. 'Is he allowed crisps? I didn't really expect him to eat it, to be honest. I thought he'd just give it a sniff.'

'He's allowed crisps.' I thought back to Emily admonishing me for so much as allowing him to look at my food. 'He's allowed whatever he likes, he has quite an unusual palate actually. And he's so fussy. I think that might even be the first thing he's eaten today.'

'What a strange boy.' She smiled and picked up the wine I'd put down in front of her. 'Cheers!' We clinked glasses and both took a couple of enormous gulps.

There was a brief moment of silence and I held my breath, waiting for her to ask me why I'd taken off in the middle of the night or why I'd been so shit at responding to her, but she didn't. Instead she asked, 'So, do you live here with your mum and dad?'

I took another sip of my wine.

'Just my dad actually. It used to be Mum and Dad, but now she's dead, so she er . . . doesn't live here anymore.'

I watched Jo recoil. 'Oh gosh. I'm so sorry. I can't believe I didn't know that.'

'Oh no it's OK, she was horrible.'

'What? Was she really?'

'Er no, no. I was just . . . trying to . . . just joking. No, she was the best. It's really shit that she died. It should have been my dad.'

'What?! Why?'

'No, I'm just . . . not really. My dad's great.'

'Right.' She looked exhausted and a bit suspicious. 'Well, it's a lovely house,' she said eventually, perhaps deciding it was safer to not ask any more questions.

'Yeah, it's nice. It makes me sad to think of my dad being here on his own. I don't think he's changed anything since Mum died.'

'Was it a long time ago?'

'Yeah.' I took a moment to figure it out. 'Fifteen years now.' She'd missed more of my life than she'd seen. It was a strange thought.

'What was she like?'

I paused before answering. I didn't really talk about her very often. It was hard to sum her up in a few words.

'She was so much fun,' I settled on in the end. 'She was so much fun, she made everything come to life. She had this perspective on things and this laugh . . . it was infectious. I'd be in bed sometimes and I could hear her telling stories and my dad just howling with laughter. He thought she was just the best thing in the world. He adored her.'

Jo looked at me sadly.

'She sounds wonderful, Ally. You must both miss her so much.'

I nodded. 'I do and I know Dad does even though he doesn't really talk about it.'

'I bet he loves having you here.'

'I think he does and he doesn't. He likes the company, but he wishes it was under different circumstances.'

'That makes sense.' She popped a crisp in her mouth and chewed thoughtfully. 'Has he met anyone since your mum?'

I shook my head. 'Not that I know of. He's a mysterious man though. He does have a lot of girl friends, a lot of women from school who have a soft spot for him.'

'How would you feel if he met someone?'

'Happy that he wasn't by himself, I think. But I'd hate her, obviously.'

'Oh, obviously.'

'What about you? Parents, dead or alive?'

'Both alive the last time I checked, living together. One brother, but he doesn't live at home anymore, and one dog.'

'Checks out. Do you get on with them?'

She tilted her head to the side as if she'd never considered the question before.

'I suppose so,' she said eventually. 'Yes, in that we don't really argue, but no in that sometimes that's because we just repress everything. They like everything to be good all the time, which can be quite stressful.'

'Ah, well that's the benefit of one of them dying, it's like breaking the fourth wall. No one can pretend it's all good all the time, you can just let everything be shit.'

'Lucky.'

'Sorry for boasting.'

'I've never met anyone like you, Ally.' She said this quickly and with a shy smile on her face. She shoved a handful of crisps in her mouth. Ever the elegant eater.

'In a good way, right?'

'A very good way.'

'Phew.' I downed the last of my wine. 'Right. So shall we make dinner?'

Jo screwed up her face.

'OK, confession time.' She took a deep breath. 'I can't cook.'

'Oh,' I waved her confession away, 'of course you can.'

'No, I *really* can't. I am a terrible cook. I can barely even cook pasta.'

'Jo . . . that is literally just . . . boiling some water.'

'Yes. That's what I'm saying.'

'What do you eat?'

She shrugged.

'The cake you bring me. Um, toast? Pizza? Microwave rice, microwave anything really.' She stopped and then clicked her fingers triumphantly. 'Cereal! Lots of cereal.'

I looked her up and down, inspecting her for signs of scurvy.

'Right. Well not to worry because, sorry to blow my own trumpet' – ugh, I had definitely been spending too much time with my dad – 'but I'm a great cook, so you can be my sous chef. All you need to do is follow my instructions.'

'OK,' she said dubiously. 'But don't blame me if it all goes horribly wrong.'

I set her to work chopping and then, after she passed back

the board to reveal an onion that looked like it had been run over by a car and broken into twenty different large and uneven pieces, I gave her the more important job of laying the table and passing me things. I was making risotto, so after a while it was all just stirring. She stood next to me, sweating by the hob instead of sitting at the kitchen table.

'So basically,' she said, 'it's just chop chop chop, put it all in the pan, add some water . . .'

'Stock . . .'

'Yes, stock water. And then stir it all up and *voilà!*'

'Yeah, I mean I suppose that *is* it, but there's a bit . . .'

'Amazing! Thank you! OK, next time I'll have to cook for *you*.'

'Wow. OK. Let's see.'

'So,' she said, leaning with her back against the counter and squinting across the room at all the magnets on the fridge. There I was, screaming my head off on Space Mountain about to be spectacularly sick. 'Is this your usual . . . thing?'

'My thing?'

'Mmm, your move.'

'Is my move to make risotto for people?'

'To cook for them. Show off your skills.'

'Yes,' I said and glanced at her. 'Is it working?'

'Well, I haven't tasted it yet.'

'True.'

'Did you use to cook for Emily a lot then?'

I was surprised that she'd asked about Emily. I looked at her, but she was staring resolutely at her wine glass.

'Well yeah, of course. We lived together.'

'Was she a good cook too?'

'Yeah, I suppose she was. We liked . . . different things.'

I thought about some of the meals we'd eaten together. Emily serving me a dessert made of cashews on a Sunday evening just after Christmas from one of the recipe books she'd been given as a present. 'Wow, it's so . . . it tastes so much like . . . cashews.'

'I know!' she'd said, thrilled.

When we sat down to eat, Jo poured us some more wine and was suitably impressed with the risotto. She continued to marvel over how easy it was to make, which I decided to let go.

We talked more about family. She told me she'd always felt that her older brother wished she'd been a boy and to some extent her parents did too. I told her that I always thought that my mum and dad wished that they'd had another baby. I wished that they had too, so there hadn't been so much pressure on me. At some point, she found my foot under the table. The tips of our toes touched, and stayed there.

When we'd finished I got up to clear the plates away.

'Let me help you!' Jo leapt up and sent a fork crashing to the floor.

'No, I can do it. You're my guest! Shall we go and sit in the living room? We can have dessert through there if you fancy it?"

'Oooh!' Her face lit up. 'What's dessert?'

'I just threw together this salted chocolate tart thing. Super easy.'

I'm not sure why I said that. It was not super easy, it was

notoriously tricky to work with chocolate pastry. I'd been worried that it might fall apart, although now I knew Jo would be happy with a bowl of Frosties, I felt much more relaxed about it.

'Yes please, sounds amazing.' Jo headed towards the kitchen door.

'It's just at the end of the hall. It's the only other room down here, so quite hard to miss. I'll meet you in there.'

As she headed off down the hall I shouted after her, 'Do you want to put some music on? My phone's in there. Password is 1234.'

'Yes!' she yelled back.

I pottered around the kitchen for a bit, topping up Malcolm's bowl and getting myself a glass of water before slicing two perfect pieces of chocolate tart, pastry intact. The wine had gone to my head already, but I felt significantly less twitchy than I had before dinner, which was a bonus. I opened a second bottle and refilled our glasses and then, thinking I'd be sensible, put them on the tray with some water.

'Your dessert, *madame*,' I announced in a terrible French accent as I walked down the hall. It really had gone to my head.

When I got into the living room and placed the tray on the table, Jo was perched on the edge of the sofa staring at my phone. There was no music playing.

'Did you decide what to put on? I know, I know I've got some terrible playlists on there, but they're only for when I'm running, I promise. I'm very cool.'

She didn't reply. Just continued to stare at the phone, occasionally scrolling downwards, her brow furrowed.

'Jo?' An icy feeling settled in my stomach.

Eventually she looked up at me, her eyes steely.

'Jeremy messaged you. I went to swipe it away but it opened your chat.'

She pushed the phone towards me forcefully. I looked at the screen and my stomach dropped.

'OK,' I said, 'it's not . . .'

She looked up at me again. She had tears in her eyes, but I could see that she was furious.

'It's not what?'

'I can explain.' My voice was shaking.

'I don't think you need to explain, it's all very clear actually. This was all to make Emily jealous. You've made up stuff about me that never even happened to make Emily jealous. Is that about it? Have I missed anything?'

'No, that's not it! Jeremy and I were just messing about . . . I didn't expect . . .'

'You didn't expect me to find out?'

'No! Well, no I didn't expect that. But I mean, I didn't expect that you'd be so . . . that I would end up liking . . .'

'Oh how lovely, lucky me!'

'No, I mean, I always liked you. From the moment we met I liked you. I just sort of . . . got caught up with getting Emily back and lost sight of . . .' I trailed off. I sounded pathetic, and she was shaking her head furiously.

'You know, I felt really sorry for you. I thought, how could someone treat this sweet person so badly? She doesn't deserve that. But you're not a sweet person. Obviously you're just as bad as her. Or maybe you were the shitty one all along.'

She got up and snatched my phone off me so she could look again before flinging it down so that it slipped off the arm of the sofa and hit the side table with a crack on the way to the floor. I winced and she glared at me.

'Do you not have anything to say for yourself?'

I could tell she was the kind of mad where it didn't matter if I did or didn't say anything, it would all be wrong. I decided to give it a punt.

'I'm just, I'm really sorry and you're a really great—'

'Ugh! Fuck off!' she interrupted me. Should have gone with silence.

'I am actually a great person and you were lucky that I liked you and you've treated that like it's nothing and taken it for granted and you've made me feel like an idiot.'

'You're not an idiot,' I said weakly, closing my eyes briefly, willing myself to shut up.

'I know I'm not an idiot!' She shouted this at me as she shoved past me to get to the front door. 'I said you've made me *feel* like an idiot.'

She hurriedly put her shoes on and I watched from the doorway of the living room as she grabbed her coat and went to the front door without even putting it on.

I wanted to say something, but had no idea what. Sorry wasn't enough. She was too angry at me.

She turned to look at me just as she was turning the door handle.

'You said you liked people too much.' She was on the verge of tears again. 'That's what you said.' She opened her mouth as if to say something else and then changed her mind. She slammed the door behind her.

I hung my head. I didn't even know what I wanted. Malcolm pottered into the hallway. He looked at me coolly and then sauntered upstairs. As ever, utterly disappointed in me. I sat back down in the living room alone, picked up my slice of tart and took a huge bite out of it. I immediately wished I hadn't, the rich chocolate cloying in my mouth. I hadn't realised how sick I felt. I contemplated calling Jeremy, but couldn't bring myself to articulate how ashamed I was.

I gingerly picked up my phone from the floor and carefully swiped the screen, which now had a neat crack right down the middle of it. She'd scrolled back pretty far.

What do you think of this Jeremy? It is too subtle? I really want her to know that we slept together but I don't want to spell it out, it feels too creepy.

AL, spell it out! Isn't this what you wanted? To make Emily jealous? Make her really jealous!

What, like I should tell her what it was like?

Yes, tell her everything! And tell her what didn't happen. Elaborate.

'Oh Emily, Jo and I, we had the most incredible night, and then we spent all day together, it was so romantic! I think I've found someone really special.'

God you're a genius. I'll use that. Emily will HATE that. It's perfect!

I drank both glasses of wine in the dark. My mind was doing somersaults and I wanted to make it stop. I thought about texting Jo to see if she'd got home safely, but I knew she didn't want to hear from me. I briefly tried on being angry with her for reading my messages, but it didn't last long. I'd have done the same thing, especially given the message that had flashed up on the screen had been:

How's it going with Jo? Better than you thought? Stop thinking about Emily! Stop it!

I couldn't believe this was the night I'd chosen to not leave my phone on airplane mode.

I Sellotaped my broken phone back together and called it a night.

14

A Bad Day for Malcolm

I managed to leave for work without bumping into my dad so he couldn't ask me about my disastrous date with Jo. But I couldn't avoid him when I arrived home, my heart sinking as I put my key in the front door. Before I could even turn it, he wrenched the door open. I knew he'd be wanting to find out how it went, but I didn't think he'd be this keen.

'Where have you been? Why aren't you answering your phone? I've been calling and calling.'

'I was just at work! And then I walked home,' I said, indignantly. I looked down at my phone, still on airplane mode. Cut off from the world just in case I got a message from Jo. Or just in case I didn't.

'Look, love,' he sat down at the kitchen table and put his head in his hands, 'I came home at lunchtime and Malcolm wasn't very well, he suddenly sort of,' he hit the back of his hand on the table to indicate he had fallen over or collapsed. Sensitive as ever. 'So I took him to the vet and he's having an operation. Right now.'

'No! Why? What's wrong?' My voice was wobbling already. Panic seized me.

'They think he's eaten something weird, which would explain why he's been off his food for the past few days.'

'I thought he just had a hairball. Oh my God!'

'I know, love.'

'Well can we go now? And see him?'

'He's still in surgery, they're going to ring us as soon as he's out.'

Waiting for the phone to ring that evening was like torture. We sat in silence. I like to think we were both thinking of our favourite Malcolm memories, but I think mostly my dad was thinking about how expensive the vets are and when would be the appropriate time to set me up with a strict repayment plan.

When it finally rang I leapt up.

'Hello?'

'Hello, is that Mr Waters?'

I was temporarily thrown.

'I . . . no! It's Ally Waters. Malcolm is my cat.'

'Ah, OK, Mr Waters,' she continued, ignoring both my correction and voice, 'I have good news and bad news.' She paused briefly, which was excruciating.

'And?' I demanded.

'And Malcolm is out of surgery, but it's touch and go. It's been

traumatic for him so he'll need to stay in overnight to be moni-
tored. We still don't know that he's out of the woods.'

'Oh my God, OK, what's the good news?'

'That he's alive,' she paused again, 'at the moment.'

'Well, what happened? What was wrong?' I turned to my
dad, wide-eyed, trying to vent some of my exasperation with
the sociopath on the phone.

'He's got a taste for elastic bands and hair ties, it's very common. We found a little ball of them in his stomach. Do you give
him elastic bands to play with?' She sounded very judgemental.

'Absolutely not,' I said, instinctively insulted even while
recalling all the times I had given him my hair ties to play with
because he loved them so much.

'Right,' she said, unconvinced. 'Well, I'll speak to you tomorrow. Either way.'

She'd hung up before I had a chance to thank her.

'I'm not going to running club without you, Al. We're in this
thing together.' Jeremy was sitting upright, pillow end of his
bed, in some new running leggings. I was stretched out length-
ways with my head dangling over the opposite end, enjoying
the blood rush.

'I feel so bad, I'm sorry. I've just ruined everything.' I was
turning purple, I could feel it. I wondered how long you'd have
to hang upside down for a vein to pop.

'You're being very dramatic. Jo will come around I'm sure and
even if she doesn't, do you even like her that much anyway?'

'I do like her, I really do.' I pulled myself up, fearing I was moments away from my head exploding. I sighed. 'I'm not sure whether I *like* her, like her. I honestly can't tell. My head's too messed up at the moment.'

'Exactly. Don't worry about it. You did one shitty thing. It's not the end of the world.'

I opened my mouth to remind him that he'd masterminded the shitty thing, but he ploughed on before I had the chance.

'You did a shitty thing and she has every right to be upset with you, but she'll get over it.'

'I just can't help but think that Malcolm getting sick is my karma for this Jo stuff. I deserve something terrible to happen to me.'

Jeremy shook his head. 'No, if it was karma for Jo, *you'd* be in the hospital now, not Malcolm. Why should he have to pay for the actions of his horrible mother?'

I knew he was just trying to make me laugh but I started to cry instead. I was a horrible mother. And a horrible person.

'Ally! Stop. I'm only messing about . . .' Jeremy leant forward as if to hug me, but I was still lying down facing the opposite way to him so he just grabbed my ankle and sort of hugged that instead.

'No, I know. I'm just so cross with myself and so worried about Malcolm. And Jo. I just feel like I've not thought about anyone but myself. I didn't notice Malcolm getting ill and I didn't care about Jo getting hurt. And that's a horrible thing to admit. I never thought about her feelings, not once. That frightens me. It's not like me. Or maybe it is like me. I don't know.'

Jeremy was silent.

'I've just been so single-minded, Jeremy. About wanting Emily back. Everything I think about is through that lens. I'm not a good person anymore.'

'Come on.'

'I'm not! Can't you see that I'm not? Jo was right. I've been feeling so sorry for myself and then I've just been behaving like a prick.'

He laughed. 'Yeah, you can still be a nice person and behave like a prick, can't you? That's what Emily did. That's what you've done. That's what everybody does. It's life.'

'What about with you and Ben?'

'Well.' He sat back again to think, releasing my leg. 'He was definitely a prick, very cold to me, especially in the end. But I was awful too. I think I was very needy. He fell out of love with me. And I didn't accept it. Haven't accepted it. I was very unkind. I mean, I didn't trick someone into sleeping with me, but . . .'

I kicked him.

'What I mean to say is, he wasn't perfect. I wasn't perfect.'

'I'll never forgive myself if Malcolm dies.'

'Well . . . he will die at some point . . .' Jeremy looked concerned that he was having to break this news to me.

'I mean if he dies now. Like today. Because I've accidentally fed him foreign objects and then not noticed he was ill.'

'He's tough. Let's try and keep positive.'

I nodded. It felt impossible.

'Look, let's get out there before it's too cold. Running club will be over by now,' he said, looking at his phone for the time. 'There's no chance we'll bump into them.'

I desperately didn't want to go, but it felt like a suitably punishing thing to do. I could hear the wind howling as we put our trainers on by the front door. It was going to be a brutal one.

We set off without headphones for once. I think Jeremy knew that there might be some wailing to attend to. About two miles into our proposed six-mile route, when we were suitably settled in, our breath somewhat steady, Jeremy turned to me.

'Do you really think I could be a teacher?'

'What?' I was struggling to hear him over my panting and the gale force wind.

'Do you really think I could teach? At primary school? It's just . . . you said. And I've been thinking about it. Or were you joking?'

I looked at him. He was nervous.

'Of course! I mean I *was* joking, but I really do think you'd be brilliant. Are you seriously thinking of doing it?'

We plodded along for a few more moments, trying to catch our breath again. We hadn't quite mastered the art of running and talking at the same time.

'I am, yeah. I've been looking at some courses.'

'That's such good news! Jeremy, that makes me so happy.'

'Really? You don't think I'll be shit? What if I've forgotten how to spell? And times tables? And making jewellery out of pasta?'

'We'll practise.'

'Yeah.'

We were quiet again for a while. Trying to find a pace we could stick to that wasn't just 'walking'. We kept waiting for the wind to be behind us instead of slapping us in the face. Eventually we turned a corner and it was like someone had turned off a switch. Jeremy turned to me as we paused at some traffic lights. We didn't need to cross the road, but every time there were lights, we liked to cross – for the break.

'I want to be happy, Al. Remember you said that you wanted to do something that didn't make you want to scream in the toilets? I want that.'

'You deserve that.' I squeezed his hand and the green man appeared. We sighed and shuffled across the road. When we hit the three-mile mark we both immediately whipped around to head back, never in any danger of taking one step over our proposed distance.

Jeremy turned to me.

'This is getting easier, right?'

I took stock of all the things that were aching – legs, feet, shoulders, lungs, and found that I was struggling to see what part was easier.

'Um . . . is it?'

'I think so. Like I feel like I'm about to die but also I know that I actually won't, if that makes sense?'

I sort of knew what he meant.

'I guess, I mean I do know that technically we can do it. My legs aren't going to give way. In that way it's easier.'

'And Al, we're chatting.'

I laughed as he started coughing, the exertion of the conversation sticking in his throat.

He pointed at me.

'And laughing!'

'True, we are laughing.'

'It's all getting easier.'

I nodded. Maybe it was.

I spent the morning at work jittery and constantly checking my phone. My dad had instructed the vets to ring me personally instead of the home phone, partly because I was Malcolm's next of kin, but also because he was worried about having to tell me that Malcolm was dead. I had once taken to my bed for an entire weekend when Smokey the hamster tragically passed away in what can only be described as a 'vacuum cleaner incident'.

At around midday my phone finally rang and I answered it on the first ring.

'Is that Alexandra Waters?' It was the same woman.

'It is, yes.'

'Malcolm's owner?'

'Yes.'

'You asked to be called on this number I believe?' She sounded bored and annoyed with me, which I hoped was a good sign.

'I did, yes, because . . . it is my number.'

'As you know, Malcolm was very poorly yesterday. Very poorly.' My heart sank.

'We did everything we could for him, but he was already so ill and we didn't get to it until it was already very serious.'

A tear slipped down my cheek. I was stunned. I had really let myself believe that he'd be OK.

'So,' she continued briskly, 'he'll need a lot of care at home and you're not to take his cone off for at least a week. At least.'

'Wait, what?' I practically shouted down the phone. 'So he's not dead?'

'No, he's not dead!' She sounded quite cross, as if I were insinuating something dreadful. 'He's very much alive.'

'Thank you, oh thank God. So I can come and get him today?'

'Yes, at your earliest convenience.' She said this as though collecting Malcolm from them was a job I'd been putting off for weeks.

I cried when I got off the phone, and Sophie, who'd been standing next to me listening in, wordlessly came and put her arms around me.

Collecting Malcolm from the vets was a relief, but also deeply traumatising. For him, all sorry for himself in his cone, but mostly for me because of the lifetime of veterinary debt I had acquired. When we got home I plucked him gently from his carrier and put him on the sofa, and he didn't move much, except to limp to his litter tray and try to knock his cone off.

Tragic. I sat next to him all afternoon in solidarity, gently scratching his chin, which he couldn't reach. I thought it probably felt quite nice. Like sticking a fork into a plaster cast. Pat sat on the other side of me wondering if she too would get chin scratches if she looked sad enough. We stayed like that all evening and most of Friday too, although Malcolm was improving quickly. He was well enough to swipe at Pat when she got too close.

My dad was off to the biggest social night of the year: the charity quiz at his school. The quiz part lasted about an hour and then, notoriously, parents and teachers just got trollied and danced to cheesy music and got off with each other. My dad had always been very vocal about his disapproval of it and noisily appalled at his obligation to attend, but I could tell he secretly loved it. He had rushed home from school and spent all afternoon getting ready and had actually ironed his shirt instead of insisting it was a 'waste of time' and that it 'looked the same'.

At around 6 p.m. I was starting to think about moving from the sofa and rooting around for something to have for tea. I noticed that my dad was doing a lot of pacing up and down the hall. He would stop by the front door and hover for a bit, and then stomp back down with his phone, which was usually down the side of a chair or switched off in a drawer, glued to his hand.

'You all right, Dad? Did you order a taxi or something?'

'Hmm?' He looked up at me as if he'd never seen me before.

'I said did you order a taxi? Has it not turned up?'

'Ah no, no taxi. I'm just, ah . . . I'm waiting for someone.'

'Oh yeah.' I turned the volume down on the TV. 'Who?'

'Just someone from school.'

'Who though?'

He was blushing furiously. We were depressingly similar.

'Liz, all right? We're going to share a taxi because she lives around the corner and it just makes sense. It's just a taxi!'

'It seems like just a taxi, Dad, yeah. You're sweating. So Liz who comes around for board games, eh? Wow.'

'I'm not bloody—' He wiped his forehead with the back of his hand. 'I'm not sweating, am I?'

'No, you're fine.' The doorbell went. 'Ooh, there she is.' He was already racing up the hall. He certainly wasn't trying to play it cool.

Liz popped her head around the living-room door to see me and the invalid. She looked very dressed up for the school quiz. Her hair had been blow-dried and she was wearing heels.

'Hiya, Ally. You all right?'

'Yeah, I'm all right, Liz. He's seen better days though.' I pointed at Malcolm, who was sitting like a loaf staring at Liz menacingly.

'Oh bless him.' She stepped forward and then wobbled, as if she had been thinking about stroking him and then thought better of it.

'Listen, I wanted to say thank you for all the treats you send your dad in with. The staffroom's never seen so much cake! That one with blueberries in – lovely.'

She seemed a bit nervous. I realised she wanted to make a good impression, that it was important to her that I liked her.

'Cheers, Liz. You're welcome. I'll keep them coming then.'

'Fabulous.'

She gave me a little wave and tottered off into the kitchen, where the giggling commenced. I turned the TV back up.

Half an hour later their taxi arrived and Dad pottered in to say goodbye to me and Malcolm. He leant forward to kiss me on the cheek and I was engulfed in a fog of aftershave and pinot grigio.

'Have you been pre-drinking, Dad?' I asked him in mock disapproval.

'No, heavens no!' he exclaimed, and then, a bit giddy from excitement and booze, 'Well, maybe just one.' He smiled at me conspiratorially.

'You look great,' I said. 'And Liz looks beautiful. Have fun sharing your taxi.'

He beamed and stuck his hand into Malcolm's cone to pat him on the head. And then, pausing for a second, patted me on the head too, ruffling my hair.

'Take good care of him.' He nodded towards Malcolm.

'Dad! Of course I will.'

'He's a good boy.'

'Dad! I know!'

'OK.' He looked at me sternly and then made his way to the front door. I could still hear them laughing as they walked down the drive. I was glad my dad was having fun on his date. One of us ought to be.

*

I spent the evening in exactly the same way as I had spent the day – on the sofa surrounded by maudlin animals. I was just nodding off when I heard a gentle tapping on the front door.

I frowned. We weren't expecting anyone, but I wondered if maybe Jeremy had popped around to see Malcolm. He'd vaguely mentioned that he might. I made sure the chain was on and then opened the door a little, just so there was room enough to peek through.

'Hi, Al.'

I was stunned momentarily, and then slowly closed the door so I could unhook the chain. When I reopened it, she really was standing there. Emily.

15

Huge Romantic Gesture

I had always considered the phrase 'I couldn't believe my eyes' to be hyperbolic, but on that day it was perfectly literal. I also stopped in my tracks, was a deer caught in headlights. It simply did not make sense that Emily was standing on my dad's doorstep in front of me. I could not compute her familiar but now almost mythical face, looking up at me, tired and desperate. The Emily I had been cultivating and nurturing in my head was beautiful and glossy and somehow more alive than the one in real life. This one looked like she hadn't slept in a week. Her hair was scraped back and her face was grey. She had eyeliner smudged under her eyes as though she'd been rubbing them a lot. She was wearing her big coat even though it was fairly mild (despite tipping it down with rain) and she looked completely swamped in it, the arms almost comically puffy. She also looked on the verge of tears, and I realised as we stood there in silence that she wasn't sure if I would let her in. I wasn't sure either.

'What are you doing here?' I managed eventually.

'I needed to get Malcolm.' She broke into a bleak smile, but it didn't reach her eyes, which still looked dangerously close to tears.

'Em . . .'

'Look, can I just come in?'

I hesitated and that tiny moment seemed to tip her over the edge.

'Al, let me in,' she said, her voice breaking and a tear spilling down her cheek. 'Please! For fuck's sake, it's bloody pouring down with rain, I'm soaking wet, just bloody let me in.'

I stepped aside to let her walk past me and into the pitch-black hallway. I had a propensity when I was home alone not to realise the only light I had on was from a screen in front of me.

I went to switch on the little lamp on the table where the keys are kept and it emitted a low orange glow not unlike the glow of a candle, which really added to the dramatic mood of the evening.

I stared at Emily, who had now taken her enormous coat off and hung it over the bannister. She was bent over, facing away from me, untying her shoelaces. Her T-shirt clung to the curve of her back. She looked very thin. Or just very small. She had definitely shrunk in some way.

I still, after all those years and all that history and all those hard feelings, couldn't suppress the thrill that came with having Emily in my house. My house! Of all the houses she could be in she was in mine. This was all I had wanted for years. It should have been heartbreaking that she was there under such depressing circumstances, but it still felt as though I had a celebrity in my house, as if I'd won a competition. I wanted to reach out and touch her, to run my finger down the bones jutting out of her back. She was so close it would be easy. I kept my arms folded across my chest.

Before she had a chance to turn around, I disappeared into the kitchen, mumbling something about tea. It was the only thing I could think of to do, and something that would occupy my hands. I switched on the light under the extractor hood, and made tea by its dim glow, not wanting to disturb the darkness of the house. I'd assumed she'd follow me into the kitchen, but she never materialised. The ticking of the clock sounded much louder than usual. I took a long time stirring. I realised we didn't have any milk that she'd be able to drink, so her tea would have to be black. I swirled the amber liquid back and forth waiting for her to appear. When she didn't, I picked up the mugs and headed out into the hall to find her.

She was sitting on the edge of the couch as if she felt it would be rude to sit back properly. As though she knew I didn't want her to be too comfortable. I handed her the tea and she accepted it wordlessly, putting it straight down on the table next to her. I knew she wouldn't drink it.

Malcolm was lying tummy side up on the rug in front of her, having made himself as long as possible. He stared at Emily, cold and disinterested, somehow still managing to be deeply withering even with the enormous cone on his stupid, fluffy head. I knew he felt the same way about me and about all humans but still, in that moment, it felt as though he was on my side.

'What on earth happened to him?' She looked horrified.

'He ate some hair ties, they think,' I said, as though the jury was still out and they hadn't just removed a little ball of them from his stomach.

'Oh my God,' she said, and clasped her hand over her mouth.

I made a start on my tea. It was excruciatingly hot. In different circumstances I might have spat it out, but I persisted and, just as the throat burn really kicked in, Emily turned to face me.

'So is he going to be OK?' I think she had meant to go for 'politely enquiring', but the accusatory tone that rung out surprised us both.

'Well, yeah,' I replied, ignoring the urge to start a fight so early on in the visit, 'as long as he can keep himself away from them in the future.'

'Right, well maybe if you didn't keep hair ties on the floor that would help.'

'Oh wow, I hadn't even thought of that. Thank you so much.'

We were both quiet for a moment watching Malcolm trying to houdini himself out of his cone.

'Ally, look, I'm sorry.'

'No, it's fine,' I said instinctively, even though obviously it absolutely wasn't fine. 'I just, you know . . . I obviously didn't mean for it to happen.'

'No, I don't just mean . . . I mean,' her bottom lip began to wobble, 'I mean I'm sorry about everything.'

I opened my mouth to respond, but realised I had no idea what I wanted to say. Thankfully I was saved by Emily, who had something of a speech planned.

'When I look back at the past couple of months, I really can't believe that was me. I really can't, Al.'

She was looking directly into my eyes. She was a very good speechmaker.

'It doesn't feel real and I don't know what came over me to make me be . . . to be so cruel.' A tear slipped down her cheek, but she wiped it away crossly.

'Whatever was going on with me and with us, you didn't deserve what I did to you, it was no way to treat someone you love.'

'Loved.' I found my voice, suddenly. A flash of something shot through my stomach. Maybe sadness. Maybe anger.

She was taken aback, but nodded slowly, remembering her own words.

'OK. I know you're very angry with me and you have every right to be.' She visibly steeled herself, she had prepared for possible resistance.

'But I want you to understand. I think I was having a mid-life crisis or something.'

I burst out laughing.

'Em, you're thirty.'

'Well OK, hopefully not *mid-life* then, but definitely a crisis. I just felt like we weren't *us* anymore. Or I felt like I wasn't me anymore. Or something. Something felt very wrong and I didn't know how to fix it. And maybe I was wrong and I know I should have talked to you about it. But I felt like you didn't even want to fix it.'

She looked at me expectantly. I knew what I was meant to say. I was meant to sigh and agree and say 'perhaps, yes, there was some part of me that had given up', but I was tired, and I had been away from Emily for enough time to gather myself.

'You didn't give me a chance to fix it. You started sleeping with someone else, and then you left me. Well, actually you didn't leave me, you forced me to leave you.'

She opened her mouth to interject, but I was on a roll.

'I understand that perhaps we weren't us anymore. I agree, I didn't feel like myself either. I had no job, I felt rootless, maybe I wasn't at my best for a few months, but I wish, I *wish* you'd sat me down and talked about it.' I paused for breath. 'I'd have done anything, Emily. You know that.'

'I know. I know. I just think,' she sighed heavily, 'I just think you sometimes think of me as some kind of perfect person who just knows all the answers and knows how to do everything.'

I must have had a 'don't flatter yourself, love' expression plastered all over my face.

'ALLY, you know what I mean, come on.'

Of course I did know what she meant. I just didn't think she knew the extent of quite how much I worshipped her.

'I couldn't believe how much you loved me, it was sometimes quite overwhelming. It can be hard to talk to you. When you won't accept I might be wrong. Or struggling.'

'Right, sorry,' I said, like a petulant fifteen-year-old, embarrassed that someone had found out that I fancied them.

'Maybe loved is even the wrong word. Don't get me wrong, I know you loved me, but you have to understand that sometimes it felt like you loved me from afar. You loved an idea of me, Al, I think.'

My instinct was to protest because this sounded like such an awful thing. And such a ridiculous thing. But we both knew it was true. Because how could she live up to the version of her that existed in my head?

I simply nodded, not quite able to bring myself to agree with her out loud. The crushing weight of it all hung in the silence that I knew I was meant to fill with some kind of explanation or apology or something. Unable to sit in it, I picked up my half-drunk cup of tea and held out my hand for Emily to give me hers. She silently handed it over, making no apology for the fact that she hadn't touched it. I stood and sort of waved them in the direction of the kitchen to indicate that I needed to clear them away immediately, and I scarpered.

I placed the cups gently in the sink so as not to make a sound, and gripped the side of the counter with both hands not sure whether to laugh or cry or potentially throw up. In all the scenarios in which Jeremy and I had discussed this happening, under no circumstances did I imagine it would be like this. I thought there might be more gushing. More tears. This all just felt very grown-up and perfunctory and bleak.

I turned around and Emily was standing in the kitchen doorway, her hand on the frame at the little mark of my height aged thirteen. She had no idea that was there of course, because it was dark. And because she'd never visited before.

'I can go and get Malcolm's carrier,' I found myself saying, barely able to look at her. 'I think my dad put it in the shed, but it's no problem to go and fetch it. And he needs his medicine, I'll have to show you how to do it.' I didn't move.

She walked towards me until she stood directly in front of me. She looked very beautiful in the light of the extractor hood, her hair all curly where it had dried from the rain, her eyes shiny from crying.

I had expected when she leant forward to kiss me to feel the kind of fire you are meant to feel when you are reunited with a lost love, when the object of your desire finally reciprocates. But there were no shooting stars or swells of orchestral music. Instead it just felt familiar, inevitable even. I wasn't overwhelmed with joy, or passion, or anything really. Perhaps I felt, if anything, hopelessness. If this wasn't the thing I wanted, then what was? I even considered, for a moment, resisting. I wondered whether this was something I even wanted to happen anymore, or whether it was just something I desperately wanted to want to happen. I had spent so much time wanting. It seemed churlish, a waste of all that time and energy to feel so devoid of emotion now. I wanted to feel ecstatic, I wanted to be out of my head and in my body.

I wished, as my hand reached around her waist and pulled her closer to me, that I could tell how she was feeling. I tried to read the way she sighed as she pressed her hips against mine. Was that sigh a sign of her own sadness? I tried to switch off the constant commentary, once I'd gone past the point where I believed I might push her away, or say 'I don't think this is a good idea'.

She stopped and looked at me. 'Can we go upstairs?'

I led the way up the dark stairs in silence. It felt very strange, but I also didn't think there was any appropriate small talk for this situation; if there was then I was certain that Emily would know what to say. She usually did. Opening the door to my bedroom, I thought I'd feel embarrassed. The single bed and the faded covers from being washed so many times, the stickers on the ceiling, and the desk I'd had since I started secondary school. But I wasn't embarrassed by any of these things. This was my comfort zone, and Emily was in it, and she would have to adjust, not me. I sat down on the bed and she hovered in the doorway. It was one of the few times in my life that I've seen her look uncertain. I switched on the lamp on my bedside table and really noticed for the first time since I'd been back that the pattern on it was in fact, little Peter Rabbits. Emily continued to hover in the doorway, so I nodded towards the bed, a sort of 'get over here then', and she scurried over. Instead of sitting next to me like I thought she would, she gently pushed me back onto the bed so that my head was resting half on my pillows and half, quite uncomfortably, on the wooden bed frame. She tucked up next to me and rested her head on my shoulder, her arm draped over my stomach, her fingers gently grazing the exposed skin. I wished desperately that I was not sporting a pair of old jogging bottoms with bits of paint on them and a silver diamanté star on the hip. I wanted to explain why I was wearing them to her as her finger brushed over the stuck-on gems, but didn't want to disrupt the silence. I didn't want to breathe too loudly or even to slightly move my arm, which was at an awkward angle underneath Emily's shoulder.

Even though we'd kissed downstairs, it already felt like a lifetime ago and impossible to simply pick up where we'd left off. Eventually, after what seemed like hours of lying completely still, I tilted my head forward just slightly, partly because it felt as though I was getting a crick in my neck from sitting at a strange angle and partly to check if Emily had fallen asleep. I didn't want to wake her, but I also didn't want to have to amputate my own arm. My head, which had been doing cartwheels somehow trying to process exactly what was happening, seemed to have just accepted this alternate reality for now and I was experiencing an odd sense of calm. Sort of like what I imagine people are describing when they're close to drowning. Peace and acceptance, somewhat numb, somewhat euphoric, as if I was watching myself from above the surface. As I tilted my head down and attempted to shift it onto the pillow, Emily's head snapped up and her eyes were wide and glowing, staring up at me. She tilted her head up towards mine and I found myself shifting onto my side to face her, solving the neck and arm problem all in one. This somehow felt more intimate than kissing, feeling her breath on my lips, the tips of our noses just touching. I felt nervous, as though this was going to be our first kiss, or our last. It counted.

When you're in a relationship with someone for a long time, it can be easy to forget that, once, a kiss was not a peck on the lips as you rush out of the door, late and thinking about something else. There is a danger that a kiss becomes something so ordinary that at the end of a day together you cannot count how many times you have kissed because it would be like counting how many times you saw a red car – you either haven't noticed, or it was none at all. I don't know who nudged themselves forward that quarter of an inch first. It could have been me, but I like to think it was her. I remember feeling that I had a lot of power, that perhaps she wanted me more than I wanted her. This kiss was very different to the kitchen kiss, it was slow at first, tentative and sweet and then quickly turned into something urgent and hungry. Once we had established what was happening it was as if we knew there was a time limit, that one moment wasted meant the possibility of this all coming to an end. Her breathing changed and she bit my lip, which I always kind of hated though never mentioned, but this time the brief irritation at the pain was like a lightning bolt of something else: desire, passion, fury.

I pushed her onto her back and reached up underneath her

still damp T-shirt and pinched her nipple between my finger and thumb. She gasped, and I could tell it hurt but that the same lightning bolt seemed to be coursing through her. She grabbed me and pulled me down onto her as close as we could get, her mouth on my neck half kissing, half biting while I reached down between us to unzip her jeans. She lifted her hips up so I could pull them down and I tried to recall the last time I'd done this. The impatient fumbling, the urgent removal of clothes, the seriousness of the endeavour. I could remember us doing this in the beginning, hot hands up skirts, difficult bras pulled down to our waists, knickers tangled around our feet at the bottom of the bed. Perhaps I was giving the illusion that I was teasing her, making her wait, punishing her, when really I felt almost paralysed with something close to fear. I both wanted it all to be over immediately and for it to never end. I didn't look at Emily as I fucked her. She buried her face in my neck and her fingernails in my back. A long time ago she might have whispered in my ear, 'I love when you're inside me' or 'fuck me harder' or even, 'I love you'. But she didn't whisper anything at all. I just felt her hot breath on my ear, short and sharp. After she came, a brief noise in my ear, barely a sound, her thighs wrapped tightly around my hand. I rested against her.

She kissed me again and moved her hands towards my velour waist, but I reached out to stop her. I lowered myself down by her side and kissed her fingers instead. I couldn't give any of myself away that night and risk losing this fleeting sense of control. Emily didn't protest. Instead, she turned away from me, pulling my arm around her, placing my hand on her stomach inside her T-shirt, and seemed to fall asleep instantly. The kind of sleep when you get home from a festival and your head has barely hit the pillow before you switch off. The sleep of someone who, exhausted, finally allowed themselves to relax. Her head was tucked under my chin, the wispy hairs from her now quite dishevelled ponytail tickling my nose. Every time I breathed in, I could smell her. Her hair at the stage between washes when it still smells of sweet shampoo (organic, ethical, grown by monks or homeless dogs or similar) and that earthy, human smell that she so hated but which I loved. A mixture of sweat and grease and, on that day, rain. She was really there, right under my nose, and I couldn't believe it. I wanted to feel elated or hopeful or at least hopelessly in love. But I didn't. I felt safe and she was familiar. A strange sense of calm descended on me as I wrapped around her, my body instantly recognising and responding to all the nooks and crannies of hers. I knew her and I had loved her but it was not home in that bed with her hair up my nose. I was visiting her and it had been nice. But I was not home. I spent a few more minutes breathing her in before turning away and falling into a dreamless sleep.

When I woke up in the very early hours of Saturday morning, my open curtains letting the light from the moon and street lamps shine in, Emily was shuffling out from under my arm. She mouthed 'hi' when she saw that I was awake.

'Hi,' I whispered back.

'I can't believe I'm really here,' she said much more loudly as she pulled herself upright, perched on the edge of the bed. I instinctively shushed her, conscious of my dad presumably asleep down the hall. I wondered if he'd noticed an extra coat and pair of shoes downstairs and what he'd thought. My instinct, I realised with a flip of my stomach, was that he'd assume that they belonged to Jo.

'Sorry.' She went back to whispering. She was looking around my room, taking everything in. Some self-consciousness started seeping back in. She looked up at my ceiling stars.

'Look Al, I don't know what I want.'

'I don't either,' I hurriedly whispered. I didn't want her to think that I desperately wanted her back or that I'd just go along with whatever decision she made.

She didn't look surprised necessarily, but I could tell that this trip hadn't been quite what she'd expected. Of course, she had a version of me and of us in her head too.

'I miss you,' she said. 'And I miss our life together.' I believed her. 'It killed me to think that you were seeing someone else, which I know is hypocritical—'

'It is.' I cut her off.

'I know it is! Are you still seeing her?'

I paused, considering whether to continue to lie about Jo. The damage had already been done so I had nothing to lose but eventually I shook my head.

'No, that's not really a thing anymore.'

She didn't ask why, only nodded slowly.

'Are you still seeing Sara?' I realised with a sickness in my stomach that I already knew the answer.

'Yes.' She said this carefully. 'Well, sort of. It's very complicated. It's very complicated because I miss you and we were together for a long time and it's hard to just . . . move on.'

'I miss you too, Em. I miss you all the time.' She opened her mouth to say something but I ploughed on knowing that if I didn't say what I wanted to say then I might never say it. 'I miss you all the time, but I've had to get on with it and I've got quite used to it and on some days, Emily, I'm doing pretty well.' I sat up in bed. 'I don't think you understand what has happened to me. I know you've missed me, but you've also been shacked up with Sara,' I still couldn't help but spit out her name, 'and you've been at home, surrounded by your things and your friends and going to your same job, and you knew all this change was coming.' I paused for breath and to assess her reaction, but she was very still, just looking at me. 'You knew it was all coming, Em, and I had no idea.' Finally my voice cracked and I began to cry. 'So I had to sort of start from scratch and I don't know if I want to just throw that all away.'

She leant forward to brush a tear from my cheek and I let her. She left her hand on my face for a moment and I wondered if she was going to kiss me again. She didn't. She just held me for a moment before sitting back.

'I know,' she said, nodding. 'I know.' She sat still again and

I wondered if she was going to say anything to persuade me to come home with her. I don't think, if I'm being honest with myself, it would have taken very much at all in that moment.

'I'm going to order an Uber,' she said eventually.

'Now?' I exclaimed. 'Emily, it's practically the middle of the night.' Panic rose, I suddenly desperately didn't want her to go. It felt horribly like it was going to be the last time I was ever going to see her. 'I can't go and get Malcolm's carrier now. It's pitch black out there and I'll wake everyone up. And he's too poorly to travel. He won't fit his cone in!'

'I'm not taking Malcolm with me.' She said this breezily as she stood in front of my tiny mirror on the wall, pulling her hair into a ponytail.

'What? Why? Have you seriously come all this way and you're not going to take him?' I was completely incredulous. I don't know why I was suddenly pushing for her to take my beloved monster away.

'I can't, Al. Let's be honest, he's always preferred you anyway. Plus, I've got to go to Manchester tomorrow. I've got a conference, so there's nowhere for me to put him. I'm pretty sure he's not going to be allowed to stay in my hotel!' She smiled at me in the mirror like we might share an 'of course, how silly' moment. I glared back.

'You came here because you have a conference.' She did not read the tone in my voice at all.

'Yes. Well no, I came up north for a conference, but I made an extra stop here. I was meant to stay in Manchester last night, but I just . . . I just had to see you. I knew I had to come and see the cat and apologise to you and try to work things out and it was all just so . . .' she paused to look for the right word, 'convenient.'

'Oh my God.' I put my face in my hands and took a deep breath. To my surprise and certainly to Emily's, when I uncovered my mouth I burst out laughing.

'What? What is so funny?' She spun around to face me properly, indignant.

'I just,' I shook my head, still grinning, 'I just thought you'd come here as a huge romantic gesture to see me and now, it all just makes so much sense.'

'It IS a huge romantic gesture,' she insisted, practically stamping her foot. 'I had to get an entirely different train! I missed a night in a hotel which I had PAID for!'

'It is, it is.' I waved my hand at her, indicating I wasn't cross and also to please pipe down. 'It's romantic, Em. It's just . . . different to what I had in my head, that's all.'

'Well, isn't everything,' she said sarcastically.

'I suppose it is,' I conceded.

I crept back downstairs behind her and switched on the hall lamp so she could put her enormous coat on and wait for her Uber. I spotted my dad's shoes kicked off in the middle of the floor along with his scarf, and thought there was probably little need for whispering. He'd be out for the count all night and probably most of the morning.

'So, you know I'm running the half marathon on Sunday.'

'That's this Sunday?' Emily's head snapped up from where she was sitting on the stairs tying her shoelaces.

'Yep, it's come around so quickly.'

She nodded. 'Well, maybe I can come and cheer you on, I won't be going back to London until Sunday afternoon.'

'Yeah, maybe!' I said half-heartedly. The idea of her leaving like this and then turning up on Sunday to cheer in the crowd felt improbable, but stranger things had happened. I didn't know if I wanted her to or not. I didn't want her to leave either, but also somehow couldn't wait for her to be gone.

She turned to a black and white photo hanging on the wall. It was of Mum, Dad and me when I was a baby. Dad was holding my arms while I toddled towards Mum, who was crouched down smiling widely with outstretched arms.

'You look just like your mum, Al.'

'People used to tell me that all the time.'

She nodded and opened her mouth as if she had something else to say, but then her phone buzzed.

'OK, it's here.' She picked up her bag from the bottom of the stairs. We did a little awkward dance in the hallway, not knowing how to say goodbye. Eventually she grabbed me and pulled me in for a hug. When we pulled away she held onto my arm and took a look at the mermaid. She stroked it gently with her thumb.

'This horrible tattoo,' she said quietly, fondly.

'I'm never getting rid of it,' I said. We might have had this conversation hundreds of times before.

'Good,' she said. 'Bye Malcolm.' She waved in the direction of the living room. He had not bothered to come to see her off.

And then a sharp gust of cold air, a gentle click of the door closing behind her, and she was gone.

16

Lesbian Gossip

The idea that I might be able to go back to sleep after Emily left was absurd. I still wasn't convinced that I hadn't been asleep the whole time and that this wasn't some terrible, wonderful, unlikely fever dream. After I closed the door behind her I turned around to face the house that she had been in. I picked up my dad's shoes and put them on the rack, and hung his scarf on the end of the bannister instead of in the cupboard where it belonged, a little flag to mark the fact I knew that he'd been out and got plastered.

After I crept back up the stairs, my eyes adjusted to the dark of this ridiculous night as I stood in the doorway to my room and inspected the scene. My duvet was crumpled at the end of my bed and a single pillow lay on the floor, a minor destruction, but evidence enough that she'd been there. I heard Malcolm clumsily padding up the stairs. He sat next to me in the doorway and bumped my leg with his cone. I stepped over a pile of my clothes to pick the pillow up and my foot landed on something sharp. I recoiled and bent down to pick it up. A fat, yellow, elasticated hair tie lay flat in my hand, the metal joiner jagged where the cotton had started to fray at the edges. A final parting gift from Emily, an irresistible and potentially lethal treat for Malcolm. I clutched it in my fist for a moment, planning to throw it in the bin, but I found myself instead reaching over to my bedside table drawer, throwing the hair tie in, and slamming it shut. Too dangerous in the bin, I told myself. Malcolm could find it there.

I lay still in bed for a few hours in a daze, not trying to get back to sleep so much as trying to recharge. I felt completely drained and also more awake than I'd ever felt in my life. I had the very rare urge to tell someone, to purge every single thing that had happened and have them wallow in the knowledge too. I wanted to hear the words said out loud. I checked the clock and considered that 6.20 a.m. on a Saturday was probably not an acceptable time to call Jeremy. I thought about sending him a message, but wasn't sure that I could accurately convey the enormity of my feelings in words and emojis. I decided to leave him a voice note, something he was in the habit of leaving me most days.

Jeremy, I know you're asleep and I'm sorry but I just have to tell you something. You're not going to believe this. OK. Emily just came here. Emily was just here in Sheffield, in my house. I just opened my door and there she was. Jeremy, we SLEPT together but like . . . it was weird! No, it wasn't a dream! But it feels like a dream. But it definitely wasn't because she left her hair tie here. She came to see Malcolm but she doesn't want him anymore. I am still processing, I think. I told her she should come and watch the race but she won't, will she? No, she won't. Will she? No. No. Of course not. Would she even want to though? No. Would we even want her to come? Ugh, the race is literally tomorrow! What is happening? Anyway I know I'm seeing you later but I just had to tell you this straight away because I knew you would die. OK see you later! Bye! Argh!

I felt immediately better for having said it out loud and, I realised, thrilled to have a friend to message at all hours of the day and night. A friend who didn't know Emily. Who was interested in the minutiae of my life and I, his. I felt a sudden overwhelming surge of love for Jeremy. I hoped he felt he could message me in the middle of the night to tell me that he'd had sex with someone who turned up at his house unexpectedly.

The morning was spent jittery and anxious in that specifically unpleasant sleep-deprived, caffeine-induced way which makes you feel like your eyes are being held open *Clockwork Orange* style and that your knees might buckle at any moment. I managed to get myself showered, dressed and downstairs, and by the time Dad appeared mid-morning I was squinting at my laptop at the kitchen table. I smiled as he shuffled in wearing a pair of novelty Christmas slippers. One Rudolph's red nose was missing, the other dangled limply from the end of his foot. His hair stuck up in such a way that I'm sure it would be impossible to achieve on purpose with all the styling in the world. He did a double take at me, surprised I expect that I was a) dressed by 10 a.m. and b) not parked in front of the TV.

'Good night, was it?' I peered over the top of my glasses at him and raised my eyebrows. How the tables had turned.

'Oh, you know how these things are.' He started to busy himself getting mugs out of the cupboard and popping teabags in them. I couldn't tell if he was making one for me and him or if it was an emergency 'two teas at once' situation. 'It was fine.'

'Cool.' I looked back down at my laptop, obviously not about to be let in on the All Saints Secondary School's juiciest gossip.

After he'd put the kettle on to boil and got himself a pint of water he turned to face me, leaning against the counter and closing his eyes briefly.

'Everyone got quite drunk,' he offered eventually.

'Mmm?' I feigned nonchalance, knowing that showing any interest would shut him up immediately.

'You know Sue?'

I looked at him blankly.

'Sue! Oh Ally, you know Sue. Secretary at school, mad hair, her boys are three years below you. Sue, Sue!' He stopped and glared at me in disbelief and added one more 'Sue!' for good measure.

'All right, yes! Sue! What's going on with Sue?' I had no idea who Sue was.

'She was . . .' Dad looked at me conspiratorially, equal parts thrilled and disgusted with the information he was about to impart, 'she was *sick! Sick in the E block toilets!*'

I clapped my hand to my chest. 'Scandalous!'

'I know,' he said, not entirely missing the sarcasm but carrying on regardless. 'Well, that is what happens if you drink a bottle of red wine and you've only had a bag of Skips for your dinner. Just Skips! What was she thinking?'

'Happens to the best of us.' I felt an affinity with poor Sue, who would now be for ever known as 'You know, Sue! Sicky Sue! Skips for tea Sue! E block toilets Sue!' The world of secondary school could be as savage in the staffroom as in the playground.

'Well, actually it doesn't happen to the *best* of us,' he muttered as he turned around to pour the water in the cups.

'And did Liz have a good night?' I asked as his back was turned.

'Yes, I believe so, thank you very much.' He said this out of the kitchen window, still not facing me.

'Will you be seeing her again?'

'Yes, every day. At school.'

'Ugh, Dad!' I was unable to keep up the faux indifference. 'You know what I mean! Will you see her again just the two of you?'

'Oh I don't know, Al.' He was getting flustered. 'Probably, yes.'

'Good,' I said, satisfied. 'She seemed lovely.' I was surprised by how much I wanted my dad to spend time with this woman. It had just been such a relief to see him so happy.

Malcolm pottered in, his head dipped in his cone, bumping clumsily into the door frame and then the chair and then finally Dad's leg. Dad bent down to stroke his head while the tea brewed.

'So how was your evening?' he asked me pointedly.

I refused to give him any reaction; I remained cool as a cucumber. There was a high chance that he might be messing with me. He might just be insinuating that I'm deeply uncool because I stayed in with no plans on a Friday night while my dad went out with a date to the wildest quiz night of the year.

'Fine thanks,' I said, not looking up to catch his eye.

'Did Jeremy come around?'

'No . . .' I looked up, this felt like a trick question.

'Oh! I assumed he must have. I didn't recognise the coat in the hall,' he said breezily.

An internal scream let rip. I had overestimated his drunkenness. I briefly considered telling him the coat was mine, or that actually yes, Jeremy had come around but that I'd somehow forgotten, but I knew lying was futile.

'Oh yeah, no. Um, that wasn't Jeremy's coat.'

'So . . . did your friend Jo come around?' He was smiling now, stirring sugar into the tea but still leaning against the side, obviously with all the time in the world to interrogate me. 'It's all right if she did, I'm just interested.'

'No, actually she didn't.' Hearing Dad ask about Jo was desperately sad. I wished I'd told him what had happened.

'Ally, it's fine, you can tell me. I don't mind! I want you to be happy! I want you to tell me about these things. I'd also like to know who is coming in and out of my house.' He added this last bit with eyebrows raised.

'She didn't stay around!' I exclaimed.

Dad opened his mouth to protest, but I held up my hand at him to stop him.

'Emily did.'

He paused. Not quite knowing what to do with the information, which was understandable. I didn't know what to do with it either.

'I don't . . . what do you mean, Emily was here? Emily Emily? London Emily? Malcolm Emily?'

'Yes, Emily Emily.'

'Well, why? What happened? Are you . . . are you back together?' My dad didn't just look surprised, he looked panic-stricken. He wanted a bit of gossip that he could tease me about all day, not this. I hadn't realised that my getting back together with Emily would be something which would bother him so much.

'No, we're not back together,' I reassured him quickly.

He looked visibly relieved.

'We're not back together,' I repeated, letting those words wash over me. 'She came to see Malcolm, I think. And to see me. She was very sorry.'

My dad nodded, letting it all sink in.

'Is she still here? In Sheffield, I mean?'

'No, she left and went to Manchester, but she might come back tomorrow, although probably not.'

'Come back for Malcolm?' Dad eyed the lump who was sitting forlornly at his feet. Malcolm had taken to staring us both out hoping one of us would cave and release him from his cone prison.

'No no, she doesn't want Malcolm anymore. Come back for me – to watch the race, I mean.'

He nodded. I could tell he was desperate to say something. I let him process this in silence while he made toast and I scrolled through blog posts on half marathons trying to glean any knowledge whatsoever that might change the game at the very last minute. A miracle running cure.

'Ally, love,' he said, 'I want to talk to you.'

'Oh God, really? Again?' I thought our walk in the woods would do us for at least the next decade.

I looked across at him in his skew-whiff dressing gown and his wild hair and saw that he'd put his glasses on. He was serious. I slowly closed my laptop.

'OK, go for it,' I said, nodding at him that I was ready. I picked up my toast and took a bite.

'I don't want you to get back together with that girl.'

I opened my mouth to interject, but he shook his head at me.

'Let me say this, Ally, and then you can say your piece. I don't want you to get back together with her. I don't think she's a bad person per se,' he said this in such a way to suggest that he absolutely thought that she was the worst person on earth, 'but I think that she is bad for *you*. I don't know what happened between you two and Lord knows relationships are very complicated. But what she did was very unkind, and that is not how you deserve to be treated, ever. She is not better than you, and she is not better than us, and I want you to be yourself because you are just fine on your own.'

'I know, Dad,' I said quietly, not quite able to meet his eye. 'I do know that I didn't deserve to be treated like that. But she really isn't a bad person.' I looked up to see his incredulous face. 'She isn't, but I can understand why you might think that.'

'You do whatever you want to do, Ally, but I want you to think very carefully about it.'

'I will. Of course I will.'

'I want you to think carefully because you've come a long way and I don't want you to throw it away for Emily or,' and he said this very pointedly, 'for anyone.'

'I won't,' I said, unconvincingly.

'I want you to start taking yourself seriously.' He was nearly in full teacher mode now, which was never good. 'Now, you know I'm happy for you to stay here, especially now that you're contributing, but I want you to consider what your next move is.'

'OK I will, and I'm so grateful for that, it's just that—'

He waved away my gratitude with a piece of toast in his hand. 'I don't want you to thank me, I want you to understand what I'm saying. This has been home base for you while you get yourself sorted, but right now, Al, I would say you're pretty sorted. So what's next? Are you going to keep on working in the shop? Are you going to consider getting back into teaching?'

I shrivelled up my nose in revulsion. I hadn't even thought about that as an option.

'So if that's a no, then what are you going to say yes to?'

Self-help jargon aside, I begrudgingly conceded that he had a point. I was very good at knowing what I didn't want and not terribly good at knowing what I actually did. I didn't know if I wanted Emily anymore, which even yesterday would have been unfathomable.

'I don't know,' I said honestly, and we sat for a bit in silence while I tried to gather my thoughts. Eventually I spoke up. 'OK, so I know I can't stay here. As much as I love it and I love you. But I don't know where else I would go at the moment.'

Dad nodded but didn't try to interject.

'In terms of work, I don't know if I want to carry on working at the bakery. I really like it there and I love Sophie and Charlie, but . . . when I quit my job I really thought I'd be working towards something on my own terms, you know? And at the moment here and at work and with everything I just feel a little bit . . . stuck.'

It felt good to say out loud, and I could see that Dad was thrilled that I'd confided in him. This was a morning of telling people things I'd usually wallow in. It was interesting. I was starting to see the appeal in it.

'Well, stuck's no good.' He said this thoughtfully, but offered nothing else.

I nodded. 'I need to try to move forward, I think.'

'You tell me if there's anything at all I can help you with.'

'I will.'

'OK.' He smiled and got up to leave.

'Thanks for the intervention.'

'It's too late for an intervention, you needed the intervention before you signed up to run for thirteen bloody miles tomorrow!'

I grimaced. 'I know.'

'And you've not had any sleep!'

'I know.'

'And you're staying at Jeremy's tonight, so no sleep there either, just gossiping all night.'

'I know.' Clearly, we had come out of school teacher mode, out of life coach mode, and right back around again to full Dad mode.

'Well, make sure you eat plenty today.'

'Not a problem.'

He nodded, satisfied that I'd been dealt with sufficiently for the morning, and made his way slowly back up the stairs to wallow in his hangover.

Jeremy didn't wake up until midday. I know this because at around two minutes past twelve I received a message that consisted only of fifty question marks. He then tried to call me about the same number of times. I felt I couldn't talk about it again with my dad in the house, who was now creeping about like a guilty, secretly hungover teenager, shoving crisps into his mouth and sipping tentatively on Coke as if that's what he usually did all day on Saturdays.

I can't talk now will tell you all later

Ally nooooooo you are killing me, ok come round asap, literally now

I'll come round before tea, what shall we carb load on?

OK fine. Christ I don't even know. A loaf of bread? A bag of rice? What does Mo Farah eat?

Gah, I don't know, pizza?

Yeah pizza that's all the food groups isn't it. Come here and eat pizza and tell me all your sordid lesbian gossip

OK done. Bring your most sordid lesbian gossip too

Will do

Leaving to go to Jeremy's house that evening turned out to be a more momentous occasion than I thought it would be. I packed my bag, checked and re-checked it, the butterflies fluttering about in my tummy as I thought about all those hills. I had my running trousers that squeezed me in like a sausage, my special socks, which worked, as far as I could tell, in the exact same way as regular socks, and my waterproof in case of rain. I also had a little tag that you were meant to tie to your shoe which would record your time. I had no idea how to do it so planned to do it with Jeremy once we'd watched a YouTube video about it.

I thought briefly of Jo and the first day that we'd met, when she sold me these expensive, ridiculous things. A pang of regret hit me thinking about the fact I'd never go to running club again. All that was ruined now. It would have been inconceivable mere weeks ago that I would be mourning going to a running club, although of course it was much more than that. As I heaved my rucksack onto my back at the front door, I called out that I was leaving to Dad who was holed up in the living room, and he rushed to say goodbye to me, fussing that I had enough food, that I'd packed a hat, that I didn't want a lift around to Jeremy's to save my legs for tomorrow.

'I think I'll walk, I'd like the fresh air. Plus I'm not even sure if it's safe for you to drive yet.'

'All right, don't be cheeky.'

'It's fine, it'll do me good to stretch out a bit. You know, I'm quite nervous.'

'You'll whizz around,' he said confidently. 'You'll absolutely whizz around. You know,' he looked up at the ceiling, suddenly uncomfortable, 'she'd be so proud, Al.'

I nodded. 'I know. Thanks, Dad.'

I noticed that he had a map of the route printed off on the little table by the front door and I thought my heart might explode. Instead of crying all over him, I grabbed him and hugged him as tightly as I could.

'See you tomorrow, tell me where you're going to be standing.' I knew he and Jeremy's mum had made a plan of action.

'We're going to move around so we can see you at different points, we've got a plan! But yes, we'll text you,' he said.

'Love you,' I called out into the wind, facing away from him and setting off down the drive.

'Love you, Al,' I thought I could just about make out, as I turned to walk down the hill.

I barely had a chance to knock on the door at Jeremy's before he wrenched it open and ushered me in.

'Come in, come in, come in, come upstairs, I want to hear

everything.' He was practically hopping up and down in anticipation.

'All right, at least let me take my shoes off first!'

'Offer her something to drink, Jeremy, my goodness!' Jeremy's mum popped her head around the living-room door. I could see Molly lying on the sofa, her phone held above her head. She didn't look at me.

'Hi Ally, love, you all right?' Jeremy's mum asked.

'I'm all right, are you?'

'Oh, I'm fine, but then I don't have to do this mad race tomorrow, do I? What on earth possessed you both to sign up I'll never understand.'

'Yeah, I can't think . . .' I shot a look at Jeremy, who was standing on the stairs impatiently waiting for this exchange to be over.

'Jeremy!'

'What, Mum?'

'Drink!'

'Ugh. Ally, do you want a drink?' Jeremy said in the least hospitable way possible.

'Um, no thanks. I'm fine?' I said, guessing that was the correct answer.

'See, she's *fine*.'

'I want a drink,' Molly called from the living room. She rolled over onto her side so she could look at me. She gave me a sarcastic smile.

I very nearly went to get her a drink myself. Any drink. All of the drinks.

'Oh yeah, good one,' Jeremy said as he turned to walk upstairs.

'Jeremy! Get your sister a drink! What do you want, Mol?'

'Tea please. Two sugars. And I'll have a biscuit as well,' Molly said, sweet as anything. 'Thanks, Mum.'

'Fuck's sake.' Jeremy spun around and stormed into the kitchen.

'What's that, Jeremy?' his mum said.

'Nothing!' he yelled back.

She turned to me and rolled her eyes. If it was time for me to move out of my dad's house then that due date was long past for Jeremy.

When he'd delivered Molly's tea we clambered up the stairs to his room and threw ourselves down on his bed. His single bed was pushed up against the wall to make way for a blow-up mattress for me.

Jeremy noisily opened up a bag of Percy Pigs (part of our pre-dinner carb loading plan) and looked at me. He waited approximately one second before impatiently waving the bag of sweets at me.

'OK go! Tell me!'

I managed to get through the entire Emily saga, from the second she entered the house until the second she left, without him interrupting me. The only sound he made was furious pig chewing.

'So now she's gone, and I haven't heard from her all day and I weirdly asked her if she wanted to come tomorrow so I guess she might show up, but I don't think she will.'

'I think she will.' Jeremy finally broke his silence.

'What? Why?'

'I don't know, I just feel like she didn't get what she wanted from you. It sounds like you showed her that you're all cool and doing fine and she probably expected you to be a complete mess.'

'So you think she'll come to the race to . . . see me in a complete mess?'

'No I don't think that's it, it's just to get the kind of closure she wants. No,' he thought for a moment, 'I'm not even sure that it's closure she wants, more like a . . . reopening?' He screwed up his face at the image those words had conjured.

'I don't think she wants to reopen anything. I think if she turns up it would be out of curiosity just to see if I can actually do the bloody thing, which is something I'm also quite curious about, to be honest.'

'But do you want her there?'

'Yeah. No. I don't know.' I thought about it for a moment. 'Do you care if you see Ben?'

Jeremy nodded.

'I'll care if I see him, if you know what I mean, but I'm not sure that I care if I see him or not, does that make sense?'

'I think so. So like if you get to the end of the race tomorrow and you haven't seen him you'll be fine but if you happen to see him you won't be able to be like "you all right, mate?" and just move on?'

'Yeah, exactly that.'

'How have you, I mean, I'm sorry, I don't want to dredge

stuff up, but Ben is the whole reason we're doing this thing and now you just don't even care if you see him? That's a pretty big deal.'

He nodded thoughtfully, twirling a jelly pig around with his fingers.

'I know, it's mad to think that this was about Ben. Now it feels like it's about so much more, don't you think? Like I'm going to do this stupid thing that I couldn't have done three months ago. I feel like even if my brain sometimes gets stuck, I can still move forward, you know? Like I can physically drag myself forward?'

'I get it. Don't get me wrong, I am never running again after tomorrow, but for some reason I feel like I absolutely *have* to finish it. It's like a compulsion. Literally everything else feels like it's gone to shit and I can't do anything about it, but I can and I will drag myself up and down all those hills tomorrow and I'm going to finish this race and it's going to be something I've bloody well achieved for myself.'

'Yes! Yes, that's it. We're going to have a medal to prove it as well. I'm going to wear it every day.'

'Same. Expecting rounds of applause everywhere I go.'

'And free drinks.'

'Do you really think we'll get free drinks?' I hadn't even considered this.

'No, babe. Absolutely not.'

'Jeremy. Do you think there's any chance that Jo will come?'

'To cheer us on you mean?'

'Well no, I think that's unlikely. I suppose I just mean, she loves running and it's a big event, so maybe she'd be there . . .'

Jeremy looked at me sadly.

'Maybe, Al. Have you spoken to her?'

I shook my head. I thought about showing him my phone notes filled with draft texts, but out of all the things I'd told him it felt the most tragic.

'Do you want to see her there?'

'Probably not, I don't need someone telling me to go and fuck myself from the crowd.'

Jeremy laughed.

'She'd never do that.'

'I know,' I said. 'She never would. She's too nice.'

'She's been brought up well,' Jeremy said. 'To respect her elders.'

'OK thank you. Very comforting.'

I thought about what it might feel like to look into the crowd and see Jo there. Cheering for us. Or cheering for someone else. I felt something stir deep in my stomach but I couldn't quite work out what it meant. Nerves or regret or perhaps the unfamiliar emptiness of my having barely eaten anything all day.

'Jeremy,' I said, putting a protective hand over my unhappy stomach, 'I'm starving.'

'Same.' He put down the empty bag of Percy Pigs and licked his fingers. 'Wait.' He looked at me accusingly. 'You have been carb loading, haven't you?'

I thought back to everything I'd eaten that day and my eyes opened wide with horror.

'Ally – what did you have for lunch?'

I shook my head and whispered, 'Nothing.'

Jeremy closed his eyes and put his hands to his temples. He took a deep breath in and exhaled slowly, audibly counting to ten.

'Don't panic,' he said eventually, his eyes wild with panic.

'I'll eat more now. A whole pizza. Two pizzas!'

He nodded, still doing his deep breathing exercises.

'It'll be fine. Everything will be absolutely fine.'

I watched him, his cheeks flushed, frantically typing into his phone, presumably googling 'last-minute carb loading', and chose to believe him.

17

King of the Hill

I stood naked in front of the full-length mirror in Jeremy's mum's bathroom. It was one of the thin, wiggly ones which in the early 2000s every single teenage girl I knew had in their bedrooms. A sort of fun-house mirror that didn't distort you so much as cut bits of you off at the sides. I looked tired. I had not slept well in the unfamiliar room on the squeaky mattress on the floor. Every time I closed my eyes, moments from the previous night with Emily replayed in my mind like a film. It was surely impossible that she'd been there and I'd touched her and she was so sorry but that it barely even mattered. My stomach lurched at the thought that I might see her again today. In all the ruminating about Emily I had all but forgotten to obsess over Jo, which was, at least, a bonus.

I had woken up at 5 a.m. unable to get back to sleep in anticipation of our 6 a.m. 'eat as much breakfast as possible' alarm, and was debating whether it would wake up the entire house if

I was to either flush the toilet or have a shower. I desperately wanted to do both. I also couldn't decide whether it made any sense to shower before running thirteen miles, so I stood in limbo, shivering, pyjamas strewn on the floor, considering my options. I was nauseous with nerves. Not being able to have a shower conjured a sort of homesickness I hadn't felt since I was a teenager at a sleepover I didn't want to be at. I wished longingly for the familiarity of my dad's house where I could shower with wild abandon and flush the toilet whenever I felt like it. I wanted to look at myself without the sides cut off.

Jeremy woke up just before the alarm went off every bit as jittery as I was and we went downstairs to try to eat some porridge. Jeremy stood at the hob in his navy-blue dressing gown stirring in grim silence as if he were cooking our last meal on earth. He poured us two huge glasses of orange juice and plonked a jar of honey and a bag of raisins on the kitchen table. And then, almost as an afterthought, a jar of Nutella.

'I never thought I'd struggle to eat a huge breakfast,' I said, lifting a spoonful of porridge glistening with honey up and letting the fat oats slip off the spoon into the bowl again.

'You have to, Al,' Jeremy said very seriously, barely finishing a mouthful of orange juice before sticking a tablespoon into the Nutella jar. 'It's very important that we have enough energy so that we don't hit a wall.'

'All right, coach, I think you mean "*the* wall".'

'No, seriously,' he said, completely ignoring me. 'This might not be the right time to tell you this, but I've been reading all these running forums and stuff and look, people who've never run half marathons before, they sometimes,' he paused, looking utterly stricken, and then pointed his spoon at me, almost accusingly, 'they shit themselves, Al.'

'No they don't.' I put down my spoon altogether, desperately not wanting to believe it was true.

'They do! They do, they shit themselves, so that's why we just have to eat foods we'd normally eat and take it steady. Don't run too fast, try not to be too nervous. Don't drink too much coffee maybe.'

'Bloody hell, Jeremy. You seriously owe me for this.'

He smiled and scooped a very generous teaspoon of sugar into his cup of tea.

'We've had fun though, haven't we? Go on, admit it.'

'Depends on your definition of fun.'

We were both quiet for a moment while we dutifully shovelled our fuel in.

'OK, it has been quite fun.' I smiled despite myself. 'And honestly, I don't know what else I would have done.'

'Exactly! And look at this,' Jeremy pulled his tartan pyjama bottom all the way up to the knee and stretched his leg up on the table to rest next to my bowl, 'a muscle!'

He began flexing his foot backwards and forwards to show off his newly hench calf for a couple of seconds before I slapped it away.

'Very impressive, that is the calf of a half marathon winner I'd say.'

'I know, I look so good in my running shorts, I might just start wearing them full time.'

'Them and your medal?'

'Yes.' He grinned at me, a wide-eyed ball of nervous chatter and excitement with a splodge of Nutella at the corner of his mouth.

In that moment, I just loved him.

Once we'd got into our running gear, checked and rechecked our bumbags, we decided to get the tram into town. There were an awful lot of brightly coloured, Lycra-clad people joining us on our trudge to the tram stop. It was an odd feeling, and as ridiculous as it might sound, before I saw all these people with their drawstring bags filled with flapjacks, touching their toes at the tram stop, it had felt as though this was just a challenge created for me and Jeremy. It didn't feel quite real that we were going to share this experience with other people, let alone thousands of other people. I found myself scanning the crowd for Jo even though I knew she wasn't running the race. My association between her and Lycra was very strong. Jeremy stared straight ahead, popping Lucozade tablets into his mouth like they were Tic Tacs, trying to get into 'the zone'.

We got on right in the middle of the packed tram and crammed ourselves in opposite an elderly couple and their enormous shopping bag on wheels. As the conductor asking who needed to buy a ticket headed our way, without even looking at each other we wordlessly decided to hold our breath and act casual as if we'd been on the tram for hours already. The conductor breezed past us without so much as a glance in our direction and, as he made his way to the back of the tram, Jeremy slapped me on the knee triumphantly.

'Well *that's* surely got to be a good omen, hasn't it?'

I nodded, peering behind me to check the conductor hadn't heard him.

'I think the universe must be on our side today, Jeremy.' I squirmed in my seat like a child. 'I really need a wee.'

He nodded grimly. 'Me too.'

'I feel like . . . no matter how many times I go, I will just always need a wee. That kind of wee.'

'Yep, same. It's fine, it's just nerves. We'll just go to the loo as soon as we get there.'

I nodded, a running race rookie, trusting this would be as easy as it sounded.

The loos, as it turns out, were easily located thanks to the vast queues of chilly and excitable runners in front of them. Hundreds of people all nervously crossing their legs and squealing about making it to the start line in time. We resisted joining for a couple of minutes, just intermittently saying 'no' at each other as if this couldn't really be happening and looking around us in search of the real toilets with no queues and perhaps a mirror to look in for a quiet moment of reflection. In the end, we gave up and joined a queue behind what felt like 75,000 people. Everyone, and I mean everyone, including the men in tutus and a woman dressed as Elsa from *Frozen*, appeared to be better prepared than me and Jeremy. They all somehow seemed to know how to tie their little tracking tag into their shoes and were wearing special watches that they were all checking and constantly stabbing the little buttons of. There was a non-stop cacophony of watch bleeps. We fell into a rare silence as we waited, both contemplating our fates.

'Al,' Jeremy said eventually, looking briefly up at the sky as if checking for a god out there listening, 'are we making a massive mistake?'

'Don't you say that now! We are literally one wee away from the start line!'

'I know, I know, I'm sorry, it's just everything feels very . . .'

'Yes, it feels very real. I know, Jeremy, I am literally here with you about to wet myself before running for ten hours.'

A man jogged past us in a Winnie the Pooh costume.

'Look it's going to be fine.' I softened, seeing his genuine fear. 'If he can do it, we can do it.'

'As if, he's running before the race. Save your energy man!' Jeremy called after him, shaking his head.

'I know, what is he thinking?'

But as soon as we'd said it, we realised that there were an awful lot of people jogging before the race. Jogging past us. Jogging on the spot. Jogging around in circles.

'They're all mad,' I said to Jeremy, rolling my eyes, 'completely mad.' We stood completely still, conserving our energy.

*

Not even half an hour later, we found ourselves not jogging so much as full-on sprinting to our designated zone. Having finally got into the Portaloos, a voice had come over the loud-speakers telling runners it was the final call to get into our zones and that the race was about to begin. We ducked under the barrier, out of breath and sweating before the clock had even started. It was in our zone that we spotted Winnie the Pooh for a second time and another man dressed as a bottle of tomato ketchup who was trying to bend over and touch his toes. In other circumstances, I would have found this very funny, but I could not even muster a smile. Two women joined together with the same cardboard box around their middle bounced about on their toes like boxers who were just entering the ring. There was also a man who looked like he might be eighty years old in the tiniest running shorts I'd ever seen, and a wiry woman of approximately the same age in head-to-toe pink and white Lycra, wearing huge sunglasses. These were our running peers, our fellow competitors.

We looked at each other in horror. When it had just been the two of us running around the streets of Sheffield it had been easy to believe that we were becoming quite the athletes.

'Oh my God, oh my God. I'm going to get outrun by bloody Barney the Dinosaur, aren't I,' Jeremy whimpered, gesturing at a giant purple shape in front of us who appeared to be necking the best part of a can of Red Bull.

'No, of course not,' I said, entirely unconvincingly, as I eyed up two elderly women wearing matching baseball caps who were confidently setting their watches and keeping an eye on the big clock that was strapped to a van at the side of our zone.

'We are in the prime of our lives, Jeremy. Our bodies are built to run. We are definitely not going to get beaten by anybody in a costume or who uses a bus pass.'

'OK fine, yes yes.' He shook his arms out and took a deep breath. 'Yes, you're right, prime of our lives. That's going to be our mantra when the going gets tough, yes?'

'Yes! Prime of our lives!' Just saying it seemed to inject us with a boost of confidence.

The extremely irritating MC of the race was still bellowing through the giant speaker next to us about being sponsored by Hallam FM when all of a sudden a horn sounded and people started to shuffle forward very slowly in front of us.

'Is this it?' Jeremy exclaimed, looking at me completely baffled.

'I guess so.' I began to shuffle very slowly along with everyone else. It all seemed so mundane. Did they not know how much it had taken for us to be there? That for some of us this was momentous?

As we got closer to the actual start line where the super fast runners must have been, the crowds were much bigger. Just as we were about to turn a corner away from the starting tunnel I heard a shriek.

'Ally!' It was our parents, verging on hysterical, waving furiously at us from the sidelines.

'Go on Ally and Jeremy!' my dad yelled. He was wrapped up

warmly and clutching a Thermos, a detail which for some reason immediately brought a lump to my throat.

We waved back, grinning stupidly at him as we turned the corner.

'See you soon!' I heard him yell as the horns and screams began to fade into the distance.

'Your dad,' Jeremy began and then paused, already out of puff, 'is the cutest.'

'Yeah,' I managed to say, not wanting to waste any precious lung capacity talking about my dad, but also knowing if I said much more I'd lose it barely a mile into the race.

Running down Eccleshall Road and past the Botanical Gardens felt doable, it all felt fine. Not good but fine. I looked at the bars and thought of all the past Allys stumbling out of taxis and screaming and laughing obnoxiously in the street as a teenager. All those times I'd confidently walked into student nights as a cocky sixteen-year-old. I jogged past a spot where I had kissed a girl in her third year of university when I was just seventeen. She had been dressed as a lemur and as she turned away from me to get the bus home, promising to call me on the wrong number I had just given her, had promptly thrown up in a bush.

I couldn't stop myself scanning the crowd obsessively for Emily. I tried to figure out where she might stand. Tried to work out if I were coming from the station where I might position myself. Perhaps she'd meet me at the end. Perhaps she wouldn't meet me at all.

Every now and then I glanced at Jeremy, who was beetroot red, to see if he was looking at the runners for Ben. He didn't seem to be. And anyway, there is no way Ben would be back here with us and Ketchup.

Around the three-mile mark I high-fived a little kid outside Endcliffe Park and accepted a Haribo fried egg off him. I felt jubilant. This is what the other runners were doing, I was one of those runners! I was a part of this thing. I had run for three miles, only ten to go. No sign of a stitch, only moderately out of breath, only moderately needing a wee, definitely not shitting myself. And now, a hero to this child. So far, a success. It didn't even faze me that it was about to rain.

I was aware of the 'King of the Hill' section of the race in a sort of vague way, the sort of awareness you have when you hear or read something mildly interesting that has nothing whatsoever to do with you. But as we turned off Eccleshall Road and wound up towards Ringinglow Road, it hit me with horrifying clarity. I wondered, as my legs began to burn before we had even reached the road, whether I had known all along on some deep unconscious level. This was a part of the city that we fastidiously avoided throughout our training despite knowing that we'd be running through it.

I looked up at Jeremy and he was looking down at me with pure terror in his eyes.

'King of the Hill,' he whispered, his breath ragged.

The other runners around us were bracing themselves, staring straight on at the slope ahead. There were people shouting encouragement in the crowds still, but no one was stopping to take their sweets or even wave at them. Everyone was suddenly very focused.

Winnie the Pooh had long faded into the distance. He shot off as soon as the horn had sounded at the beginning of the race to join the more serious runners, but now I saw a yellow speck in the distance. I wondered if the hill had broken Winnie.

Our slow jogs turned into a shuffle as we began the one-mile climb.

'Prime of our lives,' I shouted at Jeremy as the first drops of rain began to fall from the cloud that had been threatening to burst all morning.

'Prime of our lives,' he shouted back enthusiastically if not entirely convincingly.

Those would be the last words we'd say to each other until we'd reached the top of the hill. The longest mile of our lives. Every step was punctuated with a grunt or a moan. My legs were on fire and felt as though they might buckle under me at any moment. I thought I had experienced being out of breath before, but I was wrong. Running up that hill, in the rain, with a bumbag flapping around my middle, gasping for oxygen, my lungs screaming and my head spinning, that was out of breath. I thought of Emily and was glad she couldn't see me in that moment. Every time I thought we were close to the top and it would all be over soon, another voice chimed in reminding me that actually at the top of this hill we would only be five miles into the race. Somebody overtook us every couple of seconds.

As the five-mile marker came into our sights I grunted at Jeremy. Jeremy nodded and grunted back, and with everything we had we charged up the rest of the hill, desperate for it all to be over and for our legs to return to solid matter. As soon as we hit the marker, we grabbed a bottle of water each and tried to aim it in the general direction of our mouths. We were now pretty soggy from the rain so it actually didn't matter that a lot of it ended up down our fronts. We both instinctively stopped, Jeremy bent over, his hands on his knees, trying to catch a breath.

'Don't stop now, don't stop!' one of the volunteers shouted at us, all bright-eyed and bushy-tailed in her waterproof jacket and her coffee in her KeepCup. I hated her with everything I had and gave her the most meaningful glare I could muster.

'Seriously, don't stop, it'll be much harder to keep going! Your muscles will start to seize up!' She gestured at us to move on in a sort of shooing motion.

Jeremy looked at me, amazed that we really did have to carry on, that the one excruciating mile we had just climbed didn't somehow count for twenty.

'We've got to go,' I said weakly and unzipped my bumbag to grab a handful of sticky jelly beans and thrust them at him.

He nodded as he put his open palm up to his mouth to eat all the jelly beans at once, a stray green one hanging limply from his chin before dropping to the ground. I dared to glance at my phone, which I had zipped into the back of my bumbag. We had been running for well over an hour. Despite not really having a target, I'd always somehow assumed we'd easily be able to manage five miles an hour. My heart sank as we turned ourselves back around to face the road and began to shuffle around the corner with a few other runners who had somehow, impossibly, managed not to stop at the top of the hill.

We turned the corner and I burst out laughing just as Jeremy burst into tears at the sight of yet another hill. This, we discovered, was the theme of the race: just when you thought it couldn't get any worse, it did. Think you're going to vomit running that mile? Think again! It is this next mile that will make you vomit! Fantasising about falling over and breaking both your ankles on this stretch of road? On the next stretch of road you'd actually saw off both your legs if it meant you could stop!

At some point in our journey through hell, the hills gave way to flat road and we tried to enjoy the views of Sheffield through the clouds and the drizzle, despite definitely experiencing some sort of altitude sickness. On a rare downhill stretch, we spotted my dad standing with Jeremy's mum, who was holding a home-made placard saying, 'GO JEREMY'. They gave us each a Jammie Dodger and some words of encouragement, saying they'd meet us at the end. I nearly laughed in their faces at the very notion of the end – we would never get to the end.

Our pace slowed practically to a stroll and we were finally able to chat by the tenth mile. We must have been the last people in the race apart from the walkers, but we couldn't have cared less. It did not matter to us whether we were going to get beaten by Barney the Dinosaur (we were); the only thing that mattered was somehow managing to stay on our feet and also alive.

'Three miles to go,' Jeremy said to me, 'three miles and then we can stop for ever. And I mean like, never physically move again.'

I nodded grimly. 'Three miles and then we can eat cake.'

'Yes! And have a pint.'

'And chips.'

'Chips!' Jeremy shouted the word chips as if that were our mantra.

'Do you think Ben is here?'

Jeremy shook his head.

'I don't know, Al.' He didn't seem disappointed – maybe wistful, but not disappointed. 'We won't bloody see him anyway, will we? He probably finished the race an hour ago! He's probably already on his second pint, isn't he?'

I laughed, but it was not an exaggeration. I felt quite sure that at any moment we were going to get picked up by the sweeper bus.

'No Emily,' I said.

'Not yet,' he corrected me.

'And no Jo.'

'Well, obviously not.'

'Yeah I know.'

Those three miles to the finish line took for ever, but we ran the whole way. At the ten-mile mark I saw Charlie and Sophie waving and screaming at me, rattling a Tupperware box at the side of the road containing post marathon biscuits. I waved at them wearily. I didn't have the energy to give them a hug. Their excitement brought a lump to my throat for the second time that day, but I didn't have any spare liquid in my body for tears. By that point, the stuff coming out of my pores was pure Lucozade Sport.

At the eleven-mile mark, we heard a tentative 'Jeremy' coming from our right. It was almost a question, as if the shouter wasn't quite sure he'd correctly identified Jeremy. A tall, gangly boy was standing behind the barrier all wrapped up in a huge khaki and orange parka coat so sleeping bag-like that it made his skinny legs look even skinnier. He waved bashfully and Jeremy said, 'Oh my God,' under his breath and wobbled over to him. I followed, obviously, suddenly finding a new source of energy.

'Hiya,' the boy said nervously and then as an afterthought added a, 'well done!' He nodded at me to indicate that half of the 'well done' was for me.

'Oh cool, cheers,' said Jeremy, as if it had been nothing, as if we were sailing past having a lovely time, as if he didn't have a crust of jelly bean and dried sweat coating his top lip.

'All right then, maybe see you later?' the boy said as we began to jog on the spot, our legs starting to cramp up just as that stupid, clever high-vis lady had said they would.

'Yeah yeah, text me,' Jeremy said, cool as anything.

'Cool, cool,' the boy said and raised a hand at me before wandering off into the crowd.

'What was that?' I shrieked as best I could given the lack of oxygen, as we set off again.

'Nothing!' Jeremy said. We were both so red already it was impossible to tell if he was blushing.

'Is that the boy you've been texting? What's his name?'

'No!' He waited until we'd plodded on a bit more. 'Well yeah, actually it is, I don't know why I said no. His name's Rob. What do you think?' He kept his eyes fixed on the person in front of us, who was dressed as a pirate complete with a parrot on his shoulder, which flailed about in the wind.

'I think he was very . . . quiet. And tall. And very nice.' It's hard to come up with a well-worded and tactful assessment of someone when you're out of breath and your entire body is screaming.

'Yeah, he is quiet, but I think I'm awkward around him as well, which doesn't help. He is really nice. It was really nice of him to come.'

'So lovely of him to come, on such a shit day as well. I bet he's been standing around in the rain for you.'

'Yeah.' Jeremy took a swig of his Lucozade Sport and then chucked the bottle to the ground to join the sea of other abandoned bottles. He grimaced. 'I fucking hate this stuff, my whole mouth is furry.'

We jogged in silence for a bit, trying to catch our breath.

'Anyway yeah,' Jeremy eventually said, 'it's not like romance of the century or anything. He's not my boyfriend, I don't *love* him. But that's good, you know? He's just a nice boy and we're having a nice time and like, I just think that's what I need at the moment.'

'Definitely. And Jeremy, that's what you deserve. Someone who likes you, who is nice to you. That's it.'

'You deserve that too, Al.'

I couldn't reply to that because I was only just managing to keep it together and not bawl my way to the finish line. I couldn't deal with a heart-to-heart on top of all the cheering and exhaustion.

The twelve-mile sign appeared like a mirage in the desert. Time was behaving very strangely. Even though we were some of the last people approaching the home straight, the crowd, which had been much sparser during the previous few miles, started to get louder again. There were more people and some terrible, thumping music was playing as we made our way back through the city centre and towards the finish line.

I was overwhelmed simultaneously by a desperate longing for the whole, dreadful nightmare race to be over and a deep terror of what would happen when it was. This race had been our goal; this was the end game. Everything afterwards was just a question mark. With just half a mile to go and children everywhere waving and holding out sweets and kind strangers shouting 'nearly there, love' from the sidelines, I finally gave in to the tears that had been threatening to spill over since mile one. I turned to look at Jeremy and, when he saw me crying, he burst into tears too. Now we had to cry and jog and breathe all at the same time. As we spotted the finish line and the cheers became even more urgent and excited, I grabbed Jeremy's hand and we broke into our version of a sprint. It was as graceful as if we were running a three-legged race, but it felt like an insurmountable effort to speed up in any way at all and only right that we finish this bloody thing we'd started together. Seeing the time on the giant digital clock above the finishing line, the tears turned to gasping laughter. We had beaten the sweeper bus by mere minutes. As soon as we had stumbled over the line, Jeremy screamed, 'We did it!' which obviously used up any energy he might have had left as he immediately slumped over, clutching on to the barrier for dear life. Eventually he recovered enough to stand and put his arm around my shoulders and I put mine around his waist so we could limp out of there using each other as crutches.

At some point someone put a medal around my neck, wrapped me in one of those silver blankets I'd only ever seen on *Casualty*, and handed me a banana, which I took one bite out of and spat out. A weird side effect of running thirteen miles was a total loss of appetite. Very unfair.

Jeremy spotted our parents first, huddled together under a shop front on their phones like a pair of teenagers.

'Dad!' I found myself shouting quite manically in the way that a child might follow with 'Look at me, Dad, did you see what I did? Dad!'

They looked up and started briskly walking towards us beaming, phones still clutched in their hands so they could continue to document every moment.

'Well done, kid.' My dad got to me first and grabbed me by my shoulders, pushing me back a bit so he could admire my medal before pulling me in for a hug. Once he'd released me he grabbed Jeremy, hugged him briefly and gave him a pat on the back so hard I think it might have winded him.

'I'm so proud of you both,' Jeremy's mum gushed as she passed me my big coat that they'd been carrying around all day. I put it on gratefully, realising suddenly that I was shivering. I'd not felt like this since I'd passed my GCSE Maths exam (a surprise to everyone) and I got treated like a princess all day (and very much for one day only).

'Imagine running all that way! And in this weather!' Dad was shaking his head disbelievingly and gesturing at the sky as if we'd just climbed Mount Everest in a blizzard. 'Absolutely incredible. How do you feel? Will you be doing it again?' he asked us, rubbing his hands together and stamping his feet a bit obviously, having got cold waiting for much, much longer than any of us had anticipated.

'No!' we both exclaimed in unison, and the parents tittered.

'Dad, I feel literally the most exhausted I've ever felt in my life. And also like I'm going to be sick. And also like I need to go and sit in a bath for twelve hours or my legs will fall off.'

'But does it feel good though?' Dad said, ignoring everything I'd said, utterly unconcerned.

Jeremy and I looked at each other, finding it hard to pinpoint exactly what it was we were feeling, and he sort of shrugged at me.

'Yeah, it does a bit, in a weird way,' he said hesitantly, 'what do you think, Al?'

'Yeah, in a weird way. It's just those endorphins though, isn't it? Fooling you into thinking you feel good when actually you feel like you've just been hit by a car.'

Jeremy's mum nodded sagely. This was a woman who had used the exercise bike in their garage every day religiously for twenty years and knew all about those endorphins.

'Well, do you both feel well enough to go and get something to eat? Shall we go to the pub?' my dad suggested, starting to move away before letting us answer, clearly having had quite enough of standing about in the cold for one day and in desperate need of a pint.

'Yes, I want to go to the pub!' Jeremy said before he'd even finished speaking, almost literally jumping at the chance. 'Come on, Al, you've been talking about that post run pint, haven't you?'

It was also impossible to say no to Jeremy's pleading face.

'OK yes, pub! Let's do it. Only if we can find somewhere to sit down. And only if they have chips.'

'You feel so sick you can only manage chips, eh?' My dad looked at me, eyebrows raised.

'Yes, I think chips will help.'

We made off in the direction of my dad's favourite 'old man' pub, into which he was confident no runner would ever set foot, plus it had an open fireplace, which sold it to me. It was a very slow start because in the short time we'd been standing around talking, each of my feet appeared to have turned into one giant blister and my knees felt like someone had taken a hammer to them. We limped along behind our parents, wincing with every step, our medals clanging against the zips of our coats because we had insisted on wearing them on the outside so everyone would know they were in the presence of heroes.

We'd barely made it ten steps before I heard someone calling my name.

'Ally! Ally!'

Jeremy and I both turned around very slowly as all movement was now a considerable effort.

Emily was walking towards us. Again in her enormous coat. It looked undeniably ridiculous, I observed, as I wiped dried sweat off my face with my brand new 'Sheffield Half Marathon' purple drawstring bag.

'Hi!' she said, all jolly, when she finally reached us, totally unaware of any feeling of embarrassment from us having to watch her walk towards us for what felt like an hour and a half. This was her special ability, to just feel comfortable in all situations.

'I've been ringing you. I've been here for ages, but I never saw you. You must be Jeremy!' She took a step forward and before Jeremy could say anything, enveloped him in a big hug. He patted her on the back tentatively, glaring at me for some kind of clue as to how he was meant to feel about her so he could respond appropriately. I wished that I could tell him, but I had no idea.

'It is such a pleasure to meet you, Jeremy. Ally has told me all about you.' She stood back from us, beaming. 'And huge congratulations to you both!' She clapped her hands together and then grabbed my medal to take a closer look, forcing me to take a step towards her to avoid choking. 'Wow, it's just such an achievement, such a long way! That is so wonderful. I can't believe you really did it, Al.'

She looked up at me and dropped my medal back to my chest. It landed face down and I carefully corrected it. Was it weird that she didn't hug me? Did she not want to hug me? But if she didn't want to hug me, why would she be here?

'I really did it,' I said limply. I didn't know what to say that wasn't simply, 'Why are you here?' It made no sense. This was not what I had imagined. She wasn't cheering me on in the crowd tearfully, or meeting me at the finish line and passionately kissing me, or getting down on one knee. She was greeting Jeremy and me like we were old school friends who'd lost touch, who had just happened to bump into each other. She was totally casual about it. But she had really come.

'So what are you up to now?' She looked at us both eagerly and I realised that perhaps she wasn't so casual after all. Her eyes were wild.

Jeremy spoke up. 'We were just heading to the pub, with . . . our parents.' He trailed off, not knowing whether he had said the wrong thing. When he said 'parents' we both instinctively looked behind us and saw that the two of them were standing on the corner waiting for us. They were too far away for me to make out my dad's facial expression, but I could see from his dramatic gesticulating that he was slagging Emily off to Jeremy's mum. Inviting Emily was not an option.

'Oh fab, fab.' She looked at me and I wondered if she was regretting her decision to come.

We stood in silence for just a beat too long while my exhausted brain tried to work out what to do. I looked at Jeremy.

'Can you just . . . can you just let them know I'll catch up in a bit?' I stared at him, desperately trying to relay that I was sorry and that I didn't really know what I was doing. He seemed to understand.

'Sure, OK.' He looked at Emily. 'Nice to meet you.' He turned and started walking away before she could bid him an effusive goodbye and as he passed me he squeezed the top of my arm, just hard enough to hurt a bit. I knew it meant 'you've got this' and also 'don't be stupid', which I appreciated.

I couldn't bear to turn around and see Jeremy hobble slowly towards our parents without me.

'So, where shall we go?' Emily asked me, grinning.

A flash of irritation sparked in my chest.

'I don't know, Emily. I have just run for thirteen miles. Everywhere is going to be rammed full of people, and I just need to sit down.'

She looked a bit surprised at my reaction, but nodded and started looking around as if a quiet restaurant with plenty of seats and chips might miraculously materialise.

'Look, let's just sit down there for now.' I pointed at a bench and began shuffling towards it. She followed me a couple of paces behind, which was quite some feat given how slowly I was going.

I plonked myself down on the bench and she perched beside me. I realised my mood was making her nervous, which, in a mean way, I quite enjoyed. Empowered by her hesitation and feeling high as a kite from sports drinks I turned to her and decided to ask her outright.

'Why did you come here?'

She opened her eyes wide, apparently wounded by my question.

'To support you! To cheer you on!'

'I just really thought at my house, it felt like . . . it felt like we were saying goodbye, don't you think?'

She looked confused and then crestfallen as if it was all suddenly occurring to her that this was not going to go to plan.

'But you said, you said to come . . . if I wanted to.'

I sighed and leant back on the bench, stretching my legs out, desperately wishing there was something to prop them up on.

'I did say that. I know. I'm trying to understand what it is you want from me, Em.'

'I want,' she faltered, a rare occurrence, 'I don't know what I want, but I don't want to lose you. After I left on Friday it really felt like I was losing you and I couldn't stand it.'

'You haven't lost me. Come on.'

'I have. What about that other girl? I thought you were heart-broken, Al. I thought that you'd do anything to have me back. I thought you were really fighting for me.'

'I thought so too,' I said gently, and she nodded and then leant back on the bench next to me, staring straight ahead at the cluster of pigeons fighting over all the abandoned bananas.

I wanted to squeeze her knee to comfort her, but I just didn't have the energy to be anything other than truthful, to her or to myself.

'So you don't want me back?' she said eventually, incredulously. 'Really? Definitely?'

I felt a sudden piercing clarity settle over everything.

'I don't, Emily. I can't believe I'm saying this, but I don't. I forgive you though and I really do love you.'

She began to cry. I fought the urge to apologise with everything I had.

'Well, now I feel like *I've* been dumped!' she sobbed.

'You didn't even want me back! You wanted me to want you back!'

'I've never been dumped before!' she wailed, completely ignoring me.

'Well, welcome to the club. It's rubbish, isn't it?'

She nodded, wiping away mascara streaks from her cheeks, her lips pressed tightly together. It took all my strength not to wrap her up in a hug and tell her I was only joking or that maybe I'd reconsider. I knew I had to do this.

We sat next to each other for a while in silence until we were so cold it felt like hypothermia was mere moments away. I was also quite concerned that all my muscles had now seized up and I would be moulded to that bench for the rest of my life.

'I'd better go and meet my dad and Jeremy, they'll be getting worried.' I looked in the general direction that they'd walked in and wondered if I'd be able to hobble there by myself and, crucially, whether they'd ordered me any chips.

'Oh God.' She sighed heavily. 'Your dad must really hate me.'

'He does, yeah.'

Emily nodded ruefully and pushed herself up from the bench. Without a word she reached out for my hands to haul me up, a gesture which was both kind and necessary.

Once we'd managed to get me upright we stood awkwardly in front of each other.

'Goodbye again, then,' she eventually said, and then added, 'this time for good.' It was so Bond villain that I couldn't help but laugh. She looked at me blankly, not getting it.

'Goodbye for good, Em.'

18

Houdini

I thought that having my feet up in bed would ease the throbbing of my legs but I was wrong. The pain remained just as intensely as if I were standing. My highly anticipated hot bath had not helped. The chips had not helped.

When I had finally made it to the pub after my doomed chat with Emily, everyone had already had a drink and were all considering a second, so thankfully they were in a better mood with me than I'd anticipated. My dad even patted the bench next to him and shuffled up so I could perch beside him. They had ordered me chips but worried they'd go cold, so had thoughtfully eaten them. We ordered another portion and stayed in the pub chatting and drinking until Jeremy and I, like drunk toddlers, were in danger of nodding off at the table.

We had all run out of words to say to each other by the time we got to the car park, so we just hugged for a long time, our medals clinking together.

It was only when I got into the car and sat in the back seat behind my dad so I could stretch out that he looked into the rear-view mirror and, in a roundabout way, finally asked me about Emily.

'You all right, love?'

'Yeah, I'm just really tired.'

'You're not . . . upset? About anything?' He asked this breezily, as though there was nothing in particular he was enquiring about.

'I'm just sort of wiped out.'

He nodded and thankfully asked no more questions.

I closed my eyes, wondering if I'd be able to squeeze in a nap on the way home. I was so tired I would have happily stayed in the car all night. But my stomach was fluttering and my whole body was too awake, too busy trying to repair itself from the unprecedented damage I'd done to it.

I kept my eyes closed anyway, but just as we were pulling into the drive and while Dad was still facing away from me I managed to prise them open.

'Thank you for coming today. Having you in the crowd was just . . .'

I didn't know exactly how to finish my sentence but I don't think he needed me to.

'That's all right,' my dad said gruffly. And then we got out of the car and into the warm house where our very fluffy cat greeted us, triumphantly and inexplicably free from his cone. It had been a big day for everyone.

*

I stretched and tried readjusting myself in bed so that my knees were bent or my toes were pointed out like a ballerina. Nothing helped. I heaved myself onto my side and picked up my phone. I had a voice note from Jeremy.

This will be my final message to you because I will soon be dead. Literally dead. Deceased. Al, I have never felt so rough in my entire life. I want to go to sleep but I can't. I want to eat Ben and Jerry's but I also really don't, like I think I might be sick. Why did we do this?! I honestly can't believe we were so stupid. Also Rob just texted me asking if I want to do something and I do but I also . . . can't move? Help!

I moved again to lie flat on my stomach to see if that might help. It did not. I held my phone up to my sideways face and pressed record.

This is a message sent from the afterlife. RIP me. I have never felt pain like this. I can't sleep, I can't eat. I can ALWAYS eat. It is my super power! I don't know what's wrong with me. Can't you just have Rob round to yours? Then you won't need to move will you? Ugh, I'm so jealous. I want someone to come round and rub my feet and bring me cups of tea. Maybe I should have waited one more day before sacking off the love of my life.

I thought it might feel too soon to joke about Emily, but it didn't really. It felt almost inconsequential given the rest of the day.

You definitely should have done, mate. Although I don't think he's going to want to rub my feet, they are completely disgusting. One of my toenails is black, the internet says that means it's going to drop off. OK maybe I'll see if he wants to come round here. My mum is going to be so annoying about it though.

Jeremy. Move out.

I WILL. OK night, babe, I'm going to message Rob now. I'll let you know all the gory details tomorrow.

I can't wait.

I put my phone on airplane mode and opened my notes app.

Hey, how are you? I know we haven't spoken in ages and that's my fault and I know you probably don't want to hear from me at all but I have to tell you – today it was the half marathon and I finished it! And so did Jeremy! We were very slow and I think we might possibly die tonight but we did it. I want to say thank you because I couldn't have done it without you. You believed that I could do it and so I did too. You changed everything. I'm still so sorry, Jo.

I read and reread it, and when I was satisfied I put my phone away. I'd send it in the morning if I still wanted to. That had been my plan with the others too.

I lay back with my eyes closed, resigned to my throbbing legs and stinging feet. I was just beginning to drift off when my door opened. Malcolm had been re-coned and was bumbling about trying to make his way over to my bed. Thrilled, I began patting the duvet next to me enthusiastically, a move that had never worked (he thinks it's embarrassing) but that I persist with nonetheless. After a couple of tries he eventually managed to scramble up and settle next to my feet. He sighed one of his big sighs and I found myself, ridiculously, grinning in the dark. A tear slid down my cheek and into my ear.

'Night Malcolm,' I whispered as quietly as I could so as not to irritate him. 'I'm sorry about the cone.'

I wanted to tell him that I loved him, but I knew he would hate it.

I could tell that he was already asleep. His gentle snoring amplified by the plastic megaphone around his neck.

19

'Honey, I'm Home'

Four Months Later

Malcolm was lying in a sun patch on the floor. He was stretched out with his back arched. A crescent moon of fluff. It wasn't hard to find a sun patch on the floor; the entire room was one big sun patch. The air was still and sticky and every surface was warm to the touch.

I tiptoed over to him, the wet hand towel gripped in my hands was hidden behind my back. I wanted to cool him down, concerned that he was in grave danger of overheating. I had given him an ice cube, but he had just batted it under the sofa, offended that I had offered him something so dull and inedible. I kneeled down gently beside him so as not to disturb his nap and he allowed me to stroke him under the chin before I took my chance and threw the towel over his body. I scooped him up and held him like a very hot, scratchy baby. He yowled as if I had stabbed him and started to wriggle, but I held on. When I was finally satisfied that he was at least slightly damp, I let him go and he leapt from my arms and over to the other side of the room. He glared at me furiously. He half-heartedly began to wash himself, trying to get all the places that the towel had touched, but he soon gave up and went back to the original sun spot. He plonked himself down to lie on his side as if exhausted by the effort of it all and looked at me smugly. He would not have his temperature regulated by anybody, thank you very much.

The heatwave was only meant to last a week, but here we were nearly three weeks later with no signs of it letting up. I kept trying not to complain about it, remembering the cold, rainy months and how much better it was to wake up to sunshine and how nice it was to sit outside with a glass of wine in the evenings. How eating ice cream for tea several nights in a row was a luxury not to be sniffed at. But I couldn't help but wish it would cool down just slightly when even taking three steps in my own home was causing me to sweat profusely. I had barely slept, clutching a 'cold water bottle' that had been in the freezer all day, and then when I'd finally nodded off I kept having strange dreams in which I was being lowered into boiling water like an egg.

As thrilled as I was no longer to be living at my dad's house, in the past couple of weeks I had longed for the cool living room at the back of the house, which never seemed to heat up whatever the temperature outside. This flat, at the top of an eight-storey building, was a heat trap, which, I was assured by the wormy estate agent who smelt like Lynx Africa, was a fantastic energy saver in the winter. I did not doubt it, but in the summer, it was almost unbearable to be inside, a fact he strangely enough did not pass on. I got a glass of water and went to sit on our tiny balcony, room enough for two small folding chairs and a pot plant (already sadly deceased). My dad had helped me to erect a cat net, which stretched up high from the top of the wooden railing around the balcony so that Malcolm couldn't pull any daredevil stunts. I left the door open so he could potter outside with me and he stretched out at the bottom of my chair. All was forgiven. I put my feet up on the railing and had just closed my eyes when I heard the front door slam.

'Honey, I'm home!'

'I'm out here,' I called back groggily, wiping my eyes and squinting down at the time on my phone. It was later than I'd realised.

Jeremy stepped out onto the balcony clutching a two-litre bottle of fizzy water, now half empty. He proceeded to chug most of the rest of it as he waved hello before sitting down on the folding chair next to me.

'I've got a surprise.' Jeremy grinned at me, wiping water from his mouth and onto his already soaking wet T-shirt.

'Please tell me it's a paddling pool.' I pushed my sunglasses back down onto my face. 'I can't take this anymore.'

'It's better.' He pulled back the living-room curtain that we kept closed onto the balcony and indicated for me to look inside.

I leant over him to peer in and when I saw what was sitting on the table I squealed with delight.

'A fan! This is going to change everything. Look Malcolm, a fan!' Malcolm remained entirely uninterested.

'Good isn't it? They had a deal on so I've got one for each of our rooms, it's only a little one, but it's got to make some kind of a difference, surely.' He opened the bottle again and drizzled the last dregs of water into the dead plant.

'I think that's probably past the point of resurrection, babe.'

'Hmm, I'm not sure,' Jeremy said, prodding one of the brown leaves, which promptly dropped to the ground, 'it might just be a bit hot.'

'Do you know though, if we got some tomatoes out here, they'd thrive,' I said knowledgeably, as if I was full of hot gardening tips for idiots with balconies.

'Oh, we should get some, I love the idea of growing my own food,' Jeremy said, while scrolling through his phone. I had no doubt he was googling for the hundredth time 'how to bring a plant back to life'. I was quite sure 'fizzy water' was not the answer.

We had had this conversation or a variation of it several times since we'd moved in almost six weeks ago. In fact, we discussed whether or not to get a tomato plant almost every single time we sat out on the balcony. I loved the mundanity of it. I loved that neither of us ever referenced the fact that we kept having the same conversation over and over. I loved having someone to have that conversation with. I had not realised before that the person I discussed getting a tomato plant with did not have to be Emily.

'We'd better get ready hadn't we, or we're going to be late.' I said this without making any moves to get up.

'Ugh, yeah. I obviously want to go, but I also really want to go in just my swimming trunks. Is that acceptable?'

'I'm not sure. Maybe if you wear nice shoes.'

'Hmm . . . well, what are you going to wear?'

'I've got a dress! A new one.'

'Show me!' Jeremy demanded.

'You'll see it when it's on.' I waved my hand lazily.

It was exciting to have something new. This was in fact the first purchase post break-up that wasn't made of Lycra and three sizes too small.

When we eventually dragged ourselves inside to get changed I poured us each a glass of wine left over from last night, and we stood on the sofa so we could preen ourselves in the big mirror that hung on the wall behind it, a housewarming present from Jeremy's mum. Next to it hung a photo of Jeremy and me running. It was an official half marathon photograph that my dad had bought and handed over to me wordlessly, unwrapped but in a dark wooden frame, on the day I moved out. He had one of his own displayed proudly on the mantelpiece. Jeremy and I looked, objectively, disgusting. I'm not facing the camera, but instead am staring grimly ahead. I must have been moving, but it looks like my feet are glued to the ground. Jeremy is staring at the camera like he's never seen one before. His eyes are screaming 'help'.

I tied my hair back in a ponytail so I wouldn't have a sweaty neck all evening and put the bare minimum of make-up on my face, knowing that it would all be gone by the time we'd arrived anyway. I hesitated as I pulled an old red lipstick out of my washbag. It was not mine; it was definitely one of Emily's. I decided to slap it on and smiled at myself in the mirror when I was done. Jeremy nodded approvingly, unable to say much with his mouth full of tooth whitening strips. He sipped his wine through a straw.

'Got everything?' I yelled at Jeremy as he walked back and forth between the living room and the bathroom, patting himself down to check for belongings and peering at himself in all reflective surfaces.

'Yes! Let's go now or we'll never go.'

We dashed out of the door and took the stairs. It was a relief to get outside into the fresh evening air. It was still hot, but the enjoyable kind. Despite the need to hurry, we strolled along, enjoying the feeling of having had a couple of glasses of wine and no dinner. I loved that in the warm weather people would always linger outside in the evenings, instead of hibernating inside. Children ran past us shrieking, and students walked along carrying huge clinking bags filled with booze and disposable barbeques. The city felt alive.

When we arrived at the pub I finally checked my phone, bracing myself for all the missed calls and texts telling me off for being late, but there were none, just one message from my dad.

Ally, don't forget to keep hydrated and to keep Malcolm hydrated. Is

Jeremy hydrated? It's very important to be drinking a lot of water. I'm looking forward to lunch tomorrow. Don't tell her I said anything, but Liz is hoping you'll bring a cake. She loves your baking. Anyway, let me know what time to expect you and as I say, drink some water please. You don't want to get dehydrated.

I quickly texted back.

What is 'hydrated'? We're at the pub. Lots of lovely liquids here. Will bring cake, don't worry.

We went into the garden, peering through the sea of people, wondering if they'd managed to nab a table on this ridiculously busy Friday evening. When we found them, Charlie, Sophie and Nick were already halfway through their pints. There were some quite sad-looking balloons tied to some bottles which stood on the table. They had faded pictures of popping champagne bottles on them.

'You finally bloody made it!' Charlie stood up and swung one leg over the picnic bench table so she could give me a hug.

'I know, I know, I'm sorry. You know what we're like. Let me get another round in to make up for it. What's everyone having?'

'Wait a minute. We want to talk to you about something first.' Charlie gestured for us to sit down opposite her.

'What's all this then?' I said, surveying the balloons waving about in front of us in the breeze. I gently tapped one and it sagged even more.

'Well, they were in great shape, say,' Charlie smiled and looked at her watch, 'an hour ago.'

'Sorry! They still look great, but what are they for? Shit, it's not your birthday is it?'

'No, it's not my birthday, Ally. It was my birthday in May. You came! You helped make my cake!'

'Right, right.'

'We wanted to have a little celebration for the fact that the shop is doing so well and that so much of that is down to you and your help . . .'

'Oh my God, guys, that is so . . .'

'Shut up a minute, there's more.'

I shut up.

'We're doing so well in fact that we're going to be opening another one.' She paused to look at Sophie, who nodded at her enthusiastically. 'Well . . . you are. We hope.'

Sophie pushed a set of keys across the table towards me.

I looked up at them both and then at Nick, who was looking off into the distance between me and Jeremy, unmoved.

'Are you being serious?'

'Completely serious. It's just a small space, but you'll need to hire one other person. It's up near the uni, so maybe a student – we know you get along *very* well with them.'

I laughed, which immediately turned into some quite ugly sobbing.

'I don't know how I can even . . . how do I?' I looked at Jeremy helplessly, who was wiping away a tear from underneath his sunglasses.

'Drinks!' I suddenly exclaimed. 'I need to buy you drinks!'

'No, you sit down, I'll go,' Sophie said, getting up from the table, 'I was going to the loo anyway.'

She squeezed both my shoulders as she walked past me.

'I'll help you,' said Nick quickly.

It was so surreal that I was finally going to be in charge of my own shop that I could hardly take it in. A tiny space. Big enough for two people. Perfect. I immediately started fantasising about me and my apprentice hard at work. She would be completely charmed by my teaching and in awe of my spectacular work. We would ice cakes in an obscenely sensual way like that scene from *Ghost*.

'So . . . is that a yes?' Charlie said, grinning.

'Yes! Biggest yes ever!'

'Well thank God for that,' said Charlie, taking a sip of beer, 'because you're great and we've already signed the lease on the shop.'

'Ugh,' said Jeremy, pushing his sunglasses up onto his head, 'I wish I had a lesbian power couple cheerleading me, it's so unfair.'

Charlie laughed. 'We'll cheerlead you Jeremy, just tell us where to be.'

'Thank you so much, but honestly, I have no bloody idea. I've applied for some courses, but won't hear back for a while.'

'Jeremy is going to be a primary school teacher,' I announced, beaming at him like a proud mother.

'Well maybe,' he said quickly, glaring at me and tapping the wooden table as though I'd just jinxed him. 'I might not get in,

I might be shit at it. I keep being like, can I even spell? What is one plus one?'

'You won't be shit,' I said confidently and then to Charlie, 'he won't be. He'll be great. The kids are going to love him.'

'That's such lovely news, Jeremy, everything crossed for you,' Charlie said. 'You know I thought about going into teaching, but I just wasn't sure I could hack it.'

'My dad is thrilled. He keeps saying "at least *someone* is following in my footsteps".'

Jeremy picked up his phone from the table, squinting at it and then craning his neck to scan the beer garden.

'Are you expecting someone?' Charlie asked, her eyes lit up at the merest hint that there might be some gossip on the horizon.

'Yeah, this guy I know said he might be coming down to meet us for a bit, but that was a while ago and I can't see him anywhere.' Jeremy stared hard at his open WhatsApp screen, as if he might be able to trigger a reply with the power of his mind.

'Oh, is this that Rob?'

I opened my eyes wide and gave my head the briefest of shakes. She was incapable of being cool.

Jeremy looked surprised, which was quite reasonable given that he'd never mentioned Rob to Charlie.

'It isn't actually.' He became suddenly coy, raising his eyebrows and putting his sunglasses back on, revelling in being all mysterious.

'What?' I exclaimed, spinning to face him.

At that moment, Sophie and Nick reappeared through the crowd with the drinks. Sophie plonked a bottle of rosé in the middle of the table.

'What have we missed?' she asked. 'Why do you look so scandalised, Ally?'

'Jeremy's got a secret boyfriend apparently!' I said, pouring an enormous glass of wine and taking a big gulp.

'Oh yes, Rob, isn't it?' Sophie asked innocently, glancing at Charlie, who was now doing the brief head-shake at her. Unbelievable.

'Bloody hell, man. So you've all been talking about me?' He looked around the table, feigning disappointment in us all for gossiping.

'So if it's not Rob then who is it?' I asked. We all leant in. Even Nick.

'His name's Richard. He's just started at work. He's very sweet, so don't be weird. He might be here any minute, OK?' He looked around dramatically.

'So, what happened to Rob?' asked Charlie.

Jeremy shrugged nonchalantly.

'Nothing has *happened* to Rob. It's fine, but I have told you,' he looked at me specifically, 'that we are just casual. He is not my boyfriend, nor do I want him to be. He's dating other people too. It's fine, it's no big deal.'

He took a sip of his wine and continued to scan the crowd for signs of this so-called Richard. I inspected him for any indication that he was pining for Rob or that he'd been dumped. There were none.

'What about you, Al?' Charlie said through a mouthful of Scampi Fries.

'What about me?'

'Are you meeting people? Are there nice people to meet?'

I made a noise that was somewhere between a yes and a no. It was a balancing act of not giving too much or too little away. I didn't want the end-game to be Charlie taking my phone so she could 'have a play' on Tinder on my behalf – something I had learnt in my short time as a person on a dating app that people in relationships loved to do.

'She's had a couple of dates, haven't you?' Jeremy looked at me, innocent as anything. Payback for discussing Rob with the lesbians. I had made my bed.

'A couple of dates, ooh!' Charlie looked at Sophie, thrilled. 'Same person? Different people? What did you do? Where did you go? Any sleepovers?'

Nick put his head in his hands and then stabbed the home screen on his phone to check the time, groaning audibly at how long he felt he still had to give this evening.

'Couple of dates with one person, one date with another. Nothing very special, but you know, I'm putting myself out there!' I said this in a way that I thought might signal the end of the conversation.

'Oh yeah, that one date,' Jeremy grimaced and looked at Charlie and Sophie, indicating that he knew all about it.

'What?' Charlie said, quite literally on the edge of her seat. 'What date? When was this?' And then, unable to help herself, she whined, 'You don't tell us anything!'

'I wonder why!' I exclaimed.

'We're just interested in your life because we care about you.'

'Yeah, yeah.' I took a sip of rosé. A few glasses of wine in, this wasn't a story I particularly minded telling.

'OK, so, I was messaging this girl a bit back and forth and it wasn't particularly great chat but Jeremy,' here I shot him a look but he was too busy on his phone to notice, 'Jeremy said that you can't really get the measure of people until you meet them in person and that it isn't fair to judge someone just from texts.'

Charlie and Sophie nodded enthusiastically in agreement, already enthralled.

'So I ask her to go for a drink and she says yes and I'm not that excited but she seems nice and vaguely interesting, she's a postgraduate student studying something . . . history or maybe . . . politics?' I genuinely couldn't bring to mind the subject of the thesis she had so passionately described to me.

'So we go, and it's fine. It's nice. She's quite fit in a sort of practical way. You know what I mean?'

Everyone around the table murmured in agreement, Jeremy saying simply 'sensible shoes'.

'So one drink turns into a thousand drinks and at the end of the night when the bar is closing, she told me she lives in a flat close by and that her housemate isn't there and then somehow we were just sort of there.'

I paused to take a sip of wine and to keep them all hanging on a bit longer.

'So we go up to her flat and it's just quite nondescript, just like all of those flats, same Ikea sofa, same everything. A bit like ours actually.'

Jeremy shook his head vehemently. 'No, we have made ours unique and beautiful.'

'OK fine, but you get the picture. Anyway, weirdly she pours us a whisky because it's all they've got in and it was a Christmas present. So we sit on the floor for some reason and drink this horrible whisky and have a cigarette inside the flat, which was very nice. A treat these days.'

Jeremy nodded as if I was describing a delicious meal I'd had, or a massage.

'So we start kissing and sort of fooling around.'

I noticed Nick had gone bright red.

'And it's fine. It's nice. It's not very exciting, but we were drunk and so to be fair it was always going to be a bit clumsy. Anyway we're on this really scratchy rug so eventually she goes "Shall we go into the bedroom?" which made me feel a bit ill anyway, why couldn't she just say, "Shall we go to my room?"?'

'Shall we . . . take this to the bedroom?' Jeremy said in a very low, husky voice.

'Exactly! Creepy. But anyway I *do* go into the bedroom and it's dark at first and we sort of feel our way to her bed and then she reaches over and switches on her bedside lamp and when I look around I see that every single surface, and I mean, *every single surface*, is covered in Sylvanian Families and they're all looking at me.'

'*What?*' Sophie exclaimed. 'Like those little plastic, furry animals?'

'Exactly that, my friend, exactly that. I would say there must have been more than a hundred. She had the school house, she had the boat, she had the tree house, the cottage; literally any building you can think of that would house a family of tiny, plastic hedgehogs, she had it. And like, she didn't mention it. I feel like if perhaps she'd said, "Oh yeah, by the way I weirdly collect hundreds of Sylvanian Families and display them in my room, it's just a thing I like", I might have been like "Whatever, if that's your thing", but she really had no notion that it was odd at all.'

Sophie and Nick were giggling at this point but I could tell that Charlie was after a much more sordid story.

'So what did you do?' she asked hopefully.

'I told her I suddenly felt sick and got an Uber, obviously.'

'Obviously,' Jeremy echoed.

'Oh no, I feel bad for her,' Sophie said, although she was still laughing.

'Don't, she literally could not have cared less.'

They all laughed.

'She couldn't!' I insisted. 'She was just like, "Oh no, poor you, OK bye then".'

'Not meant to be then,' Sophie said, shaking her head.

'No, I don't think so, but I'm sure she'll make some . . .' I tried to think who the right match for her might be.

'Collector?' Jeremy offered.

'Yes, I'm sure she'll make a squirrel family collector very happy one day.'

'And the other one?' Charlie asked, still after something juicier than Sylvanian Family woman.

I shook my head, concentrating on pouring the dregs of the wine out into my and Jeremy's empty glasses.

'She was nice. We just didn't really click. It doesn't matter though,' I added, noting them doing their sad faces at me, 'I'm really truly not looking for someone. I'm just enjoying being by myself for a while.'

'With your house husband,' Jeremy corrected me.

'Right yes, just me and my house husband and my horrible cat son. It's enough for me.'

They looked at me as though they didn't quite believe me, but it didn't matter. I wasn't sure if I really believed it myself, but I wanted it to be true.

We sat in the pub garden buying rounds of drinks and packets of crisps until it was properly dark and we'd started to get chilly. Jeremy's Richard had turned up at one point. Richard was the polar opposite to Rob. He was shorter and stockier and had thick blond hair, which he ran his hand through a lot when he spoke. He had a couple of drinks with us before heading off to some house party that Jeremy said we might go to later. Once they'd rung the last orders bell we all said loud goodbyes and hugged each other several times, even Nick. They absolutely insisted I take some of the pitiful balloons home, so Jeremy and I took one each.

'Hey!' I grabbed Sophie's hand as they were leaving and she and Charlie both turned around. 'I want you to know how much you guys . . . I mean, when I moved back here I could never have imagined that I would get so lucky.'

'Oh, she's had a wine hasn't she?' Charlie put her arm around me and pulled me in tightly for a hug, ruffling my hair with her other hand.

'I'm being serious!' I protested, wriggling out from Charlie's headlock.

'We got lucky too, Ally,' Sophie said, ignoring her wife cackling next to her. 'We know you'll do us proud.'

Jeremy and I started strolling home at a snail's pace, discussing our possible snack options.

'We're not going to this house party, are we?' I asked, twirling the end of the balloon string around my finger so that it started to cut off the circulation, and then unravelling it again.

'Ugh, no.' Jeremy grimaced. 'I don't think so, are we?'

'No!'

'Although . . .' Jeremy stopped walking and looked at me very seriously. I stopped too, abruptly in the middle of the pavement so that a very sober couple who were walking briskly behind tutted their way around us.

'We did say that we should be doing new things, didn't we? Meeting new people?'

'Oh God,' I whined, knowing he was right, but also desperately wanting my bed.

'Did we not, Al?' Jeremy stood in front of me, arms crossed.

'I know, we did, we did.' I sighed heavily, admitting defeat. 'Where is it? I don't want to go on a trek.'

'It's only about fifteen minutes up the road. We just have to pop in,' Jeremy said reassuringly, I think as much for his sake as for mine. 'We'll just pop in, have one drink, and if we're not having a nice time then we can leave.'

'OK that sounds fair. But don't just immediately abandon me for Richard when we get there.'

'I won't, I promise. I think it's his housemate's birthday or something, so there'll be loads of people there who won't know anyone else. You know what it's like.'

We changed direction and headed towards a student area, where the houses are massive and ten people live in each one. They're always freezing cold and extremely damp. I wondered who lived in them before they became hovels for eighteen-year-olds. Every street looked the same. We stopped off at a newsagent for a couple of bottles of warm pinot grigio and twenty Marlboro Lights.

Jeremy tentatively knocked on the huge red door, which looked so old and rickety that I was quite sure I could have broken in with one sharp kick. It was immediately wrenched open by a girl wearing a giant '30' badge pinned to her T-shirt. She was clutching a glass of wine in one hand and a phone in the other. She looked completely flustered.

'Oh!' she said, surprised to see us. 'Sorry, I thought you were someone else.' She waited a couple of beats before adding, 'Come in, come in! Sorry, how rude.'

We shuffled in past her and she shut the door behind us.

'Hi, I'm Jeremy. Richard invited us, I hope that's OK.' Jeremy stuck out his hand.

'Hi Jeremy!' Her eyes lit up with recognition. 'Richard's told me all about you! I'm so pleased you could make it.'

We followed her through to the kitchen, which was packed with people who were spilling out through the back door and into the garden. They had Beyoncé blasting through speakers perched on the plastic furniture outside.

'Richard!' she shouted over a group of people. 'Jeremy's here!' She pointed at us for Richard's benefit before disappearing into the garden.

'You came!' Richard had wriggled his way through the kitchen crowd. He was clutching two empty plastic cups and thrust them at us.

He and Jeremy had a little awkward hug.

'It's so mad in here, we didn't actually expect all these people to show up.' He looked up and smiled at someone walking past.

'Yeah, it is rammed.' I touched my finger to my top lip. Already sweating.

339

'Even all the neighbours we invited came. I've never even met half of them.' He jerked his head towards the back door. 'But at least they're just hanging out in the garden.'

I looked and saw a group standing in a circle on the lawn. Occasionally one of them would shriek with laughter.

We stood and chatted for at least an hour in the kitchen. The wine disappeared at an alarming rate and new people kept coming in to introduce themselves. All of a sudden it was unbearably hot. There was no air at all, just people's sickly alcohol breath and cigarette smoke. I desperately needed not to be standing in that kitchen.

'You stay.' I reached out and squeezed Jeremy's hand. 'I just need some fresh air.' My head was swimming and I wondered if there was any food at this party. I tried to count how many glasses of wine I'd had.

'Are you sure? I don't mind coming.' Jeremy said this with his head fully turned in the opposite direction, craning towards Richard.

'I'll be fine, I'm a big girl.' I reached out my hand and he put the packet of cigarettes in it. He held up a finger to stop me and rummaged around in his pockets and, delighted with himself, produced a lighter.

I shuffled through a group of people and out of the back door, where it was considerably less rowdy. The music had changed to something quieter and the big circle of neighbours had disbanded. Instead people were huddled in twos having deep conversations or standing on their own looking at their phones.

There was one girl in the middle of the lawn at the back of the garden having an extremely drunken emotional phone call where she kept repeating, 'but you're my best friend *and* my boyfriend,' as if the person on the other end of the line was receiving the information for the first time. I perched on the wall separating the lawn from the patio, lit a cigarette, and listened to her babbling. I closed my eyes, enjoying the relative peace and quiet of the garden. I could hear another group of people chatting and laughing a few houses down and it was nice, it felt like the whole world was up and about enjoying themselves. I'd put my phone down somewhere so I had no idea what the time was. It didn't matter. I was still processing the news from earlier. My own shop.

Sitting in that strangers' garden by myself, drunk and clammy, I felt like I was exactly where I was supposed to be.

As I was finishing my cigarette and contemplating lighting another just so I could sit there for a bit longer, I was aware of someone behind me heading down the garden path. I looked up as someone perched on the wall a few feet away from me.

'Hi,' she said, briefly looking at me and then up at the house. My eyes widened, taking in her blonde hair, shorter now. Her long legs jiggling. Her arms were wrapped around herself, clutching her shoulders as if to keep herself in place.

'Jo. How do you . . . what are you doing here?'

'I live there.' She pointed at the house to our left and then added, 'Remember?'

'I, oh God . . . yeah of course, it's just . . .' A flash of standing in her kitchen in the dark. The smell. The taste of her mouth. 'I'm not sure I quite committed the specifics to memory.'

She nodded. 'Why are you here?' She still wasn't looking at me.

'I'm here with Jeremy, he's seeing one of the guys who lives here.'

She didn't say anything. Somehow it felt like I'd given the wrong answer. I was nervous. The last time I'd seen her she'd been shouting at me.

'I live with Jeremy now,' I offered.

She looked at me then. 'Not with Emily?'

'Ah. No, no. That's all over with. I mean, it was always over with.'

She looked at me then and smiled. It wasn't a mean smile, she wasn't happy that it hadn't worked out.

'Jo, I . . .'

'No don't, don't. I don't want you to apologise. I don't want to talk about it.'

'OK. But . . .'

'Yes?'

'Your hair looks great.'

She touched her hand to her head.

'I know.'

We looked at each other. I shivered involuntarily. Shock probably. And the alcohol I'd had for dinner.

'Do you want to go back inside?'

342

I shook my head. We sat facing each other, knees pulled up to our chests. The tips of our trainers touching.

'How have you been?' I asked this tentatively. It was none of my business. I knew that.

'I've been great, actually.'

'Good.'

We were quiet for a moment longer. I knew she was expecting me to say something. Not sorry. Better than sorry.

'Can we start again? Just pretend none of this ever happened?' I was surprised by the urgency of this question. How deeply I felt it. How much I wanted her to say yes.

She shook her head.

'I can't pretend it never happened. But we can try something else.'

She gently tapped my shoe with hers.

'Tell me something about yourself.'

'I'm Ally,' I paused, 'and I have a cat called Malcolm.'

She nodded.

'I'm Jo. I'm a runner . . . and a terrible judge of character.'

I smiled and she smiled back. I wanted to reach out to her then. Tell her she could trust me. That she wasn't a terrible judge of character. That my character was good.

Instead, I held out my hand, hoping she'd play along. She took it briefly, meeting my eyes.

'It's nice to meet you, Jo.'

'Nice to meet you, Ally.'

ACKNOWLEDGEMENTS

Firstly, I want to thank the Emmas, without whom you most certainly would not be reading this book.

To my agent Emma Finn, thank you for being such an unwavering champion of my writing, for loving these characters as much as I do and for making this all happen. Also thank you for answering my hundreds of questions so patiently. I would be Moira Rose screaming much more often if it weren't for your constant positivity and kindness.

To my editor Emma Capron, thank you for seeing the potential in this novel, for making it immeasurably better and for not letting me call it 'Malcolm'. I knew as soon as I met with you and the team that I'd found the right home. Your enthusiasm and excitement are infectious and I'm so grateful that I get to work with you.

I know everyone says it takes a village to create a book but that is because it actually does take a village. In this mad time the villagers were all working from home and doing everything virtually and still managed to do a phenomenal job.

Thank you to everyone at Quercus who has worked so hard on this book, especially Milly Reid, Lipfon Tang, Charlotte Day, Tash Webber, Charlotte Webb, Rachel Wright, Kat Burdon, James Buswell, George Difford, Dave Murphy, Izzy Smith, Chris Keith-Wright and so many more.

Thank you to the Penguin WriteNow programme and the hugely supportive 2018 cohort. Special thanks to Assallah Tahir who was the first person to ever read this book and who worked so hard with me on it.

Thank you to all my managers and colleagues who have been so encouraging, supportive and excited about this adventure.

Thank you to my friends who've listened to me going on about this book for the past two years. Special thanks to Lucy and Cyd for all the nights out in Sheffield which I now count as 'research', to Katy for being the other half of my brain for the past twenty years and to Suz for being the kind of friend who is really family. Maybe one day you'll finish the book and get to this bit.

Thank you to my queer family and sweet bébés – Cyd Sturgess, Anna Dews (your review is still my favourite), Andy Garraway, Bella Qvist, Samuel Richter and Olivia Le Poidevin. Your friendship and support are, quite literally, everything.

Sarah (with an H), thank you for always cheering me on and for making me laugh about a hundred times a day. The drunken voice notes are just for you.

Thank you, Mum and Dad, for always believing that this was possible and making me believe it too. Thank you for reading to me every night when I was little and always saying yes to 'one more chapter'. Also thank you for making every single person you know buy this book. In hardback.

Finally, thank you, Jen, for being such a discerning and generous early reader of this book. When you put a heart in the margins, I really believe that you heart that bit. I'm sorry about all the aforementioned Moira Rose screaming and I'm also sorry for dedicating this book to the cat and not to you. You know it's all for you really, everything is.

Identity issues. Parental abandonment.
Fear of commitment.

And that's just the therapist . . .

TELL ME EVERYTHING

Turn the page for an exclusive look at
Laura Kay's new novel.

Prologue

'See,' Georgia says, 'it was worth the walk, wasn't it?'

She picks up a peach from the picnic basket in front of us and takes a bite. The juice dribbles down her chin.

I might lean forward and wipe it off but instead I sit back and watch her, pink from our walk in the sun, sleeves rolled up on her white T-shirt, cross-legged with her trainers kicked off. I smile despite not really believing it was worth the three hours and severe sunburn it took for us to get here.

'It was,' I say.

She sticks out a foot and nudges me gently in the thigh.

'You're not even looking at the view.'

I take my sunglasses off my head and make a show of putting them on, as though they're my actual glasses and I need them in order to properly see. I plan to say something silly but, actually, the view is spectacular. Green rolling hills and far in the distance, sparkling under the blue skies, the sea.

'It's lovely, George. Honestly.'

'Has it made up for a weekend with my family?'

We've been staying with Georgia's parents for the long week-end and though they've been nothing but lovely to me, it has felt like the longest weekend of all time. Despite being in the countryside with nothing but miles and miles of fields between us and the rest of civilisation, I've spent the past few days feeling increasingly claustrophobic, longing to be back in Brighton.

This weekend away was something I agreed to months ago when we were lying in bed together and Georgia was propped up on one arm leaning over me. In that moment I'd have said yes to anything she asked. My vague feeling of unease was so quickly dismissed, went so easily unanalysed. This trip was something someone else would have to deal with in the future. But here I am.

Georgia lobs her peach stone into the distance and comes to lie beside me. She smells like sun cream. I think she's developed a hundred more freckles since we left the house this morning.

'That might take some more making-up actually,' I say.

'Really?'

Georgia turns onto her side so she's facing me and slips her hand under my T-shirt, tracing lines on my stomach. I can feel that I'm sticky with sweat around my waistband but I don't stop her.

'Can you believe it's been a year?' Georgia says.

'No,' I say, 'I can't.'

Us having been together for a year is Georgia's favourite topic of conversation recently. It's the longest relationship I've had and she sees it as a personal accomplishment.

'A year of us,' Georgia says. I turn to look at her.

'I hate those sunglasses,' she says, 'I can't see your eyes.'

I sit up a bit, resting on my elbows. I leave my sunglasses on.

'Shall we open the wine?' I say.

I set about attempting to dislodge the cork while Georgia screws stems to the plastic wine glasses her parents insisted we brought with us.

'Cheers,' I say, tapping my glass to hers.

'To a year together,' Georgia says. Just as I've taken a sip, she adds, 'And to many more!'

The wine sticks in my throat. It tastes sour. I pick up a bottle of water and take a few large gulps. Georgia doesn't appear to notice my discomfort.

'We won't be with my parents for our anniversary next year, I promise,' Georgia says. 'But this was the only weekend we were all free. And they so wanted to finally spend some time with you.'

I nod, an agreement that we won't be here next year, that we have indeed spent some time with her parents. We sit for a while side by side, blinking into the sun. I can practically feel her contentment, a gentle hum vibrating next to me. My stomach churns, the feeling that's been festering for the past few weeks finally coming to the surface. I close my eyes, its predictable familiarity is almost a relief.

Georgia sighs.

'Couldn't you just stay here forever?'

I don't reply. I just put a hand on her knee and squeeze it, trying to impress as much meaning as I can into my fingertips. To say I wish I could. I wish I could tell you that.

Georgia picks up my hand and presses her fingers into my palm.

'You're all clammy.' She peers at me. 'Are you all right? You look a bit funny.'

I nod and wipe cold sweat from my forehead with the back of my hand.

'A bit too long in the sun, maybe.'

Without hesitation she takes her baseball cap off her head and places it on mine.

'Are you sure?' I say.

'What's mine is yours,' she says. 'Always.'

1

Two years later

It is not even 9 a.m. and our flat is already hotter than the sun. I stand by the coffee machine inserting capsules and stabbing at buttons until something happens. Georgia is bashing ice cubes out of a tray. She swears as half of them land on the floor but the ones she manages to salvage she picks up in fistfuls and piles into our coffee mugs. She walks over to the fridge and passes me the oat milk, I put a splash in her mug and fill mine up to the top. I stir hers, pass it to her and then add sugar to mine. She grabs two paper straws from the drawer where we keep all the miscellaneous things that don't have homes and places one in each of our cups. We both lean against the counter, take a sip at the same time and grimace slightly. We don't like this flavour. It's too strong. Ours is a very well-rehearsed morning coffee dance. This is the last time we'll do it.

'Want some?' Georgia says as she spoons Greek yoghurt over a bowl of blueberries.

'No thanks,' I say, 'I'm going to buy a smoothie on the way into work.'

'A smoothie?' Georgia raises her eyebrows but doesn't comment further. She licks her spoon and puts the yoghurt back in the fridge.

'Sure.'

A smoothie, a croissant, a bacon sandwich. Who's to say?

'So what time are you going to be home later, do you think?'

I glance at my phone, as if knowing the time now will provide some sort of answer to her question.

'Erm, realistically? Like . . . seven?'

'Natty!'

'What?'

I take a sip of my coffee. I know what.

'You still have to pack!'

'I will, I will.'

'Have you even started?'

'Obviously!'

'Natasha.'

She looks at me seriously.

'Look, have I physically started packing? No. But mentally I am fully on top of it. Don't worry. I'm going to have it done in minutes.'

Georgia rolls her eyes at me but ends up smiling. She's extra chipper this morning.

'Right, I'm off,' she says decisively without actually making

354

any moves to go. 'I'm having a quick drink with Zara after work and then I'll be home to help you, OK?'

'Oh, Zara's not coming this evening?'

Georgia smiles patiently.

'She'll be here first thing in the morning.'

'Of course, to escort me out.'

Georgia ignores me, puts her bowl in the sink, takes the straw out of her coffee and downs the dregs, crunching on a couple of ice cubes. I shudder.

'OK, have a great day,' she breezes past me, pausing to give me a swift kiss on the cheek on her way out. She smells nice, clean hair and perfume.

'You too,' I shout after her.

I stand in the kitchen alone for a moment, savouring the last drops of my horrible coffee for the final time.

In the end I swerve the smoothie and eat a croissant so flaky I end up inspecting myself for stray crumbs all day. The therapy room I rent is no cooler than the flat. It's on the top floor of a converted town house. I have the window open and an ancient fan whirring away but I'm pretty sure it's making things worse by pushing the thick air around the room. I've had three clients this morning – one midlife crisis, one quarter-life crisis and, finally, a terrible boyfriend. He's the kind of client where instead of saying, 'Hmm, and how does that make you feel?' I want to put down my notebook, grab him by the shoulders and say, 'Dump him! Dump him now!' Instead I power through, nod in all the right places and privately count down the hours until I can have a very cold glass of wine.

'The thing is,' David is saying, 'the thing is he's had such a hard time with relationships in the past, and that's not his fault. It's just that now when it comes to commitment he really struggles, you know?'

'Mmm,' I nod, not a yes, not a no. I wait for him to keep talking.

'So when he says it's not the right time for him to come to my mum's sixtieth birthday party, like he's too overwhelmed to do that, even though I told him that it would mean a lot, and like, even though he cancelled on the day and was going to drive us and I had to buy a train ticket and it was really expensive, that's really because of his deeper trust issues and I should respect that. Like maybe . . . maybe the issue is that I should have more empathy.'

'Remind me,' I say, 'just refresh my memory so I'm clear. How long have you and Will been dating?'

David sits back in his chair and wipes some sweaty hair from his forehead. He knows I don't need reminding.

'Three and a half years.'

I let that hang in the air for a moment.

'It's a long time,' he says eventually.

'So you consider three years a long time. I think that's valid. A lot of people would consider three years a significant amount of time. I wonder if it might be worth reflecting on just how many years you want to wait for someone to commit to you.

356

And what that commitment might look like. And whether that's something Will can offer you.'

He nods, tired. I'm tired too. This is perhaps too much for one person to reflect on in thirty-five-degree heat.

'He's not a bad person,' he says. 'I don't want you to think . . . I wouldn't want you to think badly of him.'

I nod.

'What do you think you've said to me that would make him seem like a bad person?'

I do actually think he's a bad person, a bad boyfriend anyway. This sixtieth birthday party was important. Just go and drink an Aperol Spritz with Margaret, Will. It's one afternoon!

'Just, I don't know. I talk about him letting me down a lot but none of the good stuff.'

'Do you feel let down?'

He looks at me, surprised at his own words echoed back at him.

'I do feel let down. I just want him to be . . . I want him to be . . .'

He shakes his head.

'I want him to be different.'

I nod. We're out of time.

As soon as David leaves (to catch his train to go glamping with terrible Will and terrible Will's friends) I grab my phone, order an Uber and race across town to make it in time to teach my class. Sometimes on Friday afternoons I run an Introduction to Therapy taster session. I've never committed to teaching the whole course. I don't particularly like teaching but I do particularly love regular income.

I arrive at the nondescript office building with twenty minutes to spare, enough time for me to drag some plastic chairs into two semicircles, one behind the other, and stick a sign on the door which reads, 'Please wait outside until class begins at 2pm'. Good to enforce boundaries early on. Boundaries are the bedrock of therapy. Also I don't want to make small talk with all the very keen people who arrive early. But mainly the boundaries thing. Very important.

I had hoped the temperamental air conditioning might have kicked in but, if it has, I can't feel it. I try to open the windows but they're locked shut. A safety measure. I wonder if it is possible to boil alive in an office block. It smells of old carpet and microwaved lunches. It's eerily quiet.

I decide, since I have a few minutes to myself, to eat the Twix that's been melting in my bag all day and read the news, by which of course I mean, scroll through Twitter. I have a message from Georgia asking me for the thousandth time if I'll definitely be home at seven. My stomach flips at the prospect of the evening. How long can packing really take?

I've just finished the first stick of my Twix when the door opens.

'Excuse me? Natasha?'

I wipe my mouth on the back of my hand and quickly fold the wrapper around the second stick.

A woman is standing in the doorway clutching a takeaway

coffee cup in one hand and her phone in the other. She's wearing skinny jeans. Super tight and black. I don't know how she's coping with the heat. She smiles and makes to step into the room, assuming she's found the correct one.

I stand up.

'There's a waiting area outside. Please go and take a seat and I'll call you all in at two. There's actually a sign on the door.'

It comes out much harsher than I intend it to. She stands completely still for a moment. It happens too quickly to be sure but I could swear I see a flicker of a smile play on her lips, just for a second.

'Got it,' she says as she backs out and down the hall.

I eat the rest of my chocolate hurriedly and watch the clock, waiting until it's exactly 2 p.m. to go and fetch them all. My own voice, shrill and officious, rings in my ears: *There's actually a sign on the door.*

When I pull the door open to let them in, I lean against it, making room for them all to file in past me.

'Welcome,' I say. 'You can all come in now and find a seat.'

The girl in skinny jeans is the first to make her way towards me.

I reach out my hand to shake hers and she shoves her phone in the back pocket of her jeans in order to do so.

'I'm Natasha.'

'Margot.' She says, 'Sorry about before.'

Margot. A childhood friend had a dog named Margot. 'If you catch her in the wrong mood she'll have your arm off,' my friend's mum used to say, lovingly.

'It's OK,' I say, feeling guilty about admonishing her. Should I apologise? Really it was more about Twix time getting interrupted than anything else.

'I just like to set clear boundaries right from the start,' I say. She nods.

'Of course, that makes sense.'

She brushes past me. I carry on holding the door open for everyone else but, instead of greeting them properly, I can't help but watch her as she makes her way into the room. She sits down in the seat directly in the middle of the front row and puts her bag under her chair.

I wait for everyone else to file in and find a seat. They all mumble introductions to each other as they pull brand-new notebooks and pens out of backpacks and sip from identical reusable water bottles. There's fifteen of them all together. A fairly typical bunch. Becoming a therapist is an expensive business so these courses attract a pretty homogenous crowd. Most of the women are older than me, a couple by decades. All but one are white. There are two men, perhaps in their forties. Margot is an exception to the rule. I wonder if she's rich and being funded by family or whether she plans to take my path – two jobs, no sleep, mercifully low rent.

I introduce myself and do my usual spiel about the afternoon taster session, what we'll cover and what we should hope to achieve but it's hot and it's the end of the week and I can tell I've lost some of them before I've even begun. It's a shame because I know what this taster session is costing them.

'I need a volunteer,' I say and before anyone else can even lift a finger, let alone raise a hand, Margot stands up and walks over to the empty chair next to mine, set slightly apart from the rest of the group. She takes her coffee and a bottle of water with her and places them by her feet.

'Happy to help,' she says. I can't quite identify her accent but I think it's Australian. Or maybe New Zealand. The way she says 'help', *hilp*.

I look at the rest of the group. I wonder if they're expecting me to admonish her for just walking up here and not waiting for me to choose someone or let anyone else get a look in. Should I assert my authority somehow? Set another bloody boundary? They just look weary but I can tell their interest is somewhat piqued. No one looks too put out to still be in their seats.

'Thank you for volunteering,' I say to her and then I turn to the group. 'OK so . . .'

I look at Margot as if I need her to remind me of her name. Apparently I'm going to assert my authority like I'm in high school. It's pathetic but I feel briefly back in control.

'It's Margot,' she says kindly, not breaking eye contact with me. She smiles slightly. She knows my game.

'Margot and I are going to demonstrate what an initial therapy session might look like between a client and a therapist. Now,' I turn to address Margot again, 'you obviously don't have to tell me anything you don't want to – in fact, for the purposes of this session, you don't even have to tell me anything that's true.'

Margot shrugs.

'I'm happy to tell the truth.'

I nod.

'OK then. During this exercise I am your therapist and you are my prospective client.'

She widens her eyes at me, indicating she gets it. She nods impatiently.

'And it goes without saying,' I say, 'that this is a safe space and anything you share here stays within these four walls.'

I glance around the group and everyone nods. They're all sitting up a bit straighter, pens poised. They're hoping for something juicy.

'So Margot,' I smile at her, 'how are you doing today?'

'I'm good,' she says brightly.

There's a ripple of laughter throughout the room and Margot smiles at me, not acknowledging it.

'Good.' I smile serenely back at her and then around the room, refusing to be put off. 'And how do you feel about today's assessment?'

'Fine, thanks.'

More laughter, quieter this time.

'OK, so what brings you here?'

She shrugs and takes a sip from her cup. It smells sweet, like vanilla syrup. I don't think she's being deliberately obtuse. I think she's waiting for my questions to become interesting.

'Maybe you can just start by telling me a bit about yourself?'

'Like what?'

'Like where you're from? What you do? Single? In a relationship? Are you close with your family? The basics. If you're comfortable with that, of course.'

She looks at me warily.

Christ this is going to be difficult.

'I'm from New Zealand originally but I've lived in the UK for like . . . twelve years now. My parents are still together. I love them but we're not close. I mean, we're literally eleven thousand miles apart. I'm a barista but I'm also a writer and a comic. I'm . . . dating.'

She looks at me, trying to convey some sort of meaning. It seems important to her that I know the last part. Maybe it's for the sake of our captive audience. I remain impassive.

'A writer?'

'Yep.'

'What, like, books?'

She rolls her eyes at me. They're green and almost comically expressive. Underneath them are deep, dark circles.

'I write stories, poems. Sometimes I perform them, sometimes they're in books. That kind of thing.'

'Great. And a comic? So that's like . . .'

'Jokes,' she says. 'I stand on stage and tell jokes.'

She stares at me, looking for clues of recognition or, perhaps, judgement. I hope there are no traces of my natural repulsion to performance of basically any kind on my face.

'And did you want to talk about your work in these sessions?'

'Not particularly.'

'Dating?'

A smile plays on her lips and she pushes some hair from her face. It's dark and glossy and she has a fringe that looks to be in the awkward stages of being grown out.

'No.'

'OK, well what would you like to discuss?'

She pauses. I think she's trying to decide whether to tell me something real or make something up. In the moment it's very difficult to be open in front of a group of strangers, no matter how confident you are.

'I can't sleep.'

Ah, the truth.

'Talk about that a little.'

'What is there to say? I go to bed, I read, I listen to some podcast that's meant to send you to sleep, I close my eyes, I stay awake.'

She kicks her sliders off and goes to tuck her feet underneath her on the chair but she stops with one foot still on the floor.

'Is this OK?'

'Would you be more comfortable?'

'I guess I would.'

'Then it's OK.'

She tucks the other foot underneath her. I glance around the room, the whole lot of them are taking notes. *Tucks foot under self.*

'So yeah, I've tried everything. I took sleeping pills for a while but it wasn't for me. I've been hypnotised. Yoga. Crystals. Everything you can think of. My mother thinks it's something deeper. That there's something in my psyche keeping me awake.'

'Like anxiety?'

She nods. 'Or guilt.'

'Guilt. Why guilt?'

'I guess it would keep you awake.'

'What would you have to feel guilty about?'

She shrugs.

'Everyone's guilty of something, aren't they?'

I'm aware that the room is suddenly completely silent, no one's even scribbling.

'Do you think everyone's guilty of something?'

She smiles again.

'Yes.'

I write 'intense' in my notebook and nod like I'm mulling over what she's said.

'So what would you be hoping to achieve in our sessions if we worked together?'

She sighs heavily.

'I don't think we're going to achieve anything. But what's the harm in trying? Plus . . .' she grins, she's about to put a shield up, our moment of clarity dissolving in front of us, 'it'll make my mother happy.'

'Tell me about your mother.'

She laughs and everyone else does too, relieved, the tension broken by this classic therapy line of questioning.

'Are you going to tell me that I can't sleep because I hate my mother and want to have sex with my father, is that it?'

I smile and there are more titters around the room.

'We don't have to talk about your mother if you'd prefer not to.'

She nods, shakes her coffee cup, decides it's empty and places it on the floor next to her feet.

'So what about you?'

I feel my whole body tense.

'What about me?'

'Where are you from? Single? In a relationship? The basics.'

I put my notebook down.

'We're not here to talk about me.'

This is good, I tell myself, despite my cheeks flushing. This is good because this is something I can point out later to the group. An example of setting boundaries.

'You don't tell your patients anything?'

'You're not my patient. I'm not a doctor.'

'Aha! So we know you're not a doctor.'

She looks at me hopefully, trying to make me laugh. Not uncommon for real new clients. And especially not uncommon for performers.

'That's right.'

'Are you from Essex?'

I'm temporarily thrown. Not many people can detect my accent after many years of being ironed out at university, and by spending time with people who my twin sister Natalie would describe as 'annoyingly posh'.

'I am.'

I immediately regret answering. She's thrilled, which confirms it was the wrong thing to do. I glance around the room and unbelievably they're still taking notes. *From Essex originally . . .*

'I knew it. I've been watching *Love Island*. I can recognise all the accents now. Before I moved here I thought you all – *talked like this*.' She does an impression that lands somewhere between the Queen and Dick Van Dyke.

'It seems to me that maybe you don't particularly want to be here.'

She looks straight at me, unblinking.

'Why would you think that?'

'It seems like you'd rather not talk and that you're quite sure I won't be able to help. I wonder what brought you here.'

'Um, curiosity, mainly.'

'Curiosity to see whether it would help you sleep?'

'No. More like . . . curiosity about the process. About you. Therapy in general. I'm writing something so this is like . . .'

She waves her hand around in the air, looking for the word.

'Research?' I suggest.

'Yes! Exactly that. And if it helps my sleep, then . . . bonus.'

'Right.'

I draw a big question mark in my notebook. I can't tell who I'm speaking to now, real Margot or fake client Margot.

I thank her and turn to the group to ask if they have any questions. No one raises a hand, which is ridiculous. None of them have ever done any therapy training before and they've just witnessed a car crash of a 'session'. I have questions and I'm meant to be teaching the class. They're all too hot and tired or too shy. Maybe they're nervous around Margot too.

'OK, well now we're going to have everyone split into pairs for a few minutes and have a go themselves. Remember the focus at this point is practising active listening with your partner. One person should play the role of therapist, one the prospective client, and you should interact using what you've just seen as a blueprint.'

A blueprint for a deeply dysfunctional session.

There's an odd number so there's going to have to be one group of three. Normally I'd just make the odd one out join another group. Come on, Natasha. Group of three. I open my mouth to allocate someone to join another couple but instead I find myself turning to Margot.

'There's an odd number,' I say, frowning at my notebook as if it contains some sort of complicated calculation about how to split the fifteen students in the room. 'So you stay with me.'

'Yes, ma'am.'

I look up at her and she's leaning back in her chair, seemingly utterly relaxed. She reaches up to push her hair out of her face and I see she has a couple of tattoos on her upper arm that I didn't notice when she came in. A simple line drawing of a flower and a tiny anchor.

There's a low rumble of noise as the rest of the students get started around the room but it feels oddly intimate now that we're without our audience.

'Do you want to have a go at playing the therapist?' I ask her. She shakes her head immediately.

'No. I want to see more of you in action.'

I nod. I wonder if I should insist on switching roles but instead I say, 'For your research?'

She grins and reaches up to her forehead to move the hair that's fallen in her eyes.

'Ugh, this thing is driving me insane!' She blows up at her not-quite-grown-out fringe.

I look at her and smile, trying to convey calm, to conceal my heart thudding in my chest. I scold myself. This is ridiculous. I am the one in charge here. I'm a professional woman. Be professional!

'You should clip it back.'

She waves her hand dismissively.

'I can't be bothered. I just feel like one morning I'm going to wake up and I'll be able to tuck it behind my ears. I've been growing it out for fucking ever. I feel like it's got to be over soon.'

'I'm not sure it just happens overnight.'

I find myself wanting to tell her about the time in primary school when my sister cut my fringe off right to the hairline and how I had a spiky visor growing over my face for months.

'You'll see.' She flashes me a grin and I find myself smiling dopily back.

Oh god. I look around the room at everyone diligently working. Am I really going to sit at the front of the class flirting with this incredibly annoying girl? I mean, yes? No. No. I'm going to get a grip.

'OK, so let's just pick up where we left off since we're . . . slightly more advanced than everyone else.'

I'm fully winging it now, having never role-played twice with a student and never having role-played with a student without an audience.

'Tell me, how has your week been?'

I settle back into my chair, gripping my notebook tightly.

She picks up her bottle of water and takes a sip.

'My week, my week. What have I done this week? Had a few gigs. They were fine, nothing special. I'm working on some new stuff but there's something missing at the moment. It's fine though. I'll get there. It sometimes just takes a while to click.'

She pauses to take another sip of water.

'What else? What else? I've had the flat to myself. So it's been nice to watch whatever I want on TV, leave the kitchen in a state, that kind of thing. Work is fine. I've sold a lot of iced coffee. I've been drinking a lot of iced coffee. Erm, I was going to go on a date but then I literally was too tired. Too. Tired. So that's tragic, isn't it?'

She pauses, checking to see if there's anything she's missed out. 'Yeah that's it, I think. Pretty standard week.'

She takes another sip of water.

'You?'

I ignore her.

'How's your sleep been?'

370

She smiles broadly.

'I'm sorry to have to tell you, Natasha, that your assessment approximately seven minutes ago did not cure me of my insomnia. I am still very much awake, much of the time.'

'I didn't mean that! I meant, do you experience any different patterns? Is there anything, now you've had time to reflect, that you'd like to tell me about?'

She opens her mouth to reply immediately but then closes it again. As though she's decided to actually think about what I'm saying instead of firing off some smart-arse response.

'I'm tired all the time.'

'And what does that feel like?'

'Being tired?'

'Describe it.'

She pauses again. Leans forward and puts her bottle of water down as if she can't properly think and hold it at the same time.

'It feels like wading through treacle. I'm almost used to the slow thoughts, you know? I'm always slightly foggy but it's the heaviness of my limbs. It's like I'm weighed down with rocks some days. And my eyes.'

She gently touches under her eyes with her fingers. Purple.

'My eyes sometimes feel like they're being dragged halfway down my face. They feel like that all the time. At night too and I think, this is it. I can't feel like this and stay awake, it's impossible. But I close them and my brain is just like . . . ding! It comes alive. It's like turning on an engine. It just fires up.'

She looks at me desperately then. It's so fleeting if I'd blinked I would have missed it.

'What do you mean when you say it fires up?'

'It's like a movie I can't switch off. Replaying highlights. Playing trailers. Every scenario I've ever been in, every scenario I ever could be in. Every song I've heard, person I've met, dream I've had, food I've tasted, feeling I've experienced, sensation I've felt. It's like a live action replay.'

She's tense. She has shifted in her chair now to sit upright. She has one leg crossed over the other and she's jiggling it, holding onto her knee. Her knuckles are white.

I nod. I want to convey to her that I understand. I wish I could reach over and prise her hand away from her knee and hold it until she relaxes.

'Do you go back to anything in particular?'

She's quiet for a moment.

'It's a lot. It's all different things.'

I wait. She's going to say yes. If I'm quiet.

'It's everything I've ever done wrong. No. That's not even it. It's everything I've ever worried about being wrong. Things I've said to people, the way I've looked at someone. Choices I've made that might have offended someone.'

'Do you often do things to offend people?'

'No. I don't think so. Well, I don't know. I hope not.'

'Don't you think you'd know? If you were always upsetting everyone?'

'I'm worried that I don't notice. I just think . . . what if I haven't noticed that I've said something awful and all of a sudden there are consequences?'

'Can you tell me a bit more about what you mean?'

'Oh you know . . . I've accidentally been rude to my neighbour so they throw a brick through my bedroom window. Or I bump into someone on the train and they push me onto the tracks. Or I look at someone the wrong way at work and they throw their coffee in my face.'

She reels off these scenarios as if they're off the top of her head. As if they've just come to her now in this moment. She is very good at saying them as if they're ridiculous and she knows they're ridiculous. Her eyes are so tired.

'Those are very violent ends for such minor transgressions.'

She nods.

'I'm interested about why you think the people you encounter would be so quick to be violent.'

'I don't think that really. That's what I'm saying. I don't walk around all day terrified of everyone. I'm saying this is what keeps me awake. This is what comes to me when I should be asleep. They're almost like subconscious thoughts, aren't they? Dreamlike?'

She looks at me earnestly. She's vulnerable now and I sense the shield is about to go back up. She wants me to tell her something scientific. Something concrete. I can't do it. Again I feel the urge to reach out to her.

'You were too tired to go on a date this week.'

She laughs and looks up to the ceiling. I'm worried briefly

that she's irritated with me for changing the subject but she looks relieved. She visibly relaxes.

'Yeah, I couldn't face it. I wanted to lie in bed and think about meeting a violent end for a . . . how did you so eloquently describe it?'

'A minor transgression.' I can't help but smile at her.

'Yes. I honestly decided I'd rather do that.'

'Do you often choose that over dating?'

'I often do, Natasha.'

The shield is well and truly back up. She says my name like she relishes it. Before I can ask my next question she interrupts.

'Can I call you Tash?'

'No.'

'Why? Because you love boundaries?'

'It's not . . . I don't *love* boundaries. I require them in a professional setting to have meaningful and useful relationships with clients and students.'

'So, what, you just hate the name?'

'Yes. I hate it.'

'Interesting.'

'It's not particularly interesting.'

'It is because you're an enigma. You know I'll spend a lot of time trying to figure you out.'

I can feel colour rising in my cheeks. I click the end of my pen a few times. I lift it to the page as if to note something down but I just draw a deep line down the middle of the page.

'That's common.'

'People thinking about you?'

'No. People trying to figure out their therapists.'

'Oh it's a thing, is it?'

'Yes.'

'Not just about you?'

'No.'

'I'd spend a lot of time thinking about any therapist?'

'Yes. I expect you would.'

She nods, clearly enjoying this exchange. I look around the room to see if anyone can hear us. They're all focused on their own work.

'So . . .' I say, trying to get us back on an appropriate track, 'you turn down social events because you feel too tired . . .'

'Do you know how exhausting it is to date?'

I know I shouldn't answer. It's not about me. She looks me directly in the eye.

Eventually, I nod.

'All the small talk and the same stories over and over again. And you know immediately if it's not going to work but then you have to spend at least an hour in the company of someone who is best-case scenario just incredibly boring. And it's so expensive.'

She pauses to take a breath. She's on a roll as if she's doing 'a bit' about dating. 'And then even if it does go well, then what? I have to kiss someone? I have to have sex with them? Ugh, my god it's exhausting. Do you know what it's like to have sex with a stranger?'

I stare at her and then look down at my notebook, refusing to answer that one.

'It can be fun, don't get me wrong. It's just there's so much to it. What do they like? What are they expecting? What are they into? What if they do something you're not expecting? What if you do something to embarrass yourself? You know? Sometimes I would just like the comfort of having sex with someone who knows me. For it to feel familiar and easy, you know?'

'Is that something you want in general?'

'What?'

'Comfort.'

'Oof.' She sits back like I've winded her. 'You're good. You're very good. I did not see that one coming. I didn't even know I'd said it.'

'Do you want comfort, Margot?'

'I'll have to think about that one.'

She's still joking but I can tell that she really will think about it. Very satisfying. I feel as though I have the upper hand again and then immediately catch myself. This is not meant to be a power struggle.

'We've got a couple more minutes. Is there anything else you'd like to talk about? Are you sure you don't want to swap places?'

She sits forward in her chair again and rearranges herself, crossing her legs the other way.

'No,' she says. 'I like having you tell me all about myself.'

She smiles and I find that I'm smiling back. I catch myself again and close my notebook. I glance up at the rest of the group and clear my throat to get their attention. It's an adjustment when they go quiet and look at me, it feels like an intrusion on Margot and me when, just moments ago, we were the only people in the world.

The rest of the session flies by. I think everyone is relieved when I start talking through a PowerPoint and they can just relax and take notes and dream about whatever their Friday night plans are. When it reaches six o'clock I stand at the door and see everyone out, thanking them for putting up with the heat and wishing them a great weekend. Margot is the last to leave. She stops when she gets to the door, standing between me and the frame. I press my back hard against it trying to create some space between us.

'Thank you for coming,' I say. 'I hope you found it useful for your book.'

'I did. Thank you.' She smiles and makes to head out of the door but then turns back.

'You're different to how I thought you'd be.'

'Excuse me?'

'You're not what I thought a therapist would be like. What I thought you'd be like from your website. On there you look kind of like . . . I don't know. A primary school teacher or like . . . someone who teaches yoga. But here you're . . .'

I wait for her to finish her sentence but she just smiles at me, head tilted to one side. I'm stunned. I've never been evaluated after a class before.

'You're colder than I thought you'd be. Kind of like . . . an ice queen rather than a cosy confidante.' She looks pleased with her alliteration. Bloody poets.

'OK. Well. I'm sorry you feel that way, Margot.'

'No. Don't be sorry.' She grins widely. 'I liked it. Good to meet you, Natasha.'

I stand in the doorway for a while after she leaves, dimly aware of making myself later and later for Georgia. My heart is beating so loudly I can feel it thudding in my ears. I feel something close to humiliation but it's not quite that. I feel like I'm exposed. That for whatever reason, Margot was able to see me.